# Battle for Timberfall
## (Third Path of Creation - Book 2)

By ItalianDragon

ISBN: 979-8-9907413-6-2

# DEDICATION

I want to dedicate this book to my Nana and to all my cousins.

My Nana was an amazing woman. She was strong-willed, loving, smart, an amazing cook, and hilarious. Nana was a true Italian woman who embraced her family and was the other half to the most inspiring relationship I have ever witnessed.

To my cousins: we grew up as close as siblings and I could not have asked for a better extended family. The stories we shared and shenanigans we got into still make me laugh and appreciate all of you. I may not be able to see you as much as I would like, but know you are often on my mind, and definitely in my heart!

## Contents

# ACKNOWLEDGMENTS

I want to acknowledge all the authors who have come before me. After going through the process of writing I continue better understand the joy and challenges of writing. I also want to acknowledge my reviewers and editors; their efforts have been critical in helping me get this book and other books published. I appreciate D&D and fellow gaming buddies who have helped co-create so many hilarious stories together.

# Story So Far

One man sacrifices everything to find his friend who disappeared suddenly. Deathwalker's soul gets pulled through the Sea of Chaos, the primordial space between all realities. Most souls who travel through the Sea of Chaos do not survive the trip, those that do can gain a glimpse of power. However, where others retain a few drops from the Sea of Chaos, Deathwalker drank it in leading to his transformation into a dragon and being deposited in a hidden realm.

When he wakes up in this hidden realm, Deathwalker encounters Uriel, Archangel of Knowledge and Wisdom, one of the protectors of Free Will. During this meeting our protagonist learns his friend was taken by the Dark. Deathwalker also learned if he had any hope of rescuing his friend from the Dark, he had to get stronger, a whole lot stronger.

With a new understanding of his situation, Deathwalker sets out to claim the place of power in this hidden realm. Rather than starting his journey on foot and having to fight whatever beast he might encounter, Deathwalker takes flight as a dragon. Soaring to the place of power, he discovers a massive vacant fortress city surrounding the realm's place of power known as the Infinite Nexus.

Claiming the Infinite Nexus was painful and grueling, only his strength of will and gifts from his royal bloodlines helped Deathwalker survive and claim the most unique place of power in existence. He learned this Infinite Nexus was the focal point for all magics and realities. This Hidden Realm of the Infinite Nexus is keystone to protecting the entirety of all realities from beings both within and outside of the Omniverse.

Now master of this unique realm, Deathwalker appoints Uriel the Head Librarian of the Infinite Library. If knowledge is power, then this core building is the most dangerous in existence. Anything written or documented can be found within the Infinite Library.

As a thank you, Uriel provides magic spell school books at the Grandmaster level. These books have the special ability to download knowledge directly into the mind and soul of the one that reads it. Provided with books from each spell school, Deathwalker gained an opportunity to gain a unique class during his Class Trial.

During his Class Trial, Deathwalker meets Lilandra, his arbiter, and the former queen of Djinn. She guides him through the process and in the end, he becomes the unique class: Third Path of Creation. Unclear what that truly means, Deathwalker uses the unique ability he gained from the class, Soul-Forge, to free Lilandra and change her Fate.

With Lilandra now his first disciple, they return to the Hidden Realm of Infinite Nexus. Deathwalker appoints her as the Head Portal Guardian. Uriel puts Deathwalker through an intense, nonstop training session to help him master the knowledge he gained and practice the martial skills he absorbed.

Knowing he must continue to grow stronger, Deathwalker has Lilandra open a portal to another world where he can both grow and learn to put his knowledge to practice. With his human form, he begins to hunt in the forest near a town called Timberfall. Using his unique ability known as Power of 13, he permanently gains stat points, and in rare cases, some of the abilities from the ones he kills.

Gaining the ability known as **One With The Forest (Alpha Variant)**, allows Deathwalker to end up as the Alpha for a pride of Forest Pumas, after he killed their previous Alpha. Appointing Mrrsha, Prrsha, and Frrsha as his advisors and leaders of the pride in his absence, he hunts with the Forest Pumas and continues to grow his strength. During this time Deathwalker finds a primal love of the hunt and begins to lose sight of his original goal of rescuing his friend.

Eventually, Deathwalker leaves the Forest Pumas to enter Timberfall. While in the rustic town he joins the Adventurers' guild, registered as a healer. This leads to an encounter with twin adventurers known as Cal and Mara. The two implore him to heal their friend and party defender, a dwarf by the name of Grimhold.

Deathwalker uses his healing powers to save Grimhold, putting the dwarf in his debt. Then our protagonist uses his master smithing skill to fix and improve Grimhold's mithril armor. This led to the dwarf being in his debt, twice over. Deathwalker later joins Mara, Cal, and Grimhold's party, to help them complete their guild quest.

That quest led the adventuring party to a cave and tunnel system filled with krythid, giant insect creatures that operate in a hive. Deathwalker decides to summon a Shadow Gazer as a familiar, and names him Garry. According to his new familiar, summoning him was Deathwalker's best decision ever. He sent Garry to scout their enemies. This led the team to learn of a krythid Queen. Out of concern for Timberfall, the team concocts a plan to begin to thin out the krythid numbers before they collapse the cave tunnel.

During the battle with the krythid, the team gets overwhelmed and Mrrsha, Prrsha, and Frrsha come to their rescue. Deathwalker ordered Mara and Grimhold to take an unconscious Cal and exit the cave. Once his party was safe, he collapsed the tunnel on their krythid attackers. Thinking Deathwalker is dead, the adventurers head back to Timberfall to rally the town to help.

Deathwalker survived the tunnel collapse and found the bottom half of Frrsha completely crushed. With Lilandra's help and his Soul-Forge ability transform Frrsha into a Shifter Matriarch, granting her wish to be able to turn into a 'two-legged puma'. The newly coined Savage squad, Deathwalker, Garry, Mrrsha, Prrsha, and Frrsha begin to hunt down the krythid.

In confronting and defeating the krythid queen, Deathwalker uses his Soul-Forging ability once again to change her Fate and turn her into his third disciple. She shares her story on how a cloaked shadowy figure teleported her into the mountain with enough corpses to grow her brood army to harass the nearby town. They also learned that someone from Timberfall had betrayed the town.

After reuniting with his party and learning Timberfall's betrayer was the owner of the town's mill, a lesser noble called Darrien. With the help of the rest of the town council, Deathwalker brings Darrien to justice. With no heirs, our protagonist inherits everything Darrien owns including his manor and businesses. After getting his head wrapped around the new fortune he gained, Deathwalker comes up with a new plan to expedite trade and further increase his influence and profits, portal stations.

When Lord Sebastian Dormeir learns of Deathwalker's deeds and Darrien's fate, he is overjoyed. Using the authority the king granted him, Lord Dormeir appoints Deathwalker as Timberfall's new city lord. This new position requires both men to travel to the capital to gain the royal court's final approval.

On his way to establish the portal connection between Timberfall and the capital, Deathwalker and Garry come across an attack by a large group of bandits on a carriage. They decide to lend their aid and save the people. The duo laid waste to the bandits, and gained the moniker of being seen as a shadow or death for the way they would appear out of the shadows and showed no mercy.

Learning the woman in the carriage is fatally wounded, Deathwalker heals her and the other injured. He discovers the woman he saved is Lady Emma Watson, son of Duke Watson, brother to the king. This sparks Lady Emma's interest in her savior.

After Deathwalker finished the portal connection and returned to Timberfall, he shared the news with his forces. He later shared his plans for Timberfall's growth and expansion with the remaining members of the city council. He created new positions and appointed his Head Trader Malcom, General Marius, and Commander Willis to the council and then shares the wonder of the portal station hub. After their shock wore off, they all got to work.

Lord Dormeir and his retinue came to Timberfall to meet up with Lord Deathwalker Dragonvein. They were in shock upon seeing the massive city walls and only further confused when they heard rumors the new city lord was responsible for their creation. Lord Dormeir's aide, Jeffy, comes close to violating guest rights due to his rude behavior, earning him the enmity from Deathwalker's friends and allies. Though Jeffy may not care for the new lord, Sebastian Dormeir took to the man right away, finding kinship in his straightforward attitude.

Together Sebastian and Deathwalker took the portal to the capital surprising the royal guards. Upon meeting with the royal court, Sebastian explained his reasons for appointing Deathwalker and asked the king to confirm him joining the peerage. This was met with some resistance from the court due to Deathwalker being unknown.

Deathwalker revealed his plan for his portal network shocking everyone. Duke Watson began to question the new city lord about his exploits saving his daughter. During these questions a dark arrow shot out from the shadows towards the king.

It was Deathwalker's lightning reflexes that saved the king's life. On instinct, he shaped his hand to an Omni-claw, blocking another ranged attack aimed at the Duchess Lightheart. Using Light magic, he revealed three shadowy assassins. Ordering people to safety, Deathwalker, Sebastian, and General Marius pursued the three attackers.

After a grueling fight the three assassins are vanquished, and the three men return victorious. The king asks only the queen, duchess, and dukes to remain, along with Sebastian and Deathwalker. That is when they discover Deathwalker has an ancient royal bloodline resulting in the king and queen demanding the man marry one of the noble women of the kingdom to ensure his bloodline continues within their nation. In addition, for all his achievements, Deathwalker is appointed as Duke and given the Timberfall Duchy.

# Prologue

Lilandra walked through the portal and returned to the Hidden Infinite Nexus Portal Room. As the portal closed, she heard a voice to her side.

"Now where did you run off to?"

Lilandra turned to address her 'ally'. "Just busy with my duties as first disciple."

Uriel had a look on his face that told her he did not believe a word she was saying.

Lilandra just smiled at the archangel. "How are your brothers doing?"

Uriel's facial expression turned to one of understanding. "Ahhh. You saw our meeting. Now I see."

"They do not trust master." Lilandra stated.

"My brothers mean well. They have long memories, and those memories make it hard to dismiss the past." Uriel replied.

"I remember the past too Uriel. My children are forever bound as slaves to the whims of others for their past transgressions. I have been locked away in my own prison for thousands of years. So, you'll excuse me if I have little tolerance for discussions of the past." Lilandra quipped back.

Uriel sighed. "I have no interest in discussing past transgressions either. We have a chance to move forward from those days. It is my brother Michael's duty to fight against the Dark. With such a purpose he looks for threats everywhere. Give him time, I believe he will be an ally when the time comes."

"Perhaps, but I do not serve the Dark, my loyalty is to Deathwalker. Where do your loyalties lie?"

"That is not fair, and you know it, Lilandra. I am an archangel. My duty is to the Light. That does not mean I would not do everything I could for the Master of the Infinite Nexus. He is a good man put into an impossible situation. I will help him navigate what is coming." Uriel answered.

Lilandra nodded. "If I did not believe that we would be having a different conversation. You did see to it he received some of the most powerful knowledge in the Infinite Library, and that led him to me. But... that does not mean I fully trust you."

"Fair enough for now. Let us discuss Deathwalker's friend." Uriel said.

"Then you do know?" Lilandra asked.

"I have little interest in playing this game. You have found him already." Uriel said it as a statement to let her know he already knew the answer.

Lilandra sighed. "No fun at all. Yes, it did not take me long. I saw him and the others taken."

"Then you know we cannot allow them to meet. The Dark has made their machinations known. He may be one of many they are grooming into a weapon. We both know how easily the Dark can twist one's mind and heart." Uriel explained.

Lilandra sighed. "You are asking me to defy his wishes. That is not something I can do."

Uriel's face took on a pained expression. "Deathwalker is not strong enough to face him. If they meet now, he will lose the battle. If that happens, the Dark would be one step closer to taking this place for themselves."

Lilandra let out another sigh. "So dramatic. Though I must admit you are not wrong. I will have to tell him eventually, but I can wait until he is not in his current state. You do know the others will be growing stronger too. There will be a point where their encounter will be unavoidable."

"Then I guess it is good you are seeking allies for him." Uriel said as he smiled at her.

Lilandra's shock was only present for a moment, but it was enough for the archangel to see it.

"It seems I am not the only one spying on their allies. It matters not. I have set things in motion. It is only a matter of time." Lilandra replied.

"I am not here to admonish your actions, on the contrary. I do not hold the same distrust of the fae that some of my siblings do. Deathwalker will need allies for what is coming. I am sure you have been watching what has started on Earth." Uriel answered.

"Then, we are agreed. I will not mention what has happened to his friends or his world so he may have the time to be who he is meant to be. And... we will let my sisters meet him when the time is right." Lilandra agreed.

Uriel nodded. "I am just concerned. The truth cannot be hidden for long. We walk a fine line. But enough talk of such things. I can sense that Shadow Gazer of his coming this way."

Lilandra shuddered. "Ugh, not Garry."

A few moments later the Shadow Gazer floated into the room.

"Here's Garry! He, he, he. What's up guys?"

# Chapter 1 - Duke of Timberfall

Deathwalker fidgeted. He wanted to get on the road. Though to be honest there wouldn't be too much road to start. Lord Dormeir and his men would return through the portal while Deathwalker would travel to the city of Dumont.

The king had practically begged Deathwalker to finish the portal network sooner than planned. 'The importance to trade and troop movement cannot be understated', those were the king's words. In truth Deathwalker agreed with the king, it was why he proposed the network in the first place. That and all the fees his company could charge for their use were going to make his duchy prosper and make him even richer than he already was.

All of that made logical sense, and Deathwalker was all about logic, especially since coming to this world. The level of logic, however, had Deathwalker concerned. He felt emotions, but they seemed muted somehow. Heck, he had beautiful women practically throwing themselves at him, yet his mind could not shift from calculations and risks. He had wondered if it was a side effect of being a dragon or such a high Mental Aegis attribute.

Though these thoughts concerned him, they were not what had him currently fidgeting. Deathwalker had reluctantly agreed to speed up portal construction. In return for his agreement the crown said he could recruit builders and artisans from across the kingdom. He just had to meet with each duchy and 'work out the details' as the king had called it. Now he was waiting to meet with the queen's sister, Duchess Lightheart, for the third time.

This is what had him fidgeting. At first it seemed innocent enough. They had met with some of her advisors to discuss the best way to recruit and address any concerns of leaving her duchy without Skilled laborers she needed.

The second visit was just the two of them. They had a private meal, and the duchess tried every trick she knew to learn what she could about Deathwalker. There was zero talk about resources no matter how many times he tried to bring the subject of conversation back to it. The woman was an artist when it came to talk-no-jitsu.

It was clear she had designs on him. Deathwalker also could understand it. He was a complete unknown with ancient royal bloodlines who was now a peer. At least one of those bloodlines was older than theirs, it had to be if his commands worked on them. He had inadvertently used his power on them when the throne room was attacked by assassins three days ago. The royal family made it very clear to Deathwalker that he must marry into the family and possibly marry others in the hopes of passing on such a powerful bloodline.

Now he was waiting to speak with her a third time. Deathwalker was convinced she had designs on his hand in marriage. As Sebastian had put it, 'you are the most eligible bachelor in the entire kingdom. You are a Duke now, your duchy is arguably the largest in the kingdom territory wise, and you own a thriving business. One that will be making money hand over fist with the upcoming portal network. Oh yea, and you are a magic wielder who has a hero title! I mean I could keep going my friend, but you get the picture.'

Deathwalker wasn't ready to entertain such notions yet. His libido was nonexistent, and he had a duchy to organize. Plus, he still hadn't given up on finding his friend. James was out there somewhere, and he hadn't given up hope.

The door to the waiting room opened and a well-dressed servant entered and bowed deeply to Deathwalker. "Duke Dragonvein, it is an honor to greet you, your grace. If you will allow me, I can escort you to her grace, Duchess Lightheart."

Deathwalker nodded in acknowledgement. The servant escorted him into an ornate parlor. To his surprise, Duchess Lightheart was not alone. The queen and Duke Watson were also present. It did not look like the duchess was pleased.

Greeting each one in turn. "Your majesty. Duchess Lightheart, and Duke Watson. It is good to see all of you, even if I was not expecting such a meeting."

"I had not planned on their presence either, Duke Dragonvein." Duchess Lightheart replied.

'Ah. So, this wasn't her idea.' Deathwalker thought as he took a seat.

"No, I am afraid that is my doing." The Queen stated.

"And mine." Duke Watson chimed in.

The Queen nodded her head slightly in acknowledgement. "It has come to my attention that my sister has been monopolizing your time, Duke Dragonvein."

"Please call me Deathwalker."

The Queen continued. "Very well, Deathwalker. My sister means well but she is part fey and those of us with some fey blood tend to be drawn to power. Your display of that power in saving our lives is why we have come. I feel indebted to you."

"You owe me nothing. It was my duty." Deathwalker answered.

"Ha! You are a humble one. That trait will not serve you in the days to come. Do not pass up political capital my boy." Duke Watson chimed in.

"What my brother-in-law is getting at is that you should not turn away such boons. I would not approve such a waste." Duchess Lightheart said.

"My dear husband has already offered resources from this kingdom. I offer you a chance to gain warriors from my homeland in the north, the Ljósálfar nation in the Hibernal Territory. My sister and I came here to join our two nations through marriage. I married the king and my sister married the Duke Lightheart. Sadly, her husband died in one of our last wars." The Queen explained.

Duchess Lightheart's voice held genuine sadness as she spoke. "He led from the front. In the end that got him killed."

"He was a good and honorable man." Duke Watson stated.

"Many elves have some kind of fairy blood in them. Ours comes from the Winter court. Though I have no sway over Queen Mab and her court, I do have sway over my father's. I have sent word to him and have asked for his support." The Queen explained.

"I have to ask why, and for what purpose?" Deathwalker said in suspicion.

"Simple, I married the king of this kingdom for two reasons. One, was to strengthen our ties between our two nations. Two, he held a strong royal bloodline." The Queen further explained.

"Our bloodline gives us access to earth and fire magic, as well as some limited mental magic." Duke Watson stated.

"Our bloodline gives us access to Mental magic, water magic, and limited air magic. The hope was our children might possess multiple magical affinities. Such a thing is most desirable for an elf and fairy for that matter." Duchess Lightheart replied.

Duke Watson spoke up. "The only success was my daughter, Lady Emma Watson. Her mother is, was, their sister. Pregnancy is hard on elves, it weakened her. She died not long after when Dark Elf assassins came and tried to kill my Emma. She sacrificed herself to save our daughter. Emma has been tested and she does possess the affinities. However, that same event that cost me my wife had damaged her magic channels. It prevents her from fully accessing her magic."

"You see our niece may not be able to use magic but that does not mean the bloodline is not strong." The Queen stated.

"What about you and the king?" Deathwalker asked.

The Queen sighed and her sister put her hand on the Queen's arm. "We had a son, but he died during that same assassination attempt. Any further attempts at having more children have failed. Our proposal is you consider either my sister, as they never had a chance to conceive a child, or my niece. There will be other suitors, but we ask you to consider this."

'There it is!' Deathwalker thought.

"I approve of you marrying both of us. I know my niece will one day rule this kingdom with whomever she marries. However, I have strengthened our military in my late husband's absence and can provide far more tangibles." Duchess Lightheart replied.

"If their father went through so much to merge our bloodline, imagine his attitude with your ancient royal bloodline." Duke Watson chimed in again.

Deathwalker sighed. "I knew I would have to marry for political reasons, but I am not ready just yet. Please understand that is not a no but rather give me time."

"Wise and thought out, yet politically shrewd. I approve." Duchess Lightheart commented.

"I propose a counteroffer. My understanding is you are planning a festival of sorts for your duchy." Duke Watson said.

"Yes, Sebastian and I came up with the idea to commemorate the forming of our duchy and completing the portal network. We would do a week-long festival that culminated in a series of hunts and challenges. It will also serve to reduce the monster population in the forest and give people a way to rally together. I am most looking forward to the hunt." Deathwalker explained.

Duke Watson nodded. Then I propose Lady Watson be escorted by her aunt Duchess Lightheart to the festival. They remain as guests in your home for at least the length of the festival, preferably longer."

Duchess Lightheart smiled. "If you allow some of my advisors and the completion of a portal in my primary city of Hargrave, I can coordinate my duchy from Timberfall indefinitely."

Seeing Deathwalker's look she added, "Do not worry. I would not impose for so long."

"My brother-in-law's idea is wise. This will give you and them time to get to know each other and determine if marriage is welcomed. Is the compromise acceptable to you, Deathwalker?" the Queen asked.

'I knew this would be only a matter of time. The fact that it is not a complete agreement to the marriage is a start.' Deathwalker thought before he spoke up.

"I agree to host them at my estate and spend time getting to know both. I am sure others will be making the overtures known so I must leave room open for those as well."

"Diplomatic. I approve." Duchess Lightheart commented.

The Queen looked to Duke Watson who nodded his head. "Then it is agreed. Expect news from myself or my father on the boon we shall give you. I am sure my sister and brother-in-law can coordinate directly with you on their boons."

With that the Queen rose from the table as did the Duchess and Duke. Taking that as his cue to leave, Deathwalker paid his respects and left the parlor with the servant waiting at the door. Duke Watson joined him as he had a few more things he wanted to say.

Duke Watson turned to the servant. "I know the way. I can escort my peer out."

The servant bowed and made a quick exit.

"I wanted to thank you again for what you did for my daughter and my men. I know this whole thrusting marriage on you can sour your mood. I know I wasn't happy about marrying someone I did not know, but my wife made me the happiest man in the kingdom. She gave me a wonderful daughter that is kind and brilliant herself..." Duke Watson stopped himself.

Looking at Deathwalker's face which showed no emotions, the duke realized he was getting off course. "My apologies. I was starting to get into my life's story, and I love my daughter so much, it can be hard not to boast about her. That is not why I wanted this moment. Our kingdom has a problem when it comes to assassins, as you saw a few days ago and the story of my late wife. I am convinced the attack on my daughter you thwarted was an orchestrated attack to make it look like simple bandits."

"I could see that. It was an odd mix. The bandits were well equipped and yet their clothing looked intentionally dirty." Deathwalker commented.

"Exactly. I am telling you this for multiple reasons. One, be careful who you trust. Two, with you, the duchess, and my daughter all together in one place will make you all a prime target for attack. So, please stay alert and keep my daughter safe." Duke Watson explained.

"I appreciate the warning. Someone should really look at taking these assassins out." Deathwalker replied.

"Believe me, we have tried. I am convinced we have traitors among us. As for my boon, I will have Emma deliver it when she arrives." Duke Watson said as he stuck out his hand. "One last thing, good luck, you will need it."

With that, the two dukes shook hands before Deathwalker left the estate.

– – – –

Once the two dukes left, the Queen and her sister sat back down. "Are you sure about involving father?" Duchess Lightheart asked.

"Yes. Why would I not be?" The Queen replied.

"It is not father I am concerned about. You know there are many Winter fairies in our home kingdom, and the fey are not known for not getting involved in our affairs." Duchess Lightheart explained.

"I am counting on it." The Queen answered.

"What?!" Duchess Lightheart asked in surprise.

"You must have felt it as much as I have sister. Such a bloodline is old, beyond ancient yes, but there is more to that man. Magic radiates off him, more than any elf I know or have heard of. To the fey, he will be impossible to ignore once they learn of him, especially Winter herself." The Queen explained.

"You are hoping Queen Mab or one from her court takes an interest, but why when you know my designs on him?" Duchess Lightheart asked.

"You know better than anyone war is coming to our kingdom. These assassination attempts were designed to destabilize our kingdom and our allies prior to war. Whomever is pulling these strings behind the scenes might back off some if the Winter Court sticks their noses into our kingdom's affairs." The Queen clarified.

"You play a dangerous game sister. The Winter Court is not one to bend to the whims of others. You may be inviting more ruin in time." Duchess Lightheart stated.

– – –

As Deathwalker exited the estate he was greeted by Sebastian and Marius. Sebastian was the first to speak up. "How did it go?"

"As well as we expected. Duchess Lightheart will be escorting her niece Lady Emma Watson to Timberfall. There they will stay as my guests for the festival we have planned in a few weeks." Deathwalker answered.

"That seems risky." Marius commented.

"Yes, I imagine Geeves will have an aneurysm." Deathwalker replied.

"What is an aneurysm? I have never heard of that word." Marius asked.

Deathwalker winced as he realized he had used a medical term from his world that they would not know. "Hmmm. To put it simply, it damages the brain. As a healer one must understand the brain."

"You will need extra security. I can arrange for some of my men to supplement. It would be expected as you are my Duke." Sebastian stated.

"Speaking about that. What can you tell me of the other lords now under our duchy?" Deathwalker inquired.

"Lord Simium is a good man. Older in years. He has a few children, a son and daughter that seem rather competent. I expect the man to step down soon due to failing health. Their territory specialized in grain exports as they have many lush fields. Having the extra food supply in the duchy will help during those colder winter months."

"That will help as food production can be an issue at times." Marius commented.

Sebastian nodded. "Now as to Lord Longshot. He used to be a royal court magician. The man is the best marksman in the kingdom, arguably the continent. He is loyal to the crown and was rewarded with his position for distinguished service during one of our last wars. He comes from a respected noble family. I knew his father, good man. Having him in the duchy will be an even greater boon. His territory has some animal exports, but they also have a few mines. His territory is modest, but Lord Longshot has accomplished much with it in the short time he has had it. I can tell you; he will be most excited to compete in the hunt and the archery tournament."

"Good start. My understanding is we should have one or two more landed noble lords under our duchy at some point. What do I need to know about the counts and barons?" Deathwalker said.

"Nothing at the moment. As your home territory does not yet possess any, it falls to your lords to introduce you to those under their authority and report their accomplishments. We can cover that later when you assemble your lords after your trip. Speaking about that, when do you leave, and more importantly, when are you finishing my portal? He, he, he." Sebastian chuckled.

Deathwalker laughed in return. He appreciated Sebastian's directness. "Ha, ha, ha, ha! Do not worry my friend, yours is one of the first as long as you have procured all the materials."

"Yes, Saul was very thorough. I have set aside a rather large warehouse that is easily defended and accessible by the main road in my city. Saul told me he worked with his brother to get the laborers and craftsmen sent over. It should take a few more days, a week at most. My understanding is you are needed for the final part of the construction." Sebastian replied.

"To answer your earlier question, I will be leaving today after I handle a few things. As to your implied question, though it is risky, for security reasons I must be the one that does the final work. I do have one other that could do it on my behalf but that will take some coordination, so for now I am doing the work." Deathwalker answered.

"Fair enough my friend. I just do not like the idea of you traveling alone in disguise across the kingdom. It is too dangerous, even for one as capable as you." Sebastian commented.

"Thank you for saying as much Lord Dormeir! I have been urging my liege to at least select an elite bodyguard unit to defend him. I cannot see to his safety when I do not know where he is." Marius complained.

"Don't you two start ganging up on me again. We have been over this. As much as we don't like it, this must be done for the good of our duchy and this kingdom." Deathwalker held up his hand to forestall their protests. "Now as for an elite bodyguard unit, I have an idea for whom I want and will be recruiting them personally. Do not worry Marius. I will give you the chance to test their skills. That way you can be satisfied with their capabilities."

Marius nodded in agreement.

"We will make a diplomat out of you yet Deathwalker. I'm telling you; your Charisma must be through the roof for you to have convinced our friend here to let that go so easily. Ha, ha, ha." Sebastian teased.

They arrived at what would now be known as the capital portal building. Saul and his brother Malcom were there to greet the men.

"My liege, it is good to see you. As it is good to see Lord Dormeir and General Marius." Saul greeted.

"Yes. I have much to report, your grace." Malcom stated.

Saul spoke up. "We have refreshments and other delights inside, your grace."

"How are my men doing?" Lord Dormeir asked.

"All have been well cared for under our watch, my lord." Saul replied.

Deathwalker leaned in towards Malcom. "Is he always this much of a 'salesman'?"

"You have no idea, my liege. There is a reason he is stationed here in the capital and not me." Malcom replied.

The group entered the room that was turned into a lush waiting area for future travelers, and, as Saul called them, paying customers. Jeffrey or Jeffy as Deathwalker liked to call him approached the group when he saw his lord.

"Sire! You have returned! You really should take a guard detachment with you."

Jeffy had the hardest time hiding his contempt for Deathwalker. The minor noble struggled with the fact that this adventurer was now his duke. It went against everything he believed, but he could not say anything as his lord was rather fond of the man.

"I am fine Jeffrey. I was with friends in the best guarded city in the kingdom. Besides you forget these two men have already proven themselves in combat against high level assassins." Lord Dormeir admonished.

Not wanting to deal with the weasel of a man, Deathwalker decided to leave his friend and address other matters. "If you'll excuse me, my friend. I have business to attend to. Whenever you and your people are ready then depart back to your lands. I will be there as soon as I am able."

Deathwalker clasped wrists with Sebastian before departing for Saul's office.

"See you soon, my friend. Be safe on your journey." Sebastian said before pulling Deathwalker in for a hug.

The two men had started off allies and quickly became good friends. Sebastian was impressed by Deathwalker's fighting prowess and his ingenuity. He was glad to have such a man as his duke.

Malcom and Deathwalker arrived in Saul's private office. As Deathwalker took a seat, he asked his head trader what he wanted to know. "Where are we at in construction progress at each site?"

Malcom pulled out his communications book. "Hargrave is ready now."

"That is the capital for Duchess Lightheart's duchy, correct?"

"Yes, my liege." Malcom replied.

"Deathwalker. How many times do I have to tell you when we are alone to drop all the title stuff."

"You are a duke now... I-I will try." Malcom replied after a few moments of silence.

"What is the status of the other sites?" Deathwalker asked.

"Midway should be ready in a few days. Dalton about four or five days after that." Malcom answered.

"What about the new sites we planned in our duchy?" Deathwalker inquired.

"Lord Longshot was most helpful when he heard of the invention. His city of Lorinda already had most of what we needed. The construction there will be done in a day and a half at most." Malcom reported.

"What of the other two?"

"Jeffrey..." Malcom began to reply but Deathwalker cut him off. "Jeffy. No one is allowed to call him Jeffrey. I had a friend named Jeff, he was a great guy, and I also knew a guy named Jeffy, that was a total pompous jerk. That guy is most assuredly a Jeffy."

Malcom nodded. "Very well, Jeffy has been quite difficult to work with when it came to procuring what we needed. I think he seems to have a problem with my humble background, but worry not, I am a professional. My brother is not the only one who can suck up to pompous nobles."

Malcom's face turned white as he realized what he had just told his duke. "I-I mean..."

Deathwalker raised his hand. "Please think nothing of it. I happen to agree with you. So how far behind are we at the city of Malvinas?"

After taking a moment to collect himself, Malcom continued. "Thanks to Lord Dormeir and Captain Saunders, we are only two days delayed. The construction crew should be done around the time the Midway station will be ready."

"I do like Sebastian, good man." Deathwalker commented.

Nodding in agreement, Malcom shared his thoughts. "Yes, he does seem to be rather fond of you Deathwalker. He is also far easier to deal with than some of the other nobles. Which leads me to the city of Simium, yes very unoriginal but it has been in their family since its founding."

Deathwalker waved him to continue. "It has been a bit more difficult to coordinate with the Simium family. It took us the last few days to speak with all three of them. Luckily, they were in the capital meeting with Duke Watson. They do not fully understand the purpose of the building but made it clear they did not need to understand, only do what their new Duke requires of them. A large warehouse building has been secured, along with some dedicated craftsmen. With that said, they will be one of the last portal stations to be constructed. I would predict about a week and a day before the Timberfall festival begins."

"And what about ensuring we have enough protection for each station?" Deathwalker asked.

Appreciating his liege's unwavering focus, Malcom replied. "General Marius is sending one to two squads to each new location. Luckily, he already has men in Hargrave, Midway, and Dalton. There is still some concern about someone taking control of one of the portal stations, but General Marius and I have seen to that."

"How so?"

"Both his men and the clerks we have hired have all taken multiple magically binding oaths, including, but not limited to, the death oath." Malcom explained.

"Harsh but sounds effective. I also have another security measure. I have arranged for a master portal guardian that will have final control on all traffic through the portals." Deathwalker replied.

"When... how did you have time to..." Malcom started to say but Deathwalker cut him off. "She has been involved since the beginning. Our gate in Timberfall connects to an additional location. That location will remain secret and only known to me and my personal guard when the time comes. When it is time, it will be a great boon for our people. Can you leave it at that for now Malcom?"

"Of course, my liege. I have drawn up a map that will integrate with your map and update it with all the portal station site locations."

"Excellent! Let's get that done so I can head out and make my way to Hargrave." Deathwalker said as he took his Master Explorer's map from his bag of holding.

# Chapter 2 - Ludicrous Speed, Go!

'If I'm lucky enough I can get to Hargrave and be done and on my way to Lorinda before Duchess Lightheart even knows I was there.' Deathwalker thought as he snuck out of the capital.

It was night by the time Deathwalker attempted to leave the city. Using **Shadow Teleport**, he quickly moved to some nearby trees. Once hidden, he activated his dragon wings and quickly took to the sky.

Hargrave was northeast of the capital and bordered the Hibernal Territory. It was the closest duchy to the elven nation ruled by the high elves. With a portal station in the city of Hargrave, the costs to trade between the two nations would drastically reduce, as would the time, which would result in increased trade. Deathwalker knew that would translate to greater prosperity for both nations.

Under the cover of night, Deathwalker rose high into the sky and took off at a break-neck-speed. By foot, from the capital, Hargrave was over a week away by a fast horse. It took a caravan over two weeks to three weeks of travel.

The roads and trails were not a direct shot there, which did add some additional time. A crow could fly directly there, and it would probably take it three days. However, Deathwalker calculated it would take him about a full day, maybe even less as he became more comfortable using his combination of dragon wings and magic. He used air magic to reduce wind resistance and friction. Then using gravity magic to reduce drag and shift gravity to propel him forward.

'You know I wonder if I can break the sound barrier.' Deathwalker thought as he fed power into his magic to shoot him like a cannonball forward.

The more mana he poured into the effort the faster and faster he went. Trees flew by in a blur. First the trees were individual objects, then as Deathwalker's speed kept increasing the individual trees turned into one giant green blob. Even with the friction reduction, the speed was too fast to fully compensate, and he started feeling warmer. Until...

BOOM!!!

Deathwalker's ears popped and rang as he felt the sonic boom he just created. Only the magic he had surrounded himself in protected him from the worst of the effects. Roaring as he went feeling the exhilaration of speed and power, "RROOAARRR!!!"

Realizing the edges of his shirt were starting to catch fire, Deathwalker immediately began to decelerate. As he stopped and floated in the air, he patted the spots to help stop them burning. A new notification was beckoning for his attention.

*Congratulations! Your Intuition and Creativity have helped you gain the achievement Defying Gravity! You are one of the very few who have flown faster than the speed of sound! +10 Agility, +10 Dexterity, and +10 Wisdom. Flight movement speed increased by 25%. Mana and Stamina usage reduced by 25% while flying. As this was achieved using a unique combination of Air and Gravity magic, you have created a new spell.*

A bold prompt appeared in both his vision and mind, calling for him to act.

***Please name the spell.***

Deathwalker thought of the first thing that came to him.

***Spell: Ludicrous Speed Go!***
*<u>Mana Cost</u>: Channeled*
*<u>Description</u>: Manipulate the air and gravity to protect and increase your flight speed. This is a channeled spell. Speed increased based on the amount of mana channeled into the spell. Create a Sonic Boom attack with enough mana used.*

"There it is! Ha, ha, ha, ha! This is going to be so much fun to use!" Deathwalker celebrated.

"Wait a minute, I'm here already? Man, I was flying."

It was still dark outside, allowing Deathwalker to sneak into Hargrave without detection. Dropping down into an alley near the warehouse that was used to build the portal station, he shifted to hide his wings.

'If I recall, Lt. Tomlin was the one in charge of this location.' Deathwalker thought as he walked towards the entrance gate.

When he had done this very thing at the capital, the building there only had two guards on duty. This location had four soldiers, with two patrols circling the perimeter. Deathwalker was impressed that LT Tomlin was not taking any chances.

"I bet you Garry would find some way to mess with the guards. You know, I never thought I'd say this, but I find myself missing the murderhobo." Deathwalker said to himself as he walked out of the alley.

The motion caught the guards' attention and the four soldiers instantly turned in Deathwalker's direction.

While in the capital, General Marius had informed Deathwalker that there was an added benefit to the oaths that were sworn. All of Marius' men had sworn binding oaths. Part of the magic of those agreements bound the soldiers to whomever Marius pledged his fealty to. In other words, they pledged themselves to Marius and by Marius' oath of fealty it gave Deathwalker their fealty as well.

Now what caught Deathwalker's attention, was that meant if he issued a direct command to one of Marius' men, they were compelled to follow the orders of their liege-lord. This gave Deathwalker all sorts of interesting ideas. He did have to make sure they knew it was him.

"Kneel before your Duke."

The bodies of all four men moved without question or conscious thought.

"What the?"

"Why did I just do that?"

"You idiot, he must be Duke Dragonvein!"

"Our apologies your grace!"

"Think nothing of it. You may rise. My apologies, but I could think of no better way to verify my identity." Deathwalker commented.

"Think nothing of it your grace. I can take you to LT. Tomlin." The oldest and most level-headed of the guards said.

Nodding, Deathwalker fell in behind the soldier and followed him into the building. It did not take them long to arrive at a similar office to Saul's in the capital. The soldier opened the office door.

"Lieutenant, Duke Dragonvein has arrived."

"What?! He's at least a week or two early! I just spoke to General Marius this morning!" A gruff voiced man, Deathwalker assumed was LT Tomlin said.

"I know nothing about that sir, but he is here." The soldier replied.

"Well, let him in you fool!" LT Tomlin ordered.

The soldier turned to the side and held the door open for Deathwalker to walk inside the office. Once Deathwalker took a seat the soldier shut the door and returned to his post.

LT Tomlin was a good one- and three-quarter meters tall. Well-toned, dark hair and a mustache that could give Tom Selleck and Sam Elliot a run for their money. The soldier went down on one knee with a fist over his heart, and his head bowed. "Duke Dragonvein it is an honor to have you here in Hargrave."

"Please rise Lieutenant. I have no need for followers who do not look up. You will forever be bumping into things. Please, sit, and let us converse." Deathwalker stated.

LT Tomlin rose from his kneeling position and took his seat. "General Marius warned me that you would not be like the nobles. My apologies but we did not expect you for some time. If you give me some time, I am sure I can procure a suite at the finest inns in Hargrave. Or if you prefer, I can send a messenger to Duchess Lightheart's estate. I am sure they would be honored to host you for the time you are here."

Raising his hand, Deathwalker spoke up. "I have no need of any of those things. I came here to do a job only I can do. As much as I would like to get acquainted with the town and get to know our men, I am on a bit of a tight timeline. If you will take me to the portal room."

LT Tomlin rose to his feet. "If you will follow me your grace. I can show you the way."

Without another word Deathwalker was escorted to the Hargrave portal room. This portal was just as grand and ornate as the one in the capital. They had not skimped on the opulence.

'These artists sure love to embellish, but perhaps there is some logic to it. People will expect such things, especially the nobles and wealthy merchants.' Deathwalker thought as he inspected the portal structure.

Turning to LT Tomlin, "I see the artisans did not skimp on their craft."

LT Tomlin smiled. He had been concerned his Duke would not feel the work was enough. "Yes, your grace! I made a point to remind them to do their best or we would not procure their services again. After all they were doing the work for high nobility. Many jumped at the chance, I assure you if anything is not to your liking, we can hire whomever we wish."

Deathwalker inwardly cringed. He understood many jumped at the chance to be noticed by high nobles in the hope of becoming a retainer or at least gaining a patron. That made logical sense as it was about survival and getting noticed. What he couldn't tolerate was how many patrons took advantage of that hope and treated some retainers with an attitude of borderline abuse or at the very least taking advantage of people and pushing them around.

Deathwalker decided to remove any misconceptions. "Though I appreciate the zeal Lieutenant, I want to make it clear that our craftsmen and artisans are valuable resources. I expect them to be treated as such. Sure, if someone fails repeatedly or is not up to the task, we acquire someone who is. Competency is most important in life and so that is also true here as well. But no matter one's station we can still treat them with respect. That is how you can honor me as one of my men. Is that understood?"

LT Tomlin snapped to attention and put his fist to his heart. "As you command my liege!"

Nodding, Deathwalker decided to say one more thing before dismissing the man. "I expect my people to speak up and share their concerns. I will never fault someone for such a thing. As decorum dictates, pull me aside or share your concerns in private. If it cannot wait, get my attention, and state the matter is 'duchy business'. Hopefully that is clear as well."

"Yes, your grace. It is crystal clear. Thank you for caring enough to listen to our humble concerns." LT Tomlin answered as he thought about how different this man was from the nobles he dealt with in his career as a soldier.

"Good. Now that the matter is addressed, I see everything I asked for is here. I have everything I require to finish this portal station. Please leave me and make sure I am not to be disturbed. I will notify you when I am done and ready to leave." Deathwalker replied.

LT Tomlin bowed. "As you command, my liege."

Without another word the Lieutenant left the room and ordered the guards stationed by the door to allow no one entry while their Duke worked.

Having overheard the order, Deathwalker shifted his attention to the task at hand. He knew he would have to speed up the process or at least do what he did last time and create a time bubble around the room to let him work faster. Deep down Deathwalker knew this ability was something he should spend time mastering and he added it to his mental list of things to do later.

Deathwalker chuckled at his internal thought of finding time to master time. "Ha! That sure sounds like an oxymoron."

Accessing the **Infinite Well of Time Magic** within him, Deathwalker pushed outward to surround the room in a bubble of increased time compared to the world outside. He marveled how this magic never seemed to run out and operated separately from his mana pool. It did seem to be truly infinite.

"A wonder to ponder later. I have work to do." Deathwalker said to himself as he shifted his thinking towards the rune-crafting that would consume his full attention.

As Deathwalker carved, he infused magic into each rune. On he went, one after the other. He would only pause to withdraw and consume food and drink from the rations in his bag of holding. Each time he did so, Deathwalker sent a mental thank you to Uriel for gifting him such a wonder.

By the time he finished the Hargrave portal, three days had passed inside the time bubble. Deathwalker's **Rune-Crafting** Skill had reached Adept rank, which thrilled Deathwalker greatly, as each rank reduced the effort and time required to rune-craft. He remained in the time bubble another few hours to catch up on sleep and recharge his mental batteries. When he finally deactivated the time bubble what was almost four days inside had been just shy of 4 hours for the rest of the world.

"Man, I really do have to figure out the limits of the **Infinite Well of Time Magic**. It is by far one of my most powerful abilities." Deathwalker told himself.

After telling the guards to notify LT. Tomlin, Deathwalker activated the portal gate to make the final connection to integrate the gate into his portal network. By the time LT. Tomlin returned to the portal gate room, Deathwalker had a portal between Hargrave and the capital established. Normally, traffic would have to go through Timberfall as a waypoint, however, as the owner of the network, he could bypass such restrictions.

"It is magnificent your grace!" LT. Tomlin said in astonishment. The men who followed him in all had their mouths open, staring in wonder.

"It is a means to an end for our people. I entrust the protection of this place to you and your men, Lieutenant. Trader Malcom will send someone to help coordinate and manage the accounting and transactions. Please do not hesitate to let us know if you need anything." Deathwalker instructed.

LT Tomlin put his fist to his heart and bowed his head. His men repeated the gesture. "We shall guard this place with our lives.

Deathwalker nodded.

"Thank you for your dedication and loyalty. Do not forget to let us know if you require anything." Those were the last words Deathwalker spoke before walking through the portal.

As he exited in the capital, he found Saul and several guards present. When they saw it was Deathwalker they all relaxed.

"Your grace! We were not expecting you so soon! Are you tired? Can I get you anything?" Saul immediately shifted into his comfortable salesman role.

"I am fine Saul but thank you for the offer and your attention to detail." Deathwalker replied.

"I take it the Hargrave portal station is complete." Saul stated more than asked.

"Yes, the Hargrave gate room is fully operational and ready for use. Please inform your brother and General Marius. I would like someone sent who is ready to oversee the transportation fees. Let's also send some additional guards to serve under LT. Tomlin's command." Deathwalker instructed.

"Most excellent, most excellent! May the wonders you create never cease!" Saul replied excitedly.

"Did Sebastian get back okay?" Deathwalker inquired about his friend.

"Oh yes, your grace. Lord Dormeir arrived in Timberfall without incident. Malcom went back with him. According to my brother, he was anxious to return to his territory and ensure the construction of his portal station was completed as soon as possible." Saul answered.

"Yes, once each of the territories within our duchy are connected via portal, trade and defense will become so much easier." Deathwalker commented.

"I take it you plan to leave soon your grace. Where to next?" Saul asked.

"I'm going to head towards Lorinda." Deathwalker answered.

"I can see why you came here. Lorinda is slightly closer to the capital than Timberfall, but not by much, due to the winding trail to get there." Saul commented.

What Saul did not know was for Deathwalker, who would be flying there, the distance was much shorter from the capital. 'I don't have to worry about some winding road.' Deathwalker thought, but replied, "It will give them some time to finish construction."

"Ah, very wise, as usual your grace!" Saul complimented.

Once again, Deathwalker exited the capital and snuck into some nearby trees. It was still early in the morning so many of the populace were not up yet. After checking that no one was watching, Deathwalker rose high in the air.

Making sure he was at least a good distance away from the capital, Deathwalker activated Ludicrous Speed, Go! Pumping mana into the spell the world became a blur, and he heard the sonic boom from Deathwalker breaking the sound barrier.

Nearby travelers heading to the capital caught the tail end of the sonic boom.

"What was that!"

"Are we under attack?!"

"I have never heard anything like that!"

"What?! What did you just say?! My ears are ringing!"

The band of travelers were not the only ones to catch the sonic boom. The sound impacted into a nearby cave. The echoes reverberated off the walls disturbing and waking the long slumbering dragon.

Draconis stirred for the first time in over 100 years. He had fallen into deep slumber after he reached the point of maturity. For dragons it was a significant power boost when they reached each threshold. Draconis had reached his transition from a young dragon into an adult.

Draconis yawned. "Rawrrr! What wakes me from my slumber? Perhaps it is time to see what changes have taken place since I was last awake."

Draconis flew out of his cave high in the mountains. As he surveyed the surrounding areas, the dragon noticed how much these humanoids have spread since the last time he was awake. Prior to his slumber, the closest kingdom was sparsely populated. Now Draconis saw the signs of many humanoids everywhere he looked.

Those same travelers heading to the capital saw the large dragon flying overhead. The horses attached to their carriages were frightened and very skittish.

"Oh no! A dragon!"

"We must warn the capital!"

The horses took no coaxing to pick up speed and get to the capital post haste.

Draconis watched the puny humans and horses flee. "Ha! Yes! These humans may have spread like weeds, but they still know their place. Seeing them run reminds me I could eat. Let me find some cattle nearby."

It did not take Draconis long to find a pasture with cattle grazing. He knew he had to act quickly as his natural dragon aura would scare most prey animals away. Not giving them a chance the dragon blew flames to kill multiple cattle before he landed and began devouring his prey.

The local farmer who witnessed this sent his son to warn the city and seek help. "Go son! You must get help!"

"I will not leave you, and ma!"

"You must! The nobles must be warned!"

"Those nobles do not do anything, pa!"

"They may not do anything to help us, but they believe in self-preservation! A dragon is a kingdom wide threat! Now, enough arguing. Go!"

The farmer's son bolted out the back patio and took off as fast as his legs could carry him, making a straight line towards the city.

# Chapter 3 - Lord Longshot

Deathwalker arrived in the city of Lorinda. The city was bustling with traffic from traders and travelers. The city served as a good way point for foreign trade.

Once again, Deathwalker snuck into the city and headed straight for the warehouse that was to be the city's portal station. He had zero interest in the fanfare his arrival would stir. With that said, the duke had every intention of meeting his new vassal.

'All in good time. Ah these must be the guards they hired.' Deathwalker thought as he repeated his classic move of walking out of the nearest alley to the warehouse.

"Halt!"

"Who goes there?!"

'Do these guys know any other lines? Well, let's get this resolved as quickly as possible.'

"Kneel!" Deathwalker commanded.

The guards immediately kneeled.

"What is happening?!"

"I couldn't control my body!"

Deathwalker stopped in front of the two guards. "That is because I am your duke. My apologies for using such a crude method but I am on a bit of a time crunch to get all these portal stations completed before the Timberfall festival."

The mixed look of shock and realization flashed on the guards' faces. "Our apologies your grace!"

"We were not expecting you so soon."

Deathwalker waved away their concerns. “Please rise and escort me to the portal room. Also send word to Lord Longshot I have arrived in the city and will meet with him after I have finished what I must do here.”

Both guards bowed their heads and saluted by bringing their fist to their heart. They led Deathwalker to the portal room before bowing and returning to their post. One of the guards headed for the lord’s manor to inform Lord Longshot that their duke had arrived.

Realizing he did not want to wait too long before meeting with Lord Longshot, Deathwalker tapped into his **Infinite Well of Time Magic**. Creating a sphere of Time magic around the room, Deathwalker turned his focus to rune-carving and infusing his magic into the structure. As this was the fourth portal station he worked on, the process was beginning to feel like muscle memory. This allowed him to finish the process faster than any of the others so far.

“Hmmm. That was rather easy. I feel like I’m finally getting a handle on the knowledge that is in my head.” Deathwalker said before he dropped the bubble of Time Magic and activated the Lorinda portal station.

————————

A guard burst into a clearing in the back of Lord Longshot’s manor. When the lord moved into the manor, he had this space cleared for archery targets. Lord Longshot was often found here with his men practicing and constantly honing the skills of his men while remaining sharp himself.

All the archers turned to the uninvited guest. “What is the meaning of this? You know better than to disturb our lord when he is practicing!”

The guard dropped to his knees, both to catch his breath from running the whole way here and in the hope, he would not be shot by multiple arrows. “H-he is... here. D-duke Dragonvein is... in the city!”

“Why did the gate guards not notify me of his arrival?” Lord Longshot asked.

The guard on his knees was still trying to catch his breath. "I-I do... not... know, my lord. H-he arrived... at the portal station... unguarded. Told us... to let you know... he would see you... after he was done at the station."

"That seems suspicious. You just let someone you don't know alone in the portal station! How do you know it was Duke Dragonvein?" Lord Longshot asked incredulously.

Finally catching his breath, the guard replied. "He commanded us to bow, and our bodies moved without our control. It had to be our oaths in effect."

"Not necessarily. Some possess such mind magic. It is exceptionally rare but still a possibility." Lord Longshot stated before turning to his men. "Come let us investigate. We must ensure no one is trying to ruin our duke's plans."

The guard now regretted running here. 'The duke did not seem to want to be interrupted. Am I going to catch his ire when the city lord barges in while he is working. If he felt what we did, he would not doubt the veracity of the claim that the man we met was the duke.'

Lord Longshot led 200 archers to the Lorinda portal station. These weren't ordinary archers. Every one of them could use body enhancement magic to boost their eyesight or shoot farther. Lord Longshot had special bows made that could handle the extra strain.

They flooded into the building sealing off any avenue of escape. After every exit was covered, Lord Longshot led his men into the portal room. As he and his men entered the room, they saw the arch glowing and found it filled with soldiers.

Deathwalker noticed a tall, slender, and tone man in leather armor. He exuded an aura of killing intent. Insight told him everything he needed to know.

"You must be Lord Longshot." Deathwalker said as his men immediately took defensive positions as they drew their weapons.

"Stand down men!" Lord Longshot called as he lowered his bow.

'This man must be Duke Dragonvein. How else would there be so many here.' Lord Longshot thought before kneeling and bowing his head.

All his men followed their lord, kneeling and bowing their heads.

"Forgive me your grace. I did not mean to draw arms against you. I thought it suspicious that a lone traveler would show up and not announce themselves at the gate accompanied by an honor guard. Please forgive my impudence. In fact, I would gladly give you my oaths of fealty here and now!" Lord Longshot explained.

The royal court magician turned lord saw a hand extended in his vision causing him to look up.

"I have no need for people who keep their heads down. Please rise." Deathwalker said.

Lord Longshot took the offered hand and clasped wrists with Deathwalker as he rose to his feet. His men once again followed suit and rose to their feet as well.

"Impressive. You have a well-trained force. I probably should've used the gate, but this was much faster." Deathwalker commented.

"Thank you, your grace." Lord Longshot replied.

"Eh, enough of this 'your grace stuff', let's drop the formalities, call me Deathwalker."

Lord Longshot was unsure how to proceed. What information he could gather about his new duke was that he was unconventional to say the least. "Umm. I am not sure addressing you in such a manner would be appropriate."

"Nonsense! Besides, I was told you were a straight shooter." Deathwalker said.

Lord Longshot looked even more puzzled. "I am not sure what my skill with a bow has to do with how I address you..."

Deathwalker shook his head and waved is hands in frustration. "No, no, no. That's not what I meant. Damn idioms! It's an expression that refers to how the person conducts themselves. They are direct, honest, and to the point, like someone who can shoot straight. Catch my meaning now?"

Lord Longshot smiled upon hearing his duke's explanation. "Ah! I like that expression! I must use it going forward, your grace. Yes, I do endeavor to comport myself in such a manner. But what does that have to do with how I address you, your grace?"

Sighing, Deathwalker replied, "I appreciate those that can be direct and speak honestly. I would rather hear and uncomfortable truth than a rose-covered lie."

"Then you be in the minority, your grace." Lord Longshot commented.

"Yes, so I have been told. Come let me introduce you to LT. Tom Daniels." Deathwalker said.

As if that was the soldier's cue a tall slender but well-built man in armor stepped forward and bowed his head. "My lord, it is an honor to meet you."

"LT. Daniels will be the one in charge of training the men. He will coordinate with your people until another officer can be appointed. A clerk under my Trader Malcom will also be arriving to help maintain the documentation and help with logistics." Deathwalker explained.

Lord Longshot extended his hand and clasped wrists with LT Daniels. "Well met Lieutenant."

Deathwalker nodded in approval. "Good. Now with introductions out of the way..."

Lord Longshot realized what his duke was stating. "Of course!" Once again, the man knelt. "I give my oath of fealty to Duke Deathwalker Dragonvein. I shall endeavor to serve in as honorable and noble a way as possible so as to never bring shame upon my liege. I will faithfully stand in battle and serve in whatever manner he requires. His enemies are my enemies. His allies are my allies. My lands are his."

Deathwalker was informed by Sebastian that oaths between nobles were a bit more complex and therefore much longer. "I accept your oath of fealty in the same gravity it was given. I shall provide protection and sanctuary should you or your subjects require it. Should you break faith or comport yourself in an unhonorable way, I shall do my sacred duty to protect our people. Rise and let us now be friends."

The two men clasped wrists once again. As Lord Longshot rose to his feet Deathwalker commented. "I appreciate the oath, but what I was going to say before you interrupted me was if you wanted to go somewhere to sit and get to know each other."

Lord Longshot's eyebrows shot up before he saw a smile appear on his liege's face. Both men started laughing. "Ha, ha, ha! Good one your grace. Come, I am being a poor host, you must be tired after your long journey. If you would follow me to my estate, I can have my people draw you a hot bath. Afterwards, we can enjoy a fine meal of some boar I killed just this morning."

"Oooo, forest boar. Let me talk to your cooks about something I call bacon!" Deathwalker said as Lord Longshot led him towards the city lord's manor.

———-

The two men laughed and joked as they finished their meal in the morning. The two found they had much in common, from hunting to concern for their people. They had talked through the day and night, now finishing their breakfast meal.

"I must say Deathwalker, here I am supposed to be host but this bacon you have taught my cooks to make, absolutely sensational!" Lord Longshot boasted.

"Of course! It is good to find a fellow meat eater!" Deathwalker replied.

"Yes! I agree! My mind is far sharper, and I require less sleep since I switched to an animal diet only! It is nice that someone understands and appreciates that!" Lord Longshot answered.

"Thank you, Anthony, for the tour of Lorinda. It was good to have a better understanding of the cities and people within our duchy." Deathwalker commented.

Lord Anthony Longshot nodded. "I agree. It is good to know I serve a man who cares about his people and makes a point to learn more about them. So, tell me more about these hunts and tournaments you have planned."

Deathwalker began to explain. "Ah yes. I thought you might be interested in those. I plan to start the festival with various cooking contests. Then I plan to move to tournaments for one to test their skills. The tournaments will include melee combat, archery, throwing blades, races, and feats of strength."

Lord Anthony Longshot perked up when he heard about an archery tournament. "Are there any restrictions on who can participate?"

"None. Though I will not be participating in any of the tournaments. However, I do plan to lead the hunt." Deathwalker answered.

"What are you willing to tell me about the hunt?" Lord Anthony Longshot asked.

"Monsters and beasts seem to be out of balance lately." Deathwalker began. He knew exactly what the cause was, the primary predator of the forest, his pumas, had relocated to his realm.

"The intent of the hunt is to thin some of the more aggressive monsters and animals. Then putting that meat to good use by holding a massive feast to celebrate. The winner of the cooking contest will be asked to lead the making of various dishes with the meats we collect. The rest of the materials will be sold to the local businesses and Adventurers' guild." Deathwalker explained.

“It sounds well thought out, your grace. Do you require any events be conducted at the other cities in your duchy?” Lord Longshot asked.

Deathwalker decided to not press Anthony on his use of ‘your grace’ as he figured it was habit and it was something to eventually get used to. “I would encourage such things. I want us to do this festival each year. Something else I would like to be shared with our people. I will allow two uses of the portal network for free for our people during the festival celebrations. Anything beyond that will require them to pay the transportation fees. Also, additional taxes if they are attempting to bring goods to sell beyond what they can carry.”

“That will be a great boon to our people. It is also quite wise. They will surely spread the word of the magical wonder of the portal network. This will bring traders knocking at our doors to begin using the network as quickly as they can to capitalize on the reduction in operating costs.” Lord Longshot commented.

‘This new duke must have exceptionally high Intelligence and Wisdom stats.’ Lord Longshot thought.

“I have enjoyed our time together Anthony.” Deathwalker stated.

“And I you Deathwalker.” Lord Longshot replied.

The two men clasped wrists. “Your men seem to be very loyal. That is a good sign that you care about your people. I am glad to call you an ally.” Deathwalker commented.

“It has been an honor getting to know one who is so focused on the betterment of the kingdom for all, not just the nobles. I am proud to call you, my liege.” Lord Longshot stated as he bowed his head.

As they finished clasping their wrists, Deathwalker spoke up. “Come, escort me back to the portal station so I can instruct you on its workings.”

# Chapter 4 - Savage Squad Re-Unites

"Welcome back, my hunky master." Lilandra greeted Deathwalker as he walked through the portal.

Lilandra jumped into Deathwalker's arms.

"Lilandra! Always with your antics." Deathwalker mock complained. In truth, her upbeat attitude and willingness to help him, however she could make it hard for him to truly be angry with her. Plus, his emotions were still partially muted, but every time he started to focus on that fact something would pull his attention away.

"So, which one do you want to start with?" Lilandra asked.

Rather than return to the capital, Deathwalker decided it was far past time to start the process of giving Mrrsha and Prrsha their wish.

"Do you think we can do them both at the same time?" Deathwalker queried.

"Oh master, we haven't even had time together and you already want to add two other girls... I'm game!" Lilandra teased.

Deathwalker rolled his eyes. "Very funny. You know what I mean. Mrrsha leads the pride, but Prrsha is fierce and has expressed this to be her greatest wish."

Lilandra smiled. She loved to tease her master. Like any true hunter, once he set his mind to something it was almost impossible to distract him from it. She admired that trait even if she didn't say so. "Fine. You don't know what you're missing." She fake-pouted. Just as fast she had a smile on her face. "It might be possible to 'do them' both at the same time."

"Do who? Can I join in?" Garry said as he floated into the room.

"Hey Buddy! Have you been behaving yourself?" Deathwalker said in greeting.

"I have been a pillar of cooperation and help." Garry replied.

Deathwalker turned to Lilandra with raised eyebrows. Seeing his implied question, she spoke up. "By 'cooperation and help' he means join in any fight and googly eyes at me and Frrsha. And you have no idea how creepy that can be with all those eyes!"

"What?! I'm a Shadow Gazer, I creep in the shadows, and I look at things. It's in the name!" Garry answered.

"I'm surprised you didn't turn him into something as punishment. You did threaten to do so if I recall Lilandra?" Deathwalker chimed in.

Lilandra sighed. "As annoying as he can be, your familiar is quite useful, especially when it comes to battle."

"Ah yes, you did mention fighting. Tell me more." Deathwalker inquired.

"Oh, it's been loads of fun boss! Beasts and monsters. They are dumb and plentiful. It's like shooting fish in a barrel. He, he, he." Garry replied.

"Sylpharian Tigers and Silverback Stags mostly. On the boarders of where the pumas have settled, they have also encountered some Six-legged Varnacs." Lilandra stated.

"I'm not familiar with any of those beasts. What can you tell me about them?"

"Sylpharian Tigers are fast and ferocious. They are strong with hides tough enough to hold up against a puma's claws. They seem to have some kind of connection to each other similar to the forest pumas." Lilandra explained.

"Sounds like the perfect counter to our pumas." Deathwalker said in concern.

"Except they are stupid. All muscles and claws. Pure instinct and easy to ambush." Garry commented.

Lilandra continued. “Garry is correct. They are not smart and run off pure animal instinct. Their connection to each other helps them coordinate attacks, but they only use it in the most primitive ways. The pumas out smart them each time. The only problem is it takes a few pumas to take down one tiger. That is except for Frrsha, she wipes the floor with one like they were a cub.”

“More reason to help transform my pumas into the best version of themselves.” Deathwalker confirmed.

“The Sylpharian Tigers hunt the Silverback Stags which have hair fibers interwoven with metal. They are several meters tall. Smarter than the tigers but not by much. They are more protective and tend to run in larger herds. Their antlers and hooves are sharp and hard as metal...” Lilandra continued.

Prrsha interrupted. “The combination of their numbers and antlers makes them formidable prey. It is good to see you, my alpha.”

Frrsha jumped into Deathwalker’s arms and rubbed her face into his cheek. “Alpha smells so gooood!”

“Always all over our alpha Frrsha. Let him breathe.” Mrrsha chided.

“Ha, ha, ha, ha! Alright Frrsha, it is good to see you too.” Deathwalker chuckled as he pried himself free.

Once free he greeted the other two pumas. “He, he, he! It is good to see all of you.”

“You too, my alpha!” Mrrsha leaned into Deathwalker.

“We caught the tail end of your conversation about the Silverback stags.” Frrsha said.

“Yes, as Prrsha stated, they are formidable prey.”

“And tasty too!” Garry commented.

Everyone turned to Garry.

“What?! Am I wrong?” Garry defended.

“The annoying ball of eyes is not wrong. The pride has eaten well lately.” Prrsha stated.

“Yes, and we must admit your familiar has been of great help to the pride.” Mrrsha said.

“Awe! You like me! You really like me!” Garry cheered.

“Good Mask reference buddy.” Deathwalker commented.

“Thank you, boss.” Garry smiled.

“Now you mentioned another threat. What Oh yes, Six-legged Varnacs. What can you tell me about them.”

Garry visibly shivered.

“That bad huh?” Deathwalker asked.

“They seem to be part of the shadows and the dark. Vicious, several meters long. They seem to faze partially out of existence.” Lilandra began to explain before Garry interrupted her.

“They can phase into the Shadow Realm! I can’t hide from them. They just follow me there!”

“They are Dark and Shadow aligned creatures. Brutal and cruel. Luckily, we have not encountered many of them and they seem stuck near the Shadow and Dark leylines.” Lilandra relayed.

“Well, it sounds like my realm might require more attention than I originally thought.” Deathwalker considered.

“Not yet, my hunky master. In time yes, but not for a while. Shall we?” Lilandra tilted her head towards Mrrsha and Prrsha.

“Yes Lilandra. It is time to fulfill some wishes.” Deathwalker said.

Prrsha and Mrrsha’s ears perked up.

Deathwalker smiled at them. “Yes, my patient kitties. It is time to turn you into matriarchs.”

"Truly?" Mrrsha asked.

"Alpha do not tease us. Not with something so precious to us." Prrsha lamented.

Shaking his head, Deathwalker replied. "No, I am serious. It is past time to do what I promised. If you will follow me to the Central Chamber."

Lilandra had advised her master to repeat what he did with Frrsha in the throne room central chamber where the leylines all converged. From this location, Deathwalker was master of this place. He would have the greatest control over his magic, and it would allow him to repeat the process for each.

Tapping into his core and Infinite Well of Time Magic, Deathwalker activated both his Power of 13 and Soul-Forging abilities as one hand touched Mrrsha and his other hand touched Prrsha. Magic flooded into both pumas. They both partially lifted off the ground as their bodies began to glow a bright golden white light, and then morphed into humanoid outlines.

Deathwalker quickly reviewed his notifications.

*Congratulations! Mrrsha's race has changed! She has become your 4th disciple! You may now speak with them across realms!*

*Congratulations! Prrsha's race has changed! She has become your 5th discipline! You may now speak with them across realms!*

*Congratulations! Your **Soul-Forging** ability has reached **level 65**! You can now grant your disciples the ability to help break existing bonds and create new bonds in service of you.*

As the light began to fade both Mrrsha and Prrsha now stood there in humanoid form and wobbled a bit on their now two feet. Frrsha hugged them both in a tackle. "Sisters! I am so happy for you both!"

"Th-thank you Frrsha. This form feels powerful." Mrrsha replied.

“Yes, Mrrsha. I have never felt such power thrumming through my body.” Prrsha chimed in before she broke the hug and embraced Deathwalker. “Oh, thank you alpha! Now we can stand by your side always.”

“As much as I would like that Prrsha, our alpha still has me remain with the pride and I have been a two-legged puma for much longer.” Frrsha said to help temper their expectations.

Deathwalker smiled. “Actually, I’m glad you brought that up Frrsha. My people in Timberfall are pushing me to have an honor guard. I was wondering if the three of you would like to be my personal bodyguards. What do you think?”

All three women instantly pounced on Deathwalker in a group hug and nuzzled their faces into him.

‘Hmmm. Must be a cat thing.’ Deathwalker thought.

“Oh alpha! Do you really mean it?” Frrsha asked.

“Thank you, my alpha!” Mrrsha cheered.

“This means so much, my alpha!” Prrsha said in a rare show of emotions.

“Boss is so lucky. Two of em are naked. Hey boss, can we not clothe these two at least?” Garry commented.

That was when Deathwalker realized Mrrsha and Prrsha were indeed naked. Luckily, he still had a few auto-sizing outfits he removed from his bag.

“Please put these on.” Deathwalker said as he turned around to give them privacy as they got dressed.

“It is so odd that you did not have a problem with us being naked before.” Mrrsha thought out loud.

“Yes, too distracting I believe were his words when Frrsha took this form.” Prrsha recalled.

“I think he likes us more this way.” Frrsha smiled.

"I know I do!" Garry chimed in.

Deathwalker just groaned. His mind was too focused on the next objective. He didn't have time to sort out his thoughts related to the three gorgeous cat girls that he could literally smell their pheromones.

Lilandra just giggled at the interactions. "He, he, he, he. You know you bring this on yourself, my hunky master."

"How do you figure?" Deathwalker asked.

"Simple. You keep raising your Charisma. Do not forget this has an effect on those around you. But you also keep being yourself and it is clear you genuinely care about your people." Lilandra explained.

"Of course I do. It is only logical for a person to look after those he cares about." Deathwalker replied before turning to the three matriarchs. "Now I would ask the three of you to seek out Uriel."

"What is it you require of us my alpha?" Prrsha asked.

"See if he has any magical books to help teach you how to read and write. Also, it would be good to familiarize yourself with the local laws and customs. I must finish a few more portal stations before I return and have you three join me.

"That sounds so boring." Frrsha pouted.

Mrrsha gave her sister a stern look before turning back to Deathwalker. "We shall do as you command, alpha."

"Oh, and you should try to drop that when we are around others. Though it is acceptable among beastkin, others are not as understanding of such things." Deathwalker cautioned.

The three cat girls nodded and left the throne room's Central Chamber. As Deathwalker watched them go, he thought how nice it would be to have some of his pumas by his side again. They would still need to coordinate the pride's activities, but figured out with the portal network that wouldn't be too difficult.

Checking his mana and stamina reserves, to see their levels. This had become a habit of his lately when he used large amounts of power. Deathwalker was surprised to find them both full. He knew he used massive amounts of power, and his mana pool should be practically empty right now.

“How am I already full?” Deathwalker said out loud.

“What has that master?” Lilandra asked.

“My mana pool, its full! I know I have a high regeneration but not this high!” Deathwalker replied.

Lilandra waved her hand at the chamber. “Oh, that’s simple. It is because you are in a seat at the center of your place of power. When you used your abilities, this place instinctually answers your call and comes to your aid.”

“You make it sound like it’s alive.” Deathwalker commented.

“In a way, but not how you might be thinking. This place has existed longer than many can comprehend. It serves a purpose. Anything with power that serves a purpose can seem to take on a mind of its own. In truth, when you absorbed the heart crystal and bonded with this place it gained a level of sentience with that connection. That can get tricky and may mean you may face other trials as a result.” Lilandra further explained.

“What does that mean?” Deathwalker asked in concern.

“Nothing to worry about now. When do you leave for the next portal?” Lilandra replied.

“Don’t change the subject.”

“Whatever do you mean?” Lilandra attempted to fain ignorance.

“Even I didn’t buy that one.” Garry commented.

“Lilandra!” Deathwalker chided.

Lilandra mock pouted. "Okay, fine! You are the **Third Path of Creation**, but you don't fully understand what that means yet."

"Go on." Deathwalker said when she didn't elaborate.

Exhaling, she continued. "It's not that I don't want to tell you, but it is part of your own trials. I still am technically your arbiter. What I can tell you is that you are still at the beginning of your journey."

"What does that mean?" Deathwalker asked.

Lilandra attempted to elaborate. "You gaining this place is only the beginning. Usually, you must complete quests and other achievements to fully unlock the powers and then help those powers grow. Luckily for you, all the powers unlocked when you claimed this place but that doesn't mean your quest is over. This place will reveal more when the time comes."

"Bit cryptic." Deathwalker commented.

Lilandra sighed. "It is the best I can do. Think of it this way. Uriel told you others would want this place, right?"

Deathwalker nodded so Lilandra continued. "Part of your challenge will be keeping this place. Now that they know it has been claimed, and believe me, many will know, they will try to find a way in through one of the leylines. Doesn't mean they will succeed, but there are special places like Earth that have a possible doorway to this place. It is after all how you got here."

"Well good thing Earth is oblivious to that fact. Most don't even believe in magic or spiritual things to begin with." Deathwalker commented.

Lilandra grimaced.

"What? What's with that look?" Deathwalker inquired.

"I don't know how to tell you this, but the Apocalypse started on Earth." Lilandra answered.

"WHAT?! My family! My other friends!" Deathwalker exclaimed.

"The rapture saw to most of them so do not worry. Your old world is now reaping what it sowed." Lilandra stated.

"That doesn't exactly fill me with warm and fuzzy feelings. It means I will at some point want to visit my home world to see what can be done there. This is an even greater reason to find my buddy James. Speaking about him, how goes the search to find him?" Deathwalker said.

Lilandra sighed again. "You do realize how difficult a time consuming it is to search for one person across multiple realities and worlds."

This time it was Deathwalker's turn to sigh. "Yes, I can imagine a long time but don't stop looking and notify me after you locate him. I won't abandon my duties in Timberfall but that doesn't mean I won't rush to help my friend. I won't let the Dark have him!"

Lilandra perked up at that statement. "I am glad you brought that up my master. With the Dark on the move, you must be ready. It is typical for the Dark to take multiple people and pit them against each other at the same time they are sending them to fight the Light."

"So, you're telling me that more people have been taken since James and I?"

"That is correct my master. Several in fact. Both by the Dark and now by the Light. Your journey and the challenges you must overcome are only the beginning. You gained your class and specialization at the same time, so you are still growing into your power. It takes time. Being the **Third Path** means you will deal with the Dark and the Light. Both sides may not exactly be in your corner. Which means you should recruit more disciples and allies for your faction." Lilandra answered.

Deathwalker picked up on some of what Lilandra might be getting at. "Are you trying to warn me not to trust Uriel as he is part of the Light?"

"Uriel is an honorable one. Of all the archangels, I trust him the most." Lilandra replied.

"Wait have you met other archangels?" Deathwalker asked.

"Of course, my master. Some were responsible for imprisoning my children, but do not let my past make you think I cannot give unbiased council." Lilandra said with concern.

"She's got kids?! Of course she does. Why do the hot ones tend to have kids?" Garry lamented.

Deathwalker ignored Garry's comment and waved away her concern. "I trust you, Lilandra. You are my first disciple. I would be a fool to ignore your council. You must know, I trust Uriel too. I am aware of his dual loyalties, and we have discussed it in great length. I will keep my eyes open and continue to have a flexible mind."

"That is all I can ask of you right now Deathwalker." Lilandra bowed her head.

"You actually used my name for once." Deathwalker noticed.

"A serious conversation and I wanted you to know I heard you." Lilandra answered.

"Thank you for that." Deathwalker replied.

"Okay so now that all that boring subject is out the way. What can you tell me about your baby daddy? I mean talk about a lucky man! He, he, he, he!" Garry chuckled.

Lilandra glared at Garry. "Oberon was an honorable man who gave his life to save me and many others!" Then her eyes widened as she realized she had revealed something she had not intended to.

"Oberon as in the king of the forest and the fey folk? Master craftsman and teacher of the dwarves? I mean he was known for so much. That Oberon?!" Deathwalker exclaimed.

Lilandra sighed. "Yes. He was husband to me and my sisters."

"Wait, wait, wait! This guy was married to you and others. What were the others old hags to make up for being married to such a hottie?"

"No that were their mothers. I would not call Queen Mab or Queen Titania hags. And I would caution you to not be so foolish to say such things in their presence or in front of anyone in her court." Lilandra replied.

Garry had a look of horror on his face when he realized he inadvertently might've insulted both queens of fairy. "I didn't know."

Lilandra smiled at Garry's discomfort. 'Serves him right.' She thought.

Then Garry realized something. "Wait, so this Oberon guy was married to you and the two queens of fairy? Okay boss I know I said you are the luckiest man out there with three cat girls, but this Oberon guy sounds like he had you beat."

Shaking his head at Garry's one-track mind, well two if he counted his murderhobo side, which Deathwalker definitely counted. "Lilandra, you said he gave his life for others. Are you okay to share this story? We would understand if it were too hard for you."

Lilandra nodded. "It was the last great cosmic war against the Light and Dark. So many died because of that war. It even split several of the races. This is why we have Dark Elves now as a faction of elves, they split off to join the Dark. Many of my children and the children of the fey also were seduced by the promises of the Dark. Oberon wanted to join the Light, but we, his wives, cautioned him against it. We thought of our children and not of our husband, or of what was right. We failed as wives, and it cost us everything.

"Oberon was a man of principle. He helped the dragons, dwarves, and those elves that fought for the Light. Doing so in secret. When we foolishly confronted him, Oberon said he could not completely stand by, his conscience would not allow it. Looking back, I think we broke his heart. Mab was the only one who supported Oberon's decision to help in secret. Her court was not as involved in the war as the Summer court or my children. When the Dark lost Oberon offered his life if the Light would spare his wives and all the others." Tears began to flow as Lilandra shared her story.

“What an honorable man. That seems to line up with what I heard about Oberon. Though I never heard this in any of the lore I read.” Deathwalker commented.

“Nor would you. The queens ordered it to never be spoken of again. Though I do think some did write it down in their journals so you might find it in the library. All my children and I were bound in the service of others. The fey were kicked out of Avalon and Winter was charged with holding the line against the Dark and those entities outside most realities.” Lilandra explained.

“Outside?” Deathwalker inquired.

“Your world called them Eldritch beings. Entities so foreign to many realities that they corrupt or destroy anything they touch. They have many servants and their own forces that try to find ways to break in. They are a threat to all existences. It is the one thing the Light and Dark can agree on.” Lilandra replied.

“Well, that’s good to know.” Deathwalker commented.

“Good to know?! I’m going to have nightmares for weeks thinking about that!” Garry exclaimed.

Ignoring his familiar’s ramblings, Deathwalker gave Lilandra a hug as it was clear recalling those memories still hurt her after all this time. He knew from his own experience how painful memories can be, especially of ones where he failed to make the right choice or regretted losing control. “Thank you for sharing, Lilandra. I am sorry for your loss.”

Lilandra held her master for a moment before releasing him. “Many warriors were lost in that war. We have hoped for their reincarnation one day. But enough of all that, thank you for your words and the hug. Don’t you have some portals to finish?”

A part of Lilandra wanted to blurt out her suspicions about Deathwalker. The way the pumas and others acted, the way he seemed to be the perfect hunter. She wanted to warn him that Winter would come to test him. Winter could be harsh and cruel, but their cold calculations were the best choice to see if he was the Huntsman. No, she knew she couldn't say anything. If she did it could turn Fate in the wrong direction, and she couldn't risk him outright rejecting the truth. Things were going to be difficult enough to add doubt into the mix.

"You're right Lilandra. I did what I came here to do. I have portals to finish and a festival to prepare for." Deathwalker said before turning to his familiar. "Garry, I'll have you rejoin me when I return with Frrsha, Mrrsha, and Prrsha. I figured of any of us, you would appreciate a party."

"Awe boss, you really do care! I won't pass up a party, that's for sure! I'm going to get so much stalk at that party!" Garry replied.

Chuckling Deathwalker headed towards the portal room. "Of course, that's where your mind goes, ha, ha, ha, ha! I imagine you wouldn't pass up a party, my friend. I'll see you soon."

# Chapter 5 - Midway City & Lady Emma

As Deathwalker returned to the capital, he contemplated what he had just learned. He had goosebumps the entire time Lilandra spoke about the last great war. Something stirred in him, a warning or something else he could not be certain of.

Deathwalker was so lost in thought pondering what he had learned he almost flew past Midway city. 'Man, how fast was I going? Oh well, time to get this done.'

As he walked out of the alley near the future portal station, Deathwalker saw two sets of guards arguing.

"The duke just wants to offer his help."

"We cannot allow you on the premises until we receive orders to do so."

"You do realize that you are in Duke Watson's duchy!"

Walking towards the commotion, Deathwalker interjected himself into the conversation. "Gentlemen, I doubt it is so serious to come to blows."

Several of the guards were startled and drew their weapons. "Who goes there?!"

"This is none of your business stranger. Move along before we are forced to detain you for interfering with the duke's business."

Deathwalker smiled as he asked. "Which duke?"

The question caught the soldier off guard. "What?!"

Deathwalker smiled grew wider as he spoke slower. "W-which... d-dukeee?"

One of guards in the same livery spoke up. "Duke Watson."

"Ah. I see. One tinny little problem I have with that. Last I heard Duke Watson was in the capital and I own this building." Deathwalker said.

One of the guards closest to the portal station gates spoke up. "You cannot own this building, his grace Duke Dragonvein owns this building."

"Yes, it is a pleasure to meet you." Deathwalker replied as he stuck out his hand in greeting.

The guard stared for a moment before it dawned on him, and he bowed his head and dropped to his knees. "Your grace!"

The other guard with him dropped to his knees as well. The guards, who he figured belonged to Duke Watson, had puzzled looks on their faces. The one in the lead realized he should do something as he bowed his head. "Forgive us Duke Dragonvein we were not aware you had arrived in the city."

Deathwalker waved off the guard's concerns. "I kept my entry into the city a secret."

Then Deathwalker dropped his smile. "Now tell me why you are harassing my men."

"Y-your g-grace. Lady Emma asked that we come and offer our assistance in any way possible. Her father, Duke Watson, sent a message home to inform her of your plans to come here. She was to ensure you were treated with the proper hospitality." The guard answered.

"That still doesn't answer why you were harassing my men." Deathwalker pressed.

"I was told not to return until we had ensured we could offer further protection in case you came here first. Apparently, his grace said you might come here first. It appears he was correct." The guard replied.

"That sly fox. He must've heard what I did in Hargrave. Clever man." Deathwalker said more to himself than anyone else.

Turning his attention to the guards. "I must finish the process in the station. Inform Lady Emma that I will accept her hospitality once I am finished with what I must do inside."

Looking at the sky to see it was about midday. "I figure I will require several hours. Inform Lady Emma it would be my pleasure to join her for dinner if that works for her."

The three guards in matching livery bowed as the one in charge said, "Yes, your grace! We will deliver your message right away! If you excuse us, we will take our leave, Duke Dragonvein."

Deathwalker nodded as the three men moved as fast as they could possibly move. Shrugging his shoulders, Deathwalker turned to his men. "One of you mind escorting me in and then seeing to it that I am not disturbed."

"This way my liege. I can escort you." The guard on the left stated, as he rose to his feet.

Once Deathwalker was left alone in the portal room, he activated his **Infinite Well of Time Magic**. Every time he used it, Deathwalker felt more and more comfortable. Like he was becoming in sync or more attuned. The connection became easier to use and the time differential seemed to be even higher. Smiling, Deathwalker got to work.

"That beat my last time." Deathwalker said to himself as he looked at the completed portal.

He notified Trader Malcom and General Marius that another portal station was completed and connected to the network. Deathwalker also instructed them to send more men to oversee the operation and security of the facility. His original plan was to return to the capital and then fly to Dalton. Now those plans were delayed so Deathwalker could have dinner with Lady Emma Watson.

"Well, it cannot be helped. Besides, it would be good to see how she is doing after our last encounter." Deathwalker said to himself as he thought about when he saved her life from bandits.

Exiting the portal station, Deathwalker found a whole honor guard in what he assumed was the Watson livery. He recognized the soldier in the lead as the Sergeant who was with Lady Emma when the bandits attacked.

"Sergeant it is good to see you again."

The sergeant bowed. "It is an honor to see you again Duke Dragonvein. If you would permit us, we are here to escort you to the duke's estate."

"Lead on sergeant." After a few moments, Deathwalker inquired, "By the way, how are the men doing after the attack?"

"Oh, they are doing quite well your grace. Some say they feel better than they have for years." The sergeant replied.

Deathwalker thought to himself. 'I would think so. I took the time to heal old wounds and injuries that didn't set right. It was the least I could do while I was there. Glad to hear it helped.'

As they walked to the duke's estate, Deathwalker learned from the Sergeant that many of those he saved that day expressed an interest in joining him.

"Ah here we are your grace." The Sergeant opened the double doors into a grand dining hall.

At the end of the hall Deathwalker saw Lady Emma in a dazzling canary yellow dress. Several servants and guards were also in the dining room. Everyone was standing, all attention on Deathwalker.

The Sergeant led Deathwalker to Lady Emma and bowed. "Lady Emma Watson, I present Duke Deathwalker Dragonvein."

Deathwalker took Lady Emma's offered gloved hand and kissed the top of it. "Lady Emma Watson it is good to see you again. I appreciate you being host to me while I am in the city of Midway."

"Duke Deathwalker Dragonvein, I acknowledge you as my guest while you visit the city of Midway. Let the Watson Duchy be at your service." Lady Emma Watson replied.

Deathwalker and Lady Emma both nodded at each other. She was the first to speak up. “Good, now that formalities are out of the way, come let us eat. Our cooks have prepared a grand feast for us Duke Dragonvein.”

“Please Lady Watson, call me Deathwalker.” Duke Dragonvein stated.

“Ah, yes. So informal. Very well, call me Emma.” Lady Emma replied.

A stoic older woman spoke up. “Lady Watson, such is not appropriate, you are unmarried.”

Lady Emma turned to the woman. “Ah, thank you, my lady-in-waiting. Would proper decorum allow Lady Emma?”

The old woman nodded.

Lady Emma turned her attention back to Deathwalker. “Please address me as Lady Emma. My apologies that we cannot be less formal your grace.”

Deathwalker waved off her concern. “Nonsense. I understand Lady Emma. Shall we eat?”

Lady Emma and Deathwalker both sat down near each other at the large table. Soon as they sat down servants began to bring out food and drink for them. It was clear Lady Emma was pulling out all the stops based on how much food was present.

“This is far too much food for just the two of us.” Deathwalker said.

“Do not worry Deathwalker. Any food we do not eat is given to the staff and servants. If they do not want any of it, we make it available to the less fortunate in the city.” Lady Emma explained.

Nodding at her statement, Deathwalker replied. “Good practice. I will have to see how I can implement the same thing back home. It is good to see nobles who care for the less fortunate.”

“Oh yes. Father has allowed me to implement several programs and initiatives to help those in needs.” Lady Emma answered.

"I find the best solution is to create opportunities for jobs and offer skills and training where appropriate." Deathwalker commented.

"Oh, I wholeheartedly agree. We have done similar things in our duchy. It is part of a noble's duty to help their people." Lady Emma beamed. She saw Deathwalker nodding along in genuine agreement. "It was so nice to talk to someone who understood the real duty of a noble."

"Yes, we must be the best example and do everything we can to rise above pettiness and egos and help those that want to be helped." Deathwalker stated.

"Sadly, not all nobles feel as we do Deathwalker." Lady Emma lamented.

"That's okay. It is our job to help show them a better way. You cannot fix intentional ignorance." Deathwalker commented.

Lady Emma giggled. "He, he, he, he, he! Oh, you are very blunt, Deathwalker! I so appreciate that. It lets one know where they stand."

Deathwalker gave a head-nod in Lady Emma's direction. "I am glad you appreciate my directness. I find it is easier in the long run."

"Quite right you are. So, tell me, how fare your efforts to create a 'portal', I believe father called it? Will it truly allow one to travel to another location in an instant?" Lady Emma inquired. She had been curious about the marvel since she heard about it from her father.

"Ah it is already complete." Deathwalker answered.

"Truly? It is already finished?!" Lady Emma followed up in excitement.

"I finished the final touches before I was escorted to your estate. Timberfall now has connections to the Capital, Hargrave, Lorinda, and now Midway." Deathwalker continued.

"Very impressive. Other than Dalton where else do you plan to build one of these magical marvels?" Lady Emma asked.

"After Dalton I will finish the ones in the cities of Malvanis and Simium." Deathwalker answered.

“Ah, very impressive. Each of the lords in your duchy will have a portal in their capitals. It will make those under you very prosperous.” Lady Emma commented.

“That is the hope.” Deathwalker replied.

“Are you open to constructing more of these magical marvels in other cities? Could we convince you to build some in other duchies?” Lady Emma asked.

“Perhaps in the future, but there is much to do, and I want to get merchants and our people used to the concept. They will require time to adapt. Not to mention our foreign trading partners.” Deathwalker stated.

“Shrewd. Your duchy will become the trading hub for the kingdom.” Lady Emma realized.

“That is the plan. Do not take my reply as dismissal. I want the whole of the kingdom to prosper, just give things some time.” Deathwalker replied.

Lady Emma conceded. “Very well. For now. Let us change subjects. I have another matter to discuss, and I must confess it is part of the reason I was so adamant we have dinner tonight.”

‘There it is!’ Deathwalker thought. Holding back his inner hackles he said. “Please share. I do prefer the direct approach if you do recall.”

Lady Emma bowed her head in acknowledgement. “I was raised to play politics with the best of them. It means some habits are a bit more difficult to dismiss. Please give me some latitude Deathwalker. My lady-in-waiting would contest if I was too direct.”

“Very well. I can concede the point to decorum. Please, what matter do you wish to discuss?” Deathwalker asked.

“Father has asked my aunt Duchess Lightheart to escort me to the upcoming Timberfall festival.” Lady Emma began to explain.

"Yes, I was already made aware so I could prepare properly as host." Deathwalker interrupted.

"Quite right. What you may not be aware of is the intent to have us stay beyond the festival." Lady Emma continued.

"For what purpose?" Deathwalker inquired.

"Father and Uncle call it a cultural exchange, but truth is they want us to get to know each other for a hopeful and possible courting." Lady Emma said.

Deathwalker chuckled. "Ha! Hopeful indeed. What has your father and uncle told you about me Lady Emma?"

"You laugh at that statement?" Lady Emma seemed to take offense.

Shaking his head, Deathwalker clarified. "You misunderstand me, Lady Emma. The royal family has made their intentions quite clear that I am to marry at the very least a high noble from this kingdom to ensure my bloodline is bound here. I'm sure they have told you the same?"

Lady Emma reluctantly nodded. It was clear she wasn't too happy with what she took as his dismissal of her. "Yes, father and uncle were both quite clear in their desire to see us wed."

"Does that not bother you?" Deathwalker asked.

Lady Emma looked confused. "Why would that bother me?"

"I am not one for others to determine my fate. The brief time we met and what I have learned about you tells me you are of a similar demeanor." Deathwalker answered.

"You checked up on me?" Lady Emma said in surprise before shaking her head to clear her thoughts. "No, it does not matter. I have known my whole life that I would have to marry for political reasons and not for love. It is the burden of royalty and nobility. A burden we both share."

Deathwalker sighed. "Yes, I am well aware of my duties, but I will not be rushed into anything. With that said let me be clear, I happen to think you are one of the most beautiful women I have ever laid my eyes on. From what I have also learned, you seem to genuinely care for your people, and have a sharp mind. All traits I admire."

Lady Emma went from frustrated to slightly embarrassed. Here she thought he was flippantly uninterested in her and now she was receiving compliments. "Your kind words honor me Deathwalker."

"I merely speak the truth. I am not opposed to us getting to know one another. I just cannot rush into a marriage. If you can be patient with me and give us time to get to know each other further, I would welcome the opportunity." Deathwalker explained.

"I am in no rush either Deathwalker. Courting takes time when done properly. I too welcome the opportunity for us to learn more about each other. Speaking about getting to know each other further, what I have learned so far says you too care about your people and our conversation alone tells me you are no fool." Lady Emma stated.

"Navigating a woman's heart is one of the most challenging of journeys, but also one of the most rewarding. That is if they are genuine with strong principles and moral compass." Deathwalker replied.

"The most important decision we ever make in our lives is who we partner with. That has been engrained in me since birth. To be the best version of myself, only then will I understand who that partner should be. I have strived to emulate those words and truly live by them." Lady Emma explained.

Deathwalker was impressed. Such wisdom he learned late in his past life, and it cost him much. The more he talked with Lady Emma the more he appreciated how she felt. Her caring for others did not stop her efforts at mere words, she implemented actual programs in their duchy which showed a glimpse into the strength of her character. She could be reserved and at least partially keep her emotions in check, which showed the possibility of a level head during difficult times.

Deathwalker, of course, could not ignore how beautiful she looked, but he remembered something his Nanuz would say. "Looks fade over time. Find someone who is good and strong on the inside." Then there was his uncle, "Always get a good look at their mother. That will tell you what you have in store for your future." Now Deathwalker knew Lady Emma's mom died, so seeing her was out, however, her mom was sister to the Queen and Duchess Lightheart. Both women seemed to be of strong character.

Lady Emma definitely seemed strong willed. Deathwalker admired a strong-willed woman. His mother, aunts, Nana, and grandmother were no pushovers. He respected that about them. Nanuz used to say, "Strong-willed is good, keeps life interesting. Independence is bad. It is the biggest lie the world tells you. We are not independent; we are all connected. That is doubly true in marriage. Independence kills any marriage as you must become one and always consider the other person in every decision."

Why Deathwalker was reminiscing he was not sure. Perhaps it was the fact he promised himself he would not rush into marriage again and made sure he was making the right choice. A part of him still felt incomplete, especially on the emotional side. He chalked it up to being a dragon, but that fact brought up another matter.

'Can she even marry a dragon? I know dragons have been known to take other forms and cross pollinate as they were, but I will have to reveal that secret if I do start courting her. How she or others might react to that fact could change my standing in this kingdom.' Deathwalker thought.

"You seem deep in thought Deathwalker." Lady Emma commented.

Her words snapped Deathwalker out of his internal musings. "My apologies. Our conversation has brought up old memories of my family."

"I would love to hear about your family. I know very little about where you come from or your heritage." Lady Emma said with interest.

"If you do not mind, I would prefer not to discuss them at this time. I will tell you that I am very far away from home, and I do miss them at times, but it is not logical to focus on it." Deathwalker replied.

“I understand what it is like to miss family. I feel my mother’s absence every day. As difficult as it is for father, he tells me stories about her if I press hard enough. Luckily, my aunts have told me many stories. I am blessed to have such a loving and supportive family. Not all nobles can claim the same.” Lady Emma shared.

“I too came from a loving family that pushed me and taught me things as a child I am only now realizing are absolute pearls of wisdom. It makes me miss them even more. The best I can do right now is as you say, be the best version of myself possible. That reminds me, I would like to offer you, my healing.” Deathwalker said.

Lady Emma felt the pain and loss coming from this man. The sudden change in subject confused her. “Healing? I am confused. You have already healed me.”

Deathwalker chuckled. “Ha! No. When I healed you last time, I was so focused on healing the immediate life-threatening injuries that it didn’t dawn on me until afterwards. In fact, it clicked for me after I spoke with your father and aunts. It was then I realized something could be done.”

“What do you mean? What are you referring to?” Lady Emma inquired.

Deathwalker held out his hand. “If you would please remove your glove and take my hand. Though I can heal through the clothing, it would be best this way.”

Lady Emma was uncertain what Deathwalker was speaking about, but he had already healed her once. ‘Perhaps there was something he forgot or did not realize until now.’ Lady Emma thought as she removed her glove.

Her lady-in-waiting spoke up. “Mi-lady skin to skin contact is not appropriate.”

“I appreciate your concern, but it is my hand and Deathwalker has already healed me once before. I believe exceptions are made when it comes to healing.” Lady Emma quipped back.

Deathwalker took her hand and channeled his healing magic into Lady Emma. After his power had suffused her body, he focused on her magical core. Lady Emma's core was rather large. Then he saw it, her mana channel connections had been severed. On top of that the core felt dormant, probably from lack of use her whole life.

She felt the warm soothing glow radiate throughout her body. Lady Emma remembered this feeling of peace and harmony from the last time Deathwalker healed her. It was that feeling that told her he was a good and gentle man. Even though he had just wiped out a bandit gang, his magic was gentle and promised a connection to something greater. Lady Emma did not fight this feeling and instead welcomed it in.

Lilandra spoke into Deathwalker's mind. "You could use your Soul-Forging ability to heal her, my hunky master."

"I'm trying to concentrate here Lilandra. I also was trying not to make her another disciple. In case you hadn't noticed but all my disciples so far are women." Deathwalker mentality responded.

"What's wrong with that? What man would not want to be surrounded by loyal beautiful women?" Lilandra teased.

"You know, I think you will not be happy until I have multiple mates." Deathwalker replied.

"Got to get you used to the idea now." Lilandra said offhandedly.

"What?" Deathwalker asked.

"Nothing." Lilandra changed the subject. "If you are determined to do this the hard way, I recommend strengthening her channels before you reconnect them. Maybe even remove a few of her blocks. Your Purity magic is oddly enough perfectly suited for such a thing."

"Thank you for the advice. Now time to concentrate." Deathwalker said before cutting the connection and redoubling his focus on the task at hand.

Deathwalker flooded Lady Emma with Purity magic. Of all the magic types, this resonated with him more than any other. He used it to strengthen her channels and remove the blocks from her core to her arms, then to her hands. Without thinking Deathwalker rose to his feet and put his other hand on Lady Emma's head.

The guards in the room instantly drew their weapons and moved in. Lady Emma rose her other hand. "Do not interfere! I am in no danger! Let him finish!"

Ignoring all of this, Deathwalker was too focused on this new aspect of Purity magic. He could feel the different types of magic within Lady Emma's core. He sensed **Water** and **Ice** magic as the strongest, then **Healing**, **Mind**, and **Air**, with some others like **Body Enhancement**, **Earth** and **Fire** that were all latent talents.

Deathwalker's eyes began to glow as he split his mind to focus on three aspects simultaneously. First focus, he started to use Purity magic to separate those types of magic and flood them into her magical core. His second focus was using his Master of a Place of Power to impart the spells Ice Lance, Basic Healing, and Lightning Bolt into her mind. Doing both of these things while his third focus was on repairing the connections to her core.

Lady Emma gasped as she received the notifications telling her Deathwalker had taught her three spells. 'He must be the Master of a Place of Power. He is too young to have mastered such magic. Only masters of a magic or a Master of a Place of Power can so easily impart such knowledge without a magic book. Why bother? Does he not know I cannot access magic?' Lady Emma thought until all musings were cut off when she felt it.

The room began to glow as did both Deathwalker and Lady Emma. The two radiated light that suffused the room with a welcoming warmth as though something wrong was healed and now made right. All those present dared not move a muscle for fear of breaking the tranquility they felt.

Lady Emma began to weep tears of joy as she felt Deathwalker guide her consciousness down into her core. As that happened, she felt his power connection with and infuse her own. To her it was like lighting up a dark room and as that happened, for the first time in Lady Emma's life, she felt her core and her magic!

Deathwalker broke off the connection and fell back into his chair, utterly spent. The glow in the room faded. Lady Emma felt the hint of loss when their connection broke, but that feeling was overshadowed by the power she felt within herself.

"Lady Emma, are you alright?!" Her lady-in-waiting asked with concern.

"I am better than alright. I can use magic!" Lady Emma said as she cast Ice Bolt and shattered a nearby goblet.

"LADY EMMA! You-you can use your magic! HOW?!" Her lady-in-waiting asked.

All eyes turned towards Deathwalker. He was tired and mentally exhausted. The only word he managed to get out was, "What?"

"What do you mean what?! You healed my core! I was told such a thing was impossible!" Lady Emma said in shock.

Having regained some of his mana and stamina, Deathwalker sat back up rather than remaining slouching in his chair from exhaustion. Lady Emma moved faster than her lady-in-waiting could interfere. She embraced Deathwalker in a hug. "Thank you Deathwalker! You have given me something I thought impossible."

"Lady Emma! I understand, but please, consider decorum!" Her lady-in-waiting admonished.

Untangling himself from Lady Emma, Deathwalker looked her in the eyes. "Never listen to those that tell you something is impossible. Those people should just get out of the way of those who are accomplishing said impossible. I am glad I could help."

Lady Emma shook her head. "You did more than just help! I must notify my family! They will want to reward you for such a deed! You also imparted three spells to me."

Several people in the room made audible gasps at hearing that statement.

Lady Emma's lady-in-waiting quickly spoke up as she looked at everyone in the room. "You are all sworn to secrecy! Did you hear me! This is punishable by death!"

Deathwalker thought that was a bit harsh and his face showed it. When Lady Emma spoke, Deathwalker then realized what he had done, and the mistake he had made.

"You are too young, and your level is too low for you to have mastered a school of magic. That is why magic books are so prized. The only other way a person can so easily impart knowledge of a spell is if that person is a **Master of a Place of Power**! My uncle is a **Master of a Place of Power**. That is why the capital was formed in that location. You either found a Place of Power near Timberfall or were a Master before coming to our kingdom."

Deathwalker was about to say something when Lady Emma held up her hand. "I do not want to know. Nor should you share that knowledge with anyone. People have been known to be hunted down and killed to claim such power. I will have to inform my family, but I will ask that the information remain within the family. That is the least I can do for what you have done for me today. I fear, however, that my family will push even harder to bind our fates together. I do not wish for our time tonight to end, but I must now see to everyone's oaths of silence."

"It is probably for the best my lady. That took a lot out of me, and I must retire to rest. I will take my leave." Deathwalker said as he rose to his feet. "Before I go, let me offer you an olive branch that your family may appreciate."

"Olive branch? Why are you giving me an olive branch?" Lady Emma asked in confusion.

“No, no. Ah! It’s an expression from where I come from. It means a gesture of peace or to grow relations stronger between two parties. Simply put, I noticed you have an affinity for Healing magic. I would be willing to teach and mentor you in the healing arts while you remain in Timberfall. That is, if that is something you would desire.” Deathwalker explained.

“Oh! Interesting custom. Your offer of tutoring me in the healing arts would be greatly appreciated. I would be a fool to ignore the chance to learn from such an accomplished healer. I will inform my family.” Lady Emma said as she too rose to her feet.

Deathwalker kissed her hand before they both gave a slight bow of their head in farewell. Once Deathwalker left the estate, Lady Emma gave her orders. “No one is to leave the grounds until they have sworn an oath of silence on this matter. I want that oath sworn on their lives!”

Several replied in unison. “As you command Lady Watson!”

Lady Watson realized one of the younger servant boys wasn’t there. “Wait, where did Timmy run off to?”

# Chapter 6 - Finishing the Rounds

## Capital of Nord - Royal Throne Room

Several nobles were arguing back and forth.

"Do not be a fool! It is some monster, simply hunt it down and kill it!"

"It is no mere monster! There are far too many attacks!"

"You cannot think they are related!"

"Scorch marks, huge gashes in the ground. How can you not think they are related?!"

"ENOUGH!" The King ordered.

Once the room fell silent, the king waved to Captain Julian. "Thank you, your Majesty! As I was saying, we have confirmed this latest string of attacks were committed by nothing less than a dragon."

"A DRAGON?!" Duke Alicorn exclaimed.

"A dragon has not been seen in this kingdom for over a hundred years." Duchess Lightheart stated.

"I assure you Duke and Duchess, it is a dragon. We have several eyewitnesses." Captain Julian replied.

"Could it not have been a griffin, wyvern, or even a hydra? A hydra if it is old enough can pose just as much risk as a dragon." Duke Watson said.

Captain Julian turned his attention to his king. “I assure you we were quite thorough. How does his majesty wish us to proceed?”

All eyes turned to the king. “Issue a royal decree to all nobles. Inform the Adventurers’ guild. Issue a kingdom wide quest. If we can entreat the dragon that would be preferred. If not, then drive it out of the kingdom or stop it by any means necessary.”

“As you command your Majesty!” The room said in unison.

As everyone began to file out of the throne room, the king called out. “Brother, a word.”

“Of course, brother.” Duke Watson answered.

The two brothers adjourned to a small conference room behind the throne’s dais. They were greeted by the Queen and Duchess Lightheart. Duke Watson looked at his brother after closing the door. “I take it we did not wish to discuss something in front of Duke Alicorn. Other than him and Duke Dragonvein we are all here.”

Just then the door opened to the royal suites. In walked Lady Emma. Duke Watson eyes widened in shock.

“Daughter? What are you doing here? How did you get here?”

The Queen spoke up. “Your daughter asked to arrange this family meeting in private.”

“To answer your question father. I took the portal from Midway to Timberfall, and then here to the capital. Saul arranged to keep me hidden from prying eyes.” Lady Emma explained.

“The portal in Midway is already complete?! Deathwalker is ahead of schedule it seems.” Duke Watson commented.

“No surprise with that one.” Duchess Lightheart chimed in.

“All right, my niece. Why have you asked for such secrecy?” The King asked.

"Thank you, aunt, and uncle, for agreeing to this. I learned something during my dinner with Duke Dragonvein that you will soon understand required this level of precaution." Lady Emma began.

"What happened daughter? Did he do something untoward?!"

Lady Emma shook her head. "No father, nothing like that." She held out her hand palm up on the desk.

"There is nothing in your hand daughter, what is it you... whoa!!!" Duke Watson was cut off as a shard of ice formed in his daughter's hand.

Duke Watson closed the distance and embraced his daughter in a big hug. "You can use your magic! How?!"

"Cannot... breathe... father." Lady Emma wheezed.

Duke Watson released his daughter, only to have her embraced by her two aunts. "Tell us niece, what happened?!"

"Release my niece and let me give her a hug." the king said.

After several rounds of hugs, they all settled down anxiously waiting to hear her story.

Lady Emma smiled at her family's antics. "It was Deathwalker. He informed me it was noticed when he first saved my life. He said after talking with father and my aunts Deathwalker knew what he needed to do to heal my core and allow me to finally have access to it."

"This is wondrous news. It appears I owe him another boon for what he has done." Duke Watson stated.

"He must be the greatest healer in this kingdom. No one else could do what he has done." The Queen proclaimed.

"More reason to court him." Duchess Lightheart commented.

"Auntie, please." Lady Emma groaned at her aunt's antics.

Lady Emma's aunt, Duchess Lightheart, was always a bit cold and logical, but when she focused in on something it was hard to get her to let it go. What Lady Emma was about to share wasn't going to make that any easier. "When Deathwalker healed me, he also imparted three spells. **Ice Bolt**, **Heal**, and **Lightning Bolt**."

The room fell silent once again. Lady Emma spoke up before anyone else could say anything. "Before you ask, Deathwalker already confirmed he was a **Master of a Place of Power**. Now perhaps you can see why I asked for secrecy. I already made everyone at the estate who heard anything swear an oath of silence."

'Never mind it took us hours to track down Timmy. Though he was on the grounds, so it should be fine.' Lady Emma thought.

"Very well. We will keep this between us, but what he has done for our family we cannot ignore. She may be your daughter brother, but she is my heir." The king decreed.

"My father will need to be told. He will find out one way or another and it is best it comes from us husband." The Queen shared.

"Agreed." The King replied.

"Invite him to the Timberfall festival. It would make the most sense and would allow us the opportunity to reveal the truth quietly." Duchess Lightheart proposed.

"It is a good plan. He will demand to see his granddaughter once he learns of my daughter's ability to do magic." Duke Watson stated.

"It would be good to see grandfather. It has been so long. Oh, speaking about magic, Deathwalker has offered to mentor me in the healing arts. He says I have aptitude for it." Lady Emma chimed in.

"He can determine affinities without an orb. Who is this man?" The King commented.

The Queen patted her husband's arm. "He's one of our dukes now. Other than my sister's, Deathwalker's duchy is closest to my father's kingdom, if the Harkin Mountains weren't unassailable, they might share a border."

"Ha! He will try to demand a portal be built in his lands. Let us see how well Deathwalker can negotiate with the High Elf king. Ha, ha, ha, ha!" The king chuckled at the thought and was curious which might come out on top.

---

## City of Malvanis - Portal Station

The Malvanis portal station was now complete. Deathwalker stood there admiring his work. Each time he worked on a portal it became faster and easier to complete.

Deathwalker had decided to come here instead of Dalton and was glad he did. Two portals left and then Deathwalker would take a much-needed rest before the Timberfall festival and tournaments. Resources had been diverted to the city of Simium speeding up construction by a whole week. Most of that he had Lord Longshot to thank as the man diverted his own construction crews to help lend a hand.

"I do want to visit Sebastian but technically he's not expecting me for a few more days. I could go to the city of Simium and do Dalton last. I would like to meet Lord Simium and his two children. Hmmm, no, best to get Dalton out of the way now and finish up at Simium." Deathwalker told himself.

Mind made up, Deathwalker walked through the portal. He eventually returned to Midway as it was the closest duchy to Dalton. As he was not expected and it was night, it was easy for Deathwalker to sneak out of the city of Midway.

Casting Ludicrous Speed, Go! Deathwalker flew faster than the speed of sound to the city of Dalton. This had to be one of his favorite spells so far. Sure, he had created the spell, but that wasn't the main reason the fact was Deathwalker enjoyed the thrill of being in the air and going as fast as a fighter jet. If not for his past life knowledge, love of Mel Brooks movies, and Creativity, he never would have experienced this exhilaration.

Slowing down as he approached Dalton city. This was Duke Alicorn's seat of power. Of all the high nobles, Deathwalker knew very little about the man. The city was a trading hub for the kingdom and from what Malcom told Deathwalker, the city did a lot of overseas trade. They also seemed to be a conduit for trade with some of the other nearby nations.

As Deathwalker figured, of all the nobles, Duke Alicorn would be the most dissatisfied if Timberfall became a trading hub. Timberfall had the advantage of being rich in natural resources and the portal network finally removed the biggest drawback of the territory, how remote it was compared to the rest of the kingdom. Where Timberfall was small in population, Dalton was overflowing with people, they were everywhere.

There were so many people in the city, that Deathwalker had to find an alley that didn't have traffic running through it. This was the last place he wanted to draw any attention to himself. He figured if Duke Alicorn got wind Deathwalker was here it would result in endless prattle and playing politics. After a few weeks of flying around the kingdom and being so focused on completing the portals, Deathwalker was surprised he was so cordial at his dinner with Lady Emma.

'You know, I really did enjoy that dinner. Lady Emma has a sharp mind and seems to have the right mindset, at least from what I have seen so far. Though her lady-in-waiting could stand to remove the proverbial stick lodged up her behind.' Deathwalker chuckled to himself as he navigated the streets closest to the portal station.

It did not take Deathwalker long to convince the guards he was who he said he was. Rather than make them bow and draw attention to themselves, Deathwalker commanded they shake hands and not bow. It worked like a charm, and Deathwalker was inside the portal room in less than five minutes.

Once again, Deathwalker was able to complete the Dalton portal in a few hours. His Infinite Well of Time Magic was once again proving to be a boon. He was grateful to his benefactor who gave him this ability.

One fitful night of sleep Deathwalker had what he had started calling a memory dream. They started happening a few days after he killed the shadow assassins. With all the knowledge he had obtained from the magic books, Deathwalker's mind would give him glimpses into the past lives and experiences of those different masters.

Deathwalker learned Volaxia was a disguise and not his benefactor's true form. The Primordial Celestial Dragon, turned time god, was really named Chronos. Primordial Celestial Dragons were a part of the cosmos themselves, and Chronos had a gift for **Time** and **Space** magic.

The dragon had taken on the wolf form to throw off his enemies. It gave Chronos an alias he could use to accomplish his charge of protecting time itself without others knowing it was him. The dragon was old, like the beginning of time kind of old, and in his many years of existence, he had acquired several powerful abilities. To prevent the loss of those abilities or them falling into the hands of the Dark, Chronos sacrificed himself to divide up his power.

What Deathwalker called Chronos' power generator, the **Infinite Well of Time Magic** was locked away in the special book he had acquired. The rest of his knowledge and power were split in two. Some minor knowledge of Time magic was gifted to the System, and most of his more dangerous knowledge and abilities were stored in Chronos' surviving **Primordial Celestial Dragon Core**.

Where Chronos' core was, Deathwalker did not know as the memories stopped at that point. What Deathwalker did know was Chronos had been shaken by what he saw in the possible futures. So shaken, in fact, that the Primordial Celestial Dragon sacrificed himself to ensure some terrible outcome did not come to pass. Deathwalker was not sure what those possible futures were, but he knew they had to be apocalyptic bad for the dragon to make the ultimate sacrifice.

At some point, Deathwalker promised himself he would track down Chronos' **Primordial Celestial Dragon Core**. The knowledge Deathwalker had obtained told him that if those parts were reunited, he would become a true master of time itself. Only God who fully sat outside of time would be greater, and Deathwalker was completely fine with that. What he was not okay with was the Dark gaining that kind of power. No, he would make a point to find it when the time was right, but right now he had more pressing matters.

Deathwalker felt his **Infinite Well of Time Magic** could pick up on those fragments, like tuning into the right frequency and following it to the sources. What it told him was there were two fragments of Chronos' power out there across different realities. When everything was settled down, Deathwalker would track those fragments down and use his Power of 13 to obtain them.

Something deep inside him told Deathwalker he would require all of Chronos' mastery of time and space if he hoped to remain **Master of Hidden Infinite Nexus Realm**. He wasn't sure how he knew that but the feeling that leaving that power divided was a sure-fire ticket to failure. Deathwalker refused to be the guy that destroyed all realities or let them fall under the control of the Dark or some Eldritch nightmare.

'I don't need some Cthulhu-looking thing wrecking all life as we know it.'

Shaking his head to clear Deathwalker's dark musings, he admired the results of work on the Dalton portal. His people really did great work in quick timeframes. He would have to get them moved to Timberfall to work on the various construction projects Deathwalker had planned for the capital city of his duchy.

"One portal to go. Man, I'm so tired of all this back and forth. I should go hunting with the pumas when I get back. Still surprised I am an alpha for the pride of giant pumas. What a crazy and wonderful life I am living." Deathwalker said out loud as he walked through the portal.

# Chapter 7 - Simium City

The Timberfall festival was fast approaching and Deathwalker was anxious to get back. Simium city was an interesting place from what Deathwalker observed. The place had a decent number of adventurers and the guards all seemed well dressed.

The city was well established and from what he learned from Sebastian, the Simium family was one of the oldest noble families in the kingdom. They had an abundance of food which was the city's primary export. This led to growth and prosperity for not just the nobles but the people themselves. Prosperity for farmers breeds prosperity for others. The portal would help them reach farther locations faster, adding the possible revenue the farmers could receive.

Deathwalker was a big advocate for farmers and anyone working on the land. His family worked on a farm when they were able to scrape enough money together from working in the coal mines. If Deathwalker could help these people, now his people, earn more revenue before food spoiled, he would make it happen.

Different beasts and monsters were known to pop up from time to time due to the abundance of life and animals. Hence the need for the high number of adventurers to help take on the quests in the area. The agreement Deathwalker established with Darius put an Adventurers quest board in the Timberfall hub and the other portal sites allowing for greater reach to Adventurers not from Simium coming to the farmers' aid.

The idea of allowing Darius and Clara to coordinate with the other Adventurer guild masters, and then giving discounts to guild members had increased the revenue gained from the portal network usage. With Adventurers starting to actively use the new form of transportation, this led to more merchants and traders being comfortable taking a risk on something new. Current revenue gained from the first week already exceeded Malcom's projections. Everyone wanted access and due to Deathwalker insisting on keeping the fees and taxes minor people were more inclined to use the service. This led to higher demand and those minor fees and taxes added up quickly.

The agreement with the crown was very clear. Deathwalker's company kept the portal usage fee. The revenue from the taxes were split evenly three ways between the crown, the duchy the portal was in and Timberfall. It meant the other dukes and duchess were all seeing increased revenue for their duchies. With the way things were trending, the crown would not need to raise taxes any time soon.

If anything, Deathwalker could get behind not raising taxes. For the people in Timberfall they saw no benefit from the taxes they paid prior. Now that the people had a local ruler, they received a part of the taxes to put back into the running of the town. Some nobles used most of that revenue for themselves, keeping them accustomed to the lavish lifestyle they were used to. Deathwalker had zero interest in using any of the tax money for himself, that's what his own business is for. That was going to be his first order of business when he returned, meeting with the council and determining the allocation of funds to help the people.

Deathwalker sat and admired the completed Simium portal. This had been the fastest one completed. The construction crews Lord Longshot sent over out did themselves in speed and craftsmanship.

Deathwalker was originally planning to send one of his guards to notify Lord Simium he was here, but then he recalled the way the lord responded to the building of the portal. The man did it not because he understood but rather because someone in higher authority told him to do it. Some people were like that, Deathwalker wasn't one of them, but he understood the type. Both Sebastian and Anthony had warned him that Lord Simium was a stickler for protocols and proper decorum. That is Deathwalker decided to leave the city only to enter through the front gates. He was just sitting here enjoying the moment before he had to go deal with all the politicking.

Letting out a sigh, "Well, time to get this over with."

It was little effort for Deathwalker to sneak out of the city. The sun was barely rising, and several farmhands were leaving to start their workday out in the fields. It was clear who was a morning person and who was not. Several joked and had smiles on their faces and others walked like zombies to their destination.

Deathwalker chuckled. "Ha! No matter the reality or the world, there are still morning people & night owls."

Landing out of sight, Deathwalker made his way to the main road. It did not take him long to approach the main gate into Simium city. Several guards perked up seeing someone approach so early in the morning.

"Halt! What is your business in Simium?" The guard asked.

Deathwalker was still in his travel leathers. They were of high quality and looked to be expensive thanks to Betterman's craftsmanship. 'Man, I wonder how the old guy is doing. His granddaughter Alyce was such a sweet girl, totally reminds me of my daughter when she was that age.'

"Duke Dragonvein to see Lord Simium."

The guards just stood there trying to process what they had just heard. Their lord required them to be professional, it was that training that prevented them from laughing outright. One of the other guards spoke up. "If you are the duke, where is your escort?"

"At my base of operations. I can travel faster and more inconspicuously without an escort." Deathwalker replied.

The guards talked amongst themselves.

"His leather armor looks expensive."

"I thought I heard a rumor the duke was a high-ranking adventurer."

Deathwalker spoke up, putting power behind his words. "Look gentlemen, I have been practically traveling nonstop to accomplish the task given to me by the crown. Either take me to Lord Simium or you can explain to him that you turned me away."

That seemed to do the trick. All the guards bowed. "Yes, your grace!"

"Give us a moment to gather an honor guard to escort you to his lord."

Deathwalker sighed. "I do not require an honor guard."

That seemed to be the wrong thing to say to these men.

"We assure you Sire; our men will do our best to provide sufficient protection." One of the guards said before he took off deeper into the city.

"Please, your grace, if you would step into the city so we can better protect you."

Shaking his head, but doing as they asked, Deathwalker stepped across the portcullis threshold. He had to wait about thirty minutes before a large group of soldiers approached. During his wait the gate guards would not look directly at him and made it a point to be very focused on their duties even though no one was coming up the road.

The soldier at the front got down on one knee & bowed his head. The precession of no less than fifty men all followed suit.

"Your grace! It is an honor to have you in our city. If you would follow us, we will escort you to Lord Simium, his son Knight Darantious, and his daughter Lady Maggie."

“Lead on.” Deathwalker replied. He thought this was overkill but figured Lord Simium and his men would err on the side of caution to not accidentally offend his new duke.

Lord Simium’s castle was a bit opulent to say the least. As they walked through the halls, Deathwalker could see statues, paintings, and other works of art. Some paintings appeared to be telling a story.

The head guard spoke when he noticed Deathwalker looking at the different murals. “These tell the story of Lord Simium’s family. How they founded the city. Then helped to sponsor the formation of the Adventurers’ guild. It is his family’s tradition to join the guild and learn what it means to be an adventurer.”

“Noble tradition and not what I was expecting from what I have heard of the man.” Deathwalker replied.

“Oh, I assure you, your grace, Lord Simium prides himself on being the utmost example of noble.” The guard stated.

‘How odd. I would think someone who is such a stickler for protocols would struggle with the rugged lifestyle and adaptability required to be an adventurer.’ Deathwalker thought as he continued to be guided through the various halls.

After going through so many doors and hallways Deathwalker stopped counting, just as he was about to say something in the form of ‘are we there yet?’, the guards finally lead him into an anteroom. The study was well furnished with plush chairs and multiple ornately crafted desks. The room screamed money.

A finely dressed older man sat in a comfy chair. Along with the older man, a younger man and woman in their twenties sat in their own chairs. In the corner was another older gentleman who was dressed in a butler’s garb standing and ready to serve. All three nobles rose to their feet when Deathwalker entered the room.

“Duke Dragonvein, it is my honor to introduce you to Lord Simium and his son, Knight Darantious, and his daughter, the lovely Lady Maggie.” The head guard announced.

The two noble men bowed, and Lady Maggie curtsied. All three of the nobles rose as Lord Simium spoke.

"It is an honor to have you in my home Duke Dragonvein. Please join us for breakfast."

That was when Deathwalker picked up on the subtle details he originally ignored out of boredom. Lord Simium was leaning on his cane and his shoulders were slightly hunched. Their outfits were just a bit off, as if they rushed to get dressed. All of them looked tired, making it clear this was not their normal time to be awake, or at the very least too early to entertain guests.

Deathwalker waved to them to not worry. "My apologies for the early morning visit. Please, this is your home, relax, and enjoy your breakfast. I understand you make a point to ensure proper decorum, but it is early, and I have been traveling over the last week. So, with that said, I will say we allow less formality for this visit."

Then realizing some traditions could not be overlooked continued. "I still recognize I am a guest in your home and appreciate all you have done to ensure I feel welcome." Deathwalker replied.

Lord Simium smiled at Deathwalker's words. "It is an honor to have you as a guest, Duke Dragonvein. As your host, please allow me and my family to see to your needs while here in our fair city."

That part of the tradition of guest rights seen to, Lord Simium approached Duke Dragonvein and got on his knees and bowed his head. "I pledge my oath of fealty to you Duke Deathwalker Dragonvein. Your enemies are my enemies. Your allies, I shall treat as my own. Whatever you need of me I shall do everything in my power to provide. Every command you give I shall follow."

"I accept your oath of fealty with the same gravity in which it was given. I shall provide aid or sanctuary should you ever require it. The concerns you have for the well-being of your people are now my own." Deathwalker answered.

Oath delivered and accepted, Deathwalker helped Lord Simium rise to his feet. While he held onto the man, Deathwalker performed a quick diagnostic on the lord's health. Lord Simium suffered from arthritis, wounds and breaks that did not heal right, and most alarming of all was the trace amounts of poison in the man's system.

When Lord Simium went to stand on his own, he found Deathwalker still holding on to him tightly. "Your grace?"

'No wonder he is so frail. I must address this right away.' Deathwalker thought before speaking up. "I'm sure you are aware of your numerous health issues. What you may not realize is the fact you have poison in your system."

Everyone turned their heads at such a decree.

"What?! That cannot be!" Knight Darantious exclaimed.

"Father has taste testers." Lady Maggie replied.

Deathwalker turned to the siblings. "Well then the testers are failing at their job, or someone has figured another way to get the poison into his system."

"How bad is it, your grace? How much longer do I have?" Lord Simium asked.

Deathwalker's hands began to glow, the soft light spread throughout Lord Simium's body. Not only did Deathwalker cleanse the life-threatening poison, but he also removed the arthritis and healed the old injuries that were giving the noble so many mobility problems. When the light faded so did Lord Simium's aches and pains.

"There, all better. I removed the poison and repaired the damage from your old wounds. It's the least I can do for my new vassal." Deathwalker stated.

Lord Simium made some test movements and stretches. As he did so his eyes widened, and a smile spread over his face. "I had been told you were a healer of great renown, but this is beyond expectation. I feel twenty or thirty years younger! Thank you, your grace!"

Lord Simium bowed again, this time much deeper, and Deathwalker received a relationship notification from both Lord Simium and his daughter Maggie.

*Congratulations! Your noble selfless actions to heal her father of his injuries has endeared Lady Maggie to you. +100,000 relationship points with Lady Maggie. Your relationship with Lady Maggie has reached the rank of **Ally**!*

*Congratulations! For healing Lord Simium's wounds and cleansing a poison he felt was life threatening you have proven your word true! +150,000 relationship points with Lord Simium. Your relationship with Lord Simium has reached the rank of **Steadfast Ally**!*

What Deathwalker thought most interesting about those notifications was the lack of a notification from Knight Darantious. He filed that tidbit of information away for later. Deciding to keep the conversation moving forward he spoke up. "Now that is taken care of let us sit and discuss a few things."

"Of course, of course!" Lord Simium said joy still in his voice from his recent healing session.

After everyone took their seats, Deathwalker began. "The building construction project I commissioned is a portal station. It will act as a waypoint and connect the portal inside to a larger portal network. This will allow instantaneous travel between the city of Simium and Timberfall."

They looked confused so Deathwalker continued. "I have an affinity to Space magic. This allowed me to create a portal network hub at Timberfall that will take anyone to the other portals I had built."

Their eyebrows shot up again. "We could instantly transport our grain and other food shipments without need for caravans!" Knight Darantious exclaimed in realization.

"We could feed so many more people!" Lady Maggie stated.

"Which other locations connect to Timberfall?" Lord Simium asked.

“Good question. The city of Simium was the last for me to complete. The other locations are the Capital, Hargrave, Midway, Dalton, Malvanis, and Lorinda. I wanted to ensure the lords under me had access to this network to help facilitate greater prosperity.” Deathwalker answered.

“Most impressive! We have been limited in the past due to food spoiling or being so expensive to transport the farther you get from our city. This invention of yours changes that greatly. You have given us a great boon Duke Dragonvein!” Lord Simium bowed his head in acknowledgement.

“I expect you to take the portal on a regular basis to come to Timberfall. You, Lord Dormeir, and Lord Longshot will be joining my Timberfall Council.” Deathwalker ordered.

“Timberfall Council?” Knight Dartantious inquired.

Lord Simium gave his son a dirty look. “It is not for us to question why.”

“It is fine Lord Simium. I do not mind questions. I also understand you are raising both your children in how to rule the city in your absence. The Timberfall Council is where we discuss important matters for the duchy. That is where decisions will be made for our people. Things like taxes, defense, etc. However, I will not permit anyone who has not sworn an oath to sit at the Timberfall Council.” Deathwalker explained.

“Do not worry, my liege. I will see they make their oaths when the time is right, your grace. My children are loyal.” Lord Simium chimed in.

Deathwalker made his expectations clear. “I do not doubt that, Lord Simium. I merely stated a fact. Now last order of business. I expect you to announce the portal station to your people and let them know during the Timberfall festival, the fee is waived or reduced depending on the number of times they travel to Timberfall during the festivities. This is to promote trade and allow all our citizens a chance to join in the fun. I expect to see all three of you there for the events. I have enough rooms at my estate to host all of you.”

“We have heard, and we will obey Duke Dragonvein.” Lord Simium replied.

Deathwalker rose to his feet. "Good. Now if you'll excuse me but I must return to the portal station and take my leave. I have been away too long."

"I shall have my guards accompany you to the portal station." Lord Simium stated.

Deathwalker waved his statement away. "No need. It is early. Let your men eat their breakfast. I know the way."

Before Lord Simium could protest, Deathwalker had already made a hasty exit from the room. To the dismay of multiple servants who wanted to at least escort him, Deathwalker did not slow down to give them the chance. He did not reduce his pace until Deathwalker was outside Lord Simium's estate.

'Nice guy but I'm not sure about his kids. Lady Maggie kept giving me the eye every time her dad wasn't looking. Ah well, now I can enjoy the stroll to the portal station.' Deathwalker thought as he exited the city lord's home.

Shortly after leaving the city lord's manor, multiple figures approached Deathwalker. Some dropping down from nearby rooftops. All in hooded, black leather cloaks exactly like what the assassins he encountered in the capital wore. Using his **Tremorsense**, Deathwalker detected nine people approaching him from all sides.

"Well, well, well. What do we have here?" One of the larger cloaked figures said.

"Looks like one of those uppity nobles who thinks they are better than everyone else." Another figure on Deathwalker's side commented.

"I do not have noble blood." Deathwalker replied.

"What was that?"

"You were coming out of the city lord's castle. So, either you are a noble or ye work fer one." An additional figure to Deathwalker's opposite side stated.

The larger cloaked man, Deathwalker could tell by the musculature, spoke up. "See the thing is, the lord's son owes a great deal of money to some powerful people. Those people sent us."

"How much does he owe?" Deathwalker asked.

The man in front of him seemed surprised by the question. "Why? You gonna pay his debt?... Yea, I think you will pay or at least be an example."

Deathwalker sighed. He was hoping to get some information from these people. Luckily his Insight skill yielded results.

*Level 55 bandit leader*

*Level 35 bandit Henchmen...*

'Henchmen? What kind of idiot says 'henchmen, yea that's the class for me', I mean come on. Here I thought these guys were related to the men from the capital. I wonder if I can keep this guy talking.' Deathwalker thought.

"Let's just gut him and be done with it."

"No! We have our orders!" The large bandit leader snapped.

"And what are those orders?" Deathwalker asked.

"Ha! Why would I tell you?" The bandit leader laughed.

"Because you aren't planning on letting me leave here alive." Deathwalker answered.

"Ha! You got a point there. Alright, why not. You see the spoiled noble was supposed to do something for the guys that paid us, but he reneged. So, we are supposed to make a few examples to get him back in line. If that doesn't work, we kill the little upstart." The bandit leader explained.

"Uh, Boss? Should we be telling him all that?" One of the bandit Henchmen chimed in.

"Yea why not? Like he said, we plan to kill him anyway." The bandit leader replied.

'Man, finally high Charisma benefits. Just a bit more.' Deathwalker thought as he smiled at the bandit leader.

"So, who are these guys?" Deathwalker inquired.

"Do not know. They gave us these cloaks and paid us good money." The bandit leader patted a large coin pouch on his hip.

"Boss!"

"What?! Who cares? The guy is a dead man and I enjoy gloating." The bandit leader barked back at one of his henchmen.

'Ah, finally. Bout time.' Deathwalker thought before speaking up. "Well, it sounds like you don't know who hired you, so you are no more use to me."

The bandit leader looked confused. Deathwalker turned to look past the guy and spoke. "You have my permission to kill them now."

The next thing the bandit leader knew he was being lifted off the ground and flung into a nearby wall as Garry appeared from the shadows. "HERE'S GARRY!!!"

Another bandit was instantly frozen while a different one was stabbed repeatedly with his own blade as he lost control of his arm. "Quit stabbing yourself! Ha! Ha! Ha!"

The bandits went from shock to panicked in a few seconds. The road they were on echoed Garry's maniacal laughter. "Ha, ha, ha, ha, ha!"

A few tried to fight back only to get an icicle to the face or be flung high into the air. "Let's see if you can fly?"

SPLAT

"Guess not, oh well. Who wants some? Oh, you want some?! Here you go!"

SLAM

"Garry is back bitches and I know how to make an entrance!"

Those few remaining who attempted to flee found their bellies sliced open as Frrsha, Mrrsha, and Prrsha appeared in humanoid form and finished them off in a few quick slashes.

The fight, or slaughter, only lasted for a short time. It was over so fast that Garry complained. "Awe! Man! I was just starting to have fun! He, He, He!"

Turning to his master, Garry smiled. "I sure know how to make an entrance, don't I, boss?"

"Ha! Yes, my little murderhobo, you sure do." Deathwalker replied.

"Thanks for thinking of me. I really needed this!" Garry cheered.

"I know buddy." Deathwalker said before turning to the cat girls. "Good job, ladies."

All three gave Deathwalker a hug. Frrsha spoke up first. "Thank you for finally letting us join you, Alpha!"

"Yes, it's good to see you all too." Deathwalker replied.

"Hey! I did most of the work. Shouldn't I be getting some loving?" Garry complained.

"Yes, come here, you can be my scratching post! Rrrrrr." Prrsha said as she waved her claws at Garry.

"Never mind, I'm good!" Garry quickly replied and rose higher in the air for good measure.

"People approach, Alpha!" Mrrsha cautioned.

Deathwalker put his hand on her shoulder to calm her down. "Those are the guards. Remember we talked about this. Two-legged have customs you must get used to."

Mrrsha retracted her claws. "As you command, Alpha."

"They smell weak." Prrsha commented.

That made Deathwalker laugh. "Ha, ha, ha, ha, ha! Compared to you my little huntress they are cubs."

The guards finally made it to them. The scene that greeted them left them stunned at first as they all just looked around. The guard recognized Deathwalker. "D-Duke Dragonvein! Your grace, what happened here?"

"These bandits attempted to do me harm. My personal honor guard made short work of them." Deathwalker explained.

As he was the duke and these men technically served him, they merely accepted his statement as fact. "We apologize, your grace! A contingent of soldiers should always be by your side! This is our failing!"

"They at least pay you the proper respect, Alpha." Prrsha commented.

Deathwalker waved off the guard's concern. "Nonsense. I left Lord Simium's estate in a hurry. He offered but I was quick to return home. My honor guard is here now." Gesturing to the aftermath, "and as you can see, they are quite capable of defending me."

"Your grace, I would still feel better if my men could escort you the rest of the way." The guard insisted.

To the man's dismay, Deathwalker shook his head. "No. My honor guard and I can move much quicker without an escort. Besides your men need to see to this matter." Deathwalker pointed to the bloody scene.

'Wait is that guy partially stuck in the other guy?! How did Garry get that guy's head to fit in such a tiny space?' Deathwalker thought as he paid more attention to some of the gory details.

Turning his attention back to the guard. "Inform Lord Simium of this incident. All nobles should have an honor guard present while in the city. Let him know I will want to speak to him and his children in Timberfall before the festival. At that point we will discuss some aspects of this incident I do not have time to go over currently. Make sure he knows I do not blame him for this situation, but it did happen in his city, and I will expect resolution when he comes to Timberfall."

Once the guard nodded his head, Deathwalker turned and left.

"Is there a reason why you are so interested in leaving so quickly alpha?" Mrrsha asked.

"We were being watched. I felt it since I left the city lord's castle. Someone was testing us with those bandits. It's why I didn't attack and ordered you ladies to only stop the bandits from fleeing." Deathwalker explained.

"What? You wanted me to show off my awesomeness boss?" Garry asked.

"Yes, and I was letting you have some fun. They will think you are my trump card. If they are the same people behind the attack on the capital, they won't know how I defeated their assassins. There is for sure more going on here than we know, and something tells me Knight Darantious is involved somehow."

"Shouldn't we be interrogating this Knight Doucher?" Garry asked.

"In time. It was why I was vague with the guard. I want the city lord to know he is not directly accountable but as I was a guest in his city the matter must be settled according to old traditions." Deathwalker stated.

"What traditions? Is alpha going to fight this man?" Prrsha asked.

"No, his son. It gives me a chance to demand answers in a way you cannot normally do to a noble without backlash." Deathwalker explained.

"That's our alpha, always thinking ahead." Frrsha commented.

"Now let's get back to Timberfall. There are several people I want you to meet." Deathwalker said as they made it to the Simium Portal Station.

# Chapter 8 - Preparations

Guards in the portal room of the Timberfall network hub snapped to attention as Deathwalker, Garry, Frrsha, Mrrsha, and Prrsha appeared.

"Ah, good. At ease men. You already know my familiar." Deathwalker gestured to the cat girls. "These three are my personal bodyguards. You are to follow their orders as if they came from me, understood?"

The soldiers all immediately replied, "Yes, your grace!"

"Hey boss, how come you don't tell them to follow my orders?" Garry asked.

Deathwalker gave him a look. "Really? You cannot be serious. Why do you think I might not give a murderhobo carte blanche authority?"

"Cause, you don't love fun?" Garry replied.

Deathwalker just stared at the ball of crazy.

"Okay, I see your point boss. Still a part of you has got to admit it might be funny." Garry answered.

The soldiers present shuddered at the thought.

Deathwalker chuckled. "Ha! Perhaps, but as a leader I must consider all those under my care not just my crazy murderhobo familiar. Be happy you're a part of the fun that is the Savage Squad. If that isn't enough, I could let the girls turn you into their scratching post."

Frrsha, Mrrsha, and Prrsha all flexed their claws and gave Garry a wicked grin.

Garry floated behind Deathwalker. "I'm good, boss. Don't worry, I get it. The world is not ready for all this awesomeness."

Shaking his head but smiling, Deathwalker led his squad to the interior of Timberfall Manor. He had to admit Garry helped lighten the mood, and between him and his three puma shifter matriarchs his heart felt lighter than it had been for days. Hopefully Deathwalker's new friends and allies would accept his new bodyguards.

Upon entering the main building of the manor, Deathwalker found both Geeves and Mary Sue waiting for him at the door.

"Welcome home, your grace!" Geeves greeted.

"It is great to see you looking so well your grace." Mary Sue said.

"Hello you two. Have you been waiting long?" Deathwalker asked.

"Not at all, your grace. The soldiers have a linked communications orb that notifies me, Trader Malcom, and General Marius if something is of great importance like your return." Geeves explained.

"That must've cost a pretty penny." Garry commented.

"Ah, I see you have brought your familiar and... new... guests?" Geeves studied the cat girls, not sure who they were or where they came from.

Deathwalker gestured to each matriarch. “Yes, this is Frrsha, Mrrsha, and Prrsha. They will act as my honor guard when called for. Please arrange for them to have the adjoining room next to mine. As my bodyguards, they should be close in case needed.”

Geeves’ eyes widened. “This is great to hear, your grace. They look quite formidable. It is good to see you taking your safety and security seriously.”

Geeves then bowed to the girls. “Thank you for taking up the honor to guard our duke.”

“He is our alpha, of...”

Frrsha was cut off by Mrrsha. “We gladly stand with Duke Dragonvein and it is our honor to see to his protection.”

"And guard his rear!" Prrsha teased.

Deathwalker ignored the giggling cat girls. "Please have General Marius coordinate with Mrrsha on guard duty and protection. I'm sure there are matters of state requiring my attention. Inform the Timberfall Council I have returned and invite them and my adventuring party to dinner. If you have other concerns you would like to discuss, let me get settled and then join me in my private study."

Geeves and Mary Sue both bowed before escorting the Savage squad to their quarters.

## ———-Mara———-

"Come on brother! Let's go see if it is true!" Mara said as she pulled at her brother Cal's arm.

Pulling his arm from his sister's grasp, Cal admonished his sister. "Knock it off, sister! If Deathwalker is back after traveling all around the kingdom, he must be exhausted. Let him rest! Besides, I have other plans."

Mara gave her brother a dirty look. "What plans? Going to go find a certain head maid? I believe her shift is ending soon if I recall."

"I-I do not know what you are talking about, sister." Cal stuttered.

"Sure, sure. Brother, you got it bad!" Mara teased.

"You are one to talk! You have been pining over Deathwalker practically since you met him!" Cal quipped back.

Mara gave her brother a surprised look. “I do not know what you are talking about brother! He is our party member and our friend, why would I not worry about him?”

Cal just shook his head. “It is just you and I right now Mara. I will admit my interest in that angel that is Mary Sue if you admit you have a crush on Deathwalker.”

“Silly brother, I already know you like Mary Sue. Plus, I think she likes you too.” Mara replied.

“What?!” Cal quickly exclaimed.

“Oh yes. I see how she looks at you when she thinks no one is paying attention.” Mara stated.

“Really?!” Cal began to ask before catching himself. “Hey, stop trying to change the subject. You need to tell him how you feel.”

Mara’s smile fell a little at her failed attempt to change the subject. “I do not want things to get weird between us, especially if he does not feel the same way.”

“I will tell Mary Sue of my interest if you tell our friend how you feel.” Cal proposed.

“Fine! Why not come with me?” Mara replied.

“You go share your feelings and I will go do the same. Good luck sister!” Cal said as he ducked out of the room before his sister could reply.

“That jerk. Oh well, no excuse to put it off any further.” Mara said to herself before walking out of the room and heading towards Deathwalker’s private suite in the manor.

It did not take Mara long to get to Deathwalker’s door. She paused, just standing there for a while. ‘Am I really going to do this?’ Mara thought before considering her brother.

‘If Cal can share his feelings, then I should be able to do the same.’ Mara gave one last internal pep talk to herself before opening the door.

Mara got about five steps into the room before she saw a claw swipe at her. Instincts kicked in and Mara leaned back, avoiding the claw strike. Just then another swipe came, and she blocked it. The force of the strike staggered Mara for the briefest of moments. That was all her attacker needed to press for the advantage.

A sweeping leg strike caused Mara to lose her balance. She was then grabbed by her attacker and before she knew it, Mara was unceremoniously flipped on her back. As she looked up, sharp claws were inches from her face.

Mara went for her dagger to retaliate. Mid-motion, a knee fell on her arm pinning it in place. That was when Mara looked up and saw the claws and glowing eyes of... 'a cat girl?' Mara thought as her mind tried to wrap itself around what was happening.

Mara heard Deathwalker's voice from further in the room call out. "Frrsha! Stop! That's Mara, let her up!"

The cat girl moved her face in real close to Mara, sniffed, and gave a low growl.

The cat girl spoke as she got off Mara. "Grrrr. He is not yours."

Mara tried to process what was going on when she saw Deathwalker by her side. He helped her to her feet. Once on her feet Mara noticed Garry and two other cat girls in the room beside the one, she heard Deathwalker call Frrsha.

"Sorry about that Mara. Frrsha is just doing her job as my honor guard." Deathwalker stated.

Mara turned to Deathwalker with a look of confusion. "Honor guard?"

"Yes. Since I became a Duke, everyone has been bugging me to have a set of bodyguards to protect me and watch my back." Deathwalker explained.

"Is that not the job of your adventuring party?" Mara asked incensed.

“Yes, when we are out adventuring, but around town and at formal matters, I am expected to have an honor guard.” Deathwalker replied.

“Oh... Where did they come from?” Mara asked.

“Long story. Let me introduce you properly. The one that attacked you is named Frrsha. The redhead is Prrsha and the leader of the squad when I am not around is the brunette, Mrrsha.” Deathwalker introduced.

“I do not understand why Mrrsha is in charge when you are not around alpha.” Frrsha pouted.

“Because you and I are the type to kill first, ask questions later. Mrrsha is more diplomatic.” Prrsha answered.

“Less fun if you ask me.” Garry chimed in.

Mrrsha flexed her claws towards Garry. “What was that scratching post?”

Garry backed away. “Just kidding, geez. Don’t get your undergarments twisted.”

“I am not wearing any.” Mrrsha deadpanned.

“Okay, that’s hot! I take back anything bad I ever said.” Garry replied.

Deathwalker, wanting to change the subject, spoke up. “Everyone, this is Mara, my friend. We are in an adventurer party together, along with her brother Cal, and Grimhold.”

“You’ll like Grimhold. So full of life. There is just something about his voice. It just resonates with me for some reason.” Garry chimed in.

“Thank you, Garry, for the commentary. You’ll meet the others at dinner tonight.” Deathwalker stated.

“It is still weird to think we do not kill our meal before dinner.” Frrsha commented.

Mara found that statement odd. ‘How savage are these beastkin?’

Once again Deathwalker attempted to change the subject. "What brings you to my room Mara?"

"Huh? Oh... I-I just wanted to welcome you home." Mara stuttered.

This time Prrsha gave a low growl. "Errrrr."

Mrrsha elbowed her to get Prrsha to stop. "Come, let us leave our alpha to visit with his friend." Mrrsha said as she ushered Garry, Frrsha, and Prrsha into the other room and shut the door.

Deathwalker watched the pumas and his familiar excuse themselves before he motioned for Mara to have a seat at a nearby table. "Yes... well... I appreciate the gesture. It is good to be back. The last few weeks have been a bit long, but I did get a chance to see more of the kingdom. How have things been here?"

"Quiet, yet busy. Cal, Grimhold, and I have been helping General Marius train soldiers and guards in both fighting monsters and different combat techniques. The city council, Geeves, Malcom, and to my brother's dismay, Mary Sue have all been helping prepare the city for the festival. It's kept us all busy, but other than that, it has been quiet. According to General Marius, you were not expected to return until closer to the start of the festival." Mara answered.

"Luckily, Lord Longshot was able to send his skilled workers and craftsmen to help some of the other sites. It made a world of difference on time." Deathwalker explained.

"I have heard of him. They say he is the best archer in the kingdom. I would be curious to see if that is true." Mara commented.

"You'll get the chance to find out. He will be participating in several of the tournaments. I am expecting you, Cal, and Grimhold to participate as well." Deathwalker chimed in.

"Why?" Mara asked.

"Simple. I cannot participate, so I was hoping my teammates would represent me in the tournaments." Deathwalker explained.

"Why can you not participate?" Mara asked in confusion.

"Simple, I am the primary judge over the tournaments. I will lead the hunt during the festival, as is my right as Duke, but beyond that I will be a judge with the others." Deathwalker answered.

"Others?" Mara inquired.

"Elder Martha, General Marius, his brother Darius, and Duchess Lightheart have volunteered to help me with the judging. I'm not sure if Lady Emma will be participating or judging, but I figure that can be sorted out later." Deathwalker further explained.

"Duchess Lightheart and Lady Emma, the crown princess to the kingdom? Two of the three most powerful women in the kingdom are coming here?!" Mara exclaimed in shock.

"Sure. They will be staying here in the manor. The king and queen might also pay us a visit at some point during the festivities. I believe a few of the nearby nations are also sending delegations to the events as well." Deathwalker replied.

Mara just sat there for a moment. 'Here I thought those cat girls were a problem. What hope do I have to compete with such women?'

After longer than normal Mara spoke up. "I do not know how to comport myself around such people, Deathwalker."

'Ah so that is why she got so quiet.' Deathwalker thought before answering. "Just be yourself Mara. There is only one of you, so you might as well be yourself."

"T-That is not what I mean!" Mara exclaimed.

Deathwalker raised a hand. "Be calm my friend. You have nothing to worry about. I don't know about the foreign delegations, but what I have seen of Duchess Lightheart and Lady Emma, they are kind and care about their people. You will fit right in, trust me on that."

Mara's shoulders slightly relaxed but not by much. "If you say so. I will do my best. There was... never mind."

Deathwalker gave his friend a puzzled look. “Is there something else you wanted to discuss Mara?”

“N-no! I-I realized I have to go find my brother. If you will excuse me.” Mara stuttered out before rising to her feet.

Deathwalker just rose to his feet when Mara quickly excused herself and left the suite.

The doors to the other room opened and Mrrsha, Prrsha, Frrsha, and Garry entered.

“What was that all about?” Deathwalker said out loud, more to himself than anyone else.

“She lied.” Frrsha commented.

Deathwalker turned to her. “What?”

Prrsha was the one that answered him. “You must have smelled the scent she was giving off, alpha. We know you have such abilities.”

“I do, but sometimes it can be information overload, so I block it out at times.” Deathwalker replied.

“That is not wise to do alpha. Such a thing could leave you oblivious to nearby threats.” Mrrsha admonished.

Deathwalker nodded. “That is fair. I appreciate the honesty and candid feedback. I will do better to assimilate the extra sensory information as best I can, but it will take time. So, I would appreciate any insights as I work on that.”

Frrsha finally spoke up. “She wanted to mate with you.”

“What?” Deathwalker asked.

“How does this keep happening to the boss? How high is your Charisma?” Garry chimed in.

"Not now Garry!" Deathwalker replied before turning to the pumas. "Mara is a friend. She came to see me after I was gone for a few weeks..."

"Alpha do not be naive. You may see her as a friend, but she wants more, and she lied to you about it." Prrsha stated.

"I had my suspicions, but it is not something that I can think about right now. The royal family is quite adamant I marry into their family. I may have to speak with her, so she understands." Deathwalker shook his head. "For now, I will let it be. We have other matters to prepare for."

"How about you let me console her afterwards boss?" Garry asked.

"Ha! Yea I know what you have in mind buddy. You forget, I can see inside your head. I may not like to look very often, but still." Deathwalker chuckled. He knew his familiar was just trying to lighten the mood.

Garry smiled. "I don't know what you're talking about boss. My thoughts are awesome. They are filled with so many cool things, like killing, food, Sansa, killing. You know, the good stuff!"

"Ha!" Deathwalker chuckled before full on laughing. "Ha, ha, ha, ha, ha! You may be crazy but you're my kind of crazy Garry."

"Awe, thanks boss!" Garry replied.

Turning his attention towards the pumas, Deathwalker spoke up. "This was a good test of how to interact with other two-legged people. At this point, I do not care if you call me alpha in front of others. It is a common enough practice among certain beastkin that the quirk can be easily dismissed. However, growling at those that hide their intentions is something you must work at. We do not want them to know you have such abilities. Do not forget, we can telepathically communicate. It is easy to warn me of danger that way."

"Understood alpha." Prrsha said dejectedly.

"I understand alpha." Frrsha pouted.

"Mrrsha, you seem to have greater control over your instincts and emotions. I will be looking to you to help guide the others. Remember I plan to transform the pride so they can come and go and help. The three of you are to be the examples of behavior." Deathwalker stated.

Thinking maybe he had been harsher than intended, Deathwalker swept the three cat girls up in a big hug. Noting to himself that he only did this because it was logical to keep his people feeling valued, yet he himself had little emotion about the matter. It was another instance of him noticing how muted or incomplete his emotions were. Shaking off his mental musings, Deathwalker spoke up. "All of you still did well for your first altercation. I have faith. It will get better in time."

All three women began to purr. "Rrrrr. Thank you, alpha." Frrsha said.

"I just mask my emotions better, alpha." Mrrsha commented.

"I do not like those that are not honest with their feelings, but for you alpha, I will do better." Prrsha commented.

"That is all I ask. I will soon have to marry for political reasons. It is the logical thing to do, but marriage must be more than just logic, yet I cannot seem to bring myself to see it any other way." Deathwalker explained.

"Your two-legged customs are rather odd." Prrsha commented.

"Yes. You are alpha. You are expected to have more than one wife." Frrsha stated like it was just a part of life.

"She is not wrong alpha. It is the way of nature. You are the greatest alpha our tribe has ever known. Plus, it is clear you feel at home among all of us, even the cubs." Mrrsha chimed in.

"Oh boo-who! I'm the boss, I have to marry hot women, oh darn. Woah is me. Your Luck and Charisma scores have got to be off the charts! I just want to know when some of that is going to rub off on me." Garry teased.

"Very funny Garry. Thanks for cheering me up, buddy. I appreciate that. I also appreciate you, my puma matriarchs. We will sort things out in time." Deathwalker said before breaking off the random hugging session. "For now, we must get ready for dinner. There are a few more 'strange customs' I want to familiarize you all with. First is called a fork..."

Deathwalker began to explain the proper etiquette at a formal meal. The more he explained, the further the cat girls groaned. They were convinced by the end that two-leggers just did things to add further challenges to their lives. When they started to think of it as a challenge to overcome, the cat girls became more interested, but just barely.

## ———-Timberfall Manor Dining Hall———

"Brother! It is good to see you!" Darius said as he embraced his brother General Marius in a bear hug.

"G-good to see you too brother." General Marius wheezed out.

The two men were the first to be escorted into the room. Both grew up with the importance of being on time to show proper respect for other people's time. For both men, that meant coming early to ensure they were not late.

Trader Malcom entered shortly after talking with Ron about material transportation costs. "We can reduce the cost due to not having to pay so much to transport items. Plus, it can come much faster. Though, Duke Dragonvein did send me a message saying he wanted us to explore the possibility of establishing our own mining operations in the duchy. That would dramatically reduce costs overall in the long run that is."

"I do not care how it happens, just that it has added to my profit margins. I have been able to bring on a few more apprentices to help with the increased volume. I never expected for this many people to flood into Timberfall in only a few weeks." Ron replied.

Hearing the tail end of that conversation as Paul and Clarisse entered the dining hall, Paul weighed in. "We are seeing an influx from other territories in the kingdom. However, most of our immigration is coming from outside. The highest percentage by far are coming from those fleeing the Proletariat."

"The Proletariat?" Trader Malcom asked.

"Yes. My men have interviewed many of the refugees who are fleeing their oppressive rule. The government owns everything, and the people are starving. Our neighbors lost the strip of land between us and the Proletariat so the people that lived and worked on the land had to flee for their lives. Worse, those originally from the Proletariat have also been fleeing the madness that has gripped that country." Commander Willis said as he entered the room.

Commander Willis was a wolf-beastman in charge of internal security and guards for Timberfall. He took his job very seriously, and an influx of so many people had everyone concerned. Greatest of all concerned was the man responsible for the guards protecting the city.

"I have allocated additional soldiers to assist your men, Commander." General Marius commented.

Commander Willis nodded his head in appreciation. "I thank you for that, General. My men are a bit nervous, as we are not staffed to handle the protection of so many people."

"The guild could offer some assistance for coin, Commander." Guildmaster Darius chimed in.

"I do not know if we have budget for such a thing..." Commander Willis began but was cut off by Paul.

"The council will allocate additional funds Commander. Duke Dragonvein was very clear he wanted sufficient funding for Timberfall's defense."

“Thank you, Minister of Trade.” Commander Willis said to Paul.

“I think it’s nice that so many people are coming. So many new stories and information. Paul and I both have hired assistants from the refugees. Both are hard workers with families.” Clarisse spoke up.

Paul held her hand as they sat down at the table. The two council members had recently decided to make their courtship public and as such, they have never been happier. “Clarisse is right. Many of these people are decent, hardworking people coming here for a better opportunity. We were glad to help where we could.”

“Betterman walked into the dining hall. “I too have hired some of the refugees to help me. It is only their first week, but so far, they are doing well. Business is booming and Alyce cannot do it all.”

“I have no issue with immigrants, my concern is the impact it is having in processing and vetting them. You cannot just let anyone in. Sadly, my men are so overworked, I do not think we are doing enough to conduct proper assessments.” Commander Willis replied.

“I am telling’ ya, Elder, the lumberjacks have been commenting on seeing more and more monsters around.” Samuel said as he walked in with Elder Martha.

“I have noticed more injuries from adventurers coming in as well.” Elder Martha commented.

When Elder Martha noticed Darius, she turned to him. “I would recommend updating the quests and increase the number of adventurers out there helping to keep the population down.”

“Do we know the cause?” Ron asked.

“Near as we can figure in our investigations is the giant forest pumas have vanished and that has thrown the ecosystem out of sync.” Elder Martha stated.

“It is good there is a major planned hunt as part of the upcoming festival.” Commander Willis commented.

“Yes, it will help reduce the monster and beast population.” General Marius chimed in.

“I am sure it will be fine, lass.” Grimhold told Mara as he, Mara, and Cal entered.

“Yes, sister. I am sure he chose well.” Cal offered.

“That is not the point! Where did these bodyguards come from?” Mara protested.

“Bodyguards?” General Marius asked.

“Aye. Apparently, Deathwalker has found three bodyguards.” Grimhold answered.

“That makes me feel better. I do not like our Duke walking around without protection.” Paul chimed in.

Before the rest of those in attendance could weigh in, Geeves entered to let everyone know his liege had arrived.

“I am pleased to announce Duke Deathwalker Dragonvein! Ruler of the Timberfall duchy. He is accompanied by his familiar Garry, and his honor guard Mrrsha, Prrsha, and Frrsha.”

Everyone rose to their feet.

Garry floated a bit behind Deathwalker. One cat girl walked in front, while the other two cat girls were on each side of Deathwalker. They struck an imposing figure in their leather armor and fierce expressions. The cat girls assessed the room in a glance, immediately prioritizing threats and targets.

Deathwalker greeted everyone before taking a seat. “It is good to see you all again. I feel like I have been gone far longer than I was. Geeves has already introduced my personal guards. Please be seated. Let us enjoy Mezza’s amazing cooking before we talk business.”

“I will drink to that!” Grimhold cheered.

That seemed to trigger multiple servants entering with food and drinks. Geeves announced each course before he would bring the food personally to his Duke.

"Thank you, Geeves."

"Of course, your grace. It is my honor." Geeves replied.

A silence fell in the dining hall. The only sounds heard were the clanking of silverware on plates and content noises coming from the guests. Deathwalker and the pumas too were enjoying their large portions of meat. Garry periodically would levitate a piece of food and have it fly instantly into his open mouth.

Only after everyone had their fill and dessert wine was brought out, did Elder Martha break the silence. "I take it the portal network is up and running now?"

"Indeed. We now have a portal station in every major city in our duchy. In addition, we are now connected to the Capital, Hargrave, Midway, and Dalton. Timberfall is soon to become the trade hub for the kingdom. I hope we are ready for all the influx." Deathwalker explained.

"My men have all been posted at each portal station to provide protection and keep the peace." General Marius commented.

Deathwalker nodded in his direction. "Excellent." He then turned to an empty chair at the table. "Please take a seat Geeves."

"Sire? That is not proper..." Geeves began before Deathwalker cut him off.

"The meal is over. This is Timberfall Duchy business, and my understanding is you have been working very closely with the council to prepare for the festival. I want you a part of these discussions formally."

Geeves just nodded once and took his seat. He knew better than to argue with his liege when he set his mind to something. Deathwalker smiled as Geeves sat down.

Trader Malcom spoke up. “We are already seeing high usage of the portal network. The revenue far exceeds my original estimates. Your grace will make back the money you invested far faster than originally planned. That is even accounting for the large amount of funds you are pouring into Timberfall construction and restoration projects.”

“That is good, speaking about projects, how are they progressing Minister of Trade?” Deathwalker said.

Paul spoke up. “For the most part well. We have diverted some of the resources to build housing for all the new refugees and immigrants pouring into the city. That has helped the issue but has delayed the finishing of the clinic and other buildings you wanted built.”

“Tell me about these refugees and immigrants.” Deathwalker inquired.

Commander Willis chimed in. “The Proletariat conquered the land between their nation and our duchy. Many who used to live there have fled avoiding the totalitarian rule of the new regime. Many come here with nothing. We have done our best to screen these people, but we can only do so much your grace.”

“These people suffer and many of the original settlers of Timberfall hold resentments against the new people competing for resources and jobs. I hear it often from the locals that visit my tavern.” Samuel stated.

“Many of the immigrants are families looking to make their way. Several used to live in the Proletariat and are used to being promised food and shelter by the government. Many are willing to work but there are those who, I will admit, seem entitled.” Clarisse commented.

Samuel and Commander Willis seemed surprised by Clarisse’s acknowledgement.

“What?! I am not blind. I just think we should do something to help these people.” Clarisse quipped back when she saw their expressions.

“The influx of people has brought additional labor resources. Several of the business owners and shopkeepers have hired additional resources, but there are far more immigrants than we have jobs.” Betterman explained.

“Their health is of concern as well. Many traveled here with nothing or had nothing left by the time they arrived. Malnutrition is common and due to their travel conditions; their hygiene and cleanliness has led many locals to do what they can to avoid areas where the immigrants are gathering.” Elder Martha shared.

“Not all are outside immigrants. Several have moved to Timberfall once they heard about the formation of the duchy and the portal network. Many of those seek to get in the new duke’s good graces.” Geeves chimed in.

“I have also recently seen an increase in street brawls and other related crimes. The town guard simply was not expecting such an influx of people. My men are working double shifts to try to keep up, many are tired and that does not help matters any.” Commander Willis expressed.

“Ha! Welcome back lad. Seems like the council is dumping a bunch on ya.” Grimhold joked.

“Ha, ha, ha, ha! Leave it to Grimhold to tell it like it is.” Darius spoke up for the first time.

Once the guildmaster knew he had the floor, he spoke up. “The shared guild quest boards have been a huge success. I have seen far more guild traffic and the other guildmasters I have spoken to wanted me to convey their thanks. Take that you doom and gloom council. Ha, ha, ha, ha, ha!”

“Hey! I have not even said one thing.” Ron complained.

“I believe Grimhold and Darius are just trying to lighten the room, Ron.” Elder Martha chimed in.

“Oh. Thank you for explaining that Elder.” Ron replied, the redness on his face fading.

Deathwalker sighed as he looked around the table. He could see his friends’ attempts to lighten the mood had not worked. It was time for him to step in. “Very well. I had hoped we could discuss the festival before getting into these matters, but I can tell they are weighing heavily on your minds.”

Taking a long breath, Deathwalker continued. "We cannot ignore the suffering of others, but we must remain vigilant. General Marius, I want you to provide additional support to Commander Willis and his guards. The military should join the patrols to help curtail the increased violence we are seeing."

"As you command, my liege." General Marius replied.

Deathwalker continued. "That is only going to deter the opportunistic, but it will not stop the zealot. I want every guard and soldier to pay attention to their surroundings. Make note of minor details, people's movements, and those that want to be seen and those that are making a point to avoid it. My familiar Garry and one of my personal guards will join the evening patrols."

"Oh yea, I'll make anyone who tries anything regret the day they were born!" Garry commented with a manic look in his eyes.

Raising his hand to stop Garry's train of thought. "Intel and observation only Garry. You are to find what our soldiers are guards may miss. I don't want you spooking them before we can figure out if they are planning anything."

"Awww, but I love spooking people. That immediate look of terror, it's priceless!" Garry retorted.

"We will see to it he behaves, alpha." Mrrsha chimed in as she flexed her claws.

Garry visibly gulped.

"Do you really think refugees are up to something nefarious?" Clarisse asked.

Deathwalker shrugged his shoulders. "We do not know, but Commander Willis has expressed his concern, and I will trust a guard's sense of danger. Sometimes we cannot explain yet what our mind or instincts are picking up. If it is nothing, no harm done. If a plot is afoot, then we are being prudent."

Clarisse frowned but nodded her head. Paul took her hand and squeezed to comfort her. The couple gave each other knowing looks, that said they would discuss this in private.

"Now, that does not solve the root of the problem."

"Root of the problem?" Elder Martha inquired.

"Yes. Idle hands make for the devil's work. It is a saying where I come from. The true meaning is without direction and purpose people will use their free time in less-than-ideal ways. I want us to start recruiting labor and increase the number of construction projects." Deathwalker explained.

"We do not have enough skilled foremen to oversee the jobs. It is difficult enough now to manage the projects we currently have in progress. I would ask you to reconsider, your grace." Paul objected.

Deathwalker nodded at the man. He liked it when his people spoke up and voiced their concerns and opinions. He would be mindful of how he replied to his Minister of Trade.

"My understanding is Samuel and several of the other lumber mill workers and lumberjacks have some experience in helping construct the current structures in Timberfall."

"Of course we do. The men had to figure out what worked and did not. That is what happens when you live on the fringe!" Samuel replied.

Deathwalker further explained his plan. "I want us to rank our people by experience, skill, and ability to influence or lead their peers. We will assign foreman levels based on capabilities. I am even open to any immigrants that can demonstrate they possess the necessary skills. Then we delegate and assign jobs based on complexity. Bigger jobs get more experienced workers and leaders."

"It would appease the locals but in a constructive way. They would be more likely to accept immigrant foremen and workers if they knew it was based on talent and experience. I would say it could go a long way to help remove our people's fears." Samuel agreed.

"Yes and no. It will help temper them, but it is only part of the solution. The more we increase trade and demand, the more the markets can benefit from the additional businesses. I want us to consider apprenticeship programs and setting up schools for the children to learn to read, write, critical thinking, mathematics, trade skills. We must prepare the younger generations while helping integrate the current work force."

"That is very ambitious." Elder Martha commented.

"Agreed, and I think Clarisse as the Minister of Skills would do a wonderful job. Of course, she would require plenty of help from the rest of you." Deathwalker announced.

"Minister of Skills?" Clarisse asked.

"Yes. It is a role focused on knowledge. I imagine Paul would need to help quite a bit. There are so many skills out there. We should help people learn how to acquire the skills to thrive in this world. That is why apprenticeship programs are such an important part of this effort. Think about it Clarisse, you would be exploring the nature of skills and using that knowledge to help others."

Clarisse had tears of joy in her eyes. "Thank you, Master Explorer... I mean your grace! I gladly accept if Paul can help me in the endeavor."

Paul leaned over and wrapped his arms around Clarisse. "Of course! It would be my honor!" He too had the hint of water in his eyes.

"Good. Trader Malcom." Deathwalker turned to his trader.

"Yes, your grace."

"We must increase our recruitment efforts. The crown has agreed to allow me to recruit from across the kingdom. I imagine several of those who have arrived via portal are a result of that recruitment effort. Please assist Clarisse and Paul in getting the skills people have inventoried and categorized. Now, I do not expect you to do it as you are running the network, but I trust you can find a resource to help." Deathwalker instructed.

Geeves spoke up. "If it would please you, your grace, I would gladly take on that role. Mary Sue handles most of the matters of the household now. It would give me a chance to feel more of service to you."

Deathwalker smiled. "Excellent suggestion. I approve! With that settled, let us move on to the upcoming festival and the visitors we can expect."

"Speaking about that, you should be made aware that the King of the Elven people, our queen's father, is planning to attend the festival." Elder Martha shared.

Deathwalker sighed. "I'm not surprised. I figured he would make his way to meet me once he learned I healed his granddaughter, and she can use magic now."

Elder Martha's eyes widened. "Y-you healed Lady Emma's condition?! That was said to be impossible!"

"Interesting that you knew about her condition... Elder." Deathwalker retorted.

"I have been in the kingdom a long time and know the Queen's family very well. It is my home country after all." Elder Martha replied before narrowing her eyes at Deathwalker. "Do not try to change the subject. How did you do it?"

"That I will not share, but I will say I come from a long line of healers and my healing abilities are different than most. We can discuss in private some time but not now. What can you tell me to expect from the elven king?" Deathwalker replied.

"He is firm. A bit cold but that comes from Winter's influence. The man is brilliant and shrewd, expect him to test you. Oh, and the king always has one advisor from Winter with him. Sometimes an advisor from Summer but they are not as common on this continent." Elder Martha shared.

"Fey in the court?" Deathwalker asked.

"It is common among elves as we can trace our lineage back to one fey line or another." Elder Martha explained.

"Interesting. Very well. Perhaps we can discuss it further. In terms of high-profile guests, we can also expect Lady Emma and Duchess Lightheart. Both will be staying at the Timberfall Manor, so I expect Mary Sue to attend to them Geeves." Deathwalker stated.

"The Duchess and the Crown Princess are coming here?!" Geeves asked in shock.

"Yes. Please prepare." Deathwalker answered.

"At once!" Geeves said before standing and taking off.

Deathwalker chuckled. "Ha! I didn't mean right this instant, but oh well."

"That is to be expected! They are two of the most power women in the kingdom! You act like it is no big deal!" Mara exclaimed.

"Well, the King and Queen are trying to get me to marry one of them, but that's neither here nor there." Deathwalker commented.

Grimhold spit out the ale he was drinking and everyone else in the room looked completely shocked.

Coughing, Grimhold spoke up. "Cough! Lad, you cannot just drop somethin like that on us!"

"What?!" Deathwalker said in confusion.

"What, he says! You just told us you might be the new king of this country if you marry Lady Emma!" Cal chimed in.

"Oh, that. Yea I haven't agreed to anything, but I understand the ask" Deathwalker began and raised his hand as he could see several faces wanting to speak up. "In hindsight I probably should not have said anything, so I would ask all of you to keep it quiet and not spread that rumor... please."

He could tell several were having a hard time containing themselves. Deathwalker sighed. "They are not the only dignitaries coming. Lord Longshot and Lord Semium and both his children will be in attendance, as will several delegates from our neighboring countries. We have roughly two weeks to implement the plan we discussed, while also preparing for everything. It is a lot to do, and I am counting on all of you to help make it happen."

The subject of the city's current strife brought everyone out of their musings and refocused on the tasks at hand. The gossip crisis averted, Deathwalker rose to his feet to signify the end of the meeting. "Thank you everyone. I am counting on all of you to help make it all come together. Have a good rest of your evening. Oh, General Marius, please see me in my private study to discuss some additional military activities."

General Marius nodded at his liege as Deathwalker left the dining hall.

"My party member and friend might be the new king, wow." Cal commented.

Only for him to get an elbow from Mara. "Owe! What was that for?!" Cal asked, getting an angry look in reply.

# Chapter 9 - Secret Base

As Deathwalker walked back to his private study he reached out to Lilandra. “How goes what we discussed Lilandra?”

“It goes well. The portal room was already connected to a barracks in Nexus city.” Lilandra replied telepathically.

“Really? That’s the name we are going with?” Deathwalker mentally groaned.

Garry butted in on the telepathic conversation. “What? I liked it and the name makes sense.”

“It was your suggestion and you convinced everyone I liked it.” Deathwalker commented.

“Alpha does not like the name?” Frrsha chimed in.

Mrrsha and Prrsha were still not as comfortable using telepathy, but they still listened.

“Fine, Nexus city, until we think of something cooler.” Deathwalker begrudgingly agreed.

Garry smiled. “Thanks, boss.”

Deathwalker shifted his focus back to his first disciple. “Now you were saying Lilandra.”

“Yes, Orantes has lent me several of her drones. They helped with some of the required modifications. The connected barracks leads to a training facility and practice ring. All of that has been cut off from the rest of the city until you decide to reveal the truth to those stationed there. Master, are you sure you still want to do this?” Lilandra replied.

"We require a base. I want somewhere isolated. If we can prevent them from exploring, it should work. Let's have the pumas patrol near the barracks as common practice, just to be sure." Deathwalker replied.

Before moving on with his plan, another idea struck Deathwalker. "How is Orantes doing?"

"Very well. I visit her often. She has asked that you come see her when you can. I believe she wishes to show off the work her brood has accomplished. Why do you ask?" Lilandra relayed.

"Her brood could be a force unto themselves, but we would require different types of warriors. It might be good to have a conversation with her. I wanted to bring it up to you my little genie, as you might have ideas to help achieve what I am envisioning." Deathwalker explained.

"I see the images you are sending me. It is doable but give me some time to consider it." Lilandra answered.

"Excellent! I will see you shortly." Deathwalker stated, before cutting off the telepathic conversation.

It did not take General Marius long to arrive. He headed over after bidding his brother a good night. Deathwalker gestured to the empty seat at the table.

"Please sit, General. We have much to discuss."

"As you command, my liege." General Marius said as he sat down.

"I wanted to discuss the secret base we wanted to build. Had any luck locating somewhere sufficient for our needs?"

"No, my liege. Other than training and recruiting efforts, I used much of the time while you were away to have our men scout out possible base locations deeper in the forest. Though there are some options off the beaten path, closer to the Harkin mountains, that would put them too far from Timberfall to be of use." General Marius explained.

"Harkin Mountains. Hmmm. Grimhold told me that one of the Dwarven kingdoms is within the heart of those mountains. They have a few passageways that lead to the Elven nation and Hargrave. However, my understanding is that the side of the Harkin mountains Timberfall is far from the dwarves." Deathwalker said.

"That is true, my liege. It goes to show you how massive those mountains are. It would be hundreds of miles into the mountains before you reached the dwarves. Why do you ask?" General Marius replied.

"Might be worth the effort to create a portal station or create the tunnel. Just thinking of the future. Now, back to the base. I have a proposed location for our primary military base, but one that requires the highest secrecy and strictest requirements while there." Deathwalker answered.

"If you have a location, I can send my men to scout it out and determine the feasibility." General Marius commented.

"No, that simply won't do."

"Why not, my liege?" General Marius asked.

"You'll see. I am willing to take you there personally. I already sent my bodyguards and familiar along to ensure everything was ready. I wanted us to chat first. If you agree to this, I will expect strict oaths from anyone who goes to this location. One day you will understand why." Deathwalker said before standing. "So, how about it General, care to check it out?"

Without waiting for an answer, Deathwalker exited his suite and headed towards the Portal Station. General Marius followed quickly behind. "Where are we going, my liege?"

"The portal station." Deathwalker replied.

"The portal station?! Where are we going?" General Marius asked.

"You'll see soon enough." Was all Deathwalker said before going completely silent until they reached the portal hub.

“Leave us.” Deathwalker ordered the guards insider to leave the room.

The squad of soldiers did not argue. They snapped to attention and quickly left. Once they were alone again Deathwalker turned to his general. “Where we are about to go, you must swear to never share with anyone without my permission. Anyone you bring in the future must not only give the same oath but also is required to obey the rules of those there. Am I understood?”

“Not exactly, my liege, but you have my oath.” General Marius stated.

Deathwalker nodded, grabbed the warrior by the shoulder and pulled him into a portal. When General Marius opened his eyes, he was in a grand room that was larger than any amphitheater he had ever seen. There were archways everywhere. In the center of the room was a giant raised map. Part of the map he recognized as Timberfall, the rest he was unfamiliar with.

“Where are we, my liege?” General Marius asked.

“That is something we ask you to wait for an answer. Needless to say, you are in a very secret location. I believe that was one of the critical requirements to a ‘secret’ base.” Lilandra answered.

General Marius spun around to find one of the most beautiful women he had ever seen in his life. Her skin was a lavender color, she had pointy ears, and her outfit was very distracting.

Deathwalker spoke up. “Do not stare General. Let me introduce you to my Portal Master Lilandra. She is another layer of security over our network. This is her home, and you will respect her authority in this place.”

General Marius nodded multiple times. “As you command, my liege.” Turning to the lavender woman. “It is an honor to be allowed in your home Portal Master Lilandra. My apologies for staring. This place is quite breathtaking.”

Lilandra giggled. “He, he, he. At least he is respectful. I can see why you like him, master.”

"Master?" General Marius said under his breath but both Deathwalker and Lilandra heard him.

"Yes, I am Deathwalker's first disciple." Lilandra chimed in.

"Disciple?" General Marius was getting even more confused. He could feel the power radiating off this woman. 'And she is my duke's disciple? Totally lost here.'

Seeing his general's confused look Deathwalker spoke up. "I have many secrets General. We do not have the time to cover them all."

Turning to Lilandra, "Lilandra, why don't you show us to the barracks."

A smile spread over her face. She rather enjoyed being helpful. "Follow me. I will show you the secret base we have established for our people."

Lilandra guided the two men to the barracks, training yard, and military storage. Every new building they entered, General Marius' eyes grew bigger and bigger. The barracks was massive and could easily house tens of thousands of people with room to spare. The training yard was huge with several sections for melee combat, ranged attack dummies, and magic practice zones. The military storage had racks for weapons, separate sections to house rations and other perishables.

General Marius couldn't hold back any longer. "This place is magnificent!"

"I'm glad you like it General. I will expect you to coordinate with Lilandra. Bring the soldiers and supplies to the portal and she will know." Deathwalker ordered.

"How will she know?" General Marius asked.

"I am the Master Portal Guardian. I see all that enters one of the portal stations. I will await your men. Please make it clear I will tolerate no curiosity or 'accidental exploration'. If that occurs you can expect 'accidental death', am I clear?"

"Yes ma'am!" General Marius saluted.

Deathwalker clapped his general on the shoulder. “Excellent. Let us get back. I’m mentally exhausted and could use a rest.”

“Of course, my liege. Forgive my insensitivity. I was excited at such a perfect facility.” General Marius replied before following Deathwalker and Lilandra back to the portal room.

As General Marius and Deathwalker exited the portal back to Timberfall they heard two guards talking.

“It is just a black raven. Why are you acting so weird.”

“I know of no black ravens in this forest. They are not native. So, what is it doing here?”

“Who cares? It is just a bird!”

“It gives me the creeps!”

“What are you two talking about?” Deathwalker inquired.

Both men quickly snapped to attention. “Sorry, your grace. We were just chatting.”

“Yes, I heard. What is this about a black raven?”

Both soldiers looked uncertain. General Marius, seeing this barked a quick order. “Your Duke asked you a question. Answer him!”

“Well, you see, your grace. We guard this portal every day and for the last few days we noticed a large black raven perched on the manor wall. It seems to be watching what is going on.”

“Please excuse him, your grace. I do not think he has slept well the last few days. His mind is playing tricks on him.” The second guard replied.

“It is not! I am telling you there is intelligence behind those eyes!”

“Decorum gentlemen! You are in front of your Duke!” General Marius reminded the two soldiers.

Both soldiers looked horrified and dropped to their knees. “Our apologies, your grace!”

Lilandra sent a telepathic message out of nowhere. *“Master, you should...”*

Deathwalker cut her off. He was too tired mentally to worry about this whole situation. *“Later! Too tired!”*

Turning his attention to the two guards kneeling. “Get up. It’s fine.” Deathwalker said before exiting the building.

“I will discipline them later, my liege. They must know how to act properly.” General Marius commented once they left the building.

Deathwalker was about to reply when he noticed the large black raven. It stirred something within him. The giant bird turned its head and looked straight into his eyes.

For some reason Deathwalker recalled a moment from his favorite TV show Babylon 5. The line echoed in his head. “YOU HAVE A HOLE IN YOUR MIND!”

“What the heck? Why would I recall...” Deathwalker began to say before he dropped to his knees in sudden pain.

As Deathwalker shut his eyes, a vision flashed in his mind. He recalled seeing this before. It was the same scene Uriel showed Deathwalker of his arrival to the Hidden Infinite Nexus Realm.

--------

Deathwalker exited a roiling portal before transforming from a dragon into his human form. He collapsed unconscious. This is where his vision ended the last time Uriel showed it to him. However, now the vision continued. The scene panned to the side to reveal two angels. One Deathwalker recognized Uriel, the other he did not know.

The angel Deathwalker did not know walked up to his unconscious past self, bent down and placed his hands on Deathwalker’s head and chest. The angel’s hands began to glow.

Uriel spoke up as the light faded and the unknown angel stood. "Raphael, what did you just do?"

"Do not worry brother. I put a hidden geas on his soul. You have your duties and I have mine. We have seen what this man did to track down his friend. Do you think when he wakes up, he will stop doing everything he can to find his friend? Not a chance. The man is too loyal and passionate a person." Raphael replied.

"Yes, I agree he will be focused, but that focus could help him grow." Uriel chimed in.

"His friend is in the hands of the Dark! The scales must be balanced. You are the only one who can see to his introduction. I have done what I came to do. The geas must remain unknown."

Raphael patted Uriel's shoulder. "Do not worry brother, what I have done will only help him. This must be done with the utmost care, or he will recklessly go off chasing after his friend before he is ready to face him, and all is lost." Raphael stated before disappearing in a flash.

The scene ended as Deathwalker collapsed in pain. "AHHHHH!!!"

General Marius was at his side. "MY LIEGE, ARE YOU ALRIGHT?! WHAT HAS HAPPENED?!"

The General turned to his liege's familiar Garry to ask him if he knew anything.

As he looked up, Marius heard Garry say, "Oh Crap!"

Just after uttering those words, Garry winked out of existence.

CAAW, CAAW

The last thing Deathwalker thought he heard before falling unconscious was a voice saying, "We must talk!"

# Chapter 10 - Midsummer Night's Dream

"AHHH!!!" The Winter Queen That Was cried out as she dropped to the ground.

"What has happened sister?!" I asked. 'Wait why does my voice sound off? Am I in someone's dream or memory? I do not recall anything like this since I assumed my Deathwalker persona.'

"Our Huntsman has died! They killed him!" In a rare act Queen Winter wept.

The older woman tried to get up, but she found she couldn't. Her magic was intrinsically tied to her Huntsman. She felt a wound that would not go away.

"I-I cannot stand!" The Winter Queen said in shocked realization.

I quickly withdrew something I had made. I was saving it as a gift, one for each sister. "Do not worry sister. Take this cane. It is from the Tree of Life. I crafted one for you and one for our sister. This one I made just for you. I keyed it to work with your unique ability to Unravel anything. Quickly, take it!"

I thrust the carved cane into my sister's withered hand. She took it without question. The moment her magic touched the cane I saw visible relief on her tear-stained face.

"Good, it worked perfectly. Now you shall not fade away, my sister. This should help both you and Mother Summer deal with the massive losses dealt to us by the Light this day."

I helped my sister slowly stand on wobbly legs. "This must have taken great time and skill to craft. How did you know I would need this sister?"

"I felt something in the Weave, but it was Chronos who came to me. He helped me understand what was coming. Together we connected our powers and poured them into our craft." I replied.

'Wait, Chronos? Am I re-living someone's memories? But who?'

"It is good my daughter abstained from the fighting otherwise it might have been much worse." Mother Winter commented as she got her bearings.

"Our niece may disagree." I replied.

Mother Winter spat, "Bah! Our sister's ilk have always been too hot tempered and emotional. I do not care what her daughter thinks. The war is over, we lost!"

"The Dark lost sister, not us." I clarified.

My sister gave me a scowl only she could manage. "We lost! The Dark may have been the cause, but it matters little when we still lost so many of our own people."

She then leaned on her cane, and I could feel her power flow into it, causing Mother Winter to smile. "This is quite impressive sister. It appears I now owe you and that old dragon Chronos a boon."

"Do not sound so sour about it. He, he, he, he." I chuckled.

"I am not sour about you; it is that stubborn dragon. Fate and Time are intrinsically linked, and that old coot never lets us forget it. The idea of owing him a favor is just... distasteful."

I reminded my sister of one important fact. "Well, he is gone now, so it may not matter. He gave the last vestiges of his power before sacrificing himself."

"That is what bothers me most! Now I have to see to it whomever gets his **Infinite Well of Time Magic** is worthy of such a legacy. How annoying!" Mother Winter complained.

"Ha, ha, ha, ha, ha! Leave it to you, sister, to be finally rid of the Father of Time, someone I have heard you argue with on numerous occasions. Now you are upset he is gone. You actually liked him, admit it sister!" I teased.

"I will do no such thing! Besides our sister approaches and you have a gift for her." Mother Winter said before turning around and heading to the other side of the cabin.

————

Deathwalker awoke startled and looking around. "What was that?!"

It took him a moment to realize he was back in his bed in Timberfall Manor, and he was surrounded by multiple tired faces. Mrrsha, Prrsha, and Frrsha rushed to his side when he awoke. Garry was nowhere to be seen. General Marius, Geeves and Elder Martha were also nearby.

Still feeling groggy and out of it, Deathwalker asked, "What happened?"

The three cat girls rushed to his side.

"That is what we hoped you could tell us, alpha." Mrrsha stated.

Elder Martha spoke up. "Marius sent Mrrsha after me to see if I could help in anyway. You have been unconscious for the last day. I can honestly say we have no idea what the cause was."

"Frrsha and I tried to attack the giant black bird in case it was the cause, but it just flew away faster than it should have been able to move." Prrsha shared.

"I am sorry alpha. We failed in our duty to protect you." Frrsha whined.

Deathwalker patted her hand and tried to sit up in bed.

"Careful, your grace. Let me assist you." Geeves said as he helped Deathwalker sit up and propped pillows behind him.

Still feeling off, Deathwalker checked his notifications.

***Warning you have been affected by an Unknown Effect! Insight has failed to determine the source of the effect!***

*Congratulations! Your understanding of* ***Fate*** *and* ***Time*** *Magics have increased! Continue to practice these magics to understand these fundamental forces of existence.*

'Was that from the dream I just had? Was that someone's memories forcibly coming to the surface? And what the heck is an Unknown Effect. How useful is that supposed to be to me? Like what do I do with such ambiguous information?!' Deathwalker thought.

Deathwalker was about to continue reviewing his notifications when his brain finally realized something important. "Wait where is Garry?"

General Marius answered his Duke. "He vanished after you collapsed. Your bodyguards said he was somehow unsummoned or killed."

"What?! How?!" Deathwalker replied in shock.

"We do not know alpha, but we could no longer hear the annoying floating ball in our minds." Mrrsha explained.

Checking his remaining notification he got his answer.

Your familiar Garry has been killed by Unknown Effect! As he was not killed permanently, you can re-summon him in a few days. Time remaining before re-summon possible: 2 days, 3 hours.

Deathwalker was stunned. Whatever that Unknown Effect was, it killed Garry and nearly took him out, or at least that is what his body felt like had happened.

He heard Lilandra in his mind. "Perhaps I can shed some light on things now that you are awake Master."

"You know something Lilandra?" Frrsha telepathically asked.

Deathwalker just leaned his head against the headboard. “Elder Martha, Geeves, and Marius, I find myself still quite tired. Please, for now let me rest and we can speak later. My bodyguards will remain and call on you should I require it.”

Elder Martha had a look of concern on her face, but she nodded. “As you wish, my Duke. I will check in on you in the morning just to be sure you continue to be on the mend.”

“Thank you.” Deathwalker replied.

Geeves spoke next. “Ms. Mara, Cal, and Grimhold have also expressed their concerns, having heard the rumors of your collapse. What shall I tell them, your grace?”

“The truth. I have awakened but am still tired. We think something attacked me, but we do not know anything further.” Deathwalker answered.

Geeves bowed. “Very good, your grace. I and the rest of the staff are but a moment away should you require anything.”

“Thank you, Geeves.”

Both Elder Martha and Geeves left the room. General Marius bowed. “I have extra men posted outside and I posted additional soldiers throughout the manor. I will keep watch as well.”

Deathwalker tried to shake his head but found that to be a mistake when he winced from the pain. “No. I gave you an order General. I want that secret base stocked and manned. We have already lost a day. Whatever happened, I do not think there is anything the men can do. I require rest to recover.” His voice softened a bit. “Please, my friend, see to this important work.”

“As you command, my liege.” General Marius said as he stood. He looked at the three cat girls. “Watch over him.”

All three girls gave their nods of agreement. General Marius gave his Duke one last bow before he too exited the suite. Once it was just Deathwalker and his three disciples he spoke both out loud and telepathically. "Alright Lilandra, the others have left. Please go on, but before you do, open a portal here. I would prefer this conversation face to face."

"As you command, Master." Deathwalker heard Lilandra telepathically reply as a portal opened up in his bedroom and Lilandra walked out. The portal closed behind her.

"Is it safe for her to be away from the primary portal room?" Mrrsha asked in concern.

"I am still close to the Life leyline connected to the Nexus. As the portal guardian, I can open up portals and return as long as I am close enough to certain leylines." Lilandra explained.

Mrrsha nodded her understanding.

Lilandra turned her full attention to Deathwalker. "If you will permit me, master, I will explain what I was trying to tell you earlier."

"Please do." Deathwalker answered.

Lilandra erected a barrier blocking the doors leading to the rest of the manor to ensure they were not disturbed. Once that was accomplished, she began her story. "I heard the soldiers talking about a crow or black raven. I believe that is what triggered this. I do not know what caused your collapse, but I have a feeling I know who the black raven could be."

"Who dares attack our alpha?!" Prrsha roared.

"That is just it. I do not think she would intentionally attack you. It makes no sense why she of all people would attack you." Lilandra chimed in.

Deathwalker spoke up. "It is the Morrigan isn't it?"

"H-how? How could you know that?" Lilandra asked in shock.

"When you said 'she' is when it clicked for me. In my world's myths the Morrigan was associated with crows or ravens and death, as she was a battle goddess. There are other beings associated with ravens like Odin but when you alluded to her being female it clicked for me. You wanted to tell me something before I cut you off. You were expecting her, weren't you?" Deathwalker replied.

Lilandra sighed. "Morrigan is one of the original Parcae. She was also very active in your Irish and Welsh homelands."

"What is a Parcae?" Frrsha asked.

"Sisters of Fate. They had different names in different cultures in my homeland. What was so odd is that their duties seemed very similar in those multiple cultures across the globe. They were readers of the Weave of Fate. One spun, one allotted, one unraveled. Guides to one's Destiny. It appears Fate and Time are intrinsically linked." Deathwalker explained.

"You are well informed in your world's lore, Master." Lilandra commented.

"Those who do not understand history are doomed to repeat it. That saying always stuck with me. Besides certain myths and legends seemed to call to me more than others." Deathwalker stated.

"Our alpha is wise." Mrrsha chimed in.

"Hmph. I just remember the origin of the fey and fairies. It is just another way of saying Fate or the guides and manipulators of one's Fate. That is how my people gave them their name, as a warning to not cross one or lose sight of what they were capable of. That could not be coincidence." Deathwalker said more to himself in realization than to anyone else.

Deathwalker pondered a few things that seemed to click now that he knew the Morrigan was real. "The djinn, some myths around them are similar to the fey. They can manipulate or influence one's Fate or Destiny. You all are the same species, just different offshoots, aren't you?"

He felt her trepidation before Lilandra sighed and then answered. "Yes. I did not mention it before when we talked about Oberon, but we were part of God's creation. The universe itself has fundamental forces that move it forward. Those forces can partially differ or be interpreted differently but they are still there... Some of the most important forces are Fate and Time. The two are just as intrinsically linked as Life and Death is. The forces of Growth versus Entropy. Order and Chaos. These diametrically opposed forces are tied together, my children and I, well we embrace the elemental forces of the universe. Whereas some other are focused on one principle versus another."

"What does this have to do with our alpha's question?" Prrsha asked.

"I am getting there. The races began to diverge as we embraced, no, a better word would be embodied, different aspects of the forces of the universe. The more you attempt to understand the Weave, the more it can influence you. Mother Summer, the Morrigan, and Mother Winter were the first. Mab, Titania, and I were their successors. By the time it was our turn we all had differed greatly in our paths."

"How did you end up imprisoned where I met you, Lilandra? I remember you saying Oberon sacrificed himself and you and your children were imprisoned, but that is a far cry from becoming the arbiter for the Hidden Infinite Nexus Realm."

Deathwalker's question caught the djinn and the pumas off guard. "She was imprisoned?" Frrsha asked.

Lilandra answered. "Yes, I was imprisoned, Frrsha. You see, Summer allied with the Dark and the demons in the last great cosmic war for the Omniverse. The Light killed many demons, fey, djinn, and others. I lost many children in that war. They would have killed many more had not our King interceded. He had secretly helped the Light and their forces like the dragons, high elves, and dwarves. He sacrificed his life to pay for the sins of those arrogant children who thought they knew better... You see someone had to pay the ultimate price one way or another, choices have consequences. The war had broken his heart, and he could not bear to let even more die. All this I shared with you before, master."

"As I said before, honorable leader." Deathwalker commented.

Lilandra agreed. "Yes, he was the love of my life... His royal, selfless sacrifice impressed the Light. As such, instead of being imprisoned somewhere or losing my own life, the Light gave me a choice of where to serve out my eternal sentence. The Morrigan had come to me, she had told me to be careful in what I chose, that if I picked correctly, one day I might be free... So, I took a gamble. If anyone claimed the Infinite Nexus, I knew they would have the power to free me. I was right, as you did."

"Good to know. You brought up Oberon's sacrifice for a reason. What is it?" Deathwalker asked.

Lilandra continued her tale. "One thing I must admit, is God is a god of Hope. You see, the Light agreed that one day the most precious of those lost in the war would be reborn in a time when they were most needed. This hope has been something our people have held on to over the millennia, even though we waiver, it is hard to let go of such a powerful driving force such as hope, for without it, there is only despair."

"True enough. So, God promised several of those lost would be reborn. Where are you going with this Lilandra?" Deathwalker pressed.

"I am getting there, master. I must first finish my tale. In addition to that sacred promise, those who fought for the Light; the dragons, dwarves, a few fey, and elves, were promised a future royal that would give them the prosperity and wisdom they deserved. It was believed that each of the races would receive a ruler to guide them. There were many lost, so it was not like the Light did not have enough to choose from."

"Did this ever happen?" Deathwalker asked.

Lilandra shook her head. "No. Shortly after the war the royal bloodline of dragons, the Omni-dragons were killed off. There has not been one of them for thousands of years. The dragons would never follow any other but their royal bloodline. The dwarves have had kings and queens, though they may have had prosperity at times, none seemed to be the fulfillment of prophecy. Even the fey and djinn were promised the return of some of their key warriors, including our king. Not all fey joined the Dark and the Light believed Oberon should get a chance to live again."

"So, the stories I grew up hearing were true? Oberon was king of the fey and apparently the djinn as well." Deathwalker commented.

Lilandra sighed. "Yes, he truly was the best of us. We are only here now because of him. So, after the war, all were banished from Avalon, only Oberon can claim Avalon again. The summer fey were to live close to humans and in the forests to help guide and learn the importance of life. As I mentioned before, my children and I were imprisoned, bound to no longer use our power for our own whims and instead forever forced to guide or serve others. That was the price of abusing our power and letting our emotions control us.

"However, I think Winter got the worst of it. They mostly abstained from the war. As such, Queen Mab was given the burden of protecting the Omniverse realities from the Eldritch and their abominations who seek to destroy what is so different than them. Summer must assist when called, but it is Winter who bears the brunt of the fight against the demons and those outside our realities.

"You see that is what our ignorance failed to understand. The war cracked some of the barriers between the Omniverse and the truly perverse. We garnered the attention of beings that despised our very existence and then weakened the locks for them to get in." Lilandra said with clear sadness in her voice.

"Talk about poetic justice. Do not get me wrong, thousands or years without a home, or imprisoned, or fighting an endless war, pretty harsh. But it sounds like nearly destroying all life as we know it is probably the worst thing someone could do." Deathwalker admonished.

"This we as queens understood. We accepted our burdens without complaint. It has been this way for thousands of years… I gladly gave up my freedom to give my children a chance. As much as I may not agree with the Light at times, they always keep their promises, that I cannot deny. It may not occur how and when you expect but it still happens." Lilandra finished explaining.

"Will there be backlash because I freed you?" Deathwalker asked.

Lilandra shrugged her shoulders. "Possibly. I doubt it. I did my duty as arbiter, and you have gained both your class and Specialization. Duty fulfilled."

"Fair enough. So, you want to tell me why the Morrigan would attack me?" Deathwalker inquired.

Just then, the doors to the balcony opened, and a giant, black raven flies in before it transforms into a beautiful woman. "Perhaps, I can best answer that question."

# Chapter 11 – The Unraveler

All three pumas jump up and headed straight for the intruder, claws out. They made it only a few feet before streams of frost whipped past Morrigan and hit the three bodyguards. All three cat girls were instantly frozen solid. A loud tapping could be heard as an older woman with a cane walked around from behind of Morrigan.

Clack, clack, clack.

“You did not need to freeze them.” Lilandra commented.

Mother Winter shrugged. “It is better that no one else bothers us dearie. We have much to discuss.”

Deathwalker could barely move. He still had this Unknown Effect debuff that made every part of his body ache. If he had to, he would cast as much magic in their direction as possible, but he hoped to resolve this encounter peacefully. Hope did not mean ignoring the danger. ‘Best prepare for the worst.’

With their bond, Lilandra could sense Deathwalker’s preparations to fight. Lilandra knew she had to deescalate the situation fast. “They are not dead, Master. They are merely captured.”

Deathwalker looked at his first disciple. “Lilandra, you are not sounding like you are coming to our people’s aid. They have attacked our people!”

“I am trying to deescalate the situation. I believe they are not here to hurt you.” Lilandra replied.

“Bullshit!” Deathwalker said before turning to the two intruders. “You attack me and then my people. What is this debuff that you have caused me?! I want answers!” Deathwalker exclaimed.

“Ah. Well, that was not intentional. Lilandra is right, we mean you no harm.” Morrigan answered.

“Speak for yourself sister! I have not yet decided what my intentions are.” Mother Winter countered.

Morrigan glared at her. “Not helping.”

To which the old woman gave her back a toothy grin.

“Some days.” Morrigan commented before turning her attention back to Deathwalker. “Allow me to explain a few things about what happened earlier. I will answer any questions you require and give an oath to not attack you if you do not attack me.”

Deathwalker received a prompt.

*The Morrigan has offered you a temporary* ***Oath of Nonaggression*** *backed by her power. If she attacks you, her power will be lost. If you attack her, she is free to defend herself. Beware of your actions!*

‘Well, that is not ominous at all. Never seen a prompt like that. It is as if the system is warning me. It is not like I can do much currently anyway, so why not.’ Deathwalker thought as he released the magic he was starting to channel.

Feeling him let go of the spell, Morrigan nodded at Deathwalker. “Good. Now let me start with saying we were invited here by Lilandra.”

“WHAT?!” Deathwalker exclaimed as he turned his eyes on his first disciple.

“It is not what you think, Master.” Lilandra replied.

“I do not know what to think!” Deathwalker stated in exasperation.

“Oh, pipe down, dearie. She came to us as your advocate.” Mother Winter said as she took a seat in one of the chairs in the room.

Morrigan interjected. “Before you think less of her and us, let me explain what happened earlier. You see, I watch the **Weave of Fate** very closely. As I am sure you can imagine, your travel through the Sea of Chaos and arrival at the Hidden Infinite Nexus Realm...” She paused seeing the look of shock on Deathwalker’s face. “What? You do not think such an event would go unnoticed by someone who pays attention to the ripples that directly affect the strands of fate?”

Deathwalker recalled something Uriel told him during his first encounter with the archangel. “Others will have seen your arrival...”

Morrigan smiled as she saw the realization on Deathwalker’s face. “Yes, good. Then it is time to explain further. You and your friend are not the only ones to have been taken.”

Her words clicked for Deathwalker. “My friend. How could I have forgotten all about finding him? I mean at first, I thought I just found heaven coming to a reality where stats were real, and people were all used to such things, total dream come true! Then Uriel told me I had to get stronger if I hoped to ever find my friend... I mean he did say the Dark took him, that cannot be a good thing, yet why are my emotions still muted. I care but something isn’t right! What the hell is wrong with me?!”

“Ah, he finally begins to understand. About time.” Mother Winter teased.

“I showed you what was left out of your arrival. As the Dark saw to your friend’s arrival, it was the Light’s right to see to your introduction, yet they only chose to show you part of what happened when you first arrived in the Hidden Realm. They left out something critical, which is partially for your current state predicament... You see, they put a geas on you.” Morrigan explained.

This time Lilandra spoke up before Deathwalker could. “A geas?! What? I detected no such thing!”

Morrigan answered. "That is because it was placed by Raphael. He is the **Messenger of God** and known to be a great healer. Such an archangel has the authority to place a geas on your very being without being detected by the system. I believe when I showed Raphael placing the geas on Deathwalker, it triggered some kind of defense mechanism. You were not meant to discover what happened."

"You make it sound like it is alive." Deathwalker said in concern.

Morrigan shook her head. "No. Not in that way. Think of it as a stored series of commands. One of those commands was clearly to cripple you should it be discovered. Why, I do not know."

"It is your friend." Lilandra chimed in.

"What?" Deathwalker asked in confusion.

"Uriel made it very clear you were not ready to face your friend. He was too powerful and if you two fought before you had a chance to grow stronger and master your knowledge and abilities, you would die." Lilandra explained.

"The Light's champion would be lost, and the Dark would advance." Mother Winter commented.

"My friend would never do that to me. James is a good man." Deathwalker argued.

"The Dark can twist any of us in such a way to play us for fools. They did it to my people." Lilandra spoke up with both Mother Winter and Morrigan nodding along.

"That is what the Dark does dearie. It cannot create anything so instead it twists and corrupts everything it can." Mother Winter interjected.

That was when Deathwalker remembered a famous saying back on Earth. "The road to hell is paved with good intentions."

"Very apt saying." Morrigan commented before continuing. "Your friend was the first but not the last to disappear. Since you two were the beginning, many have been taken since. They are to be lieutenants and generals in a new upcoming war between the Light and the Dark. Several of us have read the signs in the Weave. War is once again inevitable."

"But how could they just take us without our consent?" Deathwalker inquired.

"They had your consent." Lilandra answered.

"I do not recall ever consenting to such a thing." Deathwalker challenged.

Lilandra's next words sent chills down Deathwalker's spine. "No one ever reads the user agreement contract."

It was the user community's biggest complaint, you had to click the agreement three times when you first started playing and any time, they released new content. No one ever bothered reading the giant boring contract, so you would just click it and move on to gaming. "You are telling me the agreement says they can take us?"

"You see your world and reality was cut off from most magics long ago. That is except for faith magic, that is strong there. Devil worshippers and many in the Dark believe they take on no negative karmic debt if they tell the person what they are doing and then go do it. In their minds it is consensual. They believe that so strongly that they look down on those that fall for the trick, seeing them as deserving what they get. It is those same people who own the gaming company and we're working to find suitable warriors for what is coming." Lilandra further explained.

Morrigan chimed in. "There is more to it than that, but we do not have time for an in-depth philosophical discussion. Needless to say, your friend was the catalyst. But you... well... let us just say you are unexpected. The combination of bloodlines, your soul's reaction while in the Sea of Chaos, the claiming of the Infinite Nexus... it had to be intelligent design."

"What do you mean?" Deathwalker asked.

"Every few generations rare beings rise, born to do extraordinary things. Some of that comes from the hard work of the previous generations and the rest comes from what drives that person. All of that culminated Fate is in the Weave, if one knows how to read it. Some are like knots in the Weave, they pull other strands towards them, influence Fate itself, but all is still driven by some greater force..." Morrigan continued to explain but was interrupted by Mother Winter.

"Oh, just say it sister! She means God, dearie. Each of us here have connections to different primordial forces of the universe, but all of that still ties back to a design. We were arrogant fools to think otherwise, some of us..." Mother Winter looked at Morrigan, "thought ourselves gods, but that is the manipulation and corruption of those damn demons!"

Mother Winter slammed her walking stick down a few times. "Now, can we please get on with this. I have a decision to make."

Sighing, Morrigan continued. "Very well. We can discuss the rest later. Back to your geas. As a knot in the Weave, you yourself are a nexus of Fate and Destiny. However, as the **Master of the Infinite Nexus**, you have the power to heavily influence the various realities within the Omniverse. That is why the Light went all in with you, and wanted some assurance you would not fall to the Dark."

"You mean the geas that is influencing my emotions and interests." Deathwalker stated.

"Yes and no. You see, I do not think Raphael knew what would happen to someone who attempted to claim the **Infinite Nexus** with a geas in place. It took that conflict within you and made it manifest." Morrigan answered.

"What are you trying to say? Please, just get to the point." Deathwalker replied.

Mother Winter laughed. "Ha, ha, ha, ha, ha! I am really beginning to like this one. He definitely acts like one from winter. Enough of your prattling sister. I have waited long enough!"

Mother Winter then rose to her feet and walked over to Deathwalker and grabbed his face in her hand and jerked his face to within inches to her own. Their eyes locked and she stared into his eyes, as he did the same. Deathwalker could feel a cold presence wash over his body, mind, and soul. For him it was like a cool breeze or an air-conditioned room on a warm day, pleasant, even as the feeling intensified.

After a few long moments Mother Winter spoke. “Interesting. It would appear you were right sister.” She broke eye contact and turned to Morrigan. “Do not let it go to your head.”

Morrigan chuckled. “Ha, ha, ha, ha. You would never let me.”

Mother Winter, still holding on to Deathwalker’s face, turned to Lilandra. “It appears you are partially right. The geas attempts to hide much, but such a thing is trivial to the Unraveler.”

“Mind telling me what is going on?” Deathwalker asked.

Turning back to Deathwalker, Mother Winter answered. “That is fair, but do not get cheeky with me dearie. I would carve your heart out for the slightest disrespect.”

“My apologies. I meant no disrespect. I am trying to understand what is going on.” Deathwalker replied.

“That is fair. What do you know of me, dearie?” Mother Winter asked.

“You said you were the Unraveler. What I know of the Parcae, one nourishes life, one assesses and allots it, the third severs it.” Deathwalker answered.

“Basic but at least you did not say I take life. Such a moronic understanding of what I do. Those that state such a thing do not live long in my presence. I possess the ability to unravel any magic or strand in the Weave. It is a combination of entropy and part of purity. That is the authority granted to me. There are only a few beings that can withstand my powers.” Mother Winter replied.

“So, is that why Winter is seen as so cold is that it possesses an aspect of entropy? It is a different kind of Ice magic, the one that stops potential.” Deathwalker commented.

Mother Winter smiled again and turned towards Morrigan. “I like this one. He learns quickly.” Turning back to Deathwalker again. “For not insulting me and saving me the trouble of explaining in depth what I am capable of, I will tell you something you should know. My sister believes that your soul was shattered due to the geas being present while you claimed the **Infinite Nexus**. It was like having warring aspects within you. The **Infinite Nexus** made those different drivers manifest, which wounded your Mind, body, and soul.”

“I mean I felt unimaginable pain when I claimed the Infinite Nexus, but I thought that was just part of the process.” Deathwalker stated.

Morrigan spoke up. “If you had all the affinities at a high enough level, it should not have been how you described it. Further proof the geas interfered with the process.”

“What different drivers though? I am still a bit confused. What the Light did caused that much difference?” Deathwalker asked.

“The geas holds different parts to it. First, it was to help you accept this new reality you found yourself in. Some who come from realities where power is not accurately measured through a system can struggle to wrap their mind around such an existence. That aspect of the geas is simple enough.” Mother Winter explained.

“It is like a dream come true for me. I have always loved Isekai stories and role-playing games, which have these kinds of elements in them.” Deathwalker commented.

Mother Winter continued. “That is what makes this geas so dangerous. It emphasizes parts of you or mutes what is already there. Your thirst for knowledge has also been greatly emphasized.”

"That explains my multiple long and drawn out, repetitive reading sessions. I mean I love the quest for knowledge and power like anyone, but man those sessions were ridiculous. My head felt like it was going to split open. I normally love to read, but I would've spaced it out over time while searching for my friend and getting used to what power I already possessed." Deathwalker said in realization.

"You have hardly mentioned your friend, but I know your laser focus in finding him was what brought you here in the first place. I always found your lack of interest in your friend odd. At first, I just figured it might be too painful for you to discuss him, but now I realize it was far worse. The geas removed your interest and shifted your focus." Lilandra chimed in.

Mother Winter nodded. "They muted your emotions and more importantly your drive to find and save your friend."

"So, my friend is in danger?!" Deathwalker said in concern. Then like a wave, his mind wandered to thinking how fascinating Mother Winter's abilities were.

Morrigan spoke up. "Of course, he was taken by the Dark. They will do everything to create conflict and one trial after the other to bring out his inner monster. Once that is accomplished, they will do everything they can to turn him into a weapon for their cause. Manipulation and corruption remember."

"I do, yet it is so hard to keep my focus on it." Deathwalker replied.

"That is the geas." Mother Winter commented.

Morrigan spoke up again. "Things have gotten much worse for you now. The damage caused to you when you claimed the **Infinite Nexus** became exasperated when you discovered the truth about the geas, and it triggered one of its effects. The geas attacked your soul bonded familiar, killing him. That is what caused you to pass out from the pain, it was a soul wound." Seeing Deathwalker's concerned look, Morrigan raised her hands. "Do not worry, your familiar can be resummoned, as the geas stopped its attack once you passed out."

"I cannot remain under this **Unknown Effect** debuff. Plus, as annoying as that little guy is, Garry is my buddy, and I cannot risk his permanent death if something like this happens again. Can you help me, Mother Winter?" Deathwalker implored.

"I can use my ability to unravel anything, even the magic binding you to the geas. This will result in the removal of the geas. However, there could be unintended consequences of doing so. I would have to remove the geas before I could tell you the extent of the damage or determine what I wish to know. You must choose dearie."

"Please remove it." Deathwalker pleaded.

"Very well. Do not move." Mother Winter said as her other hand brought her cane up to Deathwalker's forehead and the cool icy feeling of her power came crashing into him.

The icy cold feeling spread throughout him until Deathwalker felt it land on something unknown inside him. The moment the icy sensation touched what Deathwalker assumed was the geas, it dissolved instantly. Deathwalker immediately felt the pain and aches fade away. He still did not feel completely like himself, but he felt better than he had since waking back up.

Deathwalker decided to review the prompt he received.

***Unknown Effect*** *has been removed! You once again have access to all your stats and abilities!*

'Well, that is a relief.' Deathwalker thought before he received a new notification.

***Warning! Soul Instability detected! This damage is tied directly to the Spirit. Mind and Body are also affected. Soul magic alone will not provide a solution! Seek help soon! Time until permadeath: 1 year, 13 Days, and 5 Hours!***

"I AM GOING TO DIE?!!! That is a pretty big side effect!" Deathwalker exclaimed when he read the prompt.

"WHAT?!" Lilandra asked.

Mother Winter, who was still holding on to Deathwalker spoke up. "I saw his notifications as they came up. He is in far worse shape than we thought, but I see a possible solution within him."

"Explain what you saw, sister." Morrigan replied.

"The damage has cascaded to his Spirit, Mind, and Body. He has roughly a little over a year to fix the issue. It appears the geas was holding him together after he claimed the Infinite Nexus. Now that it is gone, it is only a matter of time." Mother Winter said in an emotionless tone.

"How can this happen?!" Lilandra was clearly frustrated and upset. Perhaps more than even Deathwalker was.

"Calm down, Lilandra. I appreciate the concern, but I need solutions, not outbursts right now." Deathwalker stated before giving his attention to the tiny fey woman in front of him. "You mentioned a possible solution, Mother Winter."

Mother Winter nodded. "Yes, I did, but first we must discuss why I am here, not why Morrigan came, or what Lilandra had hoped would happen in seeking us out, but why I came."

"Then you have tested him?" Morrigan asked.

"He is as I suspected?!" Lilandra replied.

"Yes and No." Mother Winter answered.

"Tested me? What is it that you expected? You know I really don't like having things kept from me!" Deathwalker said in confusion.

Mother Winter gave a light slap on Deathwalker's face, before moving her hand to his shoulder. "Do not get impatient, dearie. This is a complicated matter."

"How is it complicated?! He is either the Huntsman, or he is not. What is so complicated about that sister?" Morrigan asked.

"Wait a minute, you thought I was the Huntsman Lilandra?! Why would you think that..." Deathwalker began to say before he thought about it seriously for a moment. "Scratch that. I can see why you would think I am him, but according to Mother Winter I'm not."

"That is not what I said, dearie. Do not make me give you a slap for real this time." Mother Winter admonished.

"This is unlike you, sister. Speak plainly and get to your true meaning. Even I am confused, and I have known you for thousands of years." Morrigan said in frustration.

Mother Winter raised one eyebrow towards her sister. "You are getting rather emotional, sister. But very well. I will attempt to explain. Deathwalker's soul has been shattered." She turned her attention back to Deathwalker. "While you are in this state it is difficult for me to confirm if you are the Huntsman reborn. The damage to your soul is too extensive. However, I sense something in you that I recognize. This gives me hope that once you fully recombine, I can confirm what we suspect."

"Recombine? What does that mean?" Deathwalker asked.

Mother Winter sighed. "I will get to that, but first a warning. Your emotions will remain partially muted while you are in this state. And you can forget about helping your friend until you help yourself. My daughter must not meet you while you are in this state."

"Why?" Deathwalker asked in curiosity this time.

"Simple. Since the death of her husband, she has fully embraced the cold logic of our kind. This coldness has even been towards my granddaughter. She may want to keep you in this state of pure logic, to have one be as she is now. No, you must be healed before you meet either queen of the fey." Mother Winter explained.

"My sister is correct. Mab has grown colder than her namesake, Winter Queen. If you are the Huntsman, in this muted emotional state, she may seek to keep you that way. Which means certain death." Morrigan commented.

"But why do my emotions still feel so muted? I thought removing the geas would've fixed that. Is the spiritual and mental damage so great that it has affected my emotions?" Deathwalker asked.

"Tell him, or I will." Lilandra said firmly.

Mother Winter shook her head. "Such defiance against your elders. You truly care for this one so much?"

Lilandra stood straighter as she answered. "I do. He freed me from my prison, and you know what I believe."

Mother Winter sighed again as she turned her attention back to Deathwalker. "Very well. Your soul has been shattered. What you do not understand about that is the fact that you are not whole. The essence of who you are... you have parts missing. That is what the geas did to you. The **Infinite Nexus** tore away parts of you and scattered them across various realities. In order for you to heal, you must either regain those parts... which may be impossible to find in the infinite number of realities out there. Which is why I have an alternative to suggest."

"What alternative?" Deathwalker asked.

"You have absorbed multiple lifetimes of experiences. One of those experiences I believe is the key to your survival." Mother Winter began but was cut off by Morrigan.

"Chronos!"

Mother Winter nodded. "Exactly. You possess the **Infinite Well of Time Magic** inside you. If you could find the other part of Chronos' power and legacy, you could use it to stay the inevitable. Become as Chronos had, master of time. With that mastery you could indefinitely pause your unraveling while you search for your missing parts of your soul.

"It is a rather ingenious idea." Lilandra commented.

“Mother Winter nodded. “Of course it is, I suggested it.” She turned deathly serious. “It is our understanding that other than the Infinite Well of Time Magic, Chronos divided his power into two other relics. One was knowledge imparted into the System to be given as a boon. The second, and most powerful fragment was his Primordial Core. If someone else has it, then you must take it from them, and I do mean kill them. It is the only way. Once that is accomplished, you could spend the countless years needed to find the parts of yourself you are missing, and I do mean that literally. The more you find the more you can heal.”

“You want me to locate Chronos’ power, kill whoever has it, then use my ability to absorb it? I don’t know if I could do that. Sure, if it is in the hands of some monster not a problem, but an innocent, I am not sure.” Deathwalker answered with honest concern. ‘Do I have the right to kill another so I can live? I do not know about that.’

“Two.” Morrigan said.

“What?” Deathwalker asked in confusion.

“As my sister mentioned, Chronos’ power was split into three. One was the **Infinite Well of Time Magic**, which you possess. The other majority of his power was in his Primordial Celestial Dragon core. Lastly, a final fraction of his power was given to the System itself so it could reward it to someone in the future. If that has been given, you must take it if you hope to survive. This means you must kill two beings to save your life.” Morrigan further explained.

“Great. So now I possibly have to kill two people to save myself. I do not know about that.” Deathwalker replied.

“Survival of the fittest. That is Winter’s way. It is the cold, hard truth. In the end, it is your choice. I will give you a warning. Do not use the **Infinite Well of Time Magic** unless you have to. Doing so without the other parts of Chronos’ power will only hasten your demise.” Mother Winter warned.

“Well, whatever I decide. I appreciate the warning and the information you have freely given. Most importantly, thank you for removing the geas. I do not like being controlled.” Deathwalker said as he stood and gave Mother Winter a big hug.

Everyone was stunned, speechless, most of all Mother Winter. She had not been hugged for thousands of years. The last time was in fact her late son-in-law. Something came over her, and Mother Winter embraced Deathwalker back. They stood there for a few moments, before Deathwalker ended the hug.

"You are both welcome here any time. I just ask you to be mindful of how you announce yourselves. In fact, I'm surprised my men have not stormed the room yet." Deathwalker said.

"Oh that. My sister cast **Winter's Long Slumber** on the whole city. They should awaken once we leave. Come sister, you can get more hugs later." Morrigan teased.

Mother Winter gave her sister a stern look. "Do not push it, sister. Yes, I must rest myself. It has been many years since I exerted myself this much. Farewell Deathwalker, try not to die before we meet again."

Morrigan gave Lilandra a hug and whispered in her ear. "You were wise to request our council. Try to keep his condition quiet, if the Dark finds out the truth, it will not end well. When the time comes, I will intercede with Summer should something occur."

Lilandra replied back, "Thank you!"

With that, Morrigan stepped away, transformed into a giant black raven. A cold gust of blinding wind spread throughout the room. When it cleared, Morrigan and Mother Winter were gone, and Mrrsha, Prrsha, and Frrsha were unfrozen.

"Where did they go?!" Prrsha asked.

"What happened?" Mrrsha inquired.

It was Frrsha who looked at Deathwalker and instantly knew. "You are wounded alpha!"

# Interlude - Elven Convoy

A Ljósálfar elven guard rode his horse up to the royal carriage. "Your Majesty, we should be in Hargrave in a few hours."

"Good. It has been too long since I have seen my daughters and only grandchild." King Alfheim replied.

The king turned to the other three people in his carriage. One was his general and friend Mineheir. Then there were his two advisors. An older elf mage named Nero, served as the king's head royal court magician. Last, but definitely not least, was a fey woman named Mona who served as the official envoy from Queen Mab. She too was a talented mage and healer.

Advisor Nero was reading a rather thick book he had pulled out of his bag of holding. He might periodically look up to check on his king, but otherwise he was engrossed in his tome. The old elf had been in that position since they left the capital.

Advisor Mona seemed completely bored. She too possessed a bag of holding and was known to withdraw a magic parchment and quill that would record various notes and comments. The king knew Mona was Queen Mab's eyes and ears, notifying her of anything of import. What that exactly meant the king did not know, other than to be always mindful he was being watched. That part he was not thrilled with, but getting a powerful mage and wise advisor had its benefits. The diminutive fey woman took out a whole war band of high leveled Forest Trolls by herself.

General Mineheir practically had his head on a swivel, looking for any possible threat. "Relax, my friend. We entered the Kingdom of Nord on a well-traveled road. These people are our allies. Besides, what could stand against you and my two advisors?"

RRROOOAAARRR!!!

Advisor Mona went from bored to alert in an instant. Advisor Nero immediately put his book away. General Mineheir jumped out of the moving carriage like it was nothing, drawing his sword as he exited.

"What is it, General?" King Alfheim asked in concern.

"Y-your majesty... it...it is... a full-grown dragon!" General Mineheir stuttered out.

"A dragon?!" King Alfheim said in shock.

It had been several hundreds of years since one was seen. Most dragons left these lands and journeyed to one of the other continents. He was aware of only a handful still remaining and the king knew none in this area.

"Your majesty, we cannot remain in the royal carriage! If the dragon is recently awakened from a long slumber, it will be hungry!" Advisor Nero exclaimed.

The king knew his advisor was correct. After a long slumber and growth spurt a dragon would be ravenous and impossible to appeal to its rational mind. "Very well. General, we are exiting the carriage!"

As the king and his advisors exited the carriage, General Mineheir barked out his orders. "YOU HEARD HIS MAJESTY! FORM UP! PROTECT OUR KING WITH YOUR LIVES!!!"

A large shape in the sky blocked out the sun and cast a shadow over the envoy.

"My god that thing is massive!"

"We are all going to die!"

King Alfheim released his aura to help combat the dragon's natural fear effect. The panic on his soldiers' faces eased but did not completely disappear. That told him one thing, this was no youngling, it was at least a fully grown dragon.

The king's theory was confirmed when the dragon landed on the ground in front of them.

THUD

The only thing keeping the horses from bolting was the king's calming aura. Just one look at the massive creature, confirmed King Alfheim's theory. 'Definitely an adult dragon. Just our luck.'

"Your Majesty, we must flee! If you die here our people will blame the Kingdom of Nord. Your daughters would be declared traitors." Advisor Nero stated.

"That thought crossed my mind as well. But we..." King Alfheim's response died as the massive dragon roared.

RROOAARR!!!!!

As the dragon roared, it shot out a breath of hot flame.

King Alfheim cast his Ice magic to create a wall of ice in front of his men. Sadly, the wall was like tissue paper as the flames melted it in seconds. A few of his men were instantly charbroiled.

Advisor Nero cast his own ice wall right after the king's. The block of ice melted faster than the king's spell. It was only when Advisor Mona added her Winter magic to the ice wall that it held against the attack.

The dragon seeing his favorite attack fail to kill all the puny humanoids flapped its wings. Rising into the air, it was pelted by arrows imbued with magic. Even with the addition of magic, the attacks did little more than annoy the mighty one. Deciding these lower life forms were not worth his time, the dragon swept down, grabbed a horse in each one of his front claws and took off into the sky to find a quieter place to enjoy his newly acquired snacks.

"THAT IS MY HORSE!!! THAT BASTARD TOOK MY HORSE!!!" The General cried as he saw his favorite mount fly off in the clutches of that beast.

"Be glad it was your horse and not your life, General." Advisor Nero commented.

"Silly mortals and their pets." Advisor Mona commented as she resumed her bored expression once again.

The fey advisor made notes on her magic tablet as she returned to the royal carriage.

King Alfheim just watched her go shaking his head. 'That woman is an enigma. In fact, that is probably the most animated I have seen her in years.'

Turning to look at the aftermath of their brief encounter, the king hung his head. They had lost five loyal guards and two horses in less than a few minutes. He would have to inform his daughter and her husband. They must rally a hunting party to deal with this continent-wide threat.

"General!" King Alfheim's stern tone broke General Mineheir out of his impotent rage. "Yes, my king?!"

Seeing he had his general's attention, King Alfheim issued his orders. "Wrap what remains and prepare to move out. We cannot remain here! I must warn my daughter! Do not worry, I will demand retribution for our fallen men."

"And my horse!" General Mineheir replied.

"Yes, and your horse, my old friend." King Alfheim said chuckling as he patted his most loyal companion on the shoulder.

# Interlude – Proletariat Base

## Near the Border of Timberfall Forest

A tall, well-built man decked out in dark armor and a shorter, slender woman in dark leather armor covered in knives enter the command building. The two have similar facial features, making no one doubt their clear sibling relationship. They both knelt before the officers in the room.

The tall brother male soldier addressed his commander. "You have called us, oh wise General Marks. What are your commands?"

"Ah Carn and Belinda, are you ready to serve the will of the people?"

"Yes, General!" The two youths replied in unison.

General Marks smiled. "A new duchy has been established in the Kingdom of Nord. Their Duke, a corrupt noble by the name of Dragonvein, is doing what all nobles and wealthy people do, exploit, and oppress those around them. This man grows more powerful by helping the wealthy merchants steal the coin of the working class. As you both know, there are only so many resources in this world. If someone has more than another it is because they are exploiting the people."

Seeing the fury in their eyes, General Marks continued. "You two suffered firsthand at the atrocities of the wealthy, barely skin and bones, while they grew fat. This Duke Dragonvein is the perfect example of noble corruption. In an act of utter cruelty, he and his exploitive business owners are throwing a festival to flaunt their wealth while they throw scraps at the people and use contests and games to distract people from the misery of living in such a corrupt system."

"Scum!" Belinda spat.

"He must be stopped!" Carn said in fury.

Both siblings remembered vividly the cruelty of nobles and merchants. When their father was injured in a monster attack and lost his arm, he took up drinking because he could no longer work as a caravan guard. Their mother was exploited by the laundry service business owner. She eventually started taking darkroot to numb the pain. Eventually their mom abandoned their father to enjoy her prime years with what she called a 'less defective' man, her darkroot dealer.

When the Proletariat took power, the siblings learned the truth. Their suffering was because of the wealthy who hoarded their wealth. There were only so many resources. If someone did not have enough that was because someone else took their share. It was the greedy nobles, business owners, and merchants who refused to share their wealth.

The Proletariat fed the children what they could. Those that embraced the ideals of equal outcome were provided additional resources to learn to fight. If a parent protested, they were removed, and the state took over. Many of the children joined the army to fight the tyranny of the wealthy.

Carn and Belinda had been some of the first to want to join the army. When their father protested, claiming to know the dangers of battle and wanting a different life for his children. The siblings did the right thing and reported their father. He was summarily executed in the town square for denying a child's right to choose.

"It is our duty as Proletariat to root out these abominations to the natural order." Belinda stated.

General Marks nodded. "Good. The two of you will lead a special unit to infiltrate the city of Timberfall. You will collect as much information as possible about the city's defenses and patrols. You must also discover who the most successful business owners are. We know they only got that way by exploiting others. This information is critical if we are to hold those accountable for their crimes against the people."

"You can count on us General." Carn replied.

"Once we have the resources from Timberfall we can reduce the burden on our people. You know the food lines have only increased back home. All because of the other countries who hog their wealth and prevent us from ever having a chance to provide for our people." General Marks said before he knelt down to put a hand behind each of them.

"I was there when we executed your father for treason. I took you both in afterwards and taught you why we do what we must. You two know better than anyone why the Proletariat must control every aspect of the people's lives. Tell me why."

"Yes, General Marks. We must give everything to the less fortunate. Only when we redistribute the wealth can we achieve the utopia we desire. That is why we must dictate every aspect of their lives. Freedom is a lie and only complete control of everything can we see the dream of equality of outcome achieved." Carn recited from memory.

"Good, very good, Carn." General Marks said before turning his attention to Belinda. "What must we do in service of the people?"

"Anything and everything that is required. It is not wrong if it helps our cause. Sometimes we must tolerate the whims of those less fortunate to help ease their suffering even if it causes suffering, as that helps others. We must also be brutal and cruel if it is to serve the people and break the will of those that are exploiting others. That is why my brother embraces his moniker of Carn the Cruel and I gladly accept my name as Belinda the Brutal." Belinda answered.

"Yes, you have learned the hard reality of life well. Now attend me before you both leave to end the wickedness in Timberfall. Your real father carries a heavy burden for the people and could use your administrations." General Marks stated as he rose from his kneeling position.

# Chapter 12 - Adventurers

Lilandra expressed her concern. "Let me remain by your side. It is clear you are still recovering from that Twist of Fate, Master."

"I appreciate your concern, my little genie. Do not worry yourself over me. I am already feeling better." Deathwalker replied as he winced when attempting to tap into his Infinite Well of Time Magic.

"Then what was that?!"

"It was nothing. The connection to the **Infinite Well of Time Magic** is still healing. Pain is to be expected." Deathwalker said as he tried to put a false smile on his face.

Lilandra and the cat girls all shook their heads. They all tried to guide him back to his lounge chair. Deathwalker stood up, planning to go for a walk and stretch his legs. His pain came when he tried to tap into the Infinite Well to use Time Magic as a test.

"You heard Morrigan, you should not be using that at all!" Lilandra said in protest.

"I was just testing the connection." Deathwalker commented when he recalled a term his first disciple had said. "Wait, you said Twist of Fate as if it was something specific. What is it?"

"Only if you will sit and rest, Master." Lilandra said as she and the three cat girls all guided him back in his lounge chair.

Deathwalker decided not to fight his disciples. He could rest the remainder of the evening. "Okay, I'm sitting, now explain."

Lilandra smiled and then sat in his lap.

"Hey, I wanted to do that!" Frrsha complained.

“Next time.” Lilandra replied to Frrsha before turning her attention back to Deathwalker to answer his question.

“What Morrigan described is called a Twist of Fate. Time and Fate are intrinsically tied together. To use one draws on the other. Until your soul can be healed, using Time magic is dangerous for you.”

“Because of my Fate?”

“Your Fate is divided, shattered or split if you will. When you use Time magic it makes your Fate shatter further. Then there is your unique Soul Forge skill.”

“What about my **Soul Forge** skill?”

“The original Parcae are powerful in the nature of Fate and Destiny, but... that pales in comparison to how your skill can completely change the momentum of one’s destiny. When you use it you are altering someone’s path and giving them a choice. You see Free Will or choice is part of Creation itself.”

“It is? You know we are going to have a longer conversation about the oaths of creation.” Deathwalker commented.

Lilandra nodded. “In time, my Master. Back to my explanation. When you used your Soul Forge skill on Mrrsha and Prrsha you are tapping into the very nature of your Path, but with your Fate shattered it made your use of the Infinite Well of Time Magic weaken the hold the geas has on you and frankly what was keeping you together.”

“And when I met Morrigan...” Deathwalker said, letting Lilandra finish what he was starting to realize.

“Exactly, the encounter with Morrigan’s presence was enough to trigger the truth of your situation. Once you knew the truth, I was able to see to the extent of the damage to your soul. I am sorry, Master, I knew you had something wrong but the severity of it was well hidden from my eyes.”

"Think nothing of it, Lilandra. I am more upset with certain angels at the moment. Uriel and I are going to have a long talk, but that will have to come much later." Deathwalker replied, weariness clear in his voice.

"Do not blame Uriel. I believe the full extent of what was done was kept from him as well. If you did not have such a high amount of relationship points with him, I might doubt that, but Uriel is honorable and a protector of Free Will. It would be against his nature to side with anything that went against one's Free Will." Lilandra explained.

"Well, that does help me feel better about the situation, not fully, but enough for me to have a civil conversation when the time comes. Now I think I will take you all up on your suggestion of rest." Deathwalker said as he picked up Lilandra like she weighed nothing and headed towards his bedroom.

"Oooo!" Lilandra commented.

"Alpha, you are injured!" Frrsha protested.

"My magic is hurt but I have far more strength than is needed to lift up a tiny thing like Lilandra." Deathwalker stated.

"Awe you know just what to say to a woman! Are you going to ravage me, master?" Lilandra teased.

Deathwalker immediately dropped Lilandra. "Silly genie!"

Rather than fall to the floor, she simply floated in the air until her feet slowly touched the floor. "No fun, Master. I merely was trying to lighten the mood." Lilandra smiled.

Ignoring his flirtatious disciple, he turned his attention to his bodyguards. "Mrrsha, please inform Geeves and the others that I will be retiring for the evening to rest. In the morning, I wish to visit the Adventurers' guild and check in with Darrius. Please see if General Marius wants to accompany me to visit with his brother."

"As you command, alpha." Mrrsha said before exiting the suite.

"Frrsha."

"Yes, alpha?"

"I want you to find Grimhold, Mara, and Cal to see if they would be open to having the three of you join our adventuring party." Deathwalker stated.

"Why me, alpha? Mrrsha is a far better negotiator." Frrsha asked in confusion.

"She is, but your pheromone abilities should help you sense their stance. Plus, if I send Prrsha, she will most likely claw Mara." Deathwalker explained.

Prrsha just smiled with a wicked grin and nod.

"Fine. Though, I would not mind a few strikes with my claws." Frrsha replied.

A quick disapproving look from Deathwalker changed Frrsha's demeanor. "I will convince them we are your bodyguards and would be a great asset to the party."

"Thank you. Now Lilandra." Deathwalker started as he shifted his attention. "Please return to the Hidden Realm. We are not yet ready to explain things and your presence would raise too many questions. I will return once I feel I can summon Garry back."

"Do you have to summon that odd floating ball?" Prrsha asked.

"Yes, I do. He is my familiar and bore the brunt of that Twist of Fate. Plus, I promised the little ball of crazy that he could enjoy the upcoming festival." Deathwalker answered.

"Having an honorable alpha who sticks to what he says can be frustrating at times." Prrsha grumbled.

"I will do as you ask, but I caution you to take it easy over the next several days." Lilandra sighed in worry.

"Do not worry. When this festival is over, and my connection to the Well heals enough, we will begin tracking down the fragments of Chronos' power." Deathwalker said in all sincerity.

He was just as worried as they were. Deathwalker had a literal countdown clock to his death if he could not find those fragments. It was the only way to stave off permadeath until he could find the missing parts of himself. To do anything else would court the final death and he had zero interest in that outcome.

Prrsha and Lilandra helped Deathwalker into his bed, before stepping outside the room. Lilandra erected a sound barrier. She wanted a chance to talk with Prrsha in private.

Sensing the magic take shape, Prrsha spoke up. "What did you do?"

"I just surrounded us in a soundproof barrier."

"Why?" Prrsha asked.

"I have watched you Prrsha. Mrrsha is the most diplomatic and will do whatever Deathwalker asks. Frrsha is too emotional and would never disobey her alpha." Lilandra began to explain.

"I will not betray our alpha!" Prrsha said in indignation.

"Nor would I allow you to live if that was the case. No, I need someone fierce who will do what is necessary to protect our master. He is so focused on helping others he may ignore his survival. With his renewed focus on finding his friend, that may become even more problematic. We may need to help find these fragments and bring them to our master." Lilandra further explained.

"That I am more than happy to do. I will cut down anyone who tries to stop us from healing our alpha!" Prrsha vowed.

Lilandra smiled. "Good. Then I will reach out to you once I have something."

She vanished in a flash, reappearing in the Portal Room. Not wasting a second, Lilandra took off towards Queen Orantes' hive. As she floated down to the Krythid queen, the drones changed paths to give the two queens a chance to chat without interruption.

"Lilandra! I always enjoy your visits. Any news of our master?" Queen Orantes inquired.

"Sadly, I do..." Lilandra replied as she began to explain what had transpired.

The krythid queen's face fell further and further as she listened to the terrible news. She had just found a new purpose for her and her brood, but now that was all in jeopardy. This was something the queen could not accept.

"There must be something we can do!"

Lilandra nodded. "There is. We must find the other two parts of Chronos' power. That will prevent our master's death until he can search the Omniverse to find the missing parts of himself."

"Then we must act without delay!" Queen Orantes exclaimed.

"That is why I am here. Our master is focused on this festival that will formally acknowledge and solidify his power in the Kingdom of Nord. After, he will most likely demand to search for his friend. We should be able to delay that journey but only so much. I will begin looking for the fragments of Chronos' power. When I find them, can I count on you and your brood to help in their retrieval?"

"Of course! Anything for our master! I will begin growing warriors, scouts, and casters!" Queen Orantes replied.

"That will be most helpful. I have recruited Prrsha to help in the hunt as well. Will your brood follow her commands when the time comes?" Lilandra asked.

"It will not be a problem. I have already programmed my brood to follow our master and any of his disciples." Queen Orantes answered.

————————————-

Deathwalker woke up the next day closer to mid-morning. It was clear to him that he needed the rest. When he exited his bedroom, he found food on his private table. Mrrsha, Prrsha, and Frrsha were already waiting for him.

“Good morning you three.”

“Good morning, Alpha.” The three cat girls said in unison.

“Were you waiting for me to wake up before you ate?” Deathwalker asked.

“It is not right for us to eat before our alpha.” Frrsha replied.

“Nonsense! I appreciate the sentiment, but all of you must keep up your strength. If I am resting and you are hungry, eat something. Understood?”

“Yes, Alpha.” The three cat girls said in unison again.

Admonishment over, they all sat down and dug into the food. Everyone seemed ravenous. It did not take very long before the table was clear of every scrap of food.

“Mom used to always comment I needed to slow down my eating, but just don’t think she understood how hungry I was, it appears I found kindred spirits, ha, ha, ha, ha.” Deathwalker chuckled.

“You do not talk much of your family.” Mrrsha commented.

“I think part of that was the stupid geas, but some of it could just be me avoiding the pain of being without my family. One day I will find my buddy and then I will figure out a way home. Guess, it is just easier to not talk about it and focus on the tasks at hand.” Deathwalker reflected.

“Would you take us with you?” Frrsha asked.

All three puma girls seemed very interested in his answer.

"Hmmm, there are no cat girls on my homeworld, but sure why not. Though we will have to find a way to hide your features, so you blend in. Perhaps Illusion Magic would work." Deathwalker stated.

"You heard him sisters, no take backs!" Frrsha commented.

Deathwalker laughed. "Ha, ha, ha, ha, ha! Thank you, Frrsha. I needed that. And I agree, no take backs. Now, let's finish eating as I have plenty to accomplish today."

"What part of take it easy do you not understand Alpha?" Mrrsha asked.

"Do not mother me woman." Deathwalker snapped back before sighing. "Sorry, Mrrsha. I know you are just concerned for my well-being, but I must be me and do what I feel I have to. Do not worry though, like last night, I will ask for help. I know I cannot do everything by myself, nor do I want to."

Mrrsha nodded and dropped the matter.

Deep down Deathwalker knew he was surrounded by people who genuinely cared for him. He would not penalize them for expressing their concerns. His frustration at finding such a blaring weakness bothered him.

'Hmmm, perhaps I just thought I was beyond such things now that I am a dragon. Guess there is more to this than I thought. Here I thought spending all that time learning different magics and skills would help me be prepared for any situation... except my own failings. You cannot plan for everything, but so what! I will turn this into something good too, I don't know how yet, but I will!' Deathwalker thought.

"He is staring off into space again sisters." Prrsha commented.

That seemed to snap him out of his musings. "Huh? What?"

"You get a look when you seem distracted and deep in thought. It is quite endearing." Mrrsha replied.

The three cat girls giggled. "He, he, he, he!"

Deathwalker smiled at the girls' antics. They rushed to let him mope, and he appreciated that. "Okay, okay, got it. Focus on the here and now. Enough teasing let's get the day started. I want to stop off at the Adventurers' guild. Oh, that reminds me, what was Grimhold's answer?"

"Ah, yes. I found all three of them together. All agreed without issue. I sensed Mara had some objection, but she never voiced it." Mrrsha replied.

"Excellent! Then let's get you registered." Deathwalker said as he rose from his chair.

———————-

"Hey Alyce! I'm surprised to see you here in the guildhall. I figured you would be at your grandfather's shoppe." Deathwalker said as he saw Alyce behind the desk.

"Mom and Darrius have me help with processing paperwork here at the guild. It helps me practice my reading and writing skills and I get to spend time helping my mom. In fact, I was the one that processed your paperwork to become an A ranked adventurer." Alyce answered.

"Hmmm. That's good to know. You're pretty busy, aren't ya?" Deathwalker replied.

"Mom and grandfather keep me pretty busy." Alyce answered.

"I've met your mom and grandfather, but you make no mention of your father." Deathwalker inquired.

"My father died in a monster incursion." Alyce said somberly.

"I'm sorry to hear that." Deathwalker replied.

"It was several years ago. That is when mom came to work at the Adventurers' guild. She wanted to help those that avenged my father's death. Darrius was the one who killed the beast and saved mom and me from the same fate as my pa." Alyce explained.

"Sounds like Darrius. He's a good man from what I've seen. Funny your grandfather never mentioned anything to me." Deathwalker commented.

"That sounds like grandfather. He acts like pa is still here. I think it was hardest on him. I was so young; I only remember so much of him." Alyce stated.

"It's hard to outlive a child, something about it is so unnatural." Deathwalker said more to himself than anyone. Turning his attention back and patted Alyce on the hand. "Thank you for sharing, Alyce. If you ever need anything you let any of my people know and they will do what they can."

Alyce blushed. Noticing the color of Alyce's cheeks, Deathwalker pulled his hand away. "Sorry about that. You just reminded me of my own child when she was your age."

"You have children? You look too young for a child older than me." Alyce asked in surprise, her previous embarrassment forgotten.

"I'm a lot older than I look. Is Darrius in?" Deathwalker said in an attempt to change the subject. He had lost himself in a memory from his past life and forgot for the briefest of moments where he was.

'Not good. I cannot believe I slipped up like that. I must be careful not to reveal too much about my past. Man, maybe that geas was doing even more to keep me focused on the here and now than I realized.' Deathwalker thought in concern.

"Sure. He should be in his office. I doubt he would mind if you went in to see him." Alyce replied, obvious to Deathwalker's musings, far to infatuated with the man.

Alyce was brought out of her own thoughts by a low growl from behind Deathwalker. For the first time she noticed three female cat beastkin. "Oh, I am sorry. I did not know you were with Deathwalker. Please forgive my rudeness."

"It is not your lack of awareness that concerns us." Prrsha stated.

"How old are you cub?" Mrrsha asked.

Puzzled, Alyce replied, "I am fourteen. I will be an adult this winter."

'They consider fifteen an adult?! I forget when the mortality rate can be so high they start life so young. I think it was the same in our medieval and harsher areas. Doesn't matter, no way I could see Alyce as anything other than like my daughter.' Deathwalker thought.

"She is but a cub." Prrsha commented.

"Ladies, leave Alyce be. I consider her and her family friends. I also expect you to honor my promise to help her and her family should they need assistance. Am I understood?" Deathwalker stated.

"Yes, alpha." The three girls said in unison.

Deathwalker dismissed the whole conversation and headed to Darrius' office. Frrsha held back just a moment. "We could smell your attraction to him. You are young so it is expected you cannot control yourself, and we understand alpha is amazing. But you have much growing up to do before we could accept you as pack."

Alyce wasn't sure if she should be upset, or embarrassed, or both. 'They could smell my interest in him. Can beastkin do that?'

"Do not worry cub. We will honor his request. If you have need of us, we will come to your aid. Just make sure you wait several years before you try anything beyond asking for help." Frrsha smiled as she turned to catch up with the others.

"Those beastkin are intense, but they do seem helpful." Alyce commented, deciding to ignore her awkward emotions and focus on the offer of help.

———-

"Deathwalker! How is my favorite city lord and Duke?!" Darrius greeted.

"Do you know any other city lords or dukes for that matter?" Deathwalker replied as they clasped their wrists together in greeting.

"Well... no, but that just makes it easier for you to be my favorite!" Darrius answered chuckling.

"Fair point. Let me introduce you to my bodyguards. This is Mrrsha, Prrsha, and... ah there is Frrsha. Everyone, this is Darrius, the Timberfall Adventurers' guildmaster." Deathwalker introduced as Frrsha entered the room.

"Nice to meet all of you." Darrius said before turning to Deathwalker. "Glad to see you finally have an honor guard."

"Yes. Everyone was quite insistent." Deathwalker replied.

"Now, what can I do for ya Deathwalker? I doubt you just came here to introduce your guards." Darrius asked.

"Indeed, my friend. I came for a few reasons. First, I wanted to get them registered with the guild and added to our adventuring party's roster." Deathwalker answered.

"Oh! That makes sense. If they are going to be by your side, they might as well get paid for it, ha, ha, ha." Darrius chuckled.

"Exactly."

"That should be easy enough. We will have to test them beforehand, but I'd be willing to have them start as Rank A and add them to your party. That is if... they can beat me in a fight." Darrius said.

"He must be joking alpha." Prrsha commented.

"No little lady! I am quite serious. I cannot give special treatment, even for my Duke. The autonomy and fairness of the guild must be maintained." Darrius replied, dropping his former mirth.

Deathwalker raised his hand to forestall any further debate. "That is fine Darrius. I wouldn't want it any other way. Before we get to that however, I wanted to know how the shared quest boards were working at our portal stations."

Darrius finally turned his head to look at Deathwalker, his early mirth returning. “Oh, that! I have got to tell you, that idea has already paid dividends! I have seen more adventurers arrive in town both to help with quests and to move to the hub of the network. I have also seen several leave and return, able to now help other parts of the kingdom without the expensive cost of time and coin to travel just to complete a quest. The discount you have offered guild members, especially higher ranked ones has helped increase what the guild can do.”

“That is great news. I am glad our shared idea is helping so much. I’m curious, any lucrative quests on the board at the moment? After the girls get tested, it would be good for us to get a quest or two in before the festival.” Deathwalker said.

“There are a few, but the one with the biggest reward is the one that is a kingdom wide quest. And that is far too risky. My brother would be rather upset with me if you took that one on, but I am sure you already know that.” Darrius replied.

“What kingdom wide quest?” Deathwalker asked in confusion.

“How do you not know?” Darrius asked, equally confused.

“I have been out of touch with the goings on in the kingdom. I’ve been too busy finishing the portal network... and recuperating.” Deathwalker answered.

“Ah yes. I heard a rumor you collapsed from exhaustion from all your running around.” Darrius said.

‘Good the rumor is I was just tired, best to keep it that way. I’m impressed Marius kept that from his brother.’ Deathwalker thought.

Mrrsha replied telepathically. “Marius seems to be rather loyal, my alpha. We had discussed this with Geeves and Elder Martha to help keep things quiet.”

“Good thinking.” Deathwalker replied mentally before turning his focus back to Darrius.

"Well seeing how you have been busy then let me tell you what has the entire kingdom in a tizzy. There have been dragon sightings recently. The king issued a quest to find and resolve the situation with the dragon." Darrius stated.

"Resolve? You mean kill?" Deathwalker asked in concern. It went against every fiber in his being to kill a dragon.

"No, not necessarily. Based on the sightings it appears this is an adult dragon. There are not many in the kingdom that can kill an adult dragon, even then they would have to get lucky or be very prepared. No, the king is hoping we can entreat it and convince it to leave our lands. Whomever can resolve the issue will be paid quite handsomely and get a few boons from the royal family." Darrius explained.

"That makes more sense. Though I'm not sure what good the boons would be. I just got saddled with more responsibility." Deathwalker commented.

Darrius chuckled. "Ha, ha, ha, ha, ha. No good deed goes unpunished. There is talk from several adventurers that asking for Lady Emma's hand in marriage is not off the table. Imagine that, slay a dragon and become the future king of the kingdom! Would that not be hilarious, ha, ha, ha!"

Deathwalker felt a cold chill run down his spine, like those words were somehow prophetic. 'Just great. I'm gonna get stuck with this somehow. I just know it.'

"What is wrong, alpha?" Frrsha asked telepathically.

"Deathwalker, are ye feeling okay. You look a bit pale." Darrius commented.

Deathwalker spoke out loud to answer both. "I'm fine. I appreciate the information. Let's move to get the girls registered and tested."

# Chapter 13 - Combat Testing

"Follow me to the training yard in the back. Sadly, someone broke our Assessment Orb, which means we cannot test your magic types and capacity the traditional way. Instead, you will come at me with all you have. I can judge the attack level." Darrius explained.

"Isn't that risky?" Deathwalker asked.

"Do not worry about your bodyguards Deathwalker. I will be careful." Darrius chuckled.

"That is not what I meant, at all in fact." Deathwalker answered. He was about to express his concern for the guildmaster's safety when Darrius spoke up.

"The enchantments here help reduce the damage dealt and should prevent any permanent harm. Though I imagine it will still hurt plenty."

Deathwalker figured he should say something. "All three of my bodyguards are equal in power level. Could one of them fight you rather than all three? That way if one succeeds you can pass the other two."

"You really are worried about the well-being of your bodyguards. I assure you that the enchantments here are quite strong." Darrius pressed.

"No, I really don't think you get my concern..." Deathwalker started but was cut off by the guildmaster.

"Fine, fine. I will fight one of them. If they do well enough, I will pass all three."

Deathwalker turned to Prrsha. "Wipe the floor with him, but don't kill him. He is an ally and I actually like the guy."

"With pleasure, Alpha!" Prrsha said before activating her **One With The Forest** ability.

"Ho, ho! A stealth skill. Impressive one as I do not sense her aura. Let the fun begin!" Darrius said in glee as he activated several body enhancement techniques.

The guildmaster slowly turned his body, Darrius actively searching for any kind of distortion or shadow that would reveal Prrsha's location. He slowly rotated himself, not seeing anything. His body moved on instinct, from years of battle-hardened experience. The strike grazed his shoulder, but that still cut him deep.

Blood splashed on the floor. As Darrius swung his counterattack, a mana-infused fist to the head, Prrsha just tilted her body back while smacking the guildmaster's hand away. Then she was gone again.

The power behind the strike warped the air as it passed. Guild members noticed the distortions and started to gather to witness their leader's skills. So more gathered as Prrsha repeated her claw attack before dodging the counter strike and vanishing again.

Rather than be upset, Darrius seemed to be having the time of his life. It was rare for him to go all out on an opponent. After the first few minutes he did not expect to have several cuts and gashes without landing a single hit on the cat girl. "That stealth skill is very effective. If you did not have it I think things would be going very differently, he, he, he, he."

"Alright Prrsha, enough toying with him! No more use of your stealth! Go head-to-head!" Deathwalker yelled out.

Prrsha immediately made herself visible, a wicked smile on her face. "As you command, Alpha."

"I would not be so happy. Let me show you what a level 100 S ranked adventurer can do!" Darrius said as he practically flew in the cat girl's direction.

His punch missed and Prrsha used his momentum to flip the guildmaster, sending him crashing into the building. The big man left a sizable dent in the wall. Other than some dust and torn clothes, Darrius stepped out of the dent he made.

“Now we are talking!” The battle-crazed man said as he rushed Prrsha. Every punch and kick would miss, no match for the cat like reflexes. Her claw strikes left gashes and cuts but not as many now that she wasn’t using her stealth ability.

“Okay, let’s wrap this up. I have other matters to attend to.” Deathwalker called out.

As if on cue, Prrsha grabbed the guildmaster’s extended arm after dodging another punch. She pulled the man while flipping her body up and wrapping her legs around his neck. This time she drove his head into the ground while pulling the arm and neck tight. Darrius hit the ground headfirst and saw stars.

He lay there for a moment. With his high strength Darrius could lift the cat girl but there was not much point to it. The results were clear, she was too agile and fast for him. The cat girl was an excellent speed-based fighter.

Darrius tapped his hand on the floor a few times. Prrsha took that as his acquiesce and released him. Other than Deathwalker and Prrsha’s sisters, everyone watching was shocked. They had never seen their guildmaster beaten.

“He did not even get a real hit in!”

“I could barely track her movements!”

“Did not know someone could move that fast!”

Darrius raised his hand to silence the crowd. “Let this be a lesson to all of you to keep practicing and leveling up. Please join me in welcoming Prrsha, Mrrsha, and Frrsha to the Adventurers’ guild as rank A adventurers!”

Everyone cheered and clapped their hands. No one was stupid enough to rush in and pat the cat girl on the back and get thrown through a wall so most gave a wide respectful distance.

"I will talk to Alyce about getting the paperwork finished. Come by later today and you and your sisters can pick up your guild cards. And welcome to the guild. Our Duke is a lucky man to have such capable bodyguards and teammates!" Darrius said as he escorted his opponent back to her group.

"You fight well. I appreciated the spar." Prrsha said as she rejoined the others.

"Well done, Prrsha." Deathwalker commented.

The cat girl just nodded, but a hint of smile could be seen on her face.

"Well done sister!" Frrsha complimented.

"Yes, you did very well." Mrrsha chimed in.

"You know Deathwalker, you might want to consider getting your party to pursue S rank. It is clear your bodyguards would meet the criteria and what I have heard of your capabilities I doubt there is a more powerful healer in all the kingdom. I also heard about your fight with those high-level assassins, quite impressive." Darrius encouraged.

"I'm not sure how the others would feel about that." Deathwalker replied.

"Why not? Grimhold should have been S rank a long time ago. He is one tough dwarf, especially now with his improved armor. Mara is one of the best archers we have, and Cal is no slouch either. The lack of healing was always what kept them back. It would do the city good to have a S ranked adventurer party based here." Darrius continued.

"Perhaps." Deathwalker answered noncommittally.

"Besides Elder Martha and I cannot be the only S ranked adventurers here. Though you will have to think of a good party name now." The guildmaster commented.

"I did not realize Elder Martha was S ranked." Deathwalker said in surprise.

"Of course, how else do you think she got such a high War Leader skill." Darrius answered.

"With her low affinity for healing, it did not cross my mind." Deathwalker replied.

"That is because you have never seen her use Air and Water magic. She is wicked with such things. I believe she used to live in the Elven nation and was one of their better mages, but she left long ago to come here. Elder Martha told me she could not stand all the politicking and..." Darrius seemed to hold back.

Deathwalker pressed the man. "And what my friend? Don't keep us in suspense."

"My understanding is the fey have a tight hold over what occurs there. It is not wise to speak about such things, especially when it comes to the Queen of Air and Darkness. She has many eyes and ears even here." Darrius whispered.

Deathwalker was not going to mention his encounter with Mother Winter, and he gave a mental command to Mrrsha, Prrsha, and Frrsha not to say anything either. "Hmmm. Interesting. Well, I will have to keep that in mind. I appreciate the information and the words of caution."

"Of course, any time." Darrius replied.

"Good day to you, my friend." Deathwalker said as he clasped wrists with the burly guildmaster.

"To you as well! And you girls come back any time. I would love a rematch!" Darrius said as they left the training area.

"I like him. He is funny." Frrsha commented.

"A good warrior too. If I had been hit by any of those strikes, I would have been in bad shape." Prrsha stated.

"Yes. I am glad he is on our side." Deathwalker chimed in.

"Alpha, what will you do about Elder Martha?" Mrrsha asked.

"You mean now that I know she is such a formidable mage?" Deathwalker replied.

"Yes." Mrrsha answered.

"Ever the strategist focused on strengthening the pack. I like it. I have some ideas. She might make a good city lord. Elder Martha will probably hate that idea, but you know I have no intention of remaining here. I have a friend to find, and I will have to consider how best to enable this territory to thrive in my absence." Deathwalker explained.

"Understood alpha." Mrrsha replied.

"Now, let's go see how the construction and restoration efforts are going in the northern district." Deathwalker said.

———————

"Paul, how goes the construction efforts?" Deathwalker asked as he approached the man.

"Ah, your grace." Paul replied giving a slight bow. "It goes well. Now that the portal stations are finished, we have been able to divert more resources to creating the various buildings we need here. Plus, several of the recent immigrants are skilled workers."

"That is good to hear." Deathwalker replied.

"Very much so. I would say we are a few days away from the clinic being opened." Paul continued.

"Oh, that is good news. Any chance some of the immigrants are healers and doctors?" Deathwalker asked.

"Actually, yes. I have worked closely with Commander Willis. There are several herbalists, a few healers, and some alchemists. Many of those came from other parts of the kingdom, but there are a few from the refugees as well. Many of the refugees are farmers and hunters, with a few craftsmen mixed in." Paul explained.

"Hey, you can never have enough farmers and hunters. We should look to get them integrated." Deathwalker commented.

"We are doing our best. Many have offered to work on these construction projects. Most of the refugees did not expect us to take so many of them in. Things are still tense, but their willingness to work and help where they can, is helping. Your suggestions have also helped ease some of the locals' concerns." Paul continued to explain.

"I'm glad it helped." Deathwalker replied.

"I must admit, your grace, I had not considered the security or other aspects you had shared. In truth, both Clarisse and I thought the locals were just being selfish and uncaring." Paul sighed.

Deathwalker put his hand on the man's shoulder. "You and Clarisse have good hearts. I admire that. We just have to temper that with logic and make sure we verify certain things. Not everyone thinks as you do. Forgetting that fact is the biggest trap people fall into. We must strive to understand and see things from multiple perspectives... yet always remain united under a common goal and set of ideals. That we cannot waiver on."

"Well said, your grace. True words of wisdom. I will endeavor to remember them." Paul replied.

"Now, where is Samuel? I thought he would be around here somewhere." Deathwalker asked.

"He had to help deal with some bar fight back at his inn. Some of the locals and refugees got into it. Things are improving but I fear not fast enough." Paul explained.

"To be expected. Talk with Commander Willis about having some extra patrols make their rounds and stopping off at the Sleepy Inn. The extra presence might help, and I need his focus on construction." Deathwalker offered.

"As you command, your grace." Paul bowed.

Shaking his head Deathwalker just said goodbye and walked away. Paul had become far more formal with him since his return, and he doubted the scribe would be the only one. It was something unavoidable, yet it made him appreciate Darrius' lack of formality even more.

"Where to now, Alpha?" Prrsha asked.

"I want to visit the barracks and then we can stop off and get some food. My main goal was to watch the city streets and get a feel for how things were without being filtered through the eyes of others." Deathwalker explained.

"You do not trust what the others have reported?" Frrsha inquired.

"Not exactly. It is more about seeing things with my own eyes." Deathwalker replied as he studied the comings and goings of those around him.

Many seemed to give him and his bodyguards a wide birth. Deathwalker could tell which people were from the kingdom and which ones were refugees. Sometimes it was a difference in dress, but mostly it was in the way they carried themselves.

With the lack of housing currently, many were put in large tents on the outskirts of town, located in the empty space in between the city wall and the current buildings. The refugees kept their heads down and many seemed lost with vacant looks in their eyes. Far too many were malnourished and that included the children. It was seeing a little girl practically skin and bones lying in an open tent with what looked like her family. They were all in rags and the mother did not look well.

Not taking his eyes off the scene, Deathwalker issued his orders. "Mrrsha, go fetch Elder Martha. Frrsha, go tell Mezza to come here. Then grab some food and water from the market. Use the silver I gave you earlier."

"Yes, Alpha!" Mrrsha and Frrsha said in unison before they took off in different directions.

Deathwalker approached the tent. That was when he noticed the younger boy who looked just as bad as the child's mother. The little girl saw their approach. "Please do not hurt us. We got nothin and momma is sick."

Kneeling down, Deathwalker spoke softly. "Do not worry child. We are here to help. What's your name?"

"I am not supposed to talk to strangers, but you have kind eyes. My name is Sasha." The little girl squeaked out.

Taking out a piece of jerky he handed it to the little girl. Her mouth practically started to salivate just at the sight of the food. She snatched it as quickly as her little arms would allow as she tried to shove the whole thing into her mouth.

"Careful little one. I know you are hungry, but you must eat it slow, or you could make yourself sick. You wouldn't want to throw all that up after just getting it now, would you?" Deathwalker said softly.

The little girl replied with a mouthful of food. "Uh, no sir." She did her best to slow down even though the hunger pains had doubled at the sight of food.

Some of the people nearby were studying what was going on. Many of them took a keen interest in the offer of food. One growl from Prrsha prevented any from approaching.

"Do you mind if I take a look at your mother and brother, Sasha? I am a healer." Deathwalker asked.

"We cannot pay you sir. Pa died helping hold the line while we all escaped. Then mom and Dylan both got sick on the way here." Sasha explained.

"Let me see what I can do." Deathwalker said as he handed the girl another piece of jerky.

Touching both the little boy and mom's foreheads, Deathwalker scanned what was wrong with them. Besides obvious malnutrition, they were suffering from a debilitating disease. The little boy, who couldn't be more than four was in bad shape. His kidneys were failing, and he had a blockage in his intestines.

Not wanting to wait another minute, Deathwalker began casting his healing spells. Glowing golden white light radiated out of the tent, drawing even more onlookers. First Deathwalker used **Cleanse Disease and Poison** to remove their affliction. Then he broke down the blockage in the boy's intestines and healed his kidneys. Finally, he sped up all three of their recoveries using **Greater Restoration**. As the glow faded, even the little girl's skin looked healthier and not as sunken in.

The mom opened her eyes and blinked. Seeing some stranger looking down on her she freaked out and screamed.

"AHHH!!!"

Deathwalker put his hands up to show he was no threat and spoke in a soft tone. "Careful now. We mean you no harm. I am healer and we saw you and your family needed help."

His soft tone seemed to defuse the woman's initial fear. That is until Prrsha spoke up. "Do not be so ungrateful! You should bow at my alpha's feet for the kindness he has just shown!"

"Calm down, Prrsha. You would be startled too if you woke up to some stranger hovering over you." Deathwalker chided.

"That is true, alpha." Prrsha begrudgingly agreed.

"M-my apologies for my rudeness earlier. My name is Valentina. Thank you for healing my family."

Just then the little boy opened his eyes. "Momma, I am so hungry."

Valentina absentmindedly hugged and patted her son. "I know baby. We will figure out something soon. Shush now."

Sasha tore off a piece of the jerky she had left and handed it to her brother. "Here Dylan, chew on this, but eat it slowly." She looked at Deathwalker, getting his nod of approval before turning back to her brother.

"Where did you get that from Sasha?" Valentina asked her daughter.

"Sorry ma'am. I hope you don't mind but I gave it to her." Deathwalker said before pulling out two more strips and handing Valentina and Sasha one each. "Here. Have some more."

"Thank you, sir. I will save this for my children." The woman replied.

"Nonsense. You cannot take care of your children if you are not well."

Elder Martha arrived as Deathwalker was helping the woman sit up. The previous light from his magic made it even easier to find him in the refugee camp. "You summoned me, your grace."

"Your grace?" Valentina asked in confusion.

Elder Martha taking the scene in and realized Deathwalker had healed this family decided to speak up loud enough for all the onlookers to hear. "Why yes, you were just healed by Duke Deathwalker Dragonvein, ruler of the Timberfall Duchy!"

It just so happened that one of the city guard patrols arrived. They too had moved to investigate the glowing light. All four men put fists to their heart and bowed their heads upon seeing their duke.

Valentina had a look of horror on her face. She had screamed at the man and was talking so informally to him. Nobles were not known for letting such slights pass without punishment. She did her best to bow, which was awkward while trying to hold her son and being in a sitting position. "Please forgive me, your grace. I apologize for any unintended offense. Please spare my children..."

Catching Valentina before she hurt something trying to prostrate herself before Deathwalker. "Now, I will have none of that! I just healed you. Don't worry, I am rather informal if you haven't figured that out yet."

“A-are you certain your grace?!” Valentina asked hesitantly.

“Yes, give me a moment to sort this out.” Deathwalker said as he stood.

“It is good to see you Elder Martha. I want you to recruit some healers and herbalists. Then I want you to start prioritizing cases for healing. Some of these people are sick and we do not want disease to run rampant through Timberfall. I will offer my help healing those who need it most.”

“That is very generous of you, your grace! I shall do that at once!” Elder Martha once again spoke loud enough for all those watching to hear before she left to recruit some assistants.

‘She is doing that to help with PR, shrewd woman. I am glad she is on my side.’ Deathwalker thought before turning to the squad leader. “Sergeant, I want you specifically to find Commander Willis and make him aware of what we will be doing. Knowing the Commander, he will want to have extra men to see to my protection and assist in this coordination.

“Yes, your grace!” the Sergeant said before turning to his squad. “You men stay here and assist anyway needed. I will go find the Commander!”

Mezza arrived just as the Sergeant was leaving. “What is goin on Deathwalker? I was just about to fix ya lunch.”

“I appreciate you coming so quickly Mezza. I want you to work with some of the street vendors and other staff. Anyone who works will get fed twice a day as part of their pay. They don’t work they don’t eat, however...” Deathwalker paused for effect and to make sure everyone was paying attention. “For today, I want you to cook and feed these people some simple stew but make sure it has meat in it! I will cover the costs for this event out of my own money!”

Mezza looked at her employer like he grew an extra head. “Are ye sure about that, Sire?”

"Yes Mezza. I won't just give out handouts without people working. Nothing in life is free but for today in celebration of the upcoming festival I want the cooks to prepare food. Recruit any help you need. I will be working with Elder Martha to heal the sick."

"As you command, yer grace!" Mezza said before taking off to find some help.

Frrsha returned with some meat skewers. "Here is the food you wanted me to purchase, alpha."

Deathwalker smiled. "Perfect timing, Frrsha. Give those skewers to Valentina, Sasha, and Dylan."

"Your grace?!" Valentina said in surprise as Frrsha just handed her the food without a second thought.

Deathwalker bent down to be more at eye level with the frazzled mother. "If you have any skills that you think could help a household, go to Timberfall Manor and ask to speak to my Seneschal Geeves. He will arrange employment and housing at the manor."

Valentina thought she was done being shocked for the day, but this trumped everything. This man had healed her family, fed them, and now was offering her family work and a place to stay. This time she did manage to prostrate herself. "Oh, thank you, your grace! Thank you! I thought all hope was lost!"

"Now, now, none of that. Get up. You want to repay me, work hard and if you ever get the chance to help someone, then pay it forward. If you excuse me, it appears my day has now been spoken for." Deathwalker said as he smiled at the woman before turning and speaking with Commander Willis who appeared to have run the whole way here.

# Chapter 14 - House Guests

“Good morning, your grace. It is good to see as well, Ms. Mrrsha, Prrsha, and Frrsha.” Geeves greeted.

Mrrsha acknowledged the seneschal first. “Hello Geeves.”

Prrsha and Frrsha just nodded as their way of greeting, clearly showing they were not morning people.

“Good morning, Geeves. How are you doing this fine day?” Deathwalker asked.

“I am well, your grace. You caused quite a stir yesterday. The whole city is a buzz about what happened.” Geeves answered.

“Oh really? What are you referring to?” Deathwalker feigned ignorance.

“Surely you jest sire. You and the other healers in Timberfall took the time to heal those in need, and not just the refugees but the locals as well. Then you had Mezza coordinate cooking a simple put nutritious meat stew that you now have her offering anyone who is working on the various projects around town.” Geeves explained.

“Yea, I hope Mezza is not too mad at me for roping her in to doing that.” Deathwalker replied.

“Not at all, your grace. So many people complimented her and the others, the gratitude was palpable. You are offering recruiting opportunities for everyone willing to work to help them get a better foundation to stand on, while we are still getting a handle on sorting everything, was a great gesture. Mezza seemed very happy to be a part of it. Defender Grimhold was even seen acting as bodyguard and her helper.” Geeves continued.

Deathwalker chuckled. “I thought I saw Grimhold in the crowd yesterday. He really is smitten with her. That and I’m sure he was eating the food too.” Turning to Geeves, “Well, I’m glad she jumped right in with no complaints. See to it Mezza gets a bonus for all her extra effort.”

“She will appreciate that, your grace. I am surprised you are not still sleeping with all the healing you did yesterday.” Geeves commented.

“Magic is my favorite aspect of life, it is a part of who I am. Healing others with it, is the greatest gifts one can have when wielding magic.” Deathwalker stated.

“Beautiful sentiment, but I would expect nothing less from our Duke.” Geeves bowed.

Deathwalker waved off the praise. “You are too kind Geeves. I appreciate you. Did a woman by the name of Valentina come by with her two children?”

“Ah, yes, sire. I got her, Sasha, and Dylan situated last night in one of the servant’s quarters. I have her working with Mary Sue on helping around the house. The children can help one of the gardeners or help run errands for the staff as needed.” Geeves answered.

“That’s good to hear. Thank you for taking care of that. I do want to make sure the children attend school to help ensure they know how to read and write. They seemed like sweet kids. They have already been through enough, so if we can help them, we should.”

Geeves smiled at his liege. He could tell how much the man genuinely cared about people, especially the children. It further made the butler feel proud to serve such a man.

“Geeves what do you know about the Proletariat?” Deathwalker asked out of nowhere.

The question caught the butler off guard. “Sire?”

“The Proletariat, what do you know of them?” Deathwalker reiterated.

Then it clicked for Geeves. The children and many others were now refugees due to the Proletariat's expansion. He had interviewed Valentina last night to better understand her situation. What he had heard was horrible.

"I have heard things from some of the traders who came from the Proletariat nation. Many say they will not dare return to the dreary place. When I asked why, they mentioned a fear of having their goods confiscated for 'the people' with no compensation. A few helped smuggle people out who were trying to escape slavery." Geeves explained.

"Slavery?!" Deathwalker asked.

"It was not called slavery, but it was pretty much the same thing. The Proletariat dictates every aspect of their people's lives. The individual has no say in how they want to live their life, the state determines what they do." Geeves further explained.

"Sadly, I'm not surprised. It is the inevitable outcome of any country that spouts socialist nonsense." Deathwalker replied.

"Socialist?" Geeves inquired.

"My people dealt with a similar situation. Any country where the government took people's hard-earned money all in the name of fairness and equality, we called socialist. It nearly destroyed us all as the elites used it to control the masses and commit horrific atrocities in the name of the good of the people. It was a very dark time in our history." Deathwalker shared.

"Sounds awful, your grace."

"It was until my ancestors rebelled, overthrew the elites and started solving their own problems without the government. Sorry, this is a sore subject and one my family ingrained in me to never forget the nightmare they barely survived. It appears this Proletariat is doing the same thing." Deathwalker replied.

"Valentina shared similar stories. Her husband died trying to give them time to escape as the Proletariat conquered their homeland. She said the younger generation actually assisted the invaders, young adults she knew since they were children turned on them. She saw one stab her husband in the back." Geeves stated.

"That is a whole other level of betrayal." Deathwalker said.

"Truly is, sire. She lost everything to the greed of others. What you have done for her, and the children, makes me even more honored to be in your service. I do think Valentina will make a fine addition to the staff." Geeves genuflected.

Deathwalker reached down to help the seneschal up. "Get up Geeves. I appreciate the sentiment, but I did what I felt was right. In fact, reach out to Paul and Clarisse about opening an orphanage. I imagine there are orphans among the refugees, and I want them taught critical thinking and how to think for themselves along with some trade skills."

"You keep thinking about the people." Geeves smiled.

"It is my choice to help others. With my success, it means little if I do not use some of that to help our people grow." Deathwalker shared.

"Our duchy will be the envy of the continent."

Deathwalker smiled at the thought. "Changing subjects, what do you think of Elder Martha?"

Geeves blushed. "Sire?"

'I didn't mean it like that. I wonder if he likes her, should I play matchmaker?' Deathwalker thought to which he heard Lilandra say "Yes! Ha, ha, ha, ha, ha!"

Shaking his head he clarified. "I was asking what you thought of her as a leader. My understanding is her title of Elder is honorific."

"Ah, yes, your grace. She received that title from the elven king. Elder Martha helped guide him in learning to wield battle magic. She also worked with the Winter Court to quell several monster attacks. She later left and became a well-known adventurer. Please keep in mind, your grace, some of what I have relayed is hearsay and rumor." Geeves answered.

"Interesting." Deathwalker said as he considered how loyal she had been towards him. She reminded him of a mixture between his two grandmothers. Wise, funny, caring, and zero tolerance for nonsense.

Geeves, seeing his liege deep in thought decided to inquire why he asked him that question. "Sire, may I know the reason you asked?"

Deathwalker looked up. "Huh? Oh, yes, of course. I am considering promoting her. Now that I am a duke, I could promote someone else as the city lord. She would officially become the mayor of the city and it would allow me to focus on other matters."

"She would be a noble already if part of the kingdom felt Queen Mab already held too much influence on the continent. Many felt with the king and two dukes marrying elven women, it was already more influence than they felt comfortable with." Geeves shared.

"Really?"

"Oh yes, your grace. With the elven nation being seen as nothing but a puppet of the Winter Court and the elven king's three daughters marrying our king and two of our dukes... well you can imagine the concern some may have." Geeves explained.

"Hmmm. Not something I had considered until now, but I could see that. However, you said some of what you shared about Elder Martha may not be fact." Deathwalker replied.

"Yes, sire, but you know rumor can sweep like wildfire." Geeves commented.

"Fair enough. You've given me much to consider. Please arrange for lunch or dinner with Elder Martha." Deathwalker ordered.

"As you command, your grace." Geeves bowed before leaving Deathwalker's study.

———————————-

"Elder Martha, it is good to see you! Did you get much rest from yesterday's activities?" Deathwalker greeted.

"Your grace, it is good to see you as well! As you know, I spent most of yesterday coordinating the other healers we found. There are a few that show great promise. Though I did use some of my magic, it was limited, not much rest was required." Elder Martha replied.

Deathwalker smiled. "That is good to hear."

"I was surprised to receive your request so soon. Of all of us who helped yesterday, none worked harder than you Deathwalker. I figured you would be sleeping until the festival started." Elder Martha commented.

"I recover quickly, Elder. Besides, I am expecting guests soon. Little time to rest before they arrive." Deathwalker stated.

"Yes, Lady Emma and Duchess Lightheart." Elder Martha recalled.

"Indeed. I also received word that King Alfheim and some of his advisors will be visiting as well." Deathwalker explained.

"King Alfheim is coming here?! How interesting." Elder Martha commented.

"My understanding is you know the king of the elves. Is that true?" Deathwalker asked.

"High Elves and Wood Elves." Elder Martha replied.

"What?" Deathwalker said in confusion to her response.

"He is the king of Ljósálfar. Elves in that country are primarily seen as elves of the light. The Dark Elves or Drow elves are not allowed in Ljósálfar, by punishment of death." Elder Martha explained.

"That seems... harsh." Deathwalker commented.

"Not really. The dark elves are known to be cunning but ruthless. They also worship a spider goddess known for treachery and working with the Dark. We elves have long memories. It is hard to forget what side the Dark Elves chose. It is one of the Winter Queen's decrees, one the king's family has adamantly agreed with for thousands of years." Elder Martha clarified.

"I did not expect such emotion about killing." Deathwalker commented.

"It is not emotion, but the cold logic of facts and paying attention to history." Elder Martha stated.

"Those who do not understand history are doomed to repeat it." Deathwalker said more to himself.

Elder Martha had heard him. "Wise words, your grace."

Deathwalker looked up from his musings. "It is a saying from my home. I will not ignore your council... however, I cannot condone the persecution of a whole race of people because of something their ancestors did. Should I encounter any Dark Elves I will be cautious but will not kill them until the individual gives me cause."

Elder Martha gave a small nod of her head. "Very well, your grace. Was King Alfheim's visit why you called me to join you for lunch?"

"In part, but not the primary reason. Before I get to that, did you get a chance to talk to or listen to the personal stories from the refugees?" Deathwalker replied.

"Some. It sounds like the Proletariat are a bunch of monsters. Some of the children had been abused, along with several of the women." Elder Martha sneered.

"Commander Willis told me yesterday that some of the more recent arrivals had shared stories that they overheard the Proletariat soldiers talking about how Timberfall was to blame for their suffering, because we would not share our wealth." Deathwalker shared.

"Propaganda and lies. To be expected of immoral butchers." Elder Martha spat.

“Oh, of that we can agree. What concerns me is Commander Willis said he knows for a fact that with how shorthanded his guard has been, he is almost certain we have spies or worse in our midst.” Deathwalker replied.

“The Commander might be a bit paranoid, wolf beastmen tend to be very protective of territory.” Elder Martha commented.

“Perhaps... but I am sure you can agree to ignore the threat of the Proletariat would be the height of foolishness.” Deathwalker stated.

Elder Martha nodded her head. “Agreed.”

Deathwalker smiled. “Good. Then we can move forward with my plans.”

“Plans, your grace?” Elder Martha asked in confusion.

“Yes. Under the guise of trade, I will be asking Grimhold and Mezza to journey to the Dwarven kingdom to make an offer.” Deathwalker began to explain.

“What kind of an offer?”

Deathwalker smile grew wider. “Under the guise of opening up trade, we will establish a tunnel to this side of the valley and a Portal Station if they are interested. The real reason is to hopefully form an alliance against the Proletariat.”

“The dwarves are rather insular. They rarely get involved in anything to do with other nations. I do not see why they would change their stance now.” Elder Martha commented.

Deathwalker laughed. He was having fun with this slow reveal. What Elder Martha did not know, in fact, no one else but himself knew was Grimhold was the nephew of the current king. He had discovered that little morsel and one other critical bit of information one night while drinking with Grimhold.

“Ha, ha, ha, ha. Because I know something others don’t. First, Grimhold has some sway with the Dwarf King. Second, I’m sure you’ve heard the rumors about the dragon sightings.”

Elder Martha's eyes widened. "Of course! Dwarves have a racially ingrained fear and reverence for dragons. You have a plan to deal with the dragon."

"Exactly." Deathwalker replied.

Elder Martha's voice took on an element of concern. "Deathwalker, dragons, especially full-grown dragons are one of the most dangerous beings in existence."

Deathwalker smile never left his face. "Speaking about adult dragons, let me inquire about some of your knowledge."

Curious, Elder Martha just replied, "Ask away, your grace."

"How big do adult dragons tend to get?"

Elder Martha pondered the question. "It depends on the type of dragon. They can range from 4 to 8 meters tall when on all fours but can easily be 26 meters in length."

"And Ancient dragons?"

Elder Martha was confused. 'Was the dragon not an adult dragon but an ancient one?'

"Ancient dragons vary greatly in size and power depending on the type. I would say easily 60 meters. Why, do you think the dragon people have been seeing is an ancient dragon?"

Deathwalker waved off her concerns. 'If I do the math translation, in my dragon form I am about 169 meters tall if I lay on my belly, which is over 554 feet. This dragon that has everyone in a tizzy is maybe 15 percent of my size while I'm laying down. On all fours I am well over 390 meters which translates to about 1,300 feet tall. A few slaps should straighten them out. Heck I'll have to be careful not to squish the little guy.'

"No, I doubt it is an ancient dragon, but one cannot be too careful. I have a plan." Deathwalker raised his hand to forestall the Elder's protest. "Please, for now leave it be. Thank you for answering my questions. Now, let's talk about the main reason for wanting to have lunch with you today.

Elder Martha looked even more confused. 'What could he want to discuss?'

Geeves entered the room with several documents. Elder Martha blushed when the old butler genuinely smiled at her. She had always liked the man, the fact that he had worked for Darrien made it impossible for them to ever pursue anything beyond a friendship.

"Thank you, Geeves." Deathwalker said as Geeves placed the paperwork in front of him.

"Of course, your grace. Is there anything else you require?"

"Yes, please remain as witness. This is new to me." Deathwalker replied as he fed magic as he signed the documents. He had Malcom and Geeves assist him in getting the language right.

Elder Martha had a puzzled look on her face. "What is new to you?"

Deathwalker just smiled as he felt the magic contained in the document. He handed the document to Geeves. "Please read this out loud."

*To the citizens of Timberfall,*

*Henceforth, Elder Martha is elevated to the noble rank of Lady and named City Noble and Mayor of Timberfall city! She will retain her title of Elder and be seen formally as an advisor to the Duke of Timberfall. Rejoice as you gain a lady with the knowledge, wisdom, and power to guide Timberfall to heights of prosperity! Join me in adding this appointment to the upcoming Timberfall Festival!*

*By the authority as Duke Deathwalker Dragonvein ruler of the Timberfall Duchy*

The document shattered into million motes of light and every sentient in Timberfall Duchy received the notification announcing Elder Martha's appointment.

"WHAT?!!!" Elder Martha cried out.

When she dismissed the notification, Elder Martha saw Deathwalker in front of her with his hand held out. She took it in a daze. He lifted the older elf to her feet and gave her a hug.

After the impromptu hug, Deathwalker held her at arm's length. "Welcome to the peerage. Now that you are formally my advisor and the mayor of Timberfall city I expect you to work closely with my seneschal Geeves." Turning is head to Geeves. "Is that understood Geeves? I expect you to work very closely with Elder Martha."

Both Geeves and Elder Martha looked at each other and blushed. They both replied, "Yes, your grace."

"Good! Now if you'll excuse me, I have to talk with Grimhold and Mezza about their upcoming mission." Deathwalker said before leaving the two stunned people awkwardly looking at each other.

'He did not just do that to get Geeves and I together, did he?'

—————

# Interlude - Hargrave

“Hello, father.” Duchess Lightheart said as she hugged King Alfheim.

“It has been too long daughter. I thought I would get to see my other daughter.”

Duchess Lightheart winced. “She wanted to be here, but these dragon sightings have called her back to the royal court.”

“Dragon?! Where?! That bastard took my horse!” General Mineheir interjected.

“Ugh, again about that horse! Mineheir, let it go.” Advisor Nero commented.

“How can you say such a thing Nero?! I raised that horse from a foal!” General Mineheir protested.

“What has happened, grandfather?” Lady Emma asked in concern.

That was when King Alfheim finally noticed his granddaughter behind Duchess Lightheart. “Is that Emma? Hmmm... Something is different about you. Come give your grandfather a hug.”

The elven king did not give Lady Emma much time as he moved quickly around his daughter and embraced his granddaughter. The moment he hugged her, King Alfheim instantly knew what was different about Emma. He pulled back, holding her at arm’s length to examine her as the king blurted out, “You can use magic now! I can feel it! How?!... When?!... This changes everything, my granddaughter! You can be my heir now!”

This proclamation interrupted Mineheir and Nero’s argument. It also caught Advisor Mona’s attention. Her eyes took on a soft wintery glow. “Interesting... It appears your granddaughter has gained access to both her Winter heritage and access to Fire from her father’s side. How interesting indeed.”

She moved quick as lightning. One minute she was standing by the royal carriage and the next the fey woman was invading Lady Emma's personal space. This caused the girl to jump back in fright. "Ah! How did you move so fast?!"

Advisor Mona waved off her question as she continued to examine Lady Emma. "I am fey, such things are a trivial matter. What I am more interested in is how you have access to your magic."

Duchess Lightheart interjected. "We will discuss that shortly. However, I would like to hear more about your journey here. It sounds like you were attacked by a dragon, is this true?"

Advisor Mona looked annoyed at her inquiry being deferred, but quickly schooled her face.

King Alfheim, seeing this spoke up. "Yes, we must learn more about this miracle, but you are right daughter, matters of security must come first." He knew better than to ignore the emissary of the Winter Queen, so he hoped this compromise would appease the fey woman, at least for now.

Turning to Mineheir the king said, "General, please relay the events of our dragon encounter."

"Yes, your Majesty." General Mineheir replied before giving his attention to Duchess Lightheart and Lady Emma.

The General summarized the attack. "We were attacked by a red dragon. It was evident that the dragon was a fully grown adult. It was red in color and blew molten hot flames... The king and advisors helped as best they could with magical barriers of protection, but we still lost something so precious... The bastard flew off with my horse!" By the end of the tale General Mineheir was shaking in rage and sobbing at the loss of his friend.

"Again, with the horse! When will you drop this nonsense!" Advisor Nero protested.

General Mineheir scowled at the advisor. "Just because you have no heart and cannot understand the companionship between a man and his horse..."

“Enough!” Advisor Mona interrupted.

‘Man, that guy loves his horse.’ Lady Emma whispered to her aunt.

“You have no idea!” Duchess Lightheart replied.

Advisor Mona turned to Duchess Lightheart. “Now that you have heard our tale, let us hear yours.”

“It is alright auntie. They will find out soon enough anyway.” Lady Emma commented.

Duchess Lightheart sighed. She knew better than to withhold information from one of Queen Mab’s spies. For that was how she always considered Mona to be, more of a spy than advisor to her father.

“Very well. One of my peers, a Duke by the name of Deathwalker Dragonvein, who is arguably the greatest healer in Nord, offered to help. He was able to heal the damage done to my niece when she was a baby. Somehow, as part of this process Duke Dragonvein was also able to impart some spells for her to know.”

“He must be a master in that magic to be able to impart knowledge of specific spells.” Advisor Nero commented.

“Not necessarily. He could just be a master of place of power, one with those magic types.” Advisor Mona reminded the old elf.

Advisor Nero nodded. “Of course, of course. Either way, his ability to heal such damage is unheard of.”

It was Advisor Mona’s turn to nod. “Indeed. I must speak with this Deathwalker.”

“He is a Duke of our kingdom and must be afforded proper decorum.” Lady Emma reminded the abrupt fey.

“I care not for such things. The Winter Queen has given me strict orders to investigate any powerful magics or individuals of interest.” Advisor Mona quipped.

King Alfheim frowned but said nothing.

Duchess Lightheart spoke up. “We are journeying to his territory of Timberfall, advisor. I do not need to remind you that we will be ‘Guests’ in his home, do I?”

Her emphasizing of the word ‘guest’ made the advisor’s blood run cold, well colder than it already was. Mona knew she had to remain mindful of the confines of guest rights. This would be trickier than she thought. ‘Though how smart can some man be in the middle of nowhere? Please.’

# Chapter 15 - Infiltration

“Come sister, we have nothing to concern ourselves with. Our spies have already bribed a sergeant in the guard, and we are guaranteed to be taken on as a few new members of their unit.” Carn said to his sister.

Belinda was not convinced. “We must not underestimate our enemy.”

“Please. They are a bunch of old greedy fools. All they care about is money.” Carn argued.

“Of that we can agree. I do not doubt their greed and I also concur they are part of the older generation, therefore know only old, outdated ideas.” Belinda replied.

“Then, what is that look on your face for?” Carn asked.

“It is what our great leader said before we left. He told me to find a few younger girls to make them examples. I do not like such things, brother. Oh, I know we must do wicked things in the pursuit of our goals, but this seems risky at best.” Belinda lamented.

Carn’s face took on a look of concern to match his sister’s. He hated that such things were necessary parts of their cause. It was what they were taught from a young age. Who were they to challenge their General, the man they considered their true parent.

“What shall we do?” Carn asked.

“Our duty! We must achieve equal outcomes for all!” Belinda said, more to psych herself up.

Carn nodded. “One thing is for sure; I will be glad to get out of this damnable forest! The beasts are overrun here.”

"Yes, the environment seems out of balance. It must be because of their corrupt and greedy logging industry. They clearly have no care for the well-being of the environment, all they care about is making a profit, they are scum!" Belinda spat.

"That must be it! Why else would the beasts be so aggressive and unchecked. They must have been driven from their homes due to excessive logging!" Carn agreed.

The twins arrived at the Timberfall gate checkpoint. Sergeant Chen was their point of contact and their way into the city. They were told he and his squad wore a red sash to help them stand out. The excuse given to their superiors was to show pride in their squad. In truth, it was to help their spies hide in plain sight yet help the Proletariat know who they could use.

Carn spotted a group of guards with red sashes. "Sister, it appears we have found our contacts."

"Yes. Time to get this over with." Belinda replied as she changed direction towards the guards.

"Ah good to see our new recruits have arrived! I am Sergeant Chen. You two will be joining my squad. Follow me and I get you registered in the city guard."

The twins looked at the Sergeant, shrugged their shoulders and followed him into the guard station by the gate.

Sergeant Chen led them to another room that seemed to house a cache of guard leathers and various spears and swords. This room had a man behind a desk writing in some kind of book or ledger. The sergeant stopped in front of the desk and waited for the man to look up.

After a few moments, the man at the desk let out a breath and put down his quill. "What do you want Chen?! Can you not see I am busy? I still have to log all the new equipment we received from Councilmen Betterman and Ron."

Sergeant Chen turned to the side to show the twins and waved to them. "I know you are a busy man Quartermaster Nelix, but my new recruits need outfitting."

Quartermaster Nelix sighed. "More new recruits. You seem to recruit more than any other Sergeant. You will make captain before you know it Chen. Let me log their names in my ledger." He turned to regard the twins. "Names?"

The twins were startled at first before Belinda spoke up first. "Belinda sir."

Carn spoke up as his sister finished speaking. "Carn sir."

"Interesting names." Quartermaster Nelix thought for a minute before dismissing whatever thought he had and hooked his thumb to point behind him. "Go pick out a set of leathers and a weapon. I will make a note of it and then you can both go with your sergeant for further instructions."

Carn grabbed a leather armor set and two shortswords.

"I said 'a' weapon boy..." Quartermaster Nelix gave the side eye to Carn for a few moments before waving him off. "Fine. We have plenty anyway thanks to Councilman Ron."

Belinda already had two daggers equipped so she decided to take something with reach.

"A spear. Good choice private." Quartermaster Nelix said as he wrote in his log.

"Private?" Belinda raised an eyebrow at the man.

"Yes, the starting rank of any soldier is private. It may not be typically used but it does not change that detail, and in my line of work details matter." The gruff quartermaster replied before turning to their new squad leader. "Alright Chen, get them out of my armory. I have plenty of work to do."

Sergeant Chen reluctantly gave a head bow. "As you command quartermaster."

Turning to his two new members, "Follow me and I will give you the tour." Sergeant Chen said as he marched them out of the nearby northern barracks.

Once they were far enough away Chen turned to the twins. "Be careful around the quartermaster. He pays attention to the details. For now, he thinks you two are recruits but, we must do everything we can to avoid his scrutiny."

"We expected to be hidden not out in the open." Belinda commented.

"City guards can go places others cannot. This disguise will allow you and the others to do what you have to without drawing too much suspicion." Chen answered.

"Very well, but from now on we are in charge of this operation." Carn stated while flashing a dagger of his own.

Sergeant Chen raised his hands. "No need for threats. I have been paid well not to care. I will show you where each of the city council members lives and works. Most of them hide their wealth by living near or in their place of business. You also need to know some key strategic locations in town."

"What about this Duke Dragonvein? Where is he?" Belinda asked.

"It is best, at least for now, that you forget about him. The man is constantly surrounded by soldiers and Timberfall Manor is guarded by his personal army. Those men cannot be bought. Believe me, we have tried." Sergeant Chen explained.

"The corrupt and greedy noble must die!" Belinda spat.

"Do not worry. Come the festival there will be multiple opportunities to strike at the greedy nobles of this kingdom. From what I have heard, Duchess Lightheart and Lady Emma will be in attendance along with the Elven King Alfheim. Just imagine what would happen if the elf king died while under the duke's protection." Sergeant Chen shared.

"It could cause war between their two nations. So that is why General Marks sent us here now." Carn commented.

"Exactly. This backwater town is growing but it has nowhere near the defenses and military forces of their capital. With this many nobles gathered here we can strike a critical blow to the wealthy." Sergeant Chen replied.

"What can you tell us of the other nobles and rich business owners who are oppressing the people?" Belinda asked.

"Come. Follow me to my office. I have temporarily been assigned to a lieutenant's office while they assess our performance as sergeants. In truth, they do not have enough officers for the city guard, and they are looking to fill out their ranks." Chen replied as he led the twins to an out of the way building in the northern district of Timberfall.

"Take a seat." Sergeant Chen said as he pointed to two chairs in front of a desk. "Now let us talk about what we have gathered. First, the Duke seems lazy and has passed off much of running this city to the council. The council is run by recently appointed Elder Martha. Duke Dragonvein gave her the rank of Lady and city mayor. She already acted in such a capacity, so it only makes sense. He is the healer for some adventuring party and leaves with them periodically to chase after coin. The man has been gone the last few weeks galavanting around the kingdom."

"Proof the noble cares nothing for the people." Carn stated.

"Another elite who only cares about money." Belinda commented.

"How soon can we take this scum out?" Carn asked.

Chen sighed. "That will be difficult."

"Why is that? He is just a healer. Can we not just ambush him and his party?" Belinda asked.

"Ambushing them may be more challenging than you think. His Adventuring party is A rank. I have heard they are quite formidable, especially their dwarf defender. If you could get the healer away from them it would be one thing." Chen answered.

"Damn thick-skulled dwarves, always sticking their beards where they do not belong!" Belinda commented.

Chen nodded in agreement. "Then there are his new bodyguards..." Chen answered.

"Bodyguards?" Carn interrupted.

Chen continued his explanation. "Yes. Three cat girls. The murderous intent that comes off of those three, especially the one called Prrsha..." Chen visibly shuddered "... is enough to make anyone steer clear. Of course, I suggest we keep an eye out for opportunities, but I am afraid we will have to deal with the duke later. Elder Martha may be just as difficult."

"How so?" Belinda pressed.

"Geeves, the duke's seneschal has taken it upon himself to interview and select the lady's staff and guard contingent. He is meticulous in his interview and assessment process. Most of those he selects are being pulled from the duke's personal army. The man has also insisted Elder Martha stay with the Duke at Timberfall Manor until a 'proper' home can be built for the mayor. I might be able to get you in once her home is built, but until then, she is just as inaccessible as the duke." Chen shared.

Belinda spat to the side. "All these elites care about is being surrounded in opulence. They should all be taken out and hung for their crimes against the people."

"In time, sister." Carn comforted her before turning back to Sergeant Chen. "What about the other council members? How accessible are they?"

"Councilman Ron is a blacksmith and due to his business being paid handsomely to produce weapons for the city, both his business and home are being well guarded." Chen raised his hands when he saw Carn point to the guard uniform he was wearing. "Before you ask, my squad does not cover that part of the city. We might be able to sneak in, but it will be difficult. Most of the other council members are also similarly protected. The easiest to get to will be Councilman Betterman. His business is on our route."

"What can you tell us about him?" Carn asked.

"He is a leatherworker. A very lucrative one. He coordinates all the other leatherworkers in the city, and you are wearing some of their work." Chen explained.

"So, another wealthy business owner exploiting the people." Carn commented.

Chen nodded and continued. "Yes. From what I learned; his son died in a monster attack some time back. He has a daughter-in-law that works at the Adventurers' guild and a granddaughter that works at his shoppe and the guild."

Belinda's interest was piqued. General Marks told her to notify him of any of the children of these rulers. "Tell me about this granddaughter."

"She cannot be more than fourteen. Her name is Alyce and if she is not working at Betterman's shoppe or the guild, she is visiting her friend Elsa, who is the daughter of Councilman Samuel." Chen answered.

"These corrupt elites always seem to run together." Carn commented.

"What else can you tell us about this upcoming waste of time they are calling a festival?" Belinda asked, making a mental note regarding Alyce and Elsa.

"It is supposed to be a weeklong celebration filled with food and games. Special tournaments will be held to test skill in archery and other forms of combat. The end of the festival will be a rather large hunt. It is said all the meat from the hunt will be shared with the people." Chen relayed.

"That is surprising. I am sure the wealthy will get the choice cuts and the poor will get the scraps." Carn rebuked.

"Oh, most assuredly. Lady Emma and Duchess Lightheart will be escorting King Alfheim and his retinue to Timberfall to help judge the competitions." Chen further explained.

"Perfect! We will cripple two kingdoms in one strike!" Carn exclaimed.

"And then the resources of this place will be ours. The will of the people shall not be denied!" Belinda agreed.

"We can start with this Betterman, but we must target other key locations in the city. It is our job to sow fear and chaos inside these walls. This must be done right before the people's army marches here and sacks this place." Carn stated.

"Yes, Timberfall will be the perfect hub to launch our invasion into the rest of this corrupt kingdom. Plus, the resources here will aid in our war efforts to bring peace to this continent! Now, let us discuss how to get our squad outside our normal patrol." Sergeant Chen replied.

# Interlude - Mother Winter & Morrigan

"You like him." Morrigan commented, stating more of a fact than a question.

"Bah!" Mother Winter spat.

"You cannot lie to me sister." Morrigan pushed.

"Fine! Yes, I like him. There is something about him. He is missing a part of himself. This makes it hard to know for sure if he is the Huntsman, but the very nature of the Earl King was being multifaceted. If it was so easy we would have found him long ago." Mother Winter answered.

"Ha! So many names for the same person. Three names, for three roles. Ah well. It would have been best if we knew for certain, but such is the way of things sometimes. Your daughter is going to be a problem. It is only a matter of time before she learns of him." Morrigan commented.

Mother Winter turned to her oldest friend and sister. "You like him too. You would not have introduced yourself and helped me with his geas."

Morrigan gave her a mock look of surprise.

Mother Winter shook her head. "Do not think I did not notice your subtle nudges of the weave. He is a dragon; they are not exactly fond of us... especially since our friend's death."

"I miss Father Time too. I wish he were still among us. If Deathwalker can find the rest of Chronos' power, he can halt his unraveling, but you saw what I did in the Weave... we will have to help him when the time comes." Morrigan replied.

Seeing Mother Winter deep in thought, Morrigan decided to prompt her sister. "Your thoughts?"

"He is the Huntsman, but he is missing part of himself. Compassion and most of those annoying feelings are fragmented and incomplete within him. He cannot be left that way. As much as I detest emotions, he will need his mind, soul, and body intact for what is to come. My daughter will try to keep him without emotion, in some ways I do not blame her, but..." Mother Winter began to say but paused in her musings.

"But... that would be a betrayal and not in his or our best interest." Morrigan finished.

Mother Winter was not looking at her and appeared to be rather distracted.

"You are up to something sister." Morrigan said.

Knowing she could not keep anything from her sister, Mother Winter spoke up. "Yes. Do you remember that dragon we sensed?"

"Aye. What about him?" Morrigan asked then realized what her sister was up to. "You got one of the winter fey to influence the direction the dragon was headed in. I thought you seemed distracted lately."

Mother Winter smiled back at her sister. "A blizzard and other random acts to subtly change the dragon's direction. He should be near Timberfall soon enough."

"Diabolical! I love it!" Morrigan chuckled.

# Interlude - Grimhold & Mezza

"I do not understand why you have to be the one to go Grimmy!" Mezza complained.

Grimhold paused in his packing to take Mezza's hands in his. "My friend has asked me to go. I owe my life multiple times over to Deathwalker. I am going, and I want you to come with me."

"What?!" Mezza asked in shock.

"Aye lass. I cannot see myself being apart from you for so long. Besides, my kin are in those mountains." Grimhold explained.

"You want me to meet yer family already?" Mezza replied.

"I am courtin' ya, am I not? No point in courtin' if I not be interested in marrying ya! That would be rather pointless!" Grimhold said as he went back to packing.

Realizing what he said the dwarf froze mid-pack. Mezza wrapped him up in a bear hug. "Oh Grimmy! Yes! Of course, I accept!"

Grimhold just smiled and hugged her back. He was originally planning on asking in a different way, but she said yes, and to him that was all that mattered.

Mezza broke the embrace and ran out the door. "Let me go pack myself. I will fix us some travel food too!"

"She said yes, and she is going to cook us something for the trip. Aye. I be the luckiest dwarf on the planet." Grimhold said to himself before resuming his packing and donning his improved Mithril armor.

It took Mezza about an hour to pack and prepare several meals for their trip. She was packed and ready at the entrance to the courtyard. Grimhold did not know how she did it, but this further solidified his belief that he was a lucky man.

Deathwalker was there to greet them. "Do you have everything you need for your journey?"

"Aye lad. Mezza made several meals for our trip; we should be set." Grimhold replied.

"You are a lucky man, my friend. Come, I'll walk you to the portal." Deathwalker said.

"Portal?" Mezza asked in confusion.

"Yes, my understanding is the main entrance to the Dwarven kingdom is at the edge of the elven nation. You two will take the portal to Hargrave. From there, I have Duchess Lightheart's personal assurance, you will be granted safe passage through her Duchy and her father's elven lands." Deathwalker explained.

It did not take them long to get to the portal room. This was Mezza's first time seeing the wonder. "We just step through that, and we end up in Hargrave?"

"Exactly." Deathwalker took out a sealed envelope and handed it to Grimhold. "Give this to the Dwarven king and do what you can to convince him of my proposal."

"How is Grimmy supposed to do that, Sire?" Mezza asked incredulously.

Deathwalker just smiled. "I have faith in my friend. Everything in my bones says war is coming. If the dwarven king accepts my proposal, activate the trinket I gave you."

The two men clasped wrists then pulled each other into a big hug. Deathwalker whispered in Grimhold's ear. "If you are in trouble activate the trinket and I will know. Thank you for doing this my friend."

"Alright, alright, enough sappy nonsense. I will see ya in a few weeks." Grimhold said as he wiped a tear from his eye.

To the gruff dwarf, Deathwalker had become family. He knew what the man was proposing was bold and outrageous, yet he trusted him completely. Besides, this gave him the perfect opportunity to get his family's marriage blessing.

Mezza pulled out two butcher knives. "Do not worry, Sire. I will make sure no one tries to hurt my Grimmy!"

"Of that I am sure, Mezza. Good journey!" Deathwalker said.

"Good journey!" The two dwarves replied in unison before stepping through the portal.

"I am going to miss those two." Deathwalker said before looking at the prompt that still sent chills through him every time, he looks at it.

***Warning! Spirit connection unstable. Soul Unraveling! Time remaining until permadeath 1 year, 9 days, 13 hours...***

**Quest:** *Find the remnants of Chronos' power (AKA: Father Time) to halt the* ***Unraveling of your Soul****. Note: This is a temporary solution until the other parts of yourself can be reclaimed.* ***1 of 3 remnants of Chronos' power obtained****.*

"Well, no time like the present to get stronger. I would say a good hunt would help take my mind off all this stuff. Plus, I need to retrieve my little murderhobo." Deathwalker said as he exited the portal room.

# Chapter 16 - Garry's Return

King Alfheim walked out of the Timberfall portal. Wonder and joy was plastered on his face. First, he learned his only grandchild could finally use magic, which meant she could finally be seen as his successor. Then, he just experienced a magical marvel, traveling instantly from one location to another.

As he and his retinue exited the portal, they were greeted by a familiar face, Elder Martha. “As mayor of this city, I welcome you, King Alfheim! It is good to see you after all these years! I see we also have your daughter, Duchess Lightheart, and granddaughter, Lady Emma.”

King Alfheim put his arm around Lady Emma. “My successor!”

Elder Martha’s eyebrows rose. “I had not heard. Congratulations!”

“Grandfather, I have not yet agreed. You know I must consider my duties for the Kingdom of Nord.” Lady Emma shook her head at her grandfather’s antics.

Since the man learned she could use magic he had been practically incorrigible, flaunting his pride at being finally able to formally acknowledge her as his kin. As magic was everything to the elves, her grandfather could not show any interest or compassion to her in public. Now it was like he had years of restrained love to shower her with. It made her both smile and shake her head in frustration.

“Nonsense! We can discuss it later.” King Alfheim said before turning to Elder Martha. “It is good to see you, my old friend. You remember my daughter, Duchess Lightheart. And of course, you remember my Advisors Mona, Nero, and General Mineheir.”

Elder Martha nodded. “It is good to see you.” She was about to say, ‘see you all’, but in truth she never trusted the king’s advisors. In her mind, one was opportunistic, and the other was clearly loyal to the Winter Court.

Elder Martha turned to introduce the others in the room. “This is General Marius, Commander Willis of the city guard, Head Trader Malcom, and Geeves, seneschal to our Duke Dragonvein.”

“Where is Duke Dragonvein?” Advisor Mona inquired.

“Yes, this is bad form for our host to not be present upon our arrival.” Advisor Nero chided.

“As I am now the mayor of Timberfall, technically you are my guests, but the duke has insisted you stay at the Manor until the mayor’s residence has been finished.” Elder Martha expertly maneuvered.

“I still wish to meet him and expected him to be here.” King Alfheim replied.

Geeves stepped forward this time. “His grace was out hunting when he received a system quest. He sent word back that hc would return as quickly as possible. I can say no more than that King Alfheim. I hope you can understand.”

“A system quest, how interesting.” Advisor Mona commented under her breath.

“Yes, most interesting. I understand the importance of a system quest, they cannot be ignored. They are rarely given so it must be of the utmost importance. Very well, please show us to our accommodations.” King Alfheim conceded.

General Mineheir stepped forward and clasped wrists with General Marius. “A fellow general, it will be good to discuss tactics. Did you know we were attacked by a dragon on the way here?”

General Marius’ eyebrows rose. “A dragon? I heard the royal court issued a kingdom wide quest to deal with the beast! Hopefully you did not lose too many men!”

“It was awful! The beast took my favorite horse! Can you believe it?!” General Mineheir lamented.

“Ugh! Again, with that damnable horse!” Advisor Nero admonished.

Not wanting to hear his advisor and general start up again, King Alfheim spoke up. “I imagine your duke had a plan should we arrive before his return.”

“You are correct, your majesty. If you and our other guests would follow me. We have a special entrance to Timberfall Manor from the portal hub for convenience and to ensure your safety.” Geeves said as he guided them out of the waiting room.

## ———-A day earlier———

"Thank you for summoning me back boss! That was horrible! It was like one of those computer game things from your memory boss, something glitched and things crashed." Garry immediately started talking the moment he rematerialized at the Infinite Nexus.

As Garry was talking horror fell across his face as he looked at Deathwalker. "W-what if I am in the Matrix and this is all some simulation?! It would explain why that guy I ate tasted like chicken..."

Deathwalker shook his head, as he cut off his familiar before he could go too far on this new tangent. "Garry you are not in the Matrix. Morrigan explained what happened. You bore the brunt of the effects of multiple strands of Fate crashing into each other as others split apart. I appreciate you taking the brunt of that effect as I barely survived the experience on my end."

"No problem, boss. Glad I could help, but can we NEVER do that again!" Garry replied.

"Agreed buddy!"

"I mean we should be the ones ripping our enemies apart, not the other way around!"

"That is something we can get onboard with as well." Prrsha held a wicked grin on her face.

"Now that you have retrieved your familiar, do you have time to visit with the pride?" Mrrsha asked.

"Yes, it would be good to see the pride but give me some time with Garry and Lilandra." Deathwalker replied.

"As you command, alpha." Frrsha answered before ushering her sisters out of the main hall of the throne room.

"What's up boss? Why did you make the hot cat girls leave?" Garry inquired.

"Ugh, did you have to re-summon him?" Lilandra rolled her eyes.

"You know you missed me! He, he, he!"

"I wouldn't go that far." Lilandra quipped.

Deathwalker just shook his head at the two of them. "To answer your question Garry, let me show you both something."

Willing his prompt to be seen by the two of them, Deathwalker shared what he had kept from the others.

"Wait?! What does this mean? Are you dying boss?! Who do I have to kill to stop this?!" Garry spewed out one question after the other.

"This is apparently part of the result of Mother Winter removing a geas that one of the archangels put on me." Deathwalker replied.

"There is more to it than that. Mother Winter is known as the Unraveler. Her power only further led to this result. It is interesting that you have a specific countdown timer." Lilandra commented.

"At some point I plan to confront Uriel. A part of me wants to do that now, but something is telling me now is not the time." Deathwalker said solemnly.

"Again, who do we have to kill to fix this?!" Garry chimed in.

"Violence is not always the answer." Lilandra shot back.

"Huh? I'm sorry, I do not understand that statement at all. Overwhelming force sounds like it is very much needed in this situation!"

Deathwalker sighed. "We must find two other fragments of Chronos' power. With it, I can use the **Infinite Well of Time Magic** to pause the clock on my unraveling soul, thereby giving me the time I need to find my own fragments across the Omniverse."

Garry turned to Lilandra. "Sure sounds like murderhobo time to me!"

Lilandra just shook her head at the crazy floating ball.

Turning back to his master, Garry asked, "so, Uh, why aren't we tracking those two fragments down right now?!"

"Simple. It is too dangerous for me to use the Well right now. I need time to recover." Deathwalker explained.

"I might have a solution. It is not without risk but here at your place of power is the best place to attempt what I am thinking." Lilandra stated.

"What solution? Does it involve killing people?!" Garry exclaimed.

Rather than fight it, Deathwalker just pointed to Garry. "What he said."

"As your first disciple and your arbiter we could link our magics. You use your **Infinite Well of Time Magic** to resonate with the other two fragments. I would tap into the extensive knowledge of planar magics within you to help us navigate to the fragments. Once I get a feel for the rough location of the fragments and familiar with the resonance, I believe I can track them down without risking your use of the **Well** for an extended period of time." Lilandra offered.

Deathwalker took a few moments to consider Lilandra's offer. On one hand, it reduced the risk and could speed up the process of finding the remnants of Chronos' power. On the other hand, he had been warned not to use **Time** magic while his **Fate** was in such flux. 'No, it is a calculated risk I have to take.'

"Very well. Let's get this over with." Deathwalker answered.

Lilandra smiled and took Deathwalker's hands in hers. "Activate the **Well** and I will observe."

As asked, Deathwalker drew on the power of the **Infinite Well of Time Magic**. Doing so caused agonizing pain to shoot through him. He held on, not willing to give up so quickly.

Seeing the pain on Deathwalker's face, Lilandra felt the strands of **Fate** and **Time** magic pulsing out of her master. Using her mind's eye, she studied what she was seeing. Two intertwined strands of **Fate** and **Time** magic shot out off into the distance.

There was like an invisible wall each line passed through. Lilandra knew these walls were the veils between realities. She grabbed hold of both strands. Picking one, she followed it to its source. Once she mentally passed the veil, she instantly knew it was the reality Deathwalker came from. Resonating with the magic she had a clear path to the source of that fragment.

Once Lilandra felt she could find her way back to the first Chronos fragment it was simple for her to mentally return to Deathwalker. The first fragment firmly fixed in her mind; she followed the second connection. She could feel Deathwalker falter, and the connection dimmed.

As fast as her mind could carry her, Lilandra did her best to lock on to the second fragment. The connection flickered and dimmed once again. It was clear Deathwalker was in agony and could not hold on much longer. Doing her best, Lilandra resonated as long as she could before mentally returning.

"You can stop now master!" Lilandra cried out.

Deathwalker cut the connection and audibly sighed in relief. "Woah that was brutal. I cannot believe it hurt so..." Pausing mid-sentence as he read the prompt in front of his eyes.

Lilandra saw the look of resignation in her master's eyes. "What is it?!"

Rather than speaking, Deathwalker mentally willed them to see his prompt.

***Warning! You have further strained your soul, hastening your demise! Time until permadeath: 9 months, 0 days, 0 hours...***

"On master, I am sorry." Lilandra apologized.

At first, she was going to give Deathwalker a few moments to recover before asking him to try again. Now, even though she knew the second fragment's location was not as clear, she could not ask him to repeat that process.

"Do not worry master. Give me some time. Go enjoy your time with the pumas as you recover." Lilandra said.

"I think I will. Are you coming Garry?" Deathwalker asked.

Lilandra intervened before Garry could reply. "Actually, I would like to speak with Garry for a few moments."

Deathwalker just shrugged. He was too tired to care. It was a level of tiredness that seemed to be more than bone deep. He knew it was his wounded soul. With such mental musings, Deathwalker had little interest in inquiring why, and just left the main hall.

"What's up? Have you finally decided to give me a chance? Believe me I keep dreaming of genie!" Garry teased.

Lilandra raised one eyebrow. "I warned you not to use that reference. I will let you get a pass, just this once as I have more important matters to discuss with you."

Garry realized Lilandra was serious and after reading his master's prompt, he figured she wanted to discuss it. He could be serious for his master.

"Boss is everything to me, how else am I to be entertained." Garry smiled at the end. 'Okay, mostly serious.'

Ignoring Garry's antics, Lilandra spoke up. "I have recruited Orantes and Prrsha to help me in recovering these fragments for Deathwalker. You saw the prompt. We do not have time to be completely subtle in retrieving them. As you are not the most diplomatic, I thought you might be interested in joining our efforts when the time comes."

"Sign me up! Mayhem and I get to help the boss, sounds like an awesome time to me!" Garry grinned.

"Good! I will call upon you when the time comes. For now, say nothing to Deathwalker."

"Why?" Garry asked.

"Because he is the type of man to have too much integrity to risk others just to save his life. If he finds out, our master will expect us to comport ourselves in a way that might hinder the retrieval of the fragments. Deathwalker would sacrifice himself to save any of us, that I do know about him. I hope you are willing to do the same for him." Lilandra explained.

"Absolutely! And I will take as many bastards with me as I can!" Garry proclaimed.

——

"Ha, ha, ha, ha!" Deathwalker laughed as he played with the puma cubs.

Mrrsha, Prrsha, and Frrsha stood there and watched their alpha. It warmed their heart to see him be so kind and playful with the children of their pride. It reinforced Prrsha's resolve to help Lilandra and Orantes find what Deathwalker needed to survive.

Garry floated up to the three matriarchs. "What'd I miss?"

"That took a while for you to return. What did Lilandra want?" Mrrsha asked.

Garry used two of his eyestalks to gesture to himself. "She just wanted all of this! It's only a matter of time until you pretty kitties want me too!"

Mrrsha flexed her claws at the Shadow Gazer. "Do not make me remind you I see you little more than a scratching post!"

Frrsha played with her blonde hair, twirling it as she never took her eyes of Deathwalker. "Why would I need you when I have alpha."

Mrrsha nodded in agreement. "Come sisters, let us help our alpha with the cubs."

Frrsha and Mrrsha began to walk away but Prrsha held back. "Go sisters. I wish to speak to our alpha's familiar." As she said the last part, she extended her claws as Mrrsha had done earlier.

Both cat girls just shrugged their shoulders figuring Prrsha was just going to scare the little floating ball of crazy. Once her sisters were far enough away Prrsha spoke. "Lilandra recruited you as well."

"Yea, she told me more about her plans to save the boss. It involves mayhem and destruction so of course I'm in!"

Prrsha pulled her red hair to the side, using the motion to look back briefly at Deathwalker and her kin. "Good. I have said nothing to my sisters. Frrsha will not be able to hide her emotions from our alpha. And Mrrsha, she will make a point to ensure he knows what we are attempting."

"Yes. Lilandra wanted to keep this from him as well. I don't get it. The boss does what he feels is necessary. I have seen the monster inside; I think he would welcome the fun!" Garry challenged.

Prrsha purred at the thought. "Yes, his fierceness is unmatched. Look at how he plays with the young from our pride. To watch that you would not know he was capable of such things. He buries that part of his power deep inside himself. Our alpha does that for our sake. Just as he uses that ferocity to protect us and the others under his care, but never just for himself."

"I already told the hot genie that I was in. Lilandra said her and Orantes would need some time to prepare. Something about the brood and having one of the portal gates, blah, blah. It was just a bunch of boring talk, and I got distracted just staring at her. I mean she is just so hot! You are too in an exotic cat girl way!" Garry teased.

Prrsha just rolled her eyes. "Just be ready when the time comes."

Conversation over, Prrsha and Garry moved to join the others. As they approached Deathwalker, finished his play wrestling with the cubs. He turned to his familiar and asked, "Are you up for a hunt, buddy?"

"Did you even have to ask? Of course!" Garry grinned.

"Perfect. Let me let General Marius know on the way out. Our secret base slash training facility is turning out well when I spoke to him last. Come my savage squad, I am in need of a hunt!" Deathwalker replied.

## ———Present time———

The day had been filled with one hunt after the other. The savage squad had journeyed further into the forest closer to the mountains, battling the whole way until they had come across a rare patch of grasslands that butted up against the mountains. That was where they had encountered their current challenge.

***Nymean Lion***

*Level 100*

*HP: 5,639/12,300*

"Man, this **Nymean Lion**'s hide is tough, and its **Strength** and **Dexterity** have to be through the roof!" Deathwalker commented as he dodged another powerful swipe from the beast.

"What roof? I see no structure!" Mrrsha asked as she too had to dodge quickly out of the deadly attack.

Everyone had some minor wound or cut from one of the creature's attacks. The **Nymean Lion**'s claws seemed to have similar armor-piercing properties as the pumas did. Though the three matriarchs could penetrate the lion's thick hide, they either could only go so deep, or the beast would heal quickly.

Most of Garry's magical attacks did little more than annoy it. This caused the **Shadow Gazer** to be high in the air, mostly taunting the beast. The **Nymean Lion** crouched down; his legs slightly glowing before it leapt into the air.

"Oh shit!" Garry barely dodged out of the way hearing snapping jaws behind him.

"That is completely unfair! Something that big should not be able to jump that high!" Garry protested.

"Quit your complaining! What is unfair is how quickly it heals from our attacks!" Prrsha stated.

The only one who had been effective against the monster was Deathwalker's **Omni-claws**. The speed and power of the **Nymean Lion**'s counterstrikes were making it difficult to get in anything but glancing blows. Yet everyone could see Deathwalker smiling, clearly enjoying himself.

"The beast appears to really not like you, Garry!" Frrsha commented.

"No surprise there! Keep doing what you do best and annoy it!" Mrrsha chimed in.

"Hey! If I didn't know you cat girls loved me, I might take that seriously!"

"We do not!" Prrsha replied.

Garry gave them a mock look of hurt before shrugging and using his **Telekinesis** to grab a nearby rock and hitting the lion in the face. "Let's rock kitty!"

The **Nymean Lion** attempted his leaping attack at Garry again. This time he was expecting it and was already in motion to move out of the way. The leap attack did not come anywhere near as close as it did the first time.

"You know he really is good at pissing that thing off." Deathwalker observed.

Using the giant beast's lack of mobility while in the air, Deathwalker landed on the **Nymean Lion**'s back. Digging in his claws right below the mane. Finally getting a critical strike and firm hold on its back, he activated his **Power of 13** ability.

The **Nymean Lion** tried to buck and twist to dislodge Deathwalker. Completely distracted by this turn of events, the beast did not dodge the renewed attacks from Frrsha, Mrrsha, and Prrsha. The three cat girls finally saw their strikes do more damage as the monster seemed to grow more and more sluggish.

Seeing the long-awaited notification told them they had finally defeated their opponent.

*Congratulations! You have defeated a level 100* ***Nymean Lion****!* ***260,000 experience*** *earned!*

***Level Up!*** *Congratulations! You are now* ***Level 65****! You have* ***+13*** *stat points to distribute!*

*Congratulations! Your* ***Power of 13*** *ability has permanently absorbed the following stats:* ***+50 Strength, +50 Agility, +50 Dexterity, +35 Constitution, +25 Endurance, +13 Luck****!*

"Luck huh? How weird." Deathwalker said as he dumped his 13 stat points into **Wisdom**, then willed to review his summary stat sheet. It had been a while since he reviewed his status and wanted to see the gains from all the adventuring and hunting.

| Name: Deathwalker Dragonvein | | Race: Ancient Omni Dragon | | Experience Needed to Level: | |
|---|---|---|---|---|---|
| Level: | 65 | Form: | Human | 787,300 | |
| Stats | | | | | |
| Health: | 4,173 | Mana: | 7,098 | Stamina: | 4,043 |
| Mana Regen. per minute | 2,028 | Stamina Regen. per minute | | 2,503.8 | |
| Primary Attributes | | | | | |
| Unused Attribute Points: 0 | | | | | |
| Strength: | 323 | Agility: | 362 | Dexterity: | 336 |

| Constitution: | 321 | Endurance: | 311 | Intelligence: | 273 |
|---|---|---|---|---|---|
| Wisdom: | 260 | Charisma: | 195 | Luck: | 195 |
| Intuition: | 78 | Creativity: | 78 | Mental Aegis: | 78 |

Deathwalker was happy with the increases. He had been dealing with too much politics and city planning lately. It was hard to see the immediate results of such efforts. Sure, he saw some with their recent healing of the refugees, but it still did not help address his drive to grow stronger. Yet now, on the hunt, he felt like he was finally moving forward.

"Well, which direction should we..." Deathwalker's question was cut off with the arrival of a new notification.

***Ruler of Timberfall Duchy**, an **Adult Red Dragon** has entered your territory! This dragon is the subject of an active **Kingdom of Nord** quest! You are called to defend your territory and protect your followers! **Objectives**: Subjugate, kill, or drive off target. A lesser reward will be granted if you negotiate with the invading dragon. **Note**: Target's location has been added to your **Explorer's map**.*

Deathwalker shared the notification with his team.

"Now we are talking! Let's go bring the smack down on a dragon!" Garry cheered.

# Chapter 17 - Stretching One's Legs

"So, uh, how big is an adult dragon boss?" Garry asked as they traversed the forest.

"I think I read that red dragons can be over six meters tall." Frrsha chimed in.

"The hot cat girl can read?!" Garry retorted.

Frrsha flashed her claws right in front of Garry's face. "Careful scratching post!"

"My bad. I was just surprised is all. Brains and beauty, yum!" Garry replied.

"Where did you learn to read?" Deathwalker asked.

"Uriel taught us to read while we were in your realm, alpha." Mrrsha commented.

"You told us you were a dragon so my sisters and I asked Uriel to recommend a few books so we could learn more." Frrsha explained.

"You know, with the bond you have with the boss, I could probably share some of the shows he used to watch..." Garry began before Prrsha cut him off.

"What are shows?"

"Think of them like moving and speaking portraits." Deathwalker offered as way of explanation.

"Yea, they are great! He has a bunch that are about dragons or have dragons in them. There are also some about dinosaurs, which are just types of dragons, but their histories got them wrong. Either way they are fun to watch! It's what I do to entertain myself when there is a bunch of boring talking going on." Garry said excitedly.

"If you could share this with us Garry, we would appreciate it." Mrrsha stated.

"Awe, that is the first time you've used my name. I knew it! I'm wearing you down!"

This time Prrsha flashed her claws at the Shadow Gazer. "Do not push your luck scratching post!"

Deathwalker was uncertain about what Garry might expose them to. "Keep it family oriented to start. Oh, and none of that nonsensical crap that depicts the dragon as the bad guy. That stuff always annoyed me."

"But the best stuff is with all the blood and guts!" Garry protested.

"Do some of the older 80s and 90s cartoons. There are some great ones about dragons that I couldn't get enough of." Deathwalker shared.

Garry pondered the suggestion. "Hmmm, that is some of the better entertainment, that and anime of course!"

Deathwalker nodded in agreement.

Garry and Deathwalker spent the next several hours of their journey explaining some of the concepts and shows to the three cat girls. They seemed fascinated by the concepts of movies and tv shows, even more so when they learned how much their alpha had enjoyed the older stuff. It was decided when they returned to Timberfall, they would take some time to explore how to have the three cat girls join the mental constructs Garry and Deathwalker had created.

They heard a roar as they entered another clearing. In front of the Savage squad, they saw the Adult Red Dragon they were looking for. It had its claws dug into some kind of animal, most likely its latest meal.

"That's a huge bitch!" Garry exclaimed.

"Who dares to call me such a thing?!" The red dragon roared back.

Warning! A dragon's roar can trigger a primal fear in the hearts and minds of lesser creatures, causing a Fear, Frightened, or Horrified status condition. All are prey before the might of an adult dragon! However, you are no prey, you are a hunter! You are immune to negative status conditions from dragons. Your disciples are also granted such protections.

"I think you pissed it off, Garry." Frrsha commented.

"No surprise there." Prrsha chimed in.

'Well that explains their cavalier attitude while staring down a giant dragon.' Deathwalker thought.

"Enough chatter sisters. Let us show this intruder what happens when someone enters our forest." Mrrsha turned to Deathwalker. "If you would allow us to deal with this... intruder."

"INTRUDER! I AM A DRAGON! Wherever we tread is ours by birthright!" The red dragon roared in fury. 'Who are these insects to act this way!'

The dragon charged the savage squad.

The cat girls and Deathwalker easily dodged out of the way, but Garry was not so lucky. As the **Shadow Gazer** attempted to move, he was clipped by the backhand of the dragon's left front claw sending him off course. This led the little ball right into the path of the dragon's open maw.

CHOMP!!!

"Garry!" Deathwalker exclaimed.

The red dragon smiled a wicked grin. Just as he turned towards his other targets the dragon's face turned up in consternation. The dragon starts coughing before spitting out the **Shadow Gazer** and multiple shards of ice.

Mrrsha jumped in the air catching Garry before he careened into a nearby tree. "Of course, he didn't like you!"

"What can I say, I'm an acquired taste." Garry grinned.

The dragon spat out a few more chunks of ice and shaking their head. "You dare to use ice on ME! Burn!"

A jet of intense fire streamed out of the dragon's mouth. Moving its head back and forth in an attempt to burn all the offenders for such insults. Swiping with its tail and claws any time the cat girls approached. 'Why are these small creatures so fast?!'

Then the dragon noticed a humanoid standing up against a tree at the edge of the clearing. As easy as a target the humanoid looked, any thought of attacking felt wrong. Shaking off the weird feeling, the dragon refocused on the quick and nimble catlike humanoids.

Constant tail swipes, claw slashes, and fire breath attacks made the red dragon the hardest fight the three matriarchs ever faced. Frustration grew on both sides as feline strikes were deflected or abandoned from the onslaught that was a red dragon. The cat girls were having difficulty landing strikes but so too the dragon struggled landing a hit beyond a glancing blow. Garry's attacks were rather ineffectual as the red dragon's scales seemed to be rather resistant to magical attacks.

"Maybe we can get it to swallow the ball of crazy again." Prrsha said in exasperation.

Frrsha looked around the clearing. The ground was scorched or had huge gouges in them. Nearby trees were busted or knocked down. "At least the dragon is smart enough not to set the entire forest on fire."

Garry telekinetically threw a large tree branch into the side of the dragon's face. The strike saved Mrrsha at the last minute by sending the dragon off course.

"Suck it!"

"Thank you, Garry!" Mrrsha said as she landed next to him.

"Eh, I owed ya one." Garry replied.

Mrrsha called out to Deathwalker. "We are at a standstill, alpha."

"Yea it's not fair dragons are so resistant to magic and so huge!" Garry complained.

Garry's words resonated with Deathwalker. "Hmmm. You just gave me an idea buddy."

"Of course, I'm awesome!... what did I suggest?" Garry replied.

Deathwalker smiled back at his familiar before calling out to Frrsha and Prrsha as he started to disrobe. "Back off and leave the dragon to me!"

The two cat girls quickly disengaged their opponent. This gave the red dragon time to register what was just said. Turning to Deathwalker, the dragon sneered. "You?! What could you do little one? Ha, ha, ha, ha!"

Deathwalker did something he wanted to do since all his level ups, even more so from their recent hunting trip, take on his true form. He jumped up high into the air and began to transform. Luckily his jumping helped his expansion upwards instead of crushing everyone around him. He grew and grew, taking on his Ancient Omni-Dragon form for the first time since coming to this new world.

Deathwalker was so massive his shadow blocked out the sun for everyone in the clearing and beyond.

The red dragon stared up in equal parts shock and horror. He was now looking up at the largest ancient dragon he had ever seen. One clawed hand the size of the red dragon's entire body, and he had just insulted the being by calling him 'little'. The aura of this being enough to bring him to his knees.

With the flick of his wrist, Deathwalker picked up the red dragon and brought him close. "Who are you calling little? He, he, he, he, he!"

The savage squad too stared in shock. They had never seen their master in his full dragon form. For them it was a matter of wonder, his aura wrapping them like a warm blanket of security and protection.

———

Animals and monsters in the area felt the opposite of the savage squad. Everywhere the aura spread out the beasts panicked and fled in the opposite direction. The power of it was so intense that it was sensed miles away from Timberfall.

Several of the higher ups in the city went on alert. Elder Martha took charge and began issuing orders. "Man, the walls! I want everyone on duty and at their post immediately!"

Commander Willis saluted. "As you command, Elder! It shall be done!"

"That power... it is a dragon!" Advisor Nero stated.

Elder Martha nodded to the advisor.

"Has the dragon returned? Let me at him!" General Mineheir said as he withdrew his sword.

"This aura feels much stronger than the one we felt before." Advisor Mona commented.

"Perhaps it was holding back its power before?" King Alfheim suggested.

"Just like that dastardly dragon to toy with us earlier! Fear not your majesty, I will vanquish this cruel foe!" General Mineheir cried.

————

Garry flew up near Deathwalker's head as he saw the genuine terror in the red dragon's face. "If you bite his head off, can I get a taste of what's left, boss?"

The red dragon visibly gulped. "Ha, ha, ha, ha! Not so big and tough are you now huh?" Garry said before turning to his master. "Hey boss, if you could do this anytime, why didn't you do this earlier? I would think in that form you'd be unbeatable!"

Deathwalker did not take his eyes off the red dragon as he waved his other arm and answered his familiar. “As you can see by all the felled trees, this form is a bit unwieldy and not exactly subtle. Plus, how I use magic in this form is a bit different, so I remain in my humanoid form. Easier to blend in too.”

“Yea, but boss, look at you! I can see the beasts in the distance running for the hills. You should definitely use this form more often.” Garry retorted.

“I’ll consider it my friend. I would need to enchant some clothing to shift with me. Luckily, I got out of my trousers and the rest of my clothes before changing.” Deathwalker answered.

“Yea but I don’t think the cat girls would mind you stripping before transforming.” Garry commented.

“No, we do not mind at all!” Frrsha called out.

“Fair enough.” Deathwalker said before turning all his attention to the red dragon in his hand. ‘Is it a hand or claw or claws? Ah, no matter.’

“Now what is your name dragon?”

“D-draconis your majesty!” Draconis stuttered.

“Not very original at all.” Garry teased.

“Hey! I was named after my father, and his father before him, you ignorant little...” Draconis replied with indignation.

Deathwalker squeezed just a bit.

“My apologies for the insult to your ally, my ancient majesty.” Draconis wheezed out.

Garry just looked at the red dragon with a smug look on his face, then stuck out his tongue.

Deathwalker spoke up. “He is my familiar. That is the second time you have called me ‘majesty’. Why is that?”

"Your aura and race... it must be what I sensed when I first laid my eyes upon you. Something told me down to my very bones not to attack you. That to do so would be wrong and the highest violation of dragon law. Now that you have taken your true form and released your aura, I understand what that feeling was. All dragons possess genetic memories passed down through our bloodlines. Every dragon knows Omni-dragons are the royalty to our kind. An ancient Omni-dragon must be venerated. May I know your name your name, your Majesty?" Draconis explained.

Sensing no killing intent from the dragon, he put the red dragon back down. "You may call me, Deathwalker."

Draconis bowed as low as he could. "Oh, ancient Deathwalker. I give my oath and pledge myself to you always! Please accept me as one of your retinue. I swear to serve you faithfully and loyally for now and eternity!"

Deathwalker accepted the oath and mentally swiped away the notification. He was just about to dismiss the next notification when it asked for his input. In all of the notifications he received this was the first to ask for his choice and not allow him to minimize it. Selection made, a new notification trumpeted in his mind and in the minds of everyone in Timberfall Duchy and the Kingdom of Nord.

***Hark and rejoice! Duke Deathwalker Dragonvein has resolved the kingdom-wide threat from an Adult Red Dragon! The details and nature of how he accomplished such a legendary feat are sealed by the System! Only a Hero can resolve a dragon threat. Deathwalker is granted the Title of Hero!***

Deathwalker immediately received another notification.

*Congratulations! You chose to spare this dragon and take him into your retinue. This is the first step to claiming your rightful place as dragon royalty and establishing your own dragon wing. Your ancient Royal bloodlines are pleased! You have won the Title **Hero & Emperor of Dragons**! This title shall be hidden and only visible to dragon-kind and those you choose to share it with.*

***Title: Hero & Emperor of Dragons***

***Description: You are not only seen as dragon royalty, but also now seen as their salvation. Dragons cannot attack or do you harm. Any magic or compulsion on a dragon will be automatically broken and overridden. Reputation with dragon kin starts positive. All reputation gains with dragons increased by 1000%. You are meant to lead and save dragon kind, bear that burden well!***

"Wow! That's some title! It is all bold and everything! Of all my titles that literally might be my favorite." Deathwalker exclaimed after reading it.

His whole life he loved dragons and now this title helped him with any future dragons he would encounter and work with. It was like a dream come true. Deathwalker knew it was a critical responsibility and he would treat it as such, but he just couldn't wipe the grin off his face.

Shifting back to his humanoid form, Deathwalker asked, "Do you know how to polymorph or shift into humanoid form? If you plan to stand by my side, you will have to blend in as I do."

"Uh, boss, I don't think you exactly blend in. I mean you kind of standout..." Garry began before Deathwalker cut him off. "You know what I mean."

"Yes, your majesty. I can take humanoid form. If it pleases you, I will take form now." Draconis replied.

Deathwalker just waved his hand in a motion that said get on with it.

Without further delay, Draconis wrapped himself in magic and wove his spell. He quickly shrunk down to a tall human kneeling. The man had broad shoulders, red hair, and a dark red and black outfit.

"How is this your majesty?"

Deathwalker clasped wrists with Draconis and hauled him to his feet. "That looks great but around other humans you will need to call me something other than majesty."

"But that is what you are! I would not dare insult you, your majesty by calling you something else." Draconis said in shock.

"They do not see me as their majesty. They call me Duke, Grace, or Deathwalker. The girls call me Alpha. Garry calls me boss or master."

"Master would be most appropriate if I cannot call you Majesty." Draconis said as he bowed at the waist.

"Fine, fine. Now let's talk about humans and other humanoid races. You cannot just kill them for any small slight you might think they make." Deathwalker explained.

"Surely, you are jesting with me, master. What punishment can I really dish out?" Draconis questioned.

Garry sighed. "No, it's sad but true."

Draconis had a new look of horror on his face.

"But sometimes the boss does let us unleash the pain!" Garry chimed in.

"I knew it! Good one your majesty, you almost had me!"

Deathwalker groaned. 'This is going to take a while.'

# Chapter 18 - DRACONIS!!!

The Savage Squad walked back into Timberfall, able to circumvent the line of people either fleeing the lands of the Proletariat or arriving for the upcoming festival.

"You have returned Duke Dragonvein!" Sergeant Chen exclaimed when he saw the high noble bypass the line.

"That's the Duke? He doesn't look like much." Carn commented under his breath.

Sadly, Carn was not quite quiet enough. Draconis immediately acted. Lightning-fast, he was in front of Carn, his hand around his throat and squeezing.

"You dare disrespect my master and your liege!"

"Oooo! Oooo! Squeeze his neck harder buddy! Let's see if you can literally make his head pop off! Oh yea, let's definitely try that! I've never seen someone's head pop, let's see how far you can get it to fly!"

"With pleasure!" Draconis growled out.

"We're going to see his head pop off! Te-hee! We're going to see his head pop off! Te-hee! Te-hee!" Garry cheered as the guard's face turned from red to purple.

"That is enough Draconis. Release him." Deathwalker ordered.

The dragon in humanoid form did as commanded and instantly released the man and wiped his hand on his coat. "Such filth."

"Awe! Just when things were getting interesting!" Garry groaned.

Carn dropped to the ground as he gasped and coughed for air. "Cough.

Sergeant Chen was right beside him. "P-please forgive my subordinate's rude behavior sire."

Draconis knelt and stared daggers at the guard still gasping for air. "If I ever hear you disrespect my master again, I'll make sure he's not around to stop me next time." The tall, well-dressed, redheaded man stood up and reassumed his position behind Duke Dragonvein.

With a flash of light Deathwalker cast a minor healing spell on the man to help the guard's recovery. "Hopefully that will help your subordinate, Sergeant."

"Thank you, your grace." Sergeant Chen bowed.

Annoyed by the confrontation, but refusing to reprimand Draconis for what could be seen as dealing with a matter of disrespect, Deathwalker just walked past and headed for his manor.

Once the Duke and his guards left the area, Belinda rushed to her brother. "Are you okay brother?!"

Sergeant Chen spoke up before Carn could reply. "That was foolish! You risked much all to express a minor insult. You must be more cautious if you want to survive this assignment."

"U-understood." Carn wheezed out.

"Who was that with him? His aura gave off a clear power. I could barely track how fast he moved." Belinda said.

"I do not know. I have never seen him before. The fact that he called the duke 'master' adds another wrinkle into our plans. It is clear the high noble is only a healer, so he will not be a problem, but this new player... we must find a way to take him out or distract him long enough for it not to matter." Sergeant Chen whispered.

———-

"Master, why did you not want me to kill that worthless trash? He insulted you!" Draconis inquired.

"They are merely words, my apprentice. Where I come from, we had sage wisdom we lived by, a mantra if you will. 'Sticks and stones may break my bones, but words will never hurt me." Deathwalker replied.

"Sticks cannot break my bones, heck the stones would have to be massive." Draconis commented.

"That's what she said! He, he, he, he!" Garry retorted.

Deathwalker just shook his head. "No, I agree our bones are stronger than such things. The point was to let insults fall off you. They are meaningless. What does some random soldier know of what we are capable of? Besides, people must be free to speak their mind, even if, no, especially if it is something you may not like. We only grow stronger that way. I want those under my command to feel free to speak their minds. Sure, he did it in an inappropriate way, but I'm sure he sees me as many do, some stuck up noble."

"Are you upset with me master?"

"Not at all. I appreciate you sticking up for me and taking swift action. Just remember that many do not think as we do, give them time. Focus on their actions and not their words." Deathwalker answered.

"That is good you are not upset with Draconis as I wanted to rip that loud mouth's throat out." Prrsha commented.

"So glad I wasn't the only one." Garry chimed in.

"Heck, I wanted to smack the idiot but that doesn't serve me in the long run. Come, we should check in and see if our guests have arrived."

————-

"Your grace, you have returned! Oh, thank the Light!" Geeves practically swelled with relief.

"Has it been that bad?" Deathwalker asked.

"No, your grace. It is just I am not accustomed to hosting foreign royalty and so many high nobles."

"Do you need us to kill somebody?" Garry asked.

"Ah, I see you have returned with your familiar, sire. No Sir Garry, that will not be necessary. In fact, please do not do that." Geeves quickly replied.

"Remember, we talked about this Garry. Killing guests is bad. You only kill them if they try to kill you first." Deathwalker chimed in.

Geeves greeted the others. “It is good to see Ms. Mrrsha, Prrsha, and Frrsha... and it appears you have a new associate.”

“Yes. This is Draconis, my new apprentice. He is not familiar with kingdom protocols so please make allowances Geeves.”

“Of course, your grace. It would be my honor to help instruct Mr. Draconis in our traditions.” Geeves bowed.

“If master requires it, I will do so." Draconis replied.

Deathwalker clapped his hands together to draw attention away from how uncomfortable his apprentice appeared. “Excellent! Why don’t you lead us to our new guests Geeves.”

“Right this way, your grace.” Geeves said as he guided them from the back room into the dining hall where their guests were having a meal.

King Alfheim had brought with him one of his chefs. With Mezza on the journey with Grimhold to entreaty with the dwarves, Deathwalker was without her amazing cooking. The elven king offered his chef as a thank you to their host while Deathwalker’s cook was on a special assignment. Luckily, the elves were not vegetarian, he wasn’t sure he could stomach the lack of meat. His body had come to crave meat, so vegetarian dishes were not an option for him.

The people sitting at the dining table all rose to their feet when Deathwalker and his retinue entered the room.

“Do not get up on my account.” Deathwalker waved them down.

“Nonsense. I for one have looked forward to this meeting Duke Dragonvein.” King Alfheim said as he made his way to Deathwalker.

The men clasped wrists. “Thank you for opening your home to us.”

Seeing Elder Martha present and approaching Deathwalker. “It is also Elder Martha’s home too, at least until her mansion is built. I was glad she could receive you in my absence.”

“Ah yes, she and your seneschal Geeves have been most gracious hosts.” King Alfheim said as they released each other’s arms.

Elder Martha used that opportunity to lean in close to Deathwalker. “You owe me so big for this.”

“I thought appointing you over the city would be enough payment.” Deathwalker whispered.

“Fair point. Fine, you are building me a mansion too.” Elder Martha teased.

“Let me introduce you to my retinue. This is Advisor Mona, Advisor Nero, and General Mineheir. You already know my daughter Duchess Lightheart and my granddaughter Lady Emma.” King Alfheim moved his hand to each person.

Advisor Mona stared at Deathwalker, so intensely, he felt a bit violated. He decided to introduce his own retinue. “This is Mrrsha, Prrsha, Frrsha, and my apprentice Draconis.”

“That’s an awfully interesting name, Draconis.” General Mineheir scrutinized the red-haired man.

“Hey what about me boss?!” Garry commented.

“Ah yes, this is my Shadow Gazer familiar Garry. If you are not already aware, Shadow Gazers tend to be very aggressive and prone to violence. Please keep that in mind as he talks.” Deathwalker explained.

“Yea we mostly ignore him.” Mrrsha chimed in.

“Hey!” Garry protested.

“He is good in a fight though.” Deathwalker spoke up for his familiar.

“Awe, thanks boss!”

“That is why you have a pet or familiar is it not, for battle!” General Mineheir had a tear in his eye. “That is why I raised my favorite horse, to ride into battle...sniff... now she is gone...”

“Ahhh, not this again! Give it up man! The horse is gone!” Advisor Nero said in exasperation.

The Savage Squad looked at the two men in confusion. Seeing their confused looks, King Alfheim added context. “My escort convoy was attacked by an Adult Red Dragon. Before it flew off, it snatched up General Mineheir’s prized horse.”

“Like a thief!” General Mineheir exclaimed.

“Errrr.” Draconis started to let out a low growl at the general’s comment.

General Mineheir approached Draconis and put his hand on the man’s shoulder. “Yes, the thought makes me growl too!”

Draconis was appalled at this elf daring to put his hand on him. He was about to reach up and forcibly remove the offending appendage, both from his shoulder and the elf’s body. As he raised his hand, Deathwalker placed his own hand on Draconis’ other shoulder.

“We are sorry for your loss General. Aren’t we apprentice?” Deathwalker squeezed as he said the last few words.

Getting the hint, Draconis dropped his arm and put a smile on his face. “I am sure General Mineheir that such a prized horse was a very tasty meal for said dragon.”

“Draconis!” Mrrsha chided.

The elven general looked more confused than angry.

“I merely mean that I am sure the dragon appreciated the honor of eating such a prized animal.” Draconis tried to clarify.

General Mineheir dropped his hand from his shoulder, but Deathwalker kept his firmly affixed. There was a light in the elf’s eyes.

“You are right about that Draconis. I appreciate that perspective.” General Mineheir replied before his voice took on a dangerous tone. “But if I ever meet that dragon again, I will bury my blade right where the sun does not shine!”

"Ha! He sounds like Garry." Prrsha commented.

Mrrsha sensing the rising tension decided to help change the subject. "Perhaps the general would like to spar later, help release some of that frustration. I am sure Garry would enjoy it and would welcome the chance to do so as well."

"I'm always up for a fight." Garry gave a wicked grin.

"Less creepy Garry." Deathwalker said to his familiar before turning to the cat girl. "Though I think that is a great suggestion Mrrsha. How about it General? Would you be up to demonstrating some of your skills? It appears some of my bodyguards would welcome the chance to spar with your esteemed self."

General Mineheir smiled. "Ah yes! That would be fun. I appreciate the offer, Duke Dragonvein. Perhaps I do need to work off some of this hurt I feel."

"Hey that's my motto, work out your frustration by beating the crap out of something." Garry chimed in.

General Mineheir stroked his chin with his thumb and forefinger in giving the Shadow Gazer's words some thought. "You know, I rather like that motto Mr. Garry. Pretty good motto indeed. Come, let us go out back and get ready to spar."

Garry turned to Deathwalker with an eager look in his eyes. "I like this guy, he appreciates me! Can I go have fun flinging him around?"

"Fine. Limit your telekinesis use. Got it?"

Garry did a weird bob in the air to signify he understood before he and the elven general left the room. Prrsha and Mrrsha followed right behind the two. Advisor Mona's interest seemed to have peaked. "If you will excuse me your majesty. I wish to see the magic the duke's Shadow Gazer uses."

After she left, King Alfheim spoke up as he watched her go. "Hmmm. I have never seen her so interested. Perhaps as old as the fey woman has been alive it is a bit of a novelty to see something new." Turning to Deathwalker, "If you are open to it Deathwalker, there are some matters I would like to speak to you alone about."

"Father! I do not approve!" Duchess Lightheart immediately protested.

"Yes, I agree with auntie! We are representatives of the Kingdom of Nord. We should be present in any diplomatic discussions." Lady Emma chimed in.

As they were near him, King Alfheim patted their hands gently. "It is my prerogative to talk to my host without others present. I assure you two I will not make any demands of the Kingdom of Nord or conduct any kingdom level diplomatic negotiations without you both present. Now would you please humor this old man?"

Both women nodded in defeat.

Elder Martha stepped in. "If the Crown Princess and Duchess would like to take a tour of the gardens and see the rest of the grounds, I would be happy to show you around."

"That would be most appreciated honored elder." Duchess Lightheart and Lady Emma both replied.

"Geeves, would you take Advisor Nero to the parlor so he may relax." Deathwalker instructed.

"As you command your grace. If you would follow me Advisor Nero." Geeves waved in the direction of the door.

Advisor Nero took one final look at his king. Receiving a head nod, the man let Geeves guide him out of the room.

"Frrsha, go check on your sisters. Draconis, go with her. Remember the general is our guest." Deathwalker said the last part while staring at Draconis.

The message was clear, restrain yourself and do not cause permanent harm or break any guest rights. Draconis visibly gulped at the intensity of his master's glare before quickly exiting the room.

Frrsha just gave Deathwalker one last look before she too left.

Taking a seat by King Alfheim, Deathwalker waited for the elven man to start the conversation.

"I find myself conflicted on where to start, but perhaps it is best to start where I am most concerned... You healed my granddaughter, allowing her to be eligible to be my successor. This could unite our two kingdoms, that is, if my people accept her."

"They would not? Is that because she is half human?" Deathwalker inquired.

"That is part of it, but not the primary. She is an unknown entity to my people. Sadly, this is my own fault as I could not formally acknowledge her without her having access to magic."

"I hope you do not mind me asking why that is." Deathwalker asked.

"Like dragons, our kind are a part of magic. To be without it or weak in it would be the equivalent of denying who and what we are. Elves live long lives and have strong ties to the winter fey of our origin. As such to choose a successor out of love and not power, they would see it as a slap to our fey allies and our origin. Emotion is not our strong suit, at least not in public. General Mineheir has a rare summer fey origin, which is why he is more emotional than some of my other kind." King Alfheim explained.

"Why is that so rare?" Deathwalker inquired.

"Simple. The summer fey are not as common in this realm, more of winter settled in the north and in this realm after the great cosmic war when they were kicked out of Avalon. Most of the summer fey in this world are more south from here in warmer climates. My friend Mineheir's family migrated to be with other elves, and he has proven himself with his battle prowess. And that brings me back to the point, whomever I did choose to lead must exemplify magic itself. Queen Mab will accept nothing less." King Alfheim explained.

"Does she have that much sway in your kingdom?"

"Of course. Crossing the Winter Queen is a fool's errand. Her power is absolute in the north and as you can see with Advisor Mona, she has eyes and ears everywhere. But it is not as bad as it might sound. Our nation has been rather sheltered from much of the turmoil within the more human nations in the south." King Alfheim answered.

"Interesting."

"Now, my granddaughter has said you are open to teaching her how to master her different types of magic, is that true? And more importantly, what are your intentions with her and my daughter?" King Alfheim pressed.

Deathwalker rubbed the back of his neck. "That is a loaded question. Your two daughters have made it clear that they expect me to bind myself in marriage to this kingdom. Beyond that, I am more interested in helping the people in general and it is clear my obligations are many."

"Why is it my daughters and my son in law are so adamant about you marrying into the family? They would not exactly say, which tells me an agreement was reached. And I know of only one thing that would drive them to do so, royal blood." King Alfheim hypothesized.

"Yes, I do have royal blood. To answer your other question, I am very willing to help Lady Emma grow her magic capabilities. I am very fond of your family from the interactions I have had. I find them most honorable with a strong sense of duty and commitment to their people." Deathwalker answered.

"You are most kind Duke Dragonvein."

"Please call me Deathwalker."

"Very well, Deathwalker. With that important family and state business addressed for now, let us shift to another question."

"What would you like to know." Deathwalker asked.

"What would it take for you to build me one of those portal stations? It would dramatically change our trade options and more importantly I could see my daughters and granddaughter far more often." King Alfheim inquired.

"I can have Trader Malcom provide your people with a list of materials to acquire. He can also arrange for some of my men to journey to your capital to build it. Sadly, I must go to the location to do the final touches and connect it to the network. However, that will also allow me to configure the security and controls for your use. I am quite surprised you would be so trusting to have such a thing built in your country." Deathwalker answered.

"That is simple, my daughters are excellent judges of character, and you did get system acknowledgement as a hero after you resolved the dragon issue. By the way, expect Mineheir to inquire what he can. As you saw, he was very upset to lose his favorite horse. He would rather enjoy hearing of any suffering inflicted." King Alfheim replied.

Deathwalker chuckled. "He, he, he, he, he. Yea, it was very clear he loved that horse."

"You have no idea." King Alfheim said in exasperation.

"Yikes. Well, is there any other matters you wish to discuss?"

King Alfheim smiled. "You risked and revealed much healing my granddaughter and teaching her those spells."

Deathwalker raised an eyebrow. "How so?"

"Simple. It revealed you are a Master of a Place of Power, one that is over multiple magic types. Your level is too low to be a master mage, so the only possibility is owning a Place of Power with at least four different magic types." King Alfheim smiled.

Deathwalker realized his mistake. His **Hide in Plain Sight** showed his level much lower than it actually was. This is the same thing that led Lady Emma to the same conclusion. It was dangerous knowledge to have out there but they did not know the details and that was what was most important.

"You are correct, but I will say no more than that."

King Alfheim nodded. "That is understandable. I only bring it up as a fellow owner of a place of power, Emma will hopefully inherit."

"I'll help her as best I can. There is something you can do for me though." Deathwalker replied.

"Oh, what is that?" King Alfheim asked.

"I sent my friend and party member Grimhold and my cook Mezza to your lands. If you could see them safely pass through your nation, I would appreciate it."

"Oh really? I would be more than happy to send word. Will you share why are they traveling through my lands?" King inquired.

Deathwalker nodded. "Grimhold and Mezza are dwarves. I sent them to negotiate on my behalf with the Dwarven king to open trade and hopefully more in the future."

King Alfheim's eyebrows rose. "The dwarves tend to keep to themselves. They trade with my nation as the main exit from their mountain kingdom enters my lands. I doubt an agreement will be reached, but I can see your people safely there."

"Thank you, King Alfheim. If that is all you wished to discuss, would you like to go see how the sparing is going?" Deathwalker replied.

"That sounds quite entertaining." King Alfheim said more under his breath, "It has to be if it caught Advisor Mona's attention."

# Interlude - Grimhold & Mezza

CRUNCH!

The Forest Wolf's skull caved in from Grimhold's warhammer. The dwarven defender spun and hit another Forest Wolf in the side sending it off course from its attack on Mezza.

"Thank you Grimmy!" Mezza thanked as she cut a big gash in the third Forest Wolf's face with her butcher's knife.

YIP!

The third Forest Wolf's head reeled back and up from the pain, leaving its throat exposed. Mezza took the opportunity to use her other blade to slice the beast's throat open. Another quick slice on its two front legs dropped the canine to the road floor, dead a moment after.

The second Forest Wolf, seeing its two pack mates dead, took off back into the forest that butted up against the main road to the Elven nation. The two dwarves listened and waited for any reinforcements. When none came, they both let out a breath.

"I do not know how you live like this Grimmy, always looking over your shoulder for a monster to attack."

"No different than dealing with nobles and people. This is just more direct. Plus, I like the sound they make when they go crunch under my hammer! Ha!"

Mezza stowed her blades and drew her skinning knife. "I guess that be true. We will eat well tonight and for a few days once I skin and butcher these two."

"You are very impressive with those blades, Mezza. Nice to know such a capable woman has my back."

Mezza beamed back at him. "Oh Grimmy! You know just what to say to a woman."

"Here. Let me help you skin those two. I may not be as good as Deathwalker, but my Skinning skill is decent."

Mezza had a curious look on her face. "Deathwalker skinned? I thought he was a healer."

Grimhold laughed. "Ha, ha, ha, ha, ha! Deathwalker is far more than a healer. The man hides his strength, but he is a powerful mage and I imagine much more than that."

"What do you mean?" Mezza asked.

"Well for starters he repaired and improved my mithril armor, so his Smithing skill is rather high to do such a feat. Then there is the fact that he would dress all our kills and was damn good at it. Then there is his cookin..."

"His cookin?" Mezza interrupted.

"Aye lass. His cookin is only second to you, my love. Before I had yer food, it was some of the most flavorful meals I ever had and made things I never heard of before." Grimhold explained.

Mezza sat there for a minute. "I will have to have a chat with him when we get back. He showed me the bacon recipe, but had I known he knew other dishes I would be mining his brain for more."

"Aye, that sounds like a good idea when we return."

The two dwarves fell into a companionable silence as they continued to butcher and dress their kills. Mezza was far more skilled at this endeavor than Grimhold and finished before he did. While she waited for him to finish, she asked him another question. "Grimmy, why do you think he hides his strength? I mean I would understand if he was trying to lay low, but he is the talk of the kingdom."

Grimhold thought a moment before answering. "I do not think he wanted the responsibility he is saddled with. I truly think he just wanted to be an adventurer, but he had to step up to deal with Darrien's betrayal..."

Mezza spat to the side upon hearing her old employer's name. "He was the worst!"

Grimhold nodded before continuing. "What I do know is the man is not one to shy away from his duty. He has saved my life multiple times over in such a short period of time." Grimhold got lost in thought for a moment. "Deathwalker was willing to sacrifice himself to give Timberfall town, now turned city, a chance to survive. I would follow him anywhere and travel to the ends of the continent if he asked me to."

Grimhold had finished dressing his kill. Mezza took his hand in Her's and pulled them to her chest. "I like him too. He is a good man, and he brought me you."

Grimhold smiled and leaned in to kiss her. As he did, he thought to himself, 'This is another thing I be thankful for. His insistence on Mezza coming with me. Now I get to have moments like this, and I will get to introduce her to my family and get their blessing.'

# Interlude - Belinda and Carn

"What now?" Carn groaned.

Sergeant Chen had entered his office with a sour look on his face. "Those damnable dwarves! I reached out to contacts we have in some of the other major trading hubs. None have spotted where they disappeared to!"

"Can we get access to this portal hub we keep hearing about?" Belinda asked.

"No. My unit is not allowed access to the facility, and it is guarded by men loyal to General Marius. Commander Willis and us guards are responsible for the rest of the city." Chen explained.

"How important can two dwarves be?" Carn replied.

"Exactly. If it was an important mission, he would have sent more than two people." Belinda chimed in.

"Our General Marks only sent you two." Sergeant Chen quipped.

"That is different. First off, you and the others are here so it is more than two. Second, they are dwarves. They tend to stick to themselves and seem to only care about mining and smithing." Belinda countered.

"Perhaps. What worries me is that they disappeared. Such a thing is risk I would rather not have." Chen replied.

"Which hub do we have the fewest spies?" Carn asked, already knowing the answer.

"That's easy, Hargrave, but you already know that brother." Belinda answered before it clicked for her. "Ah. I see what you are getting at. They most likely ended up in Hargrave."

"If that is true, why? They left before the visiting dignitaries arrived. If it was to deliver a message, why have they not retuned?" Chen chimed in.

"Good question, but not one we can answer at this time. Hargrave is a trading hub for those damn elves and even some dwarves. For all we know they are traveling through the elven nation to get to the dwarves in the mountains." Carn theorized.

"But to what end? The elf king is here, and the dwarves are not known to care about much." Chen asked.

"Perhaps it is a personal matter. If so, we do not care." Belinda suggested.

"Personal matter?" Chen asked.

"Yes. It is my understanding that dwarves take courting very seriously. Maybe they are going back to get their families' blessings." Belinda replied.

"How would you know about that sister?" Carn inquired.

"What? I do have interests other than the cause. Courting rituals have always fascinated me, especially ones where their family is involved." Belinda answered.

"We do not have family beyond ourselves, the general, and our cause." Carn admonished.

"I believe we will achieve our goals, then what?" Belinda countered.

Carn looked confused and uncertain.

Sergeant Chen just rolled his eyes. 'Ah youth. They think things will happen so quickly. They have no idea.' To them he said, "Let us focus on the matters at hand. Without knowing where the dwarves are we will have to put them out of our minds for now. Next is the determination of which council members we are to target."

"That is easy. General Marks said to target Betterman and Elder Martha." Belinda stated.

Chen spoke up. “Elder Martha, I get, especially as she is now the noble over this city. Why Betterman and not the others?”

“The general heard about Betterman’s granddaughter. He will use her to break the man. With him and Elder Martha out of the way, the others will roll over.” Belinda explained.

Chen thought about the plan. “Ron only seems to care about his craft. Paul and Clarisse aren’t fighters, and they seem to have a soft spot for the refugees. Samuel may be a problem though. His is respected by many of the lumber workers.”

“Hmmm. If that is the case, we may have to find a way to neutralize him.” Carn commented.

“Leave that to me.” Chen replied.

“What is it you have planned?” Belinda asked.

Chen smiled back. “Bar brawls are not unheard of. It should be a simple enough matter to have a stray blade ‘accidentally’ kill our beloved tavern owner.”

# Chapter 19 - Learning Something New

SLAM!

"Ugh! T-that... was... an impressive counterattack." General Mineheir coughed out as he got to his feet and dusted himself off.

Deathwalker and King Alfheim entered the courtyard right as Draconis slammed General Mineheir into the ground. The elven general had a huge grin on his face, clearly having fun sparing with the redheaded man.

Not too far from that fight, Frrsha and Prrsha were sparing. Their spar was just as brutal. It was just as evident the two ladies were enjoying themselves.

The king's two advisors and Mrrsha were standing on the sidelines watching. Deathwalker and King Alfheim approached the spectators.

"Who is winning?" Deathwalker asked.

"Prrsha and Frrsha are evenly matched, so it is difficult to say. If I had to choose, I would say Prrsha." Mrrsha replied.

"Yea! It's so hot!" Garry chimed in mentally as he appeared from the shadows.

"Why are you over there?" Deathwalker asked.

Garry pointed one of his eyestalks at Advisor Mona. "It's that fey woman. When she stares at me it is like she is looking through me. It's super creepy!"

Deathwalker just shook his head and turned back to Mrrsha. "And what about my apprentice?"

Mrrsha and Garry chuckled.

Advisor Mona spoke up. “The red-haired one is mopping the floor with the blowhard youngling.”

“Youngling? Mineheir is 200 years old.” Advisor Nero countered.

The fey woman waved the elven advisor off. “It is odd though.”

“Odd?” King Alfheim asked.

“Yes. It is as if the red-haired brute is improving as the fight goes on. Almost like he is getting comfortable with his body, that or learning to fight as time passes.” Mona replied without taking her eyes off the scene.

Advisor Nero pipped up. “I do not agree with Mona’s theory your majesty. I believe the man is just toying with Mineheir, increasing the amount skill used as the fight goes on.”

Deathwalker chuckled as he reached out mentally. “You’re using him as a training dummy, aren’t you?”

Draconis gave the slightest of a shoulder shrug. He then sped up just enough to get inside the elf’s guard and elbow him in the solar plexus. “What? This is great practice. I am still not used to this form. I feel so small.”

“That’s what she said! Ha, ha, ha, ha!” Garry chimed in over the mental conversation.

“No, Garry, I said it, not one of the girls. Are you feeling alright?” Draconis mentally replied.

“No... it is a... oh never mind!” Garry said in exasperation before asking Deathwalker, “how do you not go crazy?”

“Huh?”

“No body but you get my references. How do you not get frustrated?” Garry replied.

“Oh that. Well, it is rather simple, that is why I have you buddy.” Deathwalker answered.

“Awe, boss!”

“Is that why you keep him around?” Prrsha mentally asked.

Frrsha used the momentary distraction to flip Prrsha. “You still are not used to speaking telepathically and doing other things sister.”

Prrsha growled, but otherwise did not respond beyond increasing the ferocity of her attacks. This caught the elven king’s notice.

“Your bodyguards are most impressive.” King Alfheim commented.

“Yes, they are quite fierce. Some of the most impressive specimens of beastkin I have ever seen.” Advisor Nero chimed in.

“They are not beastkin you blind oaf. They are shifters, powerful ones at that.” Advisor Mona chided.

Mrrsha immediately froze and Deathwalker tensed up. ‘Does she have some kind of skill like my **Insight**? She has to if she was able to identify their race.’

“Interesting.” Advisor Nero replied.

“Interesting indeed. They look just like beastkin.” King Alfheim said as he studied the two cat girls fighting.

“That is one of their forms. I usually do not share such information with others, but we are allies.” Deathwalker explained.

With her alpha sharing that tidbit, Mrrsha visibly relaxed. If her alpha was okay sharing that then she had nothing to concern herself with.

“I hope we can become close allies in the future. After all you will be marrying into my family.” King Alfheim grinned mischievously at Deathwalker.

Doing everything Deathwalker could to steer the conversation away from the subject of matrimony, he asked about elven magic. "From what I have heard most elves tend to have affinities with Water and Air, is that true?"

King Alfheim did not lose his smile. "Good attempt at changing the subject. To answer your question, most elves in the north are aligned with those affinities due to the Winter fey of our heritage. There are some wood elves down south that have more Earth and Fire affinities. They also have a higher disposition to nature than some of my people. We high elves tend to be even more magically inclined than some of our wood elf brethren."

"I thought I saw General Mineheir using Fire magic." Deathwalker commented.

"Yes, you did. Mineheir's family are from the southern wood elf tribe with Summer fey heritage. Currently, he is limiting his magic to body strengthening and melee range to avoid damaging your manor courtyard." King Alfheim explained.

It was Deathwalker's turn to smile. "I had some runes carved into various locations throughout the grounds. As long as he does not use Grand Scale magic the courtyard should be fine."

"Grand Scale magic?!" Advisor Nero exclaimed.

"How interesting." Advisor Mona said as she shifted her attention from watching the fighting to scrutinizing the grounds.

"Such magical formations would have to be Grand Scale or be powered by a magic core." Advisor Nero commented.

"It could be powered by a place of power." Advisor Mona chimed in as she stared intently at Deathwalker.

Ignoring the fey's glare, Deathwalker called out to General Mineheir. "By all means general, do not hold back."

General Mineheir did not have to be told twice. He charged two Fireball spells, once in each hand. This was his signature move in battle. It was rare for someone to survive one fireball let alone two.

"BURN!" Mineheir yelled as he sent both attacks right at Draconis.

BOOM! BOOM!

"If you killed our host's apprentice, I will be most upset with you Mineheir!" King Alfheim admonished.

"B-but... your majesty... the duke said it was okay." Mineheir defended.

Advisor Mona cast a quick wind spell to clear the sparring area. She wanted to see what was left of the apprentice. As the dust and smoke cleared Draconis was standing there whole and undamaged.

Draconis used his hand to brush off some dust from his outfit. "Not bad, but you will have to do much better than that if you wish to defeat me."

General Mineheir's face went from shock to a wide grin. He covered his hands and feet in flames and charged. "With pleasure!"

Deathwalker knew the Red Dragon was immune to fire damage, but he would have to ask Draconis how he mitigated the blast damage from the two spells. The rest of his guests were far more phased by this outcome than the duke. King Alfheim was the first to speak up. "Was his survival his doing or the wards you have in place?"

"A bit of both." Deathwalker replied.

"Most impressive on both counts." Advisor Nero commented.

Advisor Mona did not say anything. She just filed that information away for later. It had been several centuries since she had this much to report to her queen.

# Interlude - Alyce & Elsa

"Did you hear? Pa said royalty is in town." Elsa shared.

Alyce nodded. "Yea. I heard. The king of the elves and Lady Emma. She is a princess you know."

"Of course, I know silly. Heir to the throne. Once a princess always a princess." Elsa replied.

"I wonder what it would be like to be a princess." Alyce said her thoughts out loud.

"Eh, I think I'd rather be the ice queen myself." Elsa stated.

"You mean the Winter queen of the fey? Careful saying such things. Grandfather says the fey have ears everywhere." Alyce warned.

"That is what I mean. A princess is required to go to a bunch of balls and dance all night, heck they are probably so dainty, they even wear glass shoes. A queen should be above all that." Elsa theorized.

"I think a queen has it harder. She must deal with a bunch of nobles." Alyce countered.

Elsa shuddered. "Nobles, yuck!"

Alyce agreed. "It is so nice catching up with you, my friend. We should try to find more time to do this."

Elsa smiled and nodded her head. "Absolutely! So, what else have you heard?"

"Oh, not much..." Alyce smiled. "Mom said they recruited extra adventurers to help with security for the festival. Guess a bunch of nobles are coming too." Alyce commented.

"Ugh. Stuck up nobles. Definitely not something we need more of here." Elsa complained.

"They are not all bad. Deathwalker is the kindest man... and those two-color eyes of his, it's like he is staring deep into your soul." Alyce said dreamily.

"Yea, he is different than any other noble I have seen. You can tell. Pa says it's the way he carries himself, whatever that means." Elsa replied.

"Well, whatever it is, he makes a point to greet me when he sees me and is always so kind and respectful. You can tell he genuinely cares." Alyce smiled.

"Did you hear about what happened in the refugee camp?" Elsa asked.

Alyce nodded. "He healed and fed all those people! Deathwalker is so amazing!"

"I heard he ordered Elder Martha to schedule routine patrols through the camp with healers to check on the overall health of the refugees. It is going to take some time for them to get on their feet." Elsa chimed in.

"Grandfather said Deathwalker also ordered Elder Martha to offer them work opportunities in the various construction projects going on in the city." Alyce shared.

"Yea with our new walls the boundaries of Timberfall have grown significantly. Pa said he thinks the city will become a trading hub. All thanks to Deathwalker's efforts." Elsa commented.

"Yea grandfather is so excited. We have gotten more business in the shoppe lately. My hands are sore from all the rush orders we received." Alyce stretched her fingers.

"Oh, I heard someone new is hanging around the duke. Have you seen anything?" Elsa asked.

Alyce nodded her head. "Deathwalker took on a new apprentice. A well-built man with red hair. I saw him recently when he walked into the Adventurers' guild."

"Really?"

"Yea. Deathwalker brought him in to be registered as an adventurer. Said his name was Draconis." Alyce answered.

"What an interesting name. I feel like I have heard it before." Elsa tapped her index finger on her chin as she tried to recall where she heard the name before.

"Mom let me watch the testing. Draconis trounced Darrius rather well. And I do not mean just beat him. He knocked the Guildmaster around like a rag doll." Alyce explained.

"Wow! Darrius is super strong! If this red-headed man was able to accomplish that with the guildmaster, the guy must be very strong!" Elsa said in awe.

Alyce nodded in agreement. "Yea. It makes sense why Deathwalker picked him as an apprentice."

The two girls chatted and gossiped about the various things they heard going on. In the end their conversations still gravitated towards the ruler of the duchy. It was clear to anyone who talked to the two teenagers that they both were rather smitten with their innocent crush.

# Interlude - Elven Border

“There is the checkpoint Grimmy! Wow! I have never seen anything like that. Is the structure growing out of the ground?” Mezza asked in wonder.

“Aye lass. The elves with Life affinity worked with some shapers to grow this guard post from the surrounding trees. I was just as impressed as you are now when I first saw it.” Grimhold answered.

Mezza looked back at her betrothed. “Really? Why did ya leave the mountains? Ya never told me.”

“Family.”

Mezza just stared at Grimhold until he explained further. “My family is big on personal achievement. Hard to do that if ya stay inside the mountains. Sure, a dwarf could fight the monsters deep in the earth, and I did that for a time... but the life of adventure called to me.”

“So, you left home.” Mezza stated more than asked.

“Aye. A few of us did. We came to Nord in the hopes of joining the guild and make a name for ourselves. The lads and I were young and dumb, but we carved our own path.” Grimhold continued.

“What happened to them?” Mezza asked.

“Eh, after a few years of adventuring, we came upon a village that had been attacked by some kind of monster. At the time we did not know what it was. The place was devastated. Very few survivors.”

Mezza took Grimhold’s hand in Her’s. “That sounds awful.”

“Aye, it not be a memory I like to recall often. The monsters returned...” Grimhold began.

“What were they?” Mezza asked.

Grimhold recalled the things he still had nightmares about. "Six-legged Varnacs..."

Mezza gasped.

"Aye. They be vicious things. The stuff of nightmares. Vicious claws that can cut through non-mithril armor like it was nothin. Teeth and powerful jaws that can shatter even a dwarf's bones..." Grimhold shuddered.

The Dwarven defender rained in his emotions and patted Mezza's hand. They had stopped moving as Grimhold retold his tale. "My boys and I were well trained and quickly fell into formation. Those creatures were fast, but I was the party's defender, and we knew how to work together. We were able to keep one of those nightmares contained, we were even adding some good wounds on our foe. That was when we heard a little girl scream..."

"Oh no." Mezza gasped.

"When we looked down the way we saw two skinny street kids. A Varnac was headed right for them... Fenrir and Narn were the closest and the ones with the highest Agility and Strength among us, they made a dash for the kids. I do not fault them for doing so, those kids woulda died... but they broke formation, the Varnac we were fighting used the opportunity to strike Fayroon... split him open, he died instantly."

"Oh, no!" Mezza exclaimed.

"I finished it off... and rushed to help Fenrir and Narn." Grimhold continued.

"Did they save the kids?" Mezza asked in anticipation.

"Aye, I rushed in and took up my stance in our formation. Sadly, by the time I got there, Narn had already lost an arm and Fenrir was sportin some nasty gashes... Yet we killed the thing! Sent that bastard straight to hell where it belongs! The kids lived, twin half-elves."

"Do not tell me..." Mezza said as realization hit her.

"Aye, Cal and Mara. They had been living on the street for years getting by after their parents had died in a previous monster attack. The lads and I took them in and helped train em! Fenrir and Narn both left shortly after that. They lost the drive for the adventurer's life after Fayroon died. I canna blame em, but Cal and Mara's excitement breathed new life into me, so I became their defender."

"I never knew that was how ya met them." Mezza commented.

"I do not like to talk about it as it brings up painful memories."

"I understand Grimmy, thank you for sharing your story with me." Mezza said as she kissed the burly dwarf on his cheek.

Grimhold smiled at that. "So, what of yer family?"

Mezza smiled back. "As ya already know I am a Hill Dwarf. My family came from the south. We moved to Nord for more opportunities for Da. Me mother worked in various inns and kitchens; I picked up her talent fer cookin! After I was old enough to make ma own way, Darrien was traveling through the town we were workin in. He had me cookin and hired me on the spot."

"At least he was smart enough to do that!" Grimhold grumbled.

"Aye, had I known what a right git he was, I would never have accepted the job." Mezza said before giving Grimhold another peck on the cheek. "Though, then I would never have met'cha"

Grimhold squeezed her hand, and they resumed their trek. It did not take long for them to reach the gates by the elaborate boarder guard post. The elven and human soldiers worked together, manning each side of the wooden wall and lookout nests.

"State your business for entering the elven nation." And elven guard asked.

"In route to the Dwarven Mountain kingdom to visit family." Grimhold answered.

"Papers." The guard said as he held out his hand.

Grimhold handed him one of the documents he received from Deathwalker. It was a letter from Duchess Lightheart. The dwarf hated to think of the politicking his liege had to go through to get that, which made him even more thankful for it.

When the guard's expression changed as he read the letter. Grimhold just chuckled. The dwarf knew the duchess was one of the elf king's daughters. Another guard approached. This one seemed to be a higher rank.

"Problem?" The new guard asked as he stuck his hand out for the note the gate guard held.

The gate guard passed the new guard the document. "L-Lieutenant."

The elven lieutenant's eyebrows rose before turning his attention to the dwarf. "You must be Grimhold and Mezza?"

"Aye, that be us! But how do ya know that? The note does not mention Mezza's name." Grimhold said with suspicion.

The elven lieutenant smiled. "No, it does not. His majesty King Alfheim sent word to the border. He seeks to strengthen his relationship with Duke Dragonvein."

The elven lieutenant waved his arm as a signal and a column of elven soldiers appeared from around the corner. "We have been instructed to escort you to the mountain entrance and ensure no harm comes to either of you. I am willing to give you a temporary Oath of Protection during this journey to assuage any concerns you might have."

Grimhold laughed. "Ha, ha, ha, ha, ha! Leave it to my liege to somehow arrange for an entire elven column as our escort! Sure, I will take yer oath!" Grimhold laughed.

# Chapter 20 - Preparations

"I do not understand the importance of why I needed to join that organization." Draconis was articulating to Deathwalker and Garry as they entered the Infinite Nexus Portal room.

Garry was the first to speak up. "It's like a license to kill. We get to hunt things down and kill em!"

"What is this license you speak of?"

"Enough of that." Deathwalker interrupted.

Draconis bowed his head. "Sorry, master."

Deathwalker waved off his apology. "No need to apologize. I want you to feel free to ask questions. That was more directed at Garry. He is trying to explain things using references from my old world. Let me try to put it in simpler terms. You like shiny stuff, right?"

"Of course! A dragon naturally likes to collect things of value." Draconis replied.

Deathwalker explained his thoughts on the matter. "Well, when we complete jobs for the Adventurers' guild we get paid in silver and gold. It is another way to acquire such wealth."

Garry smiled. "And?"

Deathwalker chuckled. "He, he, he, he. And we get to hunt and kill stuff that needs killing."

"That's a win-win in my book!" Garry chimed in.

"You have a book? What else is in this book?" Draconis asked.

“No, it’s a saying from the boss’s homeworld. Man, I have so much to teach you young grasshopper!” Garry replied before turning to Deathwalker. “Hey boss, now that Draconis is one of your disciples, mind if I take him into the mindscape and start introducing him to some stuff?”

“That’s fine. I need to have a word with Lilandra and General Marius anyway.” Deathwalker answered.

Draconis visibly shuddered. The dragon did not expect such a diminutive humanoid to trounce him so thoroughly in their spar. He had grown in size and power since his master had made him one of his disciples. ‘Apparently that was not enough of an increase to defeat the queen of the djinn. She is a terror on the battlefield. That is to be expected of master’s first disciple!’

Draconis came out of his mental musings to hear Deathwalker warn Garry about something, though the words he used did not make sense to Draconis. “Start off slow buddy, most movies and shows will require more context before you introduce him.” Deathwalker replied.

Garry waved one of his eyestalks. “Not a problem boss, I got this!”

“Come on Draconis, let me take you somewhere more comfortable as we will be in the Mindscape for a while! Man, I can’t wait to introduce you to the classics! Ha, ha, ha, ha, ha!” Garry laughed as the two walked away.

Deathwalker watched the two head off, lost in his own thoughts when, “You wanted to talk to me my hunky master?”

“Ah! I mean ahh! Are you trying to give me a heart attack Lilandra?!”

The djinn just giggled. “He, he, he, he. I couldn’t help it; you were so lost in thought.”

“Hey, you used a contraction!” Deathwalker commented on Lilandra’s use of ‘couldn’t’.

“I figured I would try to adapt to your way of speaking. It may take some time but thank you for noticing.” Lilandra smiled.

“I have been avoiding going to the Infinite Library, not sure how I want to start the conversation with Uriel.” Deathwalker explained.

Lilandra gave him a look of concern. “That is understandable, but he knows you are here.”

“He does?” Deathwalker was surprised.

Lilandra nodded. “As one who has an official position in the Infinite Nexus, he knows where the Master of the Infinite Nexus is. This happens to anyone you grant an official position to here.”

“Hmmm, that’s good to know. I am not ready yet. Soon, but not now. We returned to the Hidden Realm so you could meet and spar with Draconis. That, and the girls wanted to check on the puma pride.”

“That is why they came but I sense there is more you wish to discuss.” Lilandra surmised.

“Ever the observant one. Yes, ever since my meeting with Mother Winter and Morrigan, I can’t seem to shake a feeling.”

Lilandra gave Deathwalker a puzzled look. “A feeling?”

Deathwalker nodded. “Yes. It’s like a phantom limb or an additional sense that is on the edge of my awareness. I do not yet feel comfortable asking Uriel so I figured I would come ask you.”

“Hmmm. You said this started after your encounter with two of the original Parcae? Can you describe the feeling in greater detail?” Lilandra asked.

“It is like how people describe deja vu, yet it doesn’t feel like it’s my memories but someone else’s ability.” Deathwalker shook his head. “I’m not even sure I’m making any sense.”

Lilandra put her hand on Deathwalker's shoulder. "As we now know your soul is fragmented and unraveling. This may open you up to things we cannot explain. Your spirit is a powerful one and the Parcae are guides of Fate. Your Power of 13 could also be at play here. It is possible that your encounter opened you up to sensing the Weave. If that is true, perhaps we can help you understand what you are sensing."

"Makes sense, but that does give me pause. Would I pick up other beings' inclinations? Like what happens if I encounter a demon, would that influence me in some way?" Deathwalker said in concern.

"Fallen angels can affect those around them. Some are more susceptible to certain ones than others. I cannot say for certain what will happen, but we should try to avoid it. That means you cannot go after your friend at least until you have gained the rest of Chronos' power." Lilandra said with concern.

"Other than not dying in nine months, why should that matter? I know I still have to grow stronger, but you seem to be talking about something else." Deathwalker replied.

"Yes, demons will be near your friend. Even if hidden, they are there influencing the world around them. Until we know more, we cannot risk your exposure." Lilandra explained.

Deathwalker sighed. "Yet another delay in the rescue of my friend. It's bad enough I've taken this long."

Lilandra smiled. "Look on the bright side master! I might be able to help guide you to sense the Weave better. We djinn are intrinsically tied to Fate, well at least I am, but my children have it to a far lesser degree."

"So, how do we go about this Lilandra?"

"Close your eyes and focus on that feeling. Do your best to mentally grab on to it." Lilandra explained.

Deathwalker did as instructed. He closed his eyes and concentrated. Trying to mentally hold onto that phantom sensation felt like trying to grab a fish flopping around out of water. Just when Deathwalker thought he had it, the sensation would slip from his mental fingers.

After several frustrating moments, Deathwalker finally held on to that feeling. "I've got it Lilandra! Now what?"

Lilandra kissed him.

The shock almost made Deathwalker lose his mental grip, but he held firm. Then the world exploded around him and Deathwalker lost all sense of himself. He passed out, or at least that is what it felt like.

When Deathwalker came to he was not in the Infinite Nexus. At first it felt like he was in some structure. Then he could feel the tail-tale signs of a leyline nearby. Deathwalker blinked and he was now outside. As he looked around the realization hit him. "I'm in Timberfall! What am I doing here?"

The scene came more into focus. Deathwalker saw soldiers and citizens running around. Then out of nowhere a giant boulder flew over the walls and crashed into the building. The more he paid attention the more senses he picked up. He could hear the sounds of battle on the other side of the wall. People were screaming and crying. The smell of burning wood and flesh filled his nostrils.

A shooting pain filled his head and Deathwalker gasped as his eyes opened and he bolted upright. He was back in the Infinite Nexus. "Man, that was some kiss!"

Lilandra giggled. "He, he, he, he. Technically we only required physical contact, but I couldn't help myself."

Deathwalker waved her response off. "I wasn't complaining. Did you witness what I saw?"

Lilandra nodded. "Yes. It appears at some point war is coming to Timberfall."

Deciding to check his timer, Deathwalker saw he lost only a few days. "Interesting. It appears that vision only cost me a few days. Definitely better than the three months I lost last time I tried to use the **Infinite Well of Time Magic**."

Lilandra looked chagrined. "I am sorry master I cost you even more of your precious time."

"I'm not. I learned something valuable. I now know that Timberfall will be attacked in the future. Now that I know that I can prepare. Any idea how I can stop a catapult or arrows?" Deathwalker said as he shifted into problem-solver mode.

Lilandra nodded. "You still have that **Ancient Hydra Core**, right?"

————

"Elder, do you know why the duke asked us to join him in the Town Hall?" Lady Emma asked.

"I do not. He asked to see if you wanted to join us. Your aunt and grandfather seem to be busy discussing trade agreements. I doubt they will even notice that we are gone." Elder Martha replied.

As they entered the Timberfall Town Hall, the two ladies heard Deathwalker. "You're going to like this Draconis."

"I am sure I will master, but afterwards, may I return to..." Draconis heard approaching footsteps and decided to alter what he was about to say. "To continue to study."

Deathwalker nodded in acknowledgement before turning his attention to Elder Martha and Lady Emma. "Welcome ladies. I'm glad you could make it. I think you'll enjoy what I'm about to show you."

"Oh really? And what is that, Duke Dragonvein?" Advisor Mona said from behind him.

Deathwalker caught himself before he drove an Omni-claw through the fey.

Draconis immediately summoned fire in his hands. "You dare to sneak up on my master?!"

"It is fine. Drop the spell." Deathwalker instructed.

Reluctantly Draconis let go of the magic and the flames went out. Advisor Mona just smiled back at him.

"Are all fey this mischievous?" Draconis asked.

"What are you referring to? Are you saying you were not aware of my presence?" Advisor Mona smile grew wider.

Draconis just growled "Grrrrr." and turned away from the fey woman.

"It is good of you to join us Advisor Mona. I think you might enjoy this." Deathwalker said as he pulled the giant magic core from his bag.

Advisor Mona's eyes went wide. "Is that an Ancient Hydra core?!"

She was not the only one to be in shock. "They say an Ancient Hydra is impossible to kill!" Lady Emma commented.

It was Deathwalker's turn to smile. "Not impossible, just rather difficult." He placed the magic core on the pedestal behind him. "The core is not what I wanted to show you. No, I thought you'd enjoy seeing this."

The magic formation activated, and a beam of light shot out from the pedestal straight into the air. Then the light poured out into a dome covering the entire city. Advisor Mona rushed to the pedestal as her eyes took on a wintery glow.

"It-it is a city-wide protective barrier!" Advisor Mona said in wonder before turning her eyes on Deathwalker. "How did you know how to do this? This is beyond Grand Scale Magic!"

"Truly, Advisor?!" Lady Emma exclaimed.

"I am full of surprises." Was all Deathwalker said before turning to Elder Martha. "Inform Commander Willis and the city guard. We have a new layer of protection for the city. Something tells me we may need it someday."

Elder Martha bowed. "As you command your grace. Thank you for bestowing this gift on our city."

"Come Draconis, let us get you to return to your 'studying'. Oh, and if you are still interested in me teaching you magic, I would welcome the opportunity my lady." Deathwalker said as he passed by Lady Emma.

"Thank you, Duke Dragonvein. I will gladly take you up on that offer." Lady Emma said quickly once her brain recovered from the shock of hearing so many unbelievable statements back-to-back.

Once Deathwalker and Draconis left the upper floor of the Town Hall, Lady Emma turned to Advisor Mona. "Is it really beyond Grand Scale Magic?!"

Advisor Mona did not take her eyes off of the orb and pedestal when she replied. "Most certainly child. Here I thought Draconis might be the one behind the duke's meteoric rise to power, but no..." she tapped her finger on her chin. "This Deathwalker has layers upon layers. I guess I am going to have to peel them away to get the answers I seek."

"You are still a guest in his home." Was all the warning Elder Martha gave before she left with Lady Emma to find Commander Willis.

When Advisor Mona was alone a tiny, blue light flew into the room. A tiny humanoid no bigger than a hand bowed to the fey woman. "You have called honored Advisor?"

"Yes. Keep an eye on the one that summoned this." Advisor Mona said as she waved to the glowing orb and pedestal. "Recruit others of your kind if you must. Find out everything you can and report back to me."

"As you command, honored Advisor." The tiny fairy squeaked out.

Just as the little ball of blue light started to dart off, Advisor Mona raised her hand and the fairy stopped. "Make sure when you report to me you are not spotted. I must still keep up appearances."

The little light blinked in acknowledgement before taking off.

——————

# Chapter 21 – Eyes & Ears

"You did that on purpose, didn't you?" Draconis asked once he was alone with his master.

"He, he, he, he. You used a contraction, good job, and I did." Deathwalker replied.

"Thank you, Master. My time with your familiar is helping me understand where you came from. As for that fey woman, why specifically do that in front of her?"

"Elder Martha tells me she is more of a spy for the Winter Queen, but Advisor Mona has one weakness... her fascination with magic. This will keep her distracted." Deathwalker explained.

"You told me you wanted to not draw attention to yourself. Would this not spur her to action?" Draconis inquired.

"It was an acceptable risk. The vision I had showed Timberfall being sieged... things were not going well. I merely am helping to balance the scales. Besides, Elder Martha made it very clear I had already drawn the fey's attention. I'm just choosing where she looks." Deathwalker shared.

Just then Deathwalker got a feeling that he was being watched. Not wanting to give anything away he telepathically messaged his apprentice. "I sense we are not alone."

"I sense it too. Shall I take action, master?" Draconis mentally replied.

"No. I have a better idea." Deathwalker sent before he spoke out loud. "Come, let's go get Garry. The festival starts tomorrow, and I promised my little murderhobo he could attend."

Without saying another word Deathwalker and Draconis headed for the Portal Hub.

*"Lilandra?"*

*"Yes, my hunky master?"* Lilandra replied in his head.

*"Draconis and I are about to return home. I think someone is spying on me. If they follow us in, rather than blocking them, can you isolate them and lock down any magic or chance for escape? I'd like to interrogate them."* Deathwalker sent telepathically.

*"Easy enough. There is actually an anti-magic cell near the Portal Chamber. Once they enter the portal, I will have complete control."*

*"Good to know."* Deathwalker replied with a hint of concern but brushed it off for now.

The duke nodded to his men as he passed through into the Timberfall portal hub receiving room.

The soldiers bowed and greeted in unison. "Your grace!"

"At ease. We will return later." Deathwalker responded before walking through the portal.

There was a small flash of light shortly after. "Hey, did you see that?" One of the guards asked.

"See what?"

"It looked like a flash of light!"

"Are you seeing things again? Man do not screw up this assignment for us. It is the easiest gig we have ever had!" His comrade complained.

———

"Well, well, well. What do we have here?" Lilandra asked as she peered into the cell.

Laying on the ground, looking stunned, was a tiny humanoid with wings. The little being started to rouse from its stunned expression. It got to their feet a little wobbly.

"What is it?" Deathwalker asked before using his Insight on it.

***Timov***
*Race: Fairy (Pixie variant)*
*Level: 49*

Draconis leaned over to look at what they caught only to snarl upon seeing the captive. "Pixie! Damned fairies! They are nothing but pests and spies! They don't even make a worthy snack!"

The little Timov visibly gulped before dropping to its knees. "Please do not eat me! I beg of you!!!" Then the little creature started to sob. "Take this job they said. It is a great honor to serve one of the advisors to one of the queens! Now Timov is trapped and going to get eaten! Waaaa!"

"Ugh! See what I mean, annoying things! Let me eat it so we can shut it up!" Draconis complained.

"Are they tasty?" Garry asked as he floated into the room.

"No! Mostly bones, but at least it will be much quieter in here!" Draconis replied.

"Eh, it's small enough. I could probably just grab it telekinetically and slam it into the wall until it stops. Hmmm, I wonder if I slam the thing hard enough if it'll pop." Garry offered.

That made Timov wale even more. Tears gushing down the little creature's face.

"Ugh! I agree with Draconis, that thing is annoying! Let me smash it boss!" Garry pleaded.

Deathwalker knelt, then took up a sitting position so as to not be so intimidating. He then raised his hand before he spoke in a calm voice. "Timov, are you willing to speak with me? If you stop crying, I can promise you my friends will not be so inclined to harm you."

Deathwalker's use of the little fairy's name seemed to snap it out of their wows. "O-okay. Y-you promised they will not hurt me?"

"I can promise you as long as you do not try to cause harm, we will not do you anything harmful to you... at least while we are talking."

Those words seemed to brighten up Timov. “Okay.”

Deathwalker smiled. “Great! Now why were you spying on us? You mentioned the Advisor, were you working for Mona?”

“Y-yes.” Timov hesitantly answered.

“Ha! I knew it! She upped her game after that little display with the citywide shield. You should let me eat her.” Draconis chimed in.

“Hey if we are entertaining eating hot fey women I, I think it only fair I go first! I think my long thick tongue could do wonders, he, he, he, he.” Garry commented.

“Really? Does your tongue size increase the amount you can taste or something? Would that not be a detriment depending on the situation?” Draconis asked in confusion.

Garry smiled. “Sometimes, but usually it just adds to the enjoyment. There was this one time...”

“At band camp!” Deathwalker laughed.

“Ha, ha, ha, ha! Good one boss!”

“What is this ‘band camp’?” Draconis asked in confusion.

Garry continued. “I’ll show you later buddy. Anyway, my point before I was so hilariously interrupted, I bit the head off this traitor and the combination of crunch, brains, and blood gave this amazing flavor! If I didn’t have all those taste buds, I never would have enjoyed it to the extent I did!”

“I could see that.” Draconis agreed.

“Umm, I think all your talk is making the poor little guy turn pale.” Lilandra noted.

It was true. The more Garry and Draconis talked about eating things the sicklier the little fairy looked. When both Garry and Draconis licked their lips as they stared at the little morsel, Timov visibly gulped. ‘I am dead for sure.’

"Alright guys, you had your fun." Deathwalker strives to say with a straight face. It was clear he enjoyed the two's banter.

"Eh, he is too small anyway." Draconis replied.

"That's what she said! Ha, ha, ha, ha!" Garry laughed for a moment before catching the side eye from Lilandra. "Okay, okay. Come on buddy, let me introduce you to some of the comedy movies from our master's world."

After the two left the room Lilandra commented, "They are like two teenage boys from your world."

"The age doesn't much matter. When you think of what is at stake in our lives, we have to find humor where we can. At first my familiar's approach reminded me of an immaturity I wanted to overcome, but now... well I think it's a way of coping, and frankly, he makes me laugh." Deathwalker explained.

"It appears you are reconnecting with your emotions, at least in part. I can tolerate a little inappropriate crazy if it helps my master adapt and survive." Lilandra said before pointing to the little pixie. "Though that little one looks scared to death."

Deathwalker turned and sighed. "Please excuse my friends, Timov. They are just looking after me in their own way, and they tend to be very protective. Now tell me, are you bound by any agreements?"

## ———Deathwalker's Perspective———

"I am fairy, of course I am bound by agreements. We pixies are still like any other fairy-kind, though the arch-fey tends to not treat us that way. To them we are nothing but insects. They barely bother to use us as messengers and spies." Timov explained.

"It is true, master. The fey tend to look down on or are completely indifferent to them, even though they are distant cousins." Lilandra stated.

'No wonder the little one was so scared of us. The way their kind are treated, they expected to be killed once captured.' That thought made me ask a follow up question. “Can you speak on your agreement with Advisor Mona?”

Timov nodded. “She did not bother to require my silence. In her words 'if you are stupid enough to get caught and tortured, let them know it was I who sent you before you die.' She said it in her usual cold heartless way.”

“That seems risky to me.”

Timov shook his head. “Advisor Mona is scary, and I mean super scary. Most would not think to challenge anyone that has the ear of Queen Mab, and she knows it.”

“Arrogant, but I can use that to my advantage. What were the parameters of your agreement?” I asked.

“She did not want to deal with us lowly fairies. I was the one assigned to coordinate with other pixies. We would spy or run messages for her, all of that was coordinated through me.” Timov stood up straighter. “As the advisor could not be bothered to deal with multiple pixies, she appointed me to be her liaison. It was a high honor, but also dangerous.” Timov explained.

“Dangerous? You mean because we captured you?” I inquired.

Lilandra was the one to chime in “No, it is common for their so called 'benefactor or employer' to hurt or kill them for delivering unpleasant news.”

“Ah, sounds like they never got the old adage don't kill the messenger.”

Lilandra nodded. “Quite right.”

I turned back to the little guy or gal. It was hard to tell what sex this pixie was. 'I wonder if that would be rude to ask. Oh, well, more important things to figure out first.'

"You had no other conditions besides be a liaison and her messenger spy? Like you cannot lie or anything like that?"

"We pixies cannot lie! No fey can!" Timov stood up to their full height.

"Not telling an outright lie, is not the same as always telling the truth." Lilandra warned.

Timov nodded along. "Wise words queen of the djinn."

"You know of Lilandra?"

Timov looked incredulous. "Of course! She is one of the three queens! Any fairy with half a mind knows that."

"But she was banished and locked away for thousands of years?" I commented.

"All her children may be imprisoned, but the djinn are well known to all of fairy-kind. No one is foolish enough to tangle with one as they can warp reality and the very forces of creation. All djinns should be feared, and their queen should be respected for her sacrifice." Timov bowed as he said those last words.

Lilandra nodded in acknowledgement to the little pixie. "Thank you, Timov. I expect you to entreat with my master and give him respect just as you would with me." She then turned to me. "All fairy-kind recognize djinns, just as all djinns recognize all forms of fey. As we all have some common ancestry, it is to be expected. I cannot hide what I am from them, just as they cannot hide from me."

"As always, I appreciate your council and having you by my side Lilandra." I said thanks to my first disciple.

"Tell me Timov, how were you being paid and is there any way for you to break agreements?"

"The agreement ended the moment I was captured. Advisor Mona would not waste her time rescuing someone as disposable as I." Timov replied.

Lilandra spoke up once again. “If the agreement remained someone powerful enough could use the connection from their agreement to find and confirm her involvement. As it stands now, you have no definitive proof of her involvement. The masses do not trust or believe fairies and she is aware of that fact.”

“Why is that?”

“For the same reason I mentioned earlier, not lying is not the same thing as telling the truth. That and pixies gain power from agreements. The more magic the stronger and bigger they get over time.” Lilandra explained.

“It is a pixie’s dream to eventually become fey.” Timov said with hope in their eyes.

“That can happen?”

Lilandra nodded and motioned to the fairy. “Yes, but there is more to it than that. Give us a few moments Timov as I explain the nuances of impact and growing one’s meaning through their purpose.”

“This may take some time master so bear with me.” Lilandra telepathically said as she took my hands and we both closed our eyes.

When I opened mine, we were elsewhere. It did not take me long to realize we were in a Mindscape, a landscape where minds can meet either to share information or do battle. If she brought me here, that meant what Lilandra had to share was more complex than mere words could convey.

“Perhaps it is best to explain the power of meaning. Think of it as gravity that pulls power to you.” Lilandra waved her hand and shapes like planets and stars began to appear around us.

“Many see their purpose as the way to bring meaning into their lives. Though purpose is extrinsically tied to meaning, it is only one way to grow it. There are fundamental aspects of who we are and how we were created that give us Meaning. For example, I as a woman gain meaning by having children and being a wife. Just doing those acts gathers meaning to us, but what we purposefully do adds even greater meaning. For example. I could have a child but spend no time with it, not bother to nurture or guide their development. I gain very little meaning by doing such a thing. However, if I purposefully put focus and worked with them, both my meaning and theirs grow.”

“How does their meaning grow by what you’re doing?” I asked.

Lilandra waved her hand and a star’s light warmed a planet allowing it to grow life on its surface. “Simple, we are all connected. The more energy and attention I give something the more it will grow. If I fuel them with hate, then hate grows. Like attracts like and yet opposites will fuel the other with their constant conflict. These two approaches are why the Light and Dark are constantly at odds. The Dark creates conflict and competition to grow stronger.”

“But I have always seen conflict and competition to be healthy approaches.”

Lilandra nodded. “Conflict and competition are not by their nature evil but when fueled by darker emotions they become the very power source the Dark uses to become stronger. The Light tends to focus on cooperation, compassion, and understanding. Yet if not tempered correctly, these aspects can be corrupted and turned to serve the Dark.”

“It sounds like anything can be used to serve the Dark.” I commented.

Lilandra chuckled. “He, he, he, he. You are not wrong master, but the opposite is equally true. Anything can be used to serve the Light, even the most horrific tragedy can fuel powerful positive outcomes. That is why how we understand meaning is so important. If too much focus is given to the darker aspects of an outcome or possibility, then more meaning is given over to the Dark. Remember the Dark cannot create anything, they can only corrupt and twist it to their purposes.”

"Wise words. My Nanuz used to tell me similar things. No wonder he would constantly drill into our heads to focus on the good. Even in tragedy there is good, if you can't find it, you're not looking hard enough. Thank you, God, for giving me Nanuz who was such an amazing influence." I said the last part as a prayer of thanks and appreciation. It was another positive habit I learned from my family.

"Yes, most of this you already knew. What you were probably not as aware of was the spiritual aspects of these thoughts and actions."

"Makes sense. How does this relate to the fey and fairy-kind?"

"All of us grow stronger through the meaning we gather and what we feed. Djinn, fey, fairies, etc. all gain meaning by what they do. Granting wishes grows a djinn's power. Their manipulation of the primordial forces of the universe to grant something to another, grants them a fraction of the meaning that was created as a result. I as their queen gain a fraction of what they do."

"Awesome cosmic powers! Itty-bitty living space." I quad to quote the famous and missed Robin Williams.

Lilandra smiled and continued with her explanation. "Making agreements for the fey works in a similar way. They gain a fraction of the meaning as it goes where it was meant to be. For the pixies, the more meaning they can help others gather or create, over time the more powerful they become. Eventually, that power can result in growth. They will get larger, and a few have evolved into fey. Many beings like Morrigan, who are seen as gods became that way because of the meaning they gathered and what meaning was sent to them from their believers. This is what has helped them bend the laws of the universe to their will."

"Hmmm, very interesting. This actually helps me better understand faith magic... I have a question though."

"What is that, my hunky master?"

"You could've explained this in front of Timov. I am sure they already know this. Which means there is something else you wanted to tell me."

Lilandra's smile grew wider. "Have I told you lately how much I appreciate your mind master?"

"Hmmm, not really. You've made innuendos about different parts of my body, but not my mind." I replied.

Lilandra laughed. "Ha, ha, ha, ha, ha! I do enjoy those aspects of you too. Well, let me tell you I appreciate your mind and let me answer your unasked question. Yes, there was something very important I wanted us to discuss in private. It has to do with your nature as the **Third Path of Creation**. Your ancient royal bloodlines, **Power of 13**, and **Soul-Forging** abilities they grant you something very special... you can completely alter, transform, or move meaning around! This is what let you break my bonds; you took hold of the meaning and purified it to suit your needs. That is the real power you possess and if you do not gain the other aspects of yourself, it will destroy you." She said the last part with clear sadness in her voice.

"Well one thing at a time. What I am taking from this is I have been blessed to be able to gather meaning, therefore power at an unprecedented rate. Hence why I need the rest of Chronos' power, so I don't unravel at the seams. However, now that I have a better handle on the power of agreements you have given me some ideas. Let's head back."

In a flash, we were no longer in the Mindscape. I telepathically thanked Lilandra for her explanation of all the nuances of how fairy magic and agreements worked. With it I would be better prepared for dealing with the fey.

"Thank you, Lilandra, for always sharing your knowledge and insights. This has given me an idea." I said out loud before turning my attention back to Timov. "So, if you are not under any agreements, what about coming to work for me? I have the perfect job for you."

"Job?" Timov asked.

"Yes, a job for you and your friends."

Timov took on a serious look. “What kind of job?”

————

# Interlude - Dwarven Mountain Kingdom

"HALT! State your name and purpose for visiting." A dwarven guard ordered.

"I be here to introduce the woman I be courtin to me family!" Grimhold exclaimed and Mezza blushed.

"That be honorable. Go on through." Another guard stated.

"But we did not check their papers sir." The first guard cautioned.

"He just told ya why he was here. The kingdom is not on lock down so stop being so dramatic! Yer holding up the line! We got plenty more to vet before our shift is over. How about you save that zeal for the ones with carts?" The second guard barked.

Grimhold took Mezza by the hand, nodded at the guard, and quickly moved through the gate.

After the two were farther in Mezza asked the questions in her mind. "Why did you not mention the diplomatic mission you are on? And that guard mentioned lock down, does that happen often?"

"As far as the masses are concerned, we are here visiting family. When the time comes, I will share Deathwalker's proposal. Until then, it would be best no one knows about that."

"Yea but how are you going to get an audience with the king if you do not go through proper channels?" Mezza asked in confusion.

Grimhold just smiled at her. "Do not be worrying yourself about that. I have my ways. As for the lock downs, it happens from time to time. We usually get along well with the elves, but conflicts have been known to occur. That and there are other things far more dangerous beneath the earth than a bunch of pointy-eared pansies. For now, we should focus on more joyous things. Let me show you, my home."

Those last words brought a smile to Mezza's face. "Okay Grimmy, I will follow yer lead."

————-

The droning sounds of hammers hitting metal and anvils could be heard throughout the smithing section of the crafting halls. The crafting halls and connected marketplace were absolutely massive. Mezza had never seen the like in all her travels. Criers would do everything they could to grab the attention of onlookers and passersby. The noise was almost deafening at first. Though it did not take long before Mezza was excited, especially after they found a stall with various cooking herbs.

After purchasing far more herbs and spices than they probably needed, Grimhold guided Mezza further into the smithing section. He had heard a rumor and the dwarf had to see it with his own eyes. It did not take him long to find the forge he was looking for.

"The Iron Forge, why are we here Grimmy?" Mezza asked as they entered.

Shortly after she asked that question a young dwarf girl greeted them. "Welcome to the Iron Forge! Home of the best metalwork in the kingdom! How can we help you?"

"Best metalwork in the kingdom. That be a bold claim lass. I doubt very much yer smith be the best." Grimhold replied.

"Grimmy!" Mezza said in surprise.

The dwarf girl did not seem discouraged. "I assure ya, my da does some of the best work in the city!"

Grimhold chuckled and raised his voice so he could be heard in the back. "Ha! He probably is great with horseshoes, but I bet he is shite with armor!"

Both Mezza and the girl working at the counter looked shocked.

The hammering had stopped and a few seconds later a rather large muscular dwarf with one arm came marching in from the back. "Who dares say I be shite with armor?!"

Grimhold smiled. "I do ya one armed git!"

At this point the girl working the counter had a scowl on her face and based on her body language was clearly about to go off on Grimhold.

Mezza was unsure what to do, she would back her man, even though she had no idea why he was acting this way.

The tension was thick in the air before it was broken by the one-armed dwarf's laughter. "HA, HA, HA, HA, HA! It is good to see ya, you stubborn old dwarf!"

"It is good to see ya too, Narn! I missed ya, lad!" Grimhold replied before crossing the room and embracing his friend in a bear hug.

Mezza understood what was going on once she heard the smith's name. Sadly, the girl behind the counter looked confused. "Da?"

"Ah, sorry lass. This be one of my dear friends from my adventuring days, Grimhold." Narn explained. "Grimhold, this be my daughter Griselda."

Upon hearing the name, recognition clicked and the confusion on her face was replaced with a smile. Griselda crossed the room and gave Grimhold a hug in greeting. "Thank you for keeping da safe on yer adventures! The way he tells it, he owes you his life several times over!"

Grimhold was a bit surprised. "What nonsense you be spouting, Narn!"

"Nothing that not be the truth! I owe you my life many times over!" Narn raised his one arm. "If not for you that Varnac woulda got my other arm or worse!"

Grimhold shook his head. He still felt guilty for his friend's condition. "Nah! You saved my life plenty too!"

"Ah-hmmm!" Mezza said loudly.

Grimhold shook off his mental contemplation and walked back to Mezza. Taking her hand in his, "This is Mezza, my betrothed!"

"Narn's face lit up. "Ha! Bout time ya settled down!" The smith walked over and stuck out his hand. "Honored to meet ya! If you could tame this ornery jackass, then you must be an amazing woman!"

"Look who is talking! But yes, she is amazing and one of the best cooks I have ever met!" Grimhold countered.

"Wow, that is some high praise, coming from this bottomless pit of a stomach!" Narn pointed at his friend.

Griselda rejoined the conversation. "Da says I be the best cook he has known. Ma taught me everything!"

"Perhaps we could exchange recipes." Mezza offered.

"I would like that." Griselda smiled.

"Have ya seen yer family yet?" Narn asked.

"Not yet. I came to see ya first. I had to see if what I heard was true." Grimhold replied.

"What is it ya heard?" Narn asked.

"That yer shite with armor! Ha, ha, ha, ha, ha!" Grimhold laughed.

"Why you!" Narn mock glared at his friend. After a few moments he dropped the look. "Come, I will show ya some of what I have crafted."

Grimhold let his friend guide him to the back of the forge. "I see yer armor be improved. Who did the work? It was masterfully done." Narn said when Grimhold removed his cloak hiding his mithril armor.

"Aye, his name is Deathwalker, and he be my new liege!"

# Chapter 22 – Advisory Council

"So why are we waiting here, master?" Draconis asked.

"You get used to it. There is always some boring thing we are waiting around for. It's why I keep one eye on my surroundings and the other on the Mindscape." Garry chimed in.

"Hmmm, I should be able to do that too, that is if master does mind?" Draconis had a pleading tone towards the end.

Deathwalker waved the question off. "That's fine. I will also give you two the options to return to the manor."

"We can wait here, boss." Garry answered.

"Your apprentice and familiar have a low tolerance for politics." Elder Martha commented.

"Like their master." Lady Emma teased.

Deathwalker put his hand to his chest and put on a mocked look of shock. "Why Lady Emma, are you making a joke at my expense?"

"Yes, yes, I am. He, he, he, he." Lady Emma giggled.

"Ah to be young again." Elder Martha said.

"Oh please, I have seen you casting a Slip spell to make Betterman fall on his backside." Deathwalker retorted.

"Oh, Elder Martha you have to teach me that spell!" Lady Emma laughed.

"And to think the two of you will be leading this kingdom one day." Elder Martha smiled as she shook her head.

The mention of the kingdom's desire to see them wed squashed their playful moods. "You had to be a buzzkill, didn't you?" Deathwalker replied.

"I do not know what that is, but you both are about to receive Lords Longshot, Dormeir, and Simium. Longshot and Dormeir will not care for proper decorum, but I know Simium will. He prides himself on being one of the oldest noble families in the kingdom."

"Do not remind me Elder. His daughter can be so droll at balls." Lady Emma complained.

"Hmmm, I didn't get that from her, though I did not get much time with the Dame." Deathwalker winked at Lady Emma.

"Oh really? Elder, I really do require you to show me that Slip spell." Lady Emma smiled.

"Ugh, it is like dealing with two children."

"You are one of the only ones we can be ourselves around." Lady Emma replied.

"Fine, but they really could arrive at any moment." Elder Martha sighed.

As if on cue the portal flashed and Lord Dormeir appeared with Saunders, Jeffy, and a contingent of knights. Seeing Deathwalker, Sebastian clasped wrists with the man. "It is good to see you again my friend!"

"And you Sebastian. You know your peer and host Elder Martha."

"Madam, it is an honor to see you again." Sebastian clasped wrists with Elder Martha.

"And of course you know the Crown Princess Lady Emma." Deathwalker continued.

"My lady!" This time Sebastian went to one knee and bowed his head, all his entourage joined him in the greeting.

"Rise, honorable Lord Dormeir. It is I who should be bowing before the man that helped fight off Shadow Assassins to protect my family and the royal court." Lady said as she bowed her head to him as a sign of respect.

"You honor me greatly Lady Emma. It is Deathwalker that deserves most of the praise for that day!" Sebastian patted his friend on the shoulder.

Before they could continue their conversation, the portal flashed again and Lord Longshot was there with a few soldiers, all equipped with a bow.

"Lord Longshot, welcome to Timberfall." Deathwalker greeted.

Lord Longshot looked back to the portal before turning back and replying. "Such a marvel, your grace. It is good to see you."

"Good to see you as well. You remember Lord Dormeir." Deathwalker introduced.

The two men clasped wrists. "As one warrior greets another. It is good to see you again Sebastian."

"It is good to see you as well Anthony." Sebastian replied.

"And of course your host, Elder Martha." Deathwalker continued the introductions.

Longshot gave Elder Martha a bow at the waist to show how much he respected her battle prowess. "It is an honor to be in the presence of such a decorated warrior and tactician!"

"It is good to see you again Lord Longshot. You remember Lady Emma." Elder Martha bowed her head in greeting.

Like Sebastian, Anthony and his men bowed their heads as they dropped to one knee. "Your majesty, this humble servant greets you!"

"Please rise, Lord Longshot. Duke Dragonvein tells me you plan to enter into the archery competition."

Lord Longshot and his men got to their feet. "Yes, your majesty. I must maintain my reputation as the greatest archer in the kingdom." He then turned to his Duke. "Are we waiting on Simium?"

"Yes."

"Figures. That pompous man loves to make an entrance." Longshot complained.

"There is plenty of room at the estate and the connected barracks. If you would like to get settled in." Deathwalker offered.

"I would rather wait, but Saunders and Jeffrey can get my knights settled in." Sebastian replied.

"Sire, you should not be left unguarded." Jeffy protested.

Saunders grabbed the aide by the back of Jeffrey's garment and lifted him off the ground. "Lord Dormeir is completely safe in the presence of the 'Hero'. Stop being difficult and let us get our men settled in." Turning to Deathwalker, "Duke Dragonvein it is an honor to be in your city once again. If you are ever willing to share your story of how you defeated an Adult Dragon, I would love to hear it."

Deathwalker nodded in acknowledgement as Captain Saunders, still holding Jeffrey off the ground, led the knights to the barracks.

"Awe, I'm so going to miss Jeffy, not." Deathwalker commented.

Sebastian gave a pained expression. He knew his liege did not care for his attaché, but he could not just dismiss him without proper cause. This caused him to hesitate on what to say, giving Lord Longshot the chance to direct his men to accompany Captain Saunders. "Follow the captain as he is clearly familiar with the city."

After his men left Lord Longshot turned to his liege and ask his question. "I saw the notification saying the details were not to be shared, but can you not give some kind of hint at how you accomplished such a legendary feat?"

"Boss is so awesome he made him feel tiny in comparison, ha, ha, ha, ha, ha!" Garry laughed.

"Your familiar is quite correct master." Draconis commented.

"Ah you two are paying attention now. Sebastian, you remember my familiar Garry. Lord Longshot this is my familiar Garry, he is a Shadow Gazer. I ask that you understand his race is prone to violence and inappropriate behavior."

"Not a worry, your grace. We have a few Rangers and Beast Tamers that have animal companions, allowances must be made. It is a pleasure to meet you honorable Garry."

"He, he! I like this guy, he gets it. Sometimes allowances have to be made as some of us prefer to solve our problems more directly." Garry stated.

"And let me introduce you both to my apprentice Draconis. His has joined my personal guard and like Garry is blunt and prefers more direct ways of solving problems." Deathwalker introduced.

"It is an honor to meet you Draconis." Lord Longshot greeted.

Sebastian gave his own greeting. "Yes, it is a pleasure to meet you Draconis. Perhaps we could spar later."

"It is nice to meet you both." Draconis replied before turning to Lord Dormeir. "I would welcome a chance to spar."

"Excellent!" The noble answered eagerly.

The portal flashed again and Lord Simium, his son, daughter, and a contingent of guards appeared.

"We welcome Lord Simium and his entourage to Timberfall." Elder Martha said.

"Elder Martha it is an honor." Lord Simium bowed his head.

Seeing Lady Emma, Lord Simium and his entire entourage got down on one knee and bowed their heads. "Crown Princess Lady Emma, it is a privilege to be in your presence."

"Rise, Lord Simium. It is good to see you looking healthier than the last time I saw you." Lady Emma replied.

"Yes, it is thanks to the amazing healing gift of my liege." Simium replied.

Deathwalker stepped forward to better show himself. Lords Dormeir and Longshot did the same.

"Ah, your grace. I did not see you. It is my greatest honor to see you again. I know my children and I are excited to attend this inaugural festival."

"It is good to see you too Lord Simium. You remember Lords Dormeir and Longshot." Deathwalker greeted.

"Ah yes. It is good to see fellow high nobles."

Sebastian nodded his head in greeting.

Lord Longshot couldn't help but give the man a little dig. "What took you so long ya old coot? I thought our liege healed you. What is you excuse for making all of us wait for you?"

Lord Simium's son was about to speak up and tell the Lord off when Simium shook his head. "Ever to the heart of things, like an arrow. It is good to see you too, Anthony. My apologies if I made anyone wait, it took us some time to make arrangements before we could leave the city for an extended time."

Elder Martha decided to step in. "As we are all well aware of, we can understand the minor delay. Let us show you to your rooms and give you a little time to get all settled in. Our liege has asked us to meet with him prior to the festival opening ceremony."

The group of nobles nodded and followed Elder Martha out of the portal hub's receiving room. This left Deathwalker, Lady Emma, Garry, and Draconis alone with the portal guards. Lady Emma spoke up. "She does a rather impressive job knowing when to push and prod."

Garry opened his mouth to say something, but Deathwalker cut him off. "Don't say it."

"But boss, she left herself wide open for it." Garry groaned.

"Left myself open for what?" Lady Emma asked in confusion.

"It is a saying from where I'm from. If the statement sounds suggestive in nature, you say 'that's what she said'. It's a joke and my familiar loves to use it. He still doesn't understand you do not say such things in front of a lady." Deathwalker explained.

"Oh. Your familiar is an odd one, but you seem to surround yourself with unique yet powerful characters." Lady Emma commented.

"Yes, my master does." Draconis chimed in.

Deathwalker chuckled. "Ha! That is one way of putting it. I enjoy the diversity of thought that comes from different perspectives. Those I surround myself with bring different ways of thinking and solving problems. Those most loyal and closest to me I know will follow my lead yet give me wise counsel. Even Garry's murderhobo ways have their place. I am a monster Lady Emma, but one with values and rules that help me know when to unleash what is inside."

"I do not see a monster when I look at you Deathwalker. I see a man who genuinely cares for his people." Lady Emma countered.

"It is because I care that I am willing to be a monster when needed." Deathwalker said before sticking out his elbow. "Now however is not one of those times to unleash the monster..."

"That's what she said. Did I get that right?" Lady Emma said as she hooked her arm in his.

Deathwalker smiled. "Well done. I appreciate an intelligent woman with a good sense of humor."

Lady Emma blushed slightly as she smiled back at him.

Deathwalker started to guide her back to the manor. "Come let's see if Simium and Longshot get into it."

"It may not look like it, but they are friends, or at the very least Simium respects Longshot's skills. His son though... he might make an ass of himself if young man is not careful." Lady Emma commented.

"He, he, he, he! I like her boss, she's funny" Garry said as he and Draconis moved to follow behind them.

———————

Geeves led the nobles into the assembly hall. General Marius, Guildmaster Darrius, and Commander Willis were already present discussing logistics with Deathwalker, Elder Martha, Trader Malcom, Betterman, and Paul. After Lords Dormeir, Longshot, and Simium took their seats, Elder Martha spoke up.

"That is enough gentlemen. We can discuss the rest of these items later."

"Let me welcome you all to the first Timberfall Duchy Council meeting." Deathwalker said.

The nobles had confused looks on their faces. Seeing this Deathwalker continued. "My understanding is the rest of the kingdom is governed by the noble in charge and they may decide to collectively get together with their subordinates to discuss matters of importance, but non-nobles are rarely included in such discussions. I plan to run things a bit differently in our duchy."

"Different how, Deathwalker?" Sebastian asked.

Lord Simium seemed displeased that Lord Dormeir was being so formal with their liege. He was about to speak up when Deathwalker answered the question.

"First, thank you for not being so formal here my friend. I appreciate it. It is important that everyone here feels they can speak their minds freely. I do not want any of you to remain silent or not speak up out of concern for decorum."

Deathwalker looked at Lord Simium directly. "I know you may not be comfortable with such things Lord Simium, but I ask that you try while here in these council chambers."

"I will do my best to do as you command, your grace." Lord Simium bowed his head.

"That is all I ask. Now, to answer Sebastian's question. Those you see in this room make up most of what I am calling the Advisory Council." Deathwalker said before he began introducing those in the room.

"There are a few members from the Timberfall city council that may join us later. For now, Betterman is representing those businesses. Paul and Malcom are my Trade and Transportation ministers, they are here to coordinate our trade and transportation needs across the duchy. If you have your own trade ministers, I encourage them to work through them. You cannot have a thriving territory without a prosperous economy."

The three visiting nobles gave a slight head nod in acknowledgement of Betterman, Paul, and Malcom.

Deathwalker continued. "We must protect our citizens and our borders if we hope to have the time to grow and sustain our economy. With that in mind, General Marius shall lead all military matters in our duchy, please have your territory and house guards establish contact and magical means of communication. Commander Willis is primarily focused on Timberfall city's guards and patrols but I have asked him to establish a special forces unit that will be responsible for handling internal security matters."

"Special forces unit?" Lord Simium asked.

"Yes. As you were informed Simium, I was attacked leaving your city manor."

"What?!" Lord Dormeir exclaimed.

"How could you let such a thing happen?!" Lord Longshot stared daggers at his peer.

Deathwalker raised his hand. "It is fine. My Savage Squad wiped the floor with the would-be-assassins."

"Were they like what we faced in the capital?" Sebastian asked.

"No. They were not as high-leveled or as skilled. However, they were similarly equipped which makes me think they are related." Deathwalker explained.

"Your grace, I was beside myself when I heard of what happened. I ordered an investigation, but it turned up very little." Lord Simium apologized.

"My beastmen have heighten senses that can aid in such investigations." Commander Willis chimed in.

"Beastmen?" Lord Simium inquired.

"That is right Simium. The entire unit is made up of beast-kin. They are fierce warriors, and their enhanced senses will make them invaluable in both investigations and counter espionage. I have asked Commander Willis to send his unit to Simium city to do their own investigation. See to it that your people provide them everything they require." Deathwalker ordered.

Lord Simium bowed his head. "Of course, your grace. I shall send word right away!"

Deathwalker acknowledged the response before he waved in the direction of Guildmaster Darrius. "Lastly, I have partnered with the Adventurers' guild. They have shared quest boards at each portal station and get discounts on traveling for guild business. We do not leverage adventurers enough as a kingdom, and I encourage all of you to consider outsourcing some of your needs to the guild. It should help give adventurers more opportunities to level and be less expensive than sending your own forces to address everything."

"Wise plan, but to be expected from a former adventurer." Sebastian smiled.

"My family has long since supported the use of adventurers. In fact, our city has one of the highest populations of adventurers." Lord Simium commented.

"We are all well aware of that old man." Lord Longshot dismissed the comment.

"There are other things we can address later, as I have plans related to education and farming, but that can wait for now. A word of caution, I have uncovered some information which implies that war is coming to the kingdom." Deathwalker said as he raised his hand to forestall any questions. "I will not get into any of that at this time, I share this more as a warning. Be mindful and keep your eyes and ears open."

Everyone in the room nodded their heads.

"Good. I would like to speak with Lord Simium separately in regard to these investigations. Elder Martha would you please give the others a tour of the city. You should be proud of the rapid development and growth."

Elder Martha rose from her seat and bowed to Deathwalker. "It would be my honor to show everyone what has been going on in our city."

After everyone left the hall, only Deathwalker, Lord Simium, and Commander Willis remained. "Go ahead Commander, share what you have learned."

Lord Simium looked surprised. "You mean your men have already been conducting their investigation? Why did you keep this from me until now, your grace? Have I offended you in some way?!"

Deathwalker sighed. "It is not you Simium, but rather your son."

————

"I cannot believe it, my son?! No, there has to be a mistake." Lord Simium said in denial.

Commander Willis just finished his report outlining everything his beastmen investigators discovered. Deathwalker had to give it to Commander Willis and his men, they were thorough. The fact that the men had started calling themselves the Timberfall Hunter Squad irked the Duke a bit, but he let it go.

"Believe it Simium. I heard something similar from my would-be-attackers. Your son owes some dangerous people. What is worse is the fact that your son colluded with them to poison you." Deathwalker shared his thoughts.

"My-my own son conspired to kill me, I just..."

"He wanted to be Simium's city lord. From what Commander Willis' men uncovered, it appears this unknown shadow faction wanted someone they could control in power." Deathwalker explained.

Lord Simium just sat in silence for several moments, clearly distraught. The man finally rose his head and asked the question he feared the answer to. "What of my daughter? Is she in cahoots with these vile people?"

"We cannot be for certain, but what evidence we did find seems to suggest she has no clue what her brother was up to." Commander Willis answered.

"She always was a daddy's girl." Lord Simium commented. He sighed as though resigning himself for the inevitable. "What is it you require of me, your grace?"

"Commander Willis and his men will arrest Knight Simium. This will be done quietly. I am lending him the use of my personal bodyguards to guarantee such outcome."

"You do this to protect my family's honor. Once again, you take kindness on me, your grace." Lord Simium bowed his head to his duke.

Deathwalker waved away the comment. "Think nothing of it. As I was saying, Knight Simium will be held accountable for his actions, but to do that we require answers. Your son will be held at a secret location while we extract the information we require."

"If you would indulge your humble servant, I would like the chance to speak with him after his arrest."

Deathwalker nodded. "That can be arranged. Lady Emma has already offered to go shopping with Dame Simium today while Elder Martha is showing everyone around. I would ask that you speak with your daughter when they return."

"As your command, your grace." Lord Simium bowed again.

Turning to Commander Willis, Deathwalker gave the order. "Do it. I want it done before the opening ceremony."

"As you command, my alpha!" Commander Willis proclaimed.

# Chapter 23 – Commencement

“The arena is huge.” Dame Simium commented as her father escorted her in.

“It is rather impressive.” Lord Simium replied.

“It is a shame brother cannot be here.” Dame Simium said as they walked further into the massive coliseum arena.

“Yes, a real tragedy.” Lord Longshot said sarcastically.

Lord Dormeir shook his head at his friend and peer. The two of them walked together up to the arena stage. Deathwalker had seen to it that all the high nobles would have a seat near him. Sebastian thought it was quite clever. This gave the high nobles a place of honor among all in attendance, yet implied they supported and backed the new duke.

Deathwalker was already sitting next to King Alfheim and his retinue was sitting to the left of Deathwalker. Lady Emma, the crown princess, sat to his right, then Duchess Lightheart, followed by Elder Martha. Sebastian’s seat was next to the city ruler, with Lord Longshot next to him. Lord Simium and his daughter were next, followed by General Marius and Guildmaster Darrius.

Cal, Mara, Trader Malcom, Paul, Clarisse, Betterman, Ron, Samuel sat with Alyce and Elsa behind Deathwalker. Garry, Draconis, Mrrsha, Prrsha, and Frrsha stood behind them. Commander Willis stood with the Savage Squad and had his men stationed throughout the arena.

The stands were already filled to burst. In the front of the stage stood a podium with a magical artifact affixed to it. This magic tool would enhance and project the speaker’s voice across the coliseum and beyond.

Seeing the people taking their seats, Deathwalker and Elder Martha rose to their feet and approached the podium. Elder Martha spoke up first. “Good people of Timberfall and esteemed visitors, let me welcome you to our city.”

Cheers erupted from the stands. Elder Martha raised her hand and the crowd’s excitement died down. “It is my honor to introduce my liege, the duke of Timberfall Duchy, Deathwalker Dragonvein!”

The crown clapped and smiled as Deathwalker raised his hand, the noise quieted. “Thank you, Elder Martha. It was important to me, as you are the noble over this city that you were the one to kick this off.”

The citizens of Timberfall cheered for Elder Martha and their duke. After a few moments Deathwalker continued. “I also felt it was important to celebrate the formation of our duchy and to commemorate that with a weeklong celebration. Many have come from far and wide to enjoy this first ever Timberfall festival!”

Deathwalker gave the crowd a few moments to die down again. “During this festival there will be cooks, breweries, and cuisine from all over. The portal fees are waived for your arrival and departure each day. This is to make it easier for more people to join us in the celebration. As many traders have come for this festival, I encourage you to enjoy the market and sample the food.”

More cheering echoed through the coliseum and the streets beyond.

Deathwalker continued. “Also, I want to promote healthy competition. We will be conducting a series of tournaments here in this arena over the next several days. Anyone interested can register at the various booths surrounding the arena. There will be multiple separate competitions. To start, Timberfall is a lumber export, how could we not have a few lumberjack feats of strength and skill!”

Most of the original residents of Timberfall expressed their excitement at getting a chance to show off their craft.

“In addition, there will be tournaments in melee combat, magic, archery, cooking, and brewing!”

The crowd seemed excited by this announcement, and murmurs could be heard from people commenting on which they would try their hand at.

"Now to help keep things fair, there will be a panel of judges to help determine the winners. Please help me welcome our panel of judges; King Alfheim of the elves, Duchess Lightheart of the Hargrave Duchy, Elder Martha, Guildmaster Darrius, Betterman of Betterman Leathers, Clarisse of the Explorers League, and Samuel of the Sleepy Inn."

Each person stood up and approached as Deathwalker announced their name. Finally, he raised his hand for silence. "Last but not least, the royal family's official representative for the festival, the crown princess, Lady Emma!"

This time the crowd got louder. Everyone had heard the official news that the King and Queen made it clear Lady Emma was the successor to the throne. Many knew there were rumors of her impending betrothal to Deathwalker. Seeing Lady Emma come to stand beside him, the crowd could not help but get excited.

"Thank you, good people of Timberfall Duchy. Let me also welcome King Alfheim, my grandfather to our Kingdom of Nord. As many of you have come to learn, our Duke Deathwalker Dragonvein and his allies have accomplished much since he arrived. Please join me in our support of him and our new Timberfall Duchy!"

People took to their feet and clapped and cheered.

"Thank you, Crown Princess, Lady Emma, and all of you for your support. Much is to come for our duchy and the kingdom as we usher in a new era of prosperity. This festival is the beginning of prosperity to come. We will end this festival with a grand hunt, that I will lead. The food we catch will be prepared by the winner of the cooking competition and shared with all attendees of the Timberfall festival!" Deathwalker quickly raised his hand before the crowd could get too loud as he continued. "In addition, I will personally be buying multiple casks from the winner of the brewing competition. If they cannot supply enough, I will purchase from the runner ups. These casks will be shared freely with all of you!"

Now that made the whole arena and surrounding streets erupt praising their duke for his generosity.

Deathwalker took Elder Martha and Lady Emma's hands in his, Lady Emma took her grandfather's hand, who took his daughter's. They all raised their arms up. Deathwalker spoke first. "Now let this festival begin!"

"With our blessings enjoy!" Lady Emma echoed.

"To our kin in the Kingdom of Nord!" King Alfheim called out.

"I approve of this momentous occasion!" Duchess Lightheart said.

"Let us celebrate Timberfall!" Elder Martha called out.

"That was well done Duke Dragonvein." Dame Simium commented as her and Lord Simium approached.

"Thank you, Dame Simium. I hope you and your father enjoy the festival." Deathwalker replied before turning his attention to her father. "Lord Simium, if you are interested, I would like you to help Commander Willis with some matters while I am indisposed with the judging. Also, if you are open to it, step in to judge some of the preliminary contests in my stead when my duties do not allow me to get away."

Lord Simium bowed. "You do me much honor, my duke. I appreciate the trust you are giving me."

"You are one of my vassals and I hope in time we can consider each other friends." Deathwalker put his hand out and shook Lord Simium's hand.

"Thank you for putting your faith in our family." Dame Simium bowed as well before her father escorted her off the stage.

Lord Dormeir spoke up as he approached with Lord Longshot right on his heels. "I see you did not ask Longshot and I to be judges."

Deathwalker chuckled. "Where would the fun be for you two. Besides, how can you participate if I made you a judge?"

"I plan to win the Melee tournament." Lord Dormeir said with excitement.

"And I look forward to winning the Archery competition!" Lord Longshot had a look of determination on his face.

"Then I guess my sister and I will have to give you a run for your money!" Cal teased, as he and Mara joined the conversation.

"Ah, yes, I have heard of your quick blades Calcius. It shall be fun to see what you can do." Lord Dormeir replied.

"My brother is one of the best with the blades and I have yet to be matched with the arrow." Mara said.

Lord Longshot raised an eyebrow. "Oh really?"

Deathwalker interjected. "Lord Longshot this is Cal and his sister Mara. I am a part of their adventuring party. I do believe Mara will be tough to beat as will Cal."

Lord Longshot smiled as he shook both their hands. "This tournament shall be more fun than I expected." He then held out his elbow to Mara. "Care to accompany me to the range to warm up?"

"Sure, why not. I keep hearing you are the best in the kingdom. Let us see if that is true." Mara smiled back and hooked her arm into his elbow.

Cal tightened his hands on the hilts of his blades. 'If he tries to hurt her or is playing some game...' Cal's thoughts were cutoff by his friend's words.

"The melee competition does not start for several hours. That gives you plenty of time to escort a certain person to the festivities. It is her day off work after all."

Cal smiled at Deathwalker, nodded, and then excused himself before darting off at high speed. Lady Emma commented on the sudden change. "I am guessing Mary Sue."

Deathwalker nodded. “Yes, he is quite smitten. I think she likes him too, and who am I to stand in the way of true love.”

“I had no idea you were such a romantic Deathwalker.” Lady Emma smiled.

“And a good friend. I understand being protective, but he risked much with his brash behavior.” Lord Dormeir commented.

“He is being a protective brother. It is honorable.” Deathwalker replied.

“Oh, you are right as ever my friend, but you also know the law.”

“Yes, but Anthony does not seem one to enforce such a thing if it did come to blows.” Deathwalker answered.

“That be true enough. If you will excuse me. I must prepare and I am certain Captain Saunders will want to enter the competition as well. I must make sure he knows he has my approval.” Sebastian excused himself.

“Speaking about getting escorted to see the various festivities...” Lady Emma started to say.

Deathwalker held out his elbow. “Yes, my lady, it would be my pleasure to escort you.”

Lady Emma smiled and hooked her arm in with his. Her aunt, Duchess Lightheart, quickly approached. “Did I hear you say you are checking out the festivities? I approve.” As she said her last words, Duchess Lightheart took Deathwalker’s other arm.

Taking things in stride, he smiled and replied. “Why yes, it would be my pleasure to escort you both. Shall we see if King Alfheim wants to join us?”

Deathwalker inwardly chuckled at both of their expressions as King Alfheim spoke up. “How kind of you to offer, Deathwalker. Of course, we would like to join you.”

————

The city was filled with people. The atmosphere was jovial and filled with mirth. Minstrels could be heard playing in the streets, the very talented ones were offered coin to play near their shoppe.

All the inns were completely booked for those that wanted to stay in the city. Those that did not want to stay the night or could not find a room were happy to use the free portal service. Each connecting city found their inns completely booked and often business owners and merchants could be heard hoping this Timberfall festival turned into an annual event as it meant work for them and the many temporary workers they had to bring on.

Many set up small carts or stands near the massive coliseum arena. The area was filled with merchants. As people walked through the various rows, they could hear various people trying to hawk their wares.

"Get the finest wares in the kingdom!"

"Finest wares, ha! Do not listen to him, come to my stand! My goods are far better than anything he has!"

"Fresh kebabs! Get your fresh kebabs!"

"Ooo! Ooo! Let's get some kebabs buddy!" Garry bobbed in excitement.

"I could eat. What are these kebabs you speak of?" Draconis replied.

"From the boss's memories they are seasoned chunks of meat on a stick! He seemed to really enjoy it." Garry answered.

"If Master likes them, they must be good, he has impeccable taste." Draconis commented.

The duo made their way to the kebab stand. There was a young blonde girl working the stand and taking orders while an older gentleman was doing all the grilling. The smell coming from the grill had drawn a crowd.

Three of the male patrons were refusing to leave after they got their order. It was clear they were enamored by the young girl. One of them grabbed her by the arm.

"Come on, we will show you a good time!"

"No, I am not interested!" The girl tried to pull her arm away, but the ruffian had a firm grip.

"Hey, she said leave her alone!" The older man came to the girl's defense.

Before he could get very far, one of his buddies hit him hard in the gut. He hit him so hard the man collapsed to his knees. Not expecting the sucker punch, the old man clutched his stomach and tried not to throw up his lunch.

The other patrons in line were about to protest when some invisible force grabbed them and moved all of them to the side.

"Thank you, Garry. I refused to wait in that line." Draconis said.

The crowd was about to protest, but one look from the large red-haired man had them looking elsewhere. Nodding at the humanoids who were wise enough to find somewhere else to be, Draconis and Garry approached the commotion at the kebab stand.

The two that were not holding the girl drew weapons. "Looks like we have a couple of goody goodies!"

Draconis looked at Garry. "I think they are talking to us."

Garry laughed. "Ha, ha, ha, ha, ha! They think we are..." the Shadow Gazer used one of his eye stalks to wipe tear from his big eye. "I don't even know where to begin with how wrong a statement that is!"

"Perhaps they are brain damaged. It is clear they are not very bright." Draconis commented.

Garry looked at the one grabbing the girl. "If we were goody-goody then would we do this?"

With a mental command Garry grabbed the dagger sheathed at the man's belt. In one quick motion lifted it in the air, causing the man to turn to look at it in shock, before the blade was in the man's eye socket. He let go of the girl and moved his hand halfway to his head before he collapsed dead.

"How dare you!" One of the men called out as the remaining two rushed duo.

"Now he definitely has brain damage! Ha, ha, ha!" Garry laughed.

"Ha, ha, ha, ha, ha! That was a good one Garry." Draconis replied half paying attention to the two men rushing them. "Eh, guess it is my turn."

Draconis moved like lightning. He grabbed each of the assailants' sword arms with a vice grip. With both of his arms, he pulled the two together, driving their blades into each other. In one stroke, both men slam into each other, blade sticking out of them as they collapse to the ground dead.

"I keep forgetting how fragile these beings are." Draconis commented as he looked down at the crumpled bodies.

"Yea, it's great isn't it. He, he, he! Now let's get what we came here for." Garry floated towards the kebab stand.

"Thank you, uh... good sirs." The older cook bowed.

The little girl offered them several kebabs each. "Thank you for your help Mr Garry and Draconis."

Draconis accepted the kebabs. "How do you know who we are little one?"

Garry took his kebabs with Telekinesis and chomped down on them sticks and all. "Yummm!"

"My name is Alyce. My grandfather sits on the Council and my mother works for the Adventurers' guild." Alyce waved to the older cook. "This is a friend of his Tookin. I call him Uncle Tookin. I was taught to look out for family and friends. So, when I found out he needed help I offered."

"Huh? Did you say something? I stopped paying attention after I took a bit of these kebabs. Have you tried these things? They are delicious!" Draconis commented.

"Would you like some more? It is the least we can do for your help." Tookin offered.

"We won't say no!" Garry answered.

Multiple guards swarmed in and surrounded the group.

"Halt! Who killed these men?! You, there! You are under arrest for murder!" One of the guards ordered.

"Very good soldier." A guard in more adorned armor said before turning his attention to Garry and Draconis. "I am Sergeant Chen of the Timberfall guard and you two are going away for a long time!"

"Sergeant, these two serve the duke." Alyce chimed in.

"It does not matter! No one is above the law! Now be silent child!" Sergeant Chen barked.

"Do you think master would be upset if we killed all these men?" Draconis asked Garry.

"Eh. Maybe. The boss doesn't like to waste resources."

"How dare you threaten the guard! Men!" Sergeant Chen cried out and all the guards tightened their grips on their weapons and slowly marched closer.

"Guess we get to have a bit more fun after all, buddy. I'll take the ones on the left; you take the ones on the right." Garry commented.

"Okay, but I get to kill the annoying sergeant guy. I do not like the look of him. That and no one but our master gives me orders!" Draconis' face held a wicked grin.

"HOLD! I order you all to stand DOWN!" Commander Willis entered the area.

"But-but Commander... these men threatened us and they killed those men!" Sergeant Chen protested.

"They killed those men defending innocent people. I saw it with my own eyes from the rooftop." Commander Willis replied before turning his attention to Garry and Draconis. "Something told me to keep an eye on you two to make sure you did not get into any trouble."

"Thank you, Commander. This man was not willing to listen to reason." Alyce chimed in.

"Why you little shit!" Sergeant Chen snapped back before catching himself.

"Grrrrr! Watch your tongue, Sergeant! We do not speak to children in such a manner, especially to a family member of one of our council members. Follow me and let us have a conversation about proper etiquette befitting the town guard!" Commander Willis brokered no argument as he grabbed the sergeant by the back of the collar and started to haul him away.

Alyce stuck her tongue out at the sergeant as he was being dragged away.

'Damn that brat! I almost rid ourselves of two of the duke's pawns.' Chen vowed he would make that little girl pay one day.

"Man, I was kind of looking forward to some more mayhem." Garry said as he watched all the guards follow behind their squad leader.

Draconis just shrugged his shoulders. "Eh, let us eat some more of those kebabs."

"Please follow us. It is our pleasure." Tookin offered.

"Uncle Tookin is hoping to enter the cooking contest. If you could spread the word about how good his kebabs are I am sure it will help." Alyce suggested.

"Sure! The boss loves good food." Garry replied.

"Do you think we should save some for him?" Draconis asked.

"Nah. Boss said to enjoy ourselves and that he would be busy with festival matters all day." Garry answered.

"You have a point. Then we should check out the melee competition. I am curious how some of these beings comport themselves in combat." Draconis recommended.

"Sure, why not. I am always game to watch some blood and violence." Garry said to Draconis as the two headed towards the melee competition after grabbing a few more kebabs.

Tookin watched the duo go. "Those two are rather scary."

"Yea but they helped us out when they did not half to. Just as I expect people close to Deathwalker to be, noble and honorable." Alyce smiled.

"I do believe you have a crush, my niece. You are far too young to worry about such things. You have a few more years before you are fifteen and eligible to marry. Focus on enjoying your childhood." Tookin admonished.

"I think it is so old fashioned to have to wait so long." Alyce pouted.

"Your grandfather was telling me Deathwalker told him, that where he comes from people could not marry until eighteen." Tookin shared.

"Eighteen?! They must live much longer than we do. That is crazy. Ma and pa were married at sixteen. Do you know where Deathwalker comes from?" Alyce asked.

"No, he never said, but from what your grandfather said it seemed to be very far away. Come enough daydreaming, we have kebabs to sell or give away before I can enter the cooking contest. Every chef must contribute a certain amount to the festival to help feed the people." Tookin answered.

# Interlude - Dwarven Capital

“That was very good, lass.” Grimhold stated after he finished the meal Griselda made.

Griselda beamed at Grimhold’s words, while giving a little smirk towards Mezza.

“I told ya my little Griselda could cook.” Narn boasted.

“Aye, that ya did. I can see why you married her mother.” Grimhold took Mezza’s hand in his and squeezed. “My Mezza is the best cook I have ever met, and I intend to marry her.”

Griselda’s smile slipped and turned into a tight line when she saw Mezza smiling back. “That is part of why we came here, to get his family’s blessing.”

Narn’s eyebrows rose. “Does she not...”

Grimhold cut him off. “What of our old friend? Still as pretty as ever?”

Narn, picking up on the fact his friend did not wish to talk about his family answered Grimhold’s question. “Aye, he still bears the marks from that day. The scar on his face is a testament to that.”

Grimhold grimaced at the reminder.

“He is captain of the royal guards now.” Narn finished.

“His men come by the forge often.” Griselda chimed in.

Narn pointed to his missing arm with his remaining hand. “Aye, but never Fenrir. I think he cannot stand the sight of me and feels he failed.”

“There be enough guilt to go around.” Grimhold replied.

“Enough of the self-pity. Let us drink till we canna see straight!” Narn declared.

“Now that is something I agree with!” Mezza declared as she squeezed Grimhold’s hand.

Griselda stood up to grab the keg when the door swung open. Soldiers rushed in with their weapons unsheathed, filling the room. “What is the meaning of this?!” Narn demanded.

The soldiers parted from the door allowing a well armored dwarf with a large scar on his face to enter the room. “Grimhold you are to be taken into custody and brought to the king at once!”

Mezza squeezed Grimhold’s hand as he stood. “There is no need for such a reception Fenrir. We will come with you.”

Fenrir looked at the couple holding hands. “You should have announced yourselves right away, but it appears your mind is clouded by a woman and have forgotten your duty!”

“Watch yer mouth Fenrir. This is Mezza, my betrothed, and I will not have you talking down to her in any way!”

Fenrir just turned and walked out of the room.

“Ya best go after him lad. It was nice visiting, but tradition and protocol must be adhered to.” Narn commented.

“Stubborn dwarf!” Grimhold stated.

“We are both just as stubborn.” Narn declared.

“Should we not go with them Grimmy?” Mezza asked.

“Nah, it be best to get this over with.”

# Chapter 24 - Round One, Fight

## —Deathwalker's Perspective—

As I returned to the coliseum after my tour of the various festivities with some of our esteemed guests, I found the tournaments underway. I was impressed by how much my people had handled. This was our inaugural festival, yet everything was well organized and running just as envisioned.

Making Elder Martha the city noble in charge was one of the best decisions I have made to date. Including the entire council in the planning efforts was second. Everyone pitched in and brought some great ideas for both economic growth and ease of engagement in the festivities for the overall populace. My tour showed me just how competent they were.

Lord Simium had stepped in for me to help judge the combatants while I was taking the tour. Guildmaster Darrius, his brother General Marius were helping judge the Melee competition. As I returned to the judges' booth, I asked how things were progressing.

"We have seen some impressive talent, my liege." Lord Simium replied.

"Some we may want to recruit for the army." General Marius offered.

"If you do not recruit the non-adventurers, I will." Darrius grinned at his brother.

"So, either way we win." Lord Simium surmised.

"It sounds like it." I commented.

Lord Simium leaned in so only I could hear him over the sounds of combat. "I spoke with my daughter."

"How'd it go?" I asked.

"As well as to be expected. She shared with me that she thought he was hanging around with a seedier element, but just figured he was sowing his wild oats and indulging in some vices." Simium shared.

"The real question is do you believe her?"

"My daughter has been caught up in royal court politics and gossip, but she has no interest in taking my place. My son was the ambitious one." Lord Simium explained.

"Perhaps. You will need to start grooming her now. It takes time to learn the nuisances of running a territory." I advised.

"I made her aware. She was not thrilled with the idea, but she understands the necessity." Lord Simium replied.

The announcer, who was using a magical artifact to project his voice, called out a name that caught my attention.

"Next we have Captain Saunders, head of Lord Sebastian Dormeir's soldiers, against the adventurer known as the Sunderer!"

"Oh, this should be entertaining." Darrius commented.

"You missed Lord Dormeir. He mopped the floor with his opponent." Marius informed me.

I smiled at the news of my friend's victory. "What do you know about this Sunderer?"

Lord Simium was the one that spoke up. "He does a good amount of work in my territory. He has some impressive ability and skills that let him pierce through armor. The man is typically given quests involving monsters with high defenses."

My interest was piqued.

Darrius spoke up next. “He is the best anti-defender in the guild. Saunders does not stand a chance.”

“Poor match up indeed. Captain Saunders is a knight who specializes in defense.” General Marius commented.

I had given Marius and Willis the combined assignment to learn everything they could about the forces we could call upon to defend our dukedom. If Marius was saying it was a bad match, I trusted his assessment.

Saunders was not a small man, he had broad shoulders, toned muscles, and stood at a decent height. Compared to the Sunderer however, he looked puny. The mountain of a man stood at least seven feet tall, you could put two Saunders side by side and they would not come close to the size of this man.

“BEGIN!” The announcer called out.

The two men rushed each other. Captain Saunders wore plate armor and held a sword and shield in a typical defender style. The Sunderer wore some kind of scale mail and held a massive two-handed great sword. Both men moved rather quickly for their size and the weapons and armor they used.

It was clear Saunders knew of the man as he did not try to ‘tank’ the swing from the Sunderer’s massive great sword. He dodged out of the way. I expected Saunders to be faster than the massive man, but surprisingly he was struggling to keep up.

Watching the Sunderer move was like watching a mountain move, that is if the mountain could flow like water. The man bent and flowed with far more speed and grace than someone of his size had any right to. The fight lasted roughly sixty seconds, which in combat can be an eternity, but it was clear everyone’s assessment was correct, Saunders was no match for this beast.

Saunders was just a little bit too slow on his latest dodge. He caught part of the flat of Sunderer's great sword on the swing. It was clear to me the Sunderer was not trying to kill and typically used the flat of his blade as more of a club to reduce the chance he might slice the poor knight in two. Just catching part of that hit sent the captain flying back and crashing into the coliseum wall. The magical wards made Saunders slightly bounce off the wall and land on his back.

"Cough, I concede. At least I lasted longer than I thought I would." Saunders croaked out. It was clear he was going to need some serious healing.

The Sunderer reached out his hand and lifted the heavily armored knight like he weighed nothing. "You fight well. Not many can stand against me. One day perhaps I will find one who can. From that day I will be his man."

His words surprised me and gave me some ideas. I filed that away for later.

It was time for Cal's match up. He was up against an elf. King Alfheim, Elder Martha, Duchess Lightheart, and Lady Emma were judging the magical competition, so I could not ask them why an elf chose martial combat instead of magic. It was not like someone couldn't enter multiple disciplines, but the first few rounds of the magic and melee tournaments were being held at the same time. This made it rather hard for someone to participate in both. As elves were magically inclined, this surprised me.

"What do we know about his competitor?" I asked.

"That is one of Mineheir's majors, a man by the name of Arden. He is more martially inclined. Has some body-strengthening magic but not much in the way of ranged magic. The General was telling me about him. I believe he was also going to enter the archery competition when that starts tomorrow." General Marius explained.

"Interesting." I replied just before the announcer called out, "BEGIN!"

In terms of speed the two men were evenly matched. They practically danced and flipped around the arena as they parried and dodged attacks. It was clear this elven major was rather skilled. Even when he started to activate his body strengthening, my teammate had no problem keeping up with him.

I realized how much Cal had really grown. I did what I could to join them on any quests from the Adventurers' guild. This allowed Cal to take greater risks as he knew I would be there to heal him. Greater risk, greater reward. He learned how to enhance his body using his mana and once he learned that his talent skyrocketed. It was clear the orphaned twin was driven, both to keep up with his sister and her growing capabilities and, I think, his interest in my head maid.

The two of them finally started to go out on a few dates. I made it clear to both of them that they were grown adults, and I had no expectations either way. Sure, I gave Suzie a decent amount of paid time off lately, but that was more me making up for how poorly the employment laws were in this kingdom, sure that is why and no other reason. Okay, maybe a little reason. What can I say? I could tell they both were interested in each other and the only way to allow that to blossom was to give them the time they both needed.

I heard Suzie cheering for Cal, and when he heard it, a look of greater determination took hold. A driver all men knew of that would make us push ourselves harder and risk more, all to gain greater respect from the woman he loved.

Cal's speed and the force of his blows increased. The elven major was now backpedaling as he attempted to keep up with his opponent's newfound strength.

The fight only lasted a few more moments. As with any type of combat, the scales can turn quickly. Cal had increased the tempo of the fight, but it did not take long for Major Arden to adapt.

The battle-hardened major infused his muscles with power and started to emit a faint aura. This aura created a cold that began to leech away Cal's own body-enhancement magic. Realizing the tables had quickly turned the rogue tried to draw his opponent in.

Cal made a desperate feint in a last-ditch effort to gain an upper hand, but Major Arden did not take the bait. Instead, he used Cal's temporary over extension against him by sweeping the rogue's legs out from under him. The move caught Cal completely off guard. The elf fell flat on his back and as he looked up at one of Arden's blades, which was inches from Cal's face.

"I concede!" Cal cried out.

The elven major offered Cal his hand. "Well fought!"

"Good match!" Cal commented as Arden helped the man to his feet.

"You fight well. Work on not letting your emotions get the better of you in battle, that is what defeated you, not me." Major Arden advised.

Cal was about to protest, then paused and realized he was proving the man's point. Exhaling, "Ah, you may be right. You are a tough opponent. That aura of yours is wicked."

"I have Winter Fey in my bloodline. That has its perks." Arden commented.

"I would not know. My parents died when I was young. My sister and I were street rats. There is very little we know of our heritage." Cal replied.

Then the elven major said something neither Cal nor I were expecting to hear. "Let no one speak ill of your humble origins, orphan. Yes, I know of your background. I knew your father; he would be proud of the elf you have become."

Cal just stood there in shock. He tried not to think upon those painful memories. They were so young when his parents died. He knew so little about them.

"If you ever wish to speak or hear some stories of our past adventures, seek me, Major Arden, out." The elf said as he started to walk out of the arena. "Oh, and if you are ever in elven lands and anyone disrespects or dismisses you due to your accent, tell me and I will straighten them out."

# Interlude - Capital of Nord

Duke Watson bowed to the king and queen. “Brother, why have you called me here? I was planning on visiting the Timberfall festival.”

“That can wait. We have a pressing matter to address.” The king replied.

“What has happened?”

“My father has made his intentions clear. He wishes to officially announce my niece as his successor.” The queen answered.

“That is rather fast. He learns she can cast magic and is not only ready to publicly acknowledge her, finally, but name her his heir?”

Advisor Nero walked into the small conference room. “Perhaps I can shed some light on things.”

“Advisor Nero?! I thought you were in Timberfall!” Duke Watson exclaimed.

“I was and I must return soon. His majesty entrusted me to be the one to relay this matter with the utmost discretion.” The advisor replied.

“What matter? Would someone please start making sense!”

“King Alfheim intercepted a missive from Advisor Mona. She has sent word of your daughter’s miraculous healing and her ability to use magic. The message also includes the magical wonder of the portals. All these things have been made possible thanks to a single man.” Nero explained.

“We all know of Duke Dragonvein’s talents when it comes to magic. That does not invalidate my daughter’s claim to the elven throne. I am not seeing why this required you to come in secret during the middle of the night!” Duke Watson complained.

“Tell him.” The queen ordered.

Advisor Nero nodded. “There was one other bit of information in the missive. Advisor Mona sensed residual Winter magic in Timberfall. She believes it is tied to Deathwalker, making him a prime candidate to be the Huntsman reborn.”

Duke Watson, who had yet to take his seat after entering the room fell back into his chair stunned.

“Advisor Mona has always been a spy for Queen Mab. Deathwalker is planning on ending the festival with a grand hunt, some might call that a Wild Hunt.” Advisor Nero stated.

“For her to find traces of Winter magic... when Queen Mab hears this, she will come and sweep aside anyone who dares to stand in her way. My niece, your daughter, means nothing to Mab, her heart is as cold as ice, she will take what she believes is Her’s.” the queen said.

“Their pending engagement must be dissolved.” Duke Watson finally spoke up, worry in his voice for his daughter and his nation. It was best for everyone that the Queen of Winter stayed in the north. Her very presence affected the environment around her.

“My king does not wish any harm to come to the Kingdom of Nord, but I would recommend you prepare your people and restrict travel that might cross her path.” Advisor Nero cautioned.

“How long do we have?” Duke Watson asked.

Advisor Nero answered. “The missive should already be in the Winter Queen’s hands. It will take time to mobilize her court...”

“How long?” Duke Watson pressed.

“A month if you are lucky. Realistically three weeks.”

“Thank you for delivering this message. It gives us time to prepare.” the king said.

“Please thank my father as well. We will need some time to determine what to do and how best to prepare. For now, tell him to keep this quiet.” The queen chimed in.

Advisor Nero bowed his head and left.

The three royals just sat there in silence for a time. History of this continent proved no country survived if they tried to get in between the Winter Queen and what she wanted. They would have to distance themselves from Deathwalker, Timberfall Duchy would be lost.

"The best course of action would be to withdraw troops from the area now, then after the festival, make a public announcement. To say anything now would cause a panic. Let the people of Timberfall have a chance at joy. Then we will recall Emma, Duchess Lightheart, and our guests. There is nothing Timberfall can do to stop what is coming." The king stated.

The queen nodded. "Agreed. My niece will be heartbroken. I do not wish to rush that sorrow."

Duke Watson finally spoke up. "I cannot believe Winter is coming..."

Advisor Nero had left the room but only now shut the door, a smile on his face.

A tiny flash of light zipped through the crack in the door before it closed, not noticed by anyone. The light moved as fast as its little wings could towards the portal station. 'I must warn my liege!'

# Chapter 25 - Considerations

## —Deathwalker's Perspective—

"My hunky master. I know it is late but one of the little pixies has something you will want to hear." Lilandra told me telepathically.

I was awake. I did not sleep much, and when I did it was not for very long. I had two cat girls asleep next to me. The three matriarchs had come to an agreement amongst themselves that one to two would stand watch and one or two would get to use me as a pillow. Their excuse was they had grown accustomed to sleeping near me when I used to hunt with the pride of pumas in the forest.

Sure, they were soft and comfy, but my mind could not settle down. The previous day had been a resounding success, and I could see the joy on everyone's faces. Even the refugees started to have a look of hope in their eyes. It was a good day. No, what had me worried was this nagging intuition that something was wrong. I mean technically the giant countdown to my permadeath falls into the category of significantly 'something is wrong', but it felt more than that.

For that matter, since I arrived in the Hidden Realm I haven't paid much attention to my intuition, which is odd now that I think about it. My whole life I have had a sixth sense or strong intuition and learned to trust my gut, but now that I think about it, I have pretty much been running off of pure logic and my critical thinking skills. Maybe, yet another side effect of my soul being shattered? Far too many other things to consider now, it is not like I can do anything to change it at this time.

Never mind the fact that Garry and Draconis still have not returned for the night. Last I saw them, they were drinking with Mineheir. The elven general could drink like a dwarf from what I saw. I was concerned about mixing alcohol with a murderhobo and quick to anger dragon, but when General Mineheir had slapped Draconis one too many times on the back, the dragon punched him. I thought I might have to intervene, but the General just got up, laughed and bought them another round of drinks. Like I said, I am convinced he has some dwarf in his heritage somewhere.

They seemed to be having fun and I promised my familiar I would not interfere as long as they didn't try to kill anyone. Sure, I heard about the three ruffians they killed, but that doesn't count. Anyone trying to have their way with an underage girl won't get much sympathy from me, especially little Alyce. In fact, if they hadn't already seen to their deaths I would have.

That little one had grown on me. Commander Willis told me how she stood up to the guard sergeant. Plus, she is always helping people, not just her grandfather and mother. Though those two talk about her so often that I feel like I adopted her as one of my own. Hmmm, maybe I just miss my children more than I thought. She did kind of look like one of my daughters.

I am naturally protective, and that will always be a part of who I am.

Eh, I am sure I would've heard about anything too crazy by now. Might as well get up and listen to what the little pixie has to report. I untangled myself from the two sleeping cat girls and took a seat at my desk.

The little pixie landed on my desk and did a little bow. "Oh, great and honorable one who has taken all of pixie-kind under his wing..."

I interrupted the little one. It had only been a few days, but the little fairies seemed to be rather enamored with me. I know they were not treated well before but come on! I mean I am sure a big factor is their interest in serving Lilandra, yet she swears the little guys are more interested in serving me.

Anyone capable of having the Queen of the Djinn as their disciple was someone, they were interested in serving. Factor in the fact I treat them with honor and respect, and they have flocked to me in droves. Maybe my Charisma is at play here in some way too. I do find once I overcome the initial uncertainty and am liked, that multiplies exponentially. According to Lilandra, we now have hundreds of little fairies under my employ.

"Please I appreciate the kind words, but Lilandra seemed like what you had to say was rather important."

"Oh yes your Majesty."

'Majesty? That's a new one.' I thought as the little one continued.

"As ordered, we have been keeping an eye on all the guests."

"You are being careful, right? I do not want any of you getting hurt just for my curiosity." I interrupted.

The little pixie beamed. "Your concern is truly touching your highness. No, we are very careful. Our kind are rarely noticed unless we want to be."

"That is good. Make sure the others know how I feel on this matter." I said as I turned to my personal fairy.

"Of course, your Majesty. They already know, but it will warm their hearts to hear you continue to express concern for their well-being."

I smiled back at my personal go-between with all the fairies, before turning to the little pixie excitedly waiting to tell me the rest of their story.

"Advisor Nero took the portal to the capital of Nord. There he met with the king and queen and informed them King Alfheim had intercepted a missive from Advisor Mona to Queen Mab..."

"That's not good. What did the message say?" I replied.

"It spoke of King Alfheim's intention to name Lady Emma as his heir and of her ability to use magic thanks to your amazing healing. Advisor Nero also spoke about the portal stations you have created and how you intend to end the festival with a grand hunt. Advisor Mona is convinced you are the Huntsman reborn."

"No surprise there. That fey woman has been rather fascinated with me since she got here." I commented.

"Advisor Nero also said Advisor Mona also detected remnants of Winter magic." The little fairy continued.

That brought me up short. "Some wisps of Mother Winter's magic must still be here from that massive sleep spell she cast. Now Advisor Mona is attributing that to me, just great. That will be a challenge to explain."

"Advisor Nero said Queen Mab would be coming here to Timberfall in roughly three weeks."

A chill ran down my spine. "That's not good. Mother Winter was adamant that I do not meet Mab in my current state."

The little fairy put their hand on my finger in comfort. "Worry not, majesty. Queen Mab is not coming. Well at least not yet."

"Say what now?" I was confused.

"King Alfheim never intercepted the missive. Advisor Nero had been spying on Advisor Mona and got wind of her intentions, but Advisor Mona has not sent the letter." My personal fairy chimed in.

"Okay, please explain." I instructed.

"Advisor Mona still thinks we are doing as she has asked. Most fey do not pay us much mind as you know, my liege. I may have suggested she might want to wait to see what happens with the great hunt. After all, if you cannot lead the hunt or do it poorly how can you be the Huntsman. Advisor Mona may not pay my kind much attention, but she did not become a spy for Queen Mab by being careless. She agreed to wait, but the note is written, and Advisor Nero found it." My personal fairy explained.

"Good job buddy! He did not tell King Alfheim?"

The little pixie who followed Advisor Nero shook its head. "No, your Majesty. He used some kind of crystal and then headed to speak with the human king and his elf queen."

"What game is he playing?" I asked out loud, more to myself than anyone but the little pixie answered me regardless.

"The king, queen, and Duke Watson have agreed they will probably have to back out of your engagement to Lady Emma. They also think anyone who stands in Mab's way is lost. The king gave the order to withdraw his soldiers from the path from Hargrave to Timberfall. This is to be done quietly as to not raise concerns."

"I am not surprised they would not want Lady Emma harmed, but I'm surprised they aren't letting the people know." I commented.

"They will announce the fact that Timberfall Duchy stands alone and offer anyone who wishes to temporarily relocate the opportunity to do so in the other duchies. The kingdom will not publicly state they will not interfere in the Winter Court's business."

"Smart and prudent."

Prrsha remained silent while she watched over me, but hearing this, she had to speak up. "They are no allies. To abandon you when things get tough... Makes me want to claw their eyes out!"

"I appreciate your sentiment my fierce huntress, but I do not expect those that are not part of our faction to do anything different. What I know of Mab, they are making the tough decision to save lives."

"Yes, by sacrificing yours and anyone who stands with you." Prrsha retorted.

I nodded to her in acknowledgement. "Fair point, fear makes people do dumb things. I take it Advisor Nero heard their plans?"

"Yes, your Majesty. He was smiling when he heard about the troop movements."

"You have that look on your face." Prrsha commented.

"Huh? What look?"

"The look that typically comes when you realize something or come to some sort of realization." Prrsha answered.

"Hmmm. I guess I will have to work on my poker face more."

"Poke-her face?" Prrsha asked.

"No poker, it's a game from my world that requires you to be very careful what expressions you display."

"I do not know if anyone other than my sisters and I would notice. Perhaps Lilandra as she watches you closely too."

"She is a bit of a voyeur." I said out loud knowing Lilandra was probably watching.

"Guilty as charged! Bath time is still my favorite!" Lilandra commented across the mental link.

"I like bath time too." Prrsha smiled at me.

"Okay, enough of that." I did not blush, nope not one bit. I turned to the two fairies. "Inform General Marius and Commander Willis that any reinforcements that may come to our aid from the kingdom are being moved. Make sure no one else hears this report."

"It shall be done, my liege."

"Instruct General Marius to bring any patrols back to the city. We can send them through the portal and recall them easily, but I do not want them caught outside the walls should there be an attack."

"You expect an attack, alpha?" Prrsha asked.

"I do. This cannot be coincidence. I would grab Advisor Nero but he is technically a guest so I will have to wait until he leaves the city. Sure, he could be trying to sabotage Advisor Mona as there is no love loss there, but I doubt it. For now, always keep an eye on him."

"Already done, my liege." My personal fairy replied.

"Man, you guys are fast. Great job. Also inform Commander Willis to double their efforts to detect any sabotage. If my intuition is right, we can expect an attack soon, my guess is towards the end of the festival or shortly after. I do not know who or from where, but I want our people ready. Commander Willis is to say nothing to the guards except for his intelligence squad." I turned to Prrsha. "Please work with your sisters to help the Commander out."

"Sure, I can help the canine hunt some prey." Prrsha flashed her claws and smiled.

"Well, there is no way I'm going back to sleep so I might as well start my day early."

## —Draconis & Garry—

"Do you not think we should check in with our master?" Draconis asked.

"Naaahhh. Why would we?" Garry replied.

"We have been out all night, and the sun has come up."

"He said for us to have fun during this festival and that is what we are doing." Garry stated.

"I do not know..."

"I mean think about last night. After we drunk that elf, Mineheir, under the table those guys invited us to join their game. You won all that coin playing cards and gambling!" Garry countered.

"I do like coin and it was rather fun trumping all those humans."

"Yea, what a bunch of rubes! Did they not even consider all my eyes might help me see things they didn't want us to? He, he, he, he!" Garry chuckled.

"Their leader should not have tried to strike me when they lost all their money." Draconis chimed in.

"Ha! That was the best part! Loved how you used hardened dragon scales when he punched you in the gut. Then-then he broke his hand! Ha, ha, ha, ha, ha!"

Commander Willis appeared from a nearby alley. "I appreciate the restraint you both showed."

"I thought you were following us." Garry commented.

"Worried we would make trouble Commander?" Draconis asked.

"You both do not seem surprised to see me."

"Nah, Shadow Gazer remember. I can literally look in every direction at once." Garry chimed in.

Commander Willis nodded in acknowledgement. "Fair point. To answer your question Draconis, I thought after the run in you had it would be prudent. Plus, his grace, my alpha, asked me to keep an eye out for you two."

Draconis bowed his head this time. "Deathwalker is wise. I have a low tolerance for fools."

Commander Willis pointed at Garry. "Yet, you hang out with this one."

Draconis slapped Willis on the back, sending him stumbling a few feet forward. "Ha! Good one!"

Garry laughed. "Ha, ha, ha, ha, ha! The Commander has jokes! Beware, I got plenty! Ha!"

Commander Willis smiled as he let his claws show a bit. "That is one thing I admire about you Garry, you have balls."

"He is a floating ball." Draconis said in confusion, not getting the reference.

Willis decided to change the subject. "I see you two are headed to the arena."

"Absolutely! People kicking the crap out of each other, sign me up."

"The archery competition should be good. Mara and Lord Longshot will both be going against separate competitors today. Lord Dormeir should be facing his opponent in the next round of the Melee tournament." Commander Willis explained.

"I wouldn't mind seeing that hot elf! Don't really care about the others when I can look at her." Garry commented.

"We should observe the others. They are supposed to be allies of our master. We should get a better idea of what they are capable of." Draconis chimed in.

"My thoughts exactly." Commander Willis replied.

"Fine, but I'm keeping one eye on the hot elf at all times!" Garry declared.

# Chapter 26 – Consider It Done

“Can you believe it ladies and gentlemen; Mara has gained a perfect score!” The announcer cried out in excitement after Mara hit the bullseye from so far away.

“YEA! That’s what I’m talking about you hot elf!” Garry cheered from the stands.

The archery competition rounds would put two people against each other. They were then graded on speed and accuracy. Both contestants had to hit multiple targets from various distances, some with obstacles partially blocking the way. Later rounds would have moving targets, a few with temporary camouflage enchantments on them to add to the difficulty. The duke was sparing no expense to make this a worthy challenge for the best of the best to showcase their talents and entertain the populace.

Mara winning a perfect score from the judges was something Lord Longshot took notice of. He was watching the tournament after winning his round with a perfect score. ‘Ever since I have met this woman, she has impressed me, such talent!’

“Can you believe it ladies and gentlemen?! Two contestants now have a perfect score! Here I thought no one could give our most famous archer, Lord Longshot, a true challenge! How exciting!” The announcer continued to the roar of the crowd.

“She is quite skilled.” Mrrsha said behind Lord Longshot.

The noble nearly jumped out of his skin at the comment. His intense focus on the match only made Mrrsha’s stealth abilities even more effective.

“Are you trying to give me a fright?!” Longshot exclaimed.

“Not at all, Lord Longshot.”

After Mrrsha's reply, he quickly regained his composure. "You are one of the duke's personal bodyguards, correct?"

The cat girl smiled. "Yes, I am Mrrsha if you do not remember."

"Yes, I recall. You are the more diplomatic one according to Deathwalker." Longshot replied.

"Yes, alpha has me handle the more delicate matters for him. My sister Prrsha tends to be more vicious and is working closely with Commander Willis on internal defense. Whereas my sister Frrsha prefers to not leave our alpha's side. None of us do, but she will leave his side when required to." Mrrsha stated.

"For what delicate matter has my liege sent you to me?"

"He wanted you to know he supports your interest in Ms. Mara and is willing to help two people he considers friends."

The noble was not expecting that response. "What-what are you saying? Wait... is Deathwalker making a joke or teasing me?"

Mrrsha shook her head. "Not at all. Alpha is very observant, and what he cannot catch, Garry and the rest of us help him too. Among my kind there is no shame pursuing a potential mate. Mara is quite capable." 'Not to mention, if you two get together my sister will not eventually kill her.' Mrrsha thought but did not voice that little tidbit of information.

"I am a noble Mrrsha. That means I am bound by a code..."

Mrrsha interrupted. "Alpha has been educating me in this code. You may be required to mate with one not of your choosing, but that can come from obligations to your liege or your family. Your duke is making it clear he will not interfere other than to support his friends. Anyone who pays attention can see the way you look at her."

"Surely not..." Longshot groaned. "Have I been that obvious?"

"To anyone half paying attention... Just so you know we have observed her making glances at you too since your introduction. Rarely does that happen. Our alpha does not want someone he considers a friend to ignore such a blessing." Mrrsha explained.

'I am no fool. My liege... no, my friend, is giving me his support and making sure I know it. Mara is an incredible woman and an amazing archer. Perhaps Deathwalker could help me.' Longshot thought before he made his request. "Life is too short but long enough for regrets. If we end up in the finals, would Deathwalker be willing to ask the finalists to help train our duchy's archers? Regardless, if I win or not, it will benefit the kingdom and if Ms. Mara happened to spend some significant time helping me train my men and others..."

Mrrsha raised her hand to cut him off. "Consider it done. This is something I know our alpha would gladly do. Such a thing is only a benefit to all involved. He wants you to consider any other ideas. Should you come up with something, do not hesitate to ask."

"Deathwalker must trust you completely if you can promise such a thing here and now without checking with him first."

What Lord Longshot did not know was the fact that Mrrsha and Deathwalker were in constant telepathic communication and their bond was so strong he could see and hear through his disciple's senses.

"He does. That and he thinks ahead." Was all Mrrsha said before turning and walking away.

Lord Longshot watched Mrrsha go realizing she moved without making a sound and if he did not actively use his enhanced vision the cat girl would just blend into the background. 'I would not want to tangle with her, I doubt I would survive the encounter. Such a deadly warrior, and my friend sends her to deliver a message to me, just so I know I have his support.' Shaking his head to clear his thoughts. "I am going to have to push myself even harder now if I want to win."

———-

"Oooo, that is going to leave a mark! Get a healer to that guy on the double! Well, I might as well announce the winner of that round, though with the way his opponent is bent that way..." the announcer shook his head for a moment." "Now ladies and gentlemen, please give a round of applause for the Sunderer for winning his next round!"

After the cheering died down the announcer continued. "With this being the final match for this round of the Melee competition, that gives us our four semifinalists! Please give another round of applause for Lord Sebastian Dormeir, Major Arden, Montarr, and the Sunderer!"

The announcer raised his hand to get the crowd to quiet down. "As a reminder the Melee semifinals will resume tomorrow. Our duke wishes to see the Melee tournament be the first to complete. Then we shall finish the magic and archery tournaments in the following days after that. Major Arden will face Lord Dormeir and Montarr will face Sunderer! Come back tomorrow to witness the unquestionable combat skill of these contestants!"

———

Morning came and went. The coliseum was once again packed with people. More nobles came from throughout the kingdom to witness the semifinals of the Melee tournament. Many knew of Lord Dormeir's battle prowess and were eager to see how he faired against a martial focused elf. Others were excited to see the two adventurers Montarr and the Sunderer square off.

"What can you tell me about Montarr, Darrius?" Deathwalker asked.

"He is an ex-knight who gave up his title to fight monsters." Darrius replied.

"Why would he have to give up his title?" King Alfheim inquired.

"Simple, his liege wanted him focused on protecting his interests, but Montarr could not in good conscience ignore the suffering of the people he swore to protect." Darrius explained.

"Which noble was it?" Deathwalker wanted to know who to avoid or keep any eye on.

'He is asking the right question.' Darrius knew he liked Deathwalker. "One of the lords under Duke Acorn."

"For some reason I'm not surprised."

Darrius shrugged. "I have learned to avoid nobles if I can. As for Montarr, he gave up his knightly title and joined the Adventurer's guild. The man is an excellent warrior. I have seen him fill both the role of melee fighter and defender. It will be good to see how he fairs against the Sunderer."

"BEGIN!" The announcer called out.

Montarr was a rather large man, yet he still seemed puny rushing towards the man they called Sunderer. The blows they landed on each other made the ground shake from the impacts. Each one dishing out brutal blow after blow.

From what Deathwalker had learned about the Sunderer, the rumor was the man had giant blood in him. Based on how huge the fighter was Deathwalker could see it. The fact that Montarr was still going and dishing out as much as it got was impressive. 'Sadly, it looks like Montarr is slowing and Sunderer, though bloodied, does not seem to be winded. I don't see this lasting much longer.'

Deathwalker's prediction came true. Montarr lasted another minute, which was a rather long time in such an all-out brawl. One final well-placed blow to Montarr's temple sent him down to the ground unconscious. Sunderer immediately stepped back once his opponent hit the arena floor. The ability for the man to so quickly disengage impressed Deathwalker further. Lady Emma seemed to notice as well. "The man may look like a brute, but a brute would not step back so quickly when their opponent was down."

Deathwalker nodded. "It is clear he has a code. The most dangerous of men do." 'Even more reason to go forward with my plan should he win.'

"Your statement makes me think you have a code too."

"I do." Deathwalker confirmed.

"What is your code Deathwalker?" Lady Emma inquired.

"Use my power to help or defend others. See no innocent child harmed and bring swift justice to anyone who does. Give hope to those who need it. Lastly, do not shirk my duty. That includes doing what others cannot, especially if such things would give my people nightmares. I carry that burden, so they do not have to."

Lady Emma had a look of surprise on her face. She did not expect the conversation to become so serious.

"Make no mistake, Lady Emma, I bear the burden, so others do not have to... But I am also one who is more than their code. Duty is important, it is part of one's sense of purpose. Yet God gives us more than that, there is a strong need to create and to love." Deathwalker waved out to the crowd. "This festival, these tournaments, all of it is to celebrate what we can build together."

At his final words, Deathwalker put his hand on Lady Emma's. She squeezed his back and smiled. "You are always thinking but even in your thoughts you show a concern for the people under your care. It was what impressed me the most when we first met. You came to the aid of someone you did not know and made a point to heal the others, even the horses." She squeezed his hand again. "I doubt someone comes up with a code like yours without having gone through much pain and hardship in life. Together we will bring about a new era of prosperity for the kingdom."

Deathwalker nodded. "Strong people bring about good times. Good times can create weak people if you let it. It is a variation on something someone told me once. A nugget of truth. In our efforts to help the kingdom we must help them learn self-accountability and to find ways to cope with the challenges that will come."

"Always thinking ahead Deathwalker." Lady Emma smiled back at him.

Marius and Darrius kept quiet and gave each other a knowing look. Neither man had ever heard Deathwalker summarize his code before. Both knew it further evidence he was an honorable man. His words of wisdom at the end reminded them of their family and why they each took up the role of protector in their own way.

"Oh look, it is time for Lord Dormeir to face off against Major Arden." Lady Emma commented.

"Honorable people of Timberfall Duchy. It is my pleasure to announce the next two competitors, Lord Dormeir and Major Arden! Both have given us some impressive matches these last few days, let them hear your encouragement!"

The crowd erupted. Many of the spectators called out Lord Dormeir's name, as he was from the duchy, and throughout the tournament he comported himself with honor. However, there were still several calling out Major Arden for how skilled he proved himself so far.

"This guy does such a great job." Deathwalker commented.

"It is his class." Lady Emma stated.

"Huh?"

"His class. He has Town Crier as a class. He is one of the best in the kingdom. Father uses him all the time to announce important events and deliver key messages when a personal touch is needed. My uncle sent him, figuring he would help." Lady Emma explained.

"Remind me to thank the king next time I see him."

"Let the fight... BEGIN!"

Deathwalker knew from personal experience what an impressive fighter and swordsman Sebastian was. The man was very skilled in body strengthening and enhancement magic too. When the fight started Dormeir moved faster than he ever saw him move and at first it appeared Major Arden wasn't expecting it.

Sebastian had the elf on the defensive. He would change up his attacks and fluctuate the speed mid-swing making it difficult for Arden to adapt. The lord wasn't just swinging his sword either. He was kicking, punching, and elbowing every chance he got. Each blow looked to have significant force behind it, yet he could pull a hit at the last minute if the elf got his blade in the path of the strike.

All in all, it was one of the most impressive displays of battle prowess Deathwalker and practically everyone at the coliseum had seen. The crowd went wild at the display. Many would have trouble the next day talking with how loud they were cheering.

They were a good five minutes into the fight before the elven major went on the offensive. Arden still did not have the upper hand, but he at least was able to dish out a few counterattacks.

"I am impressed a human can fight so well!" Major Arden gritted out as he blocked another blow.

"You are very skilled. It has been some time since I could go all out like this!"

"You have been a worthy opponent hu-... I mean Dormeir. However, I have no intention of losing. I figured I would save my trump card for the final fight, but you have earned it."

Major Arden quickly jumped back to disengage the fight. His body took on a bluish white sheen, like a coating of ice. Then his blade glowed blue, and ice extended out from his feet. Lord Dormeir didn't give him much time and charged in to resume the melee.

The closer Sebastian got the colder he felt. It was like the elf was projecting an aura of cold around him. Worse it made the nobleman feel sluggish.

When he got a strike on the elf's side Sebastian's sword clanged off and sent a reverberation up his arm. This was a serious development. 'Is this man invulnerable to my attacks?'

Upon closer inspection of the area he struck, there were signs of cracked ice. "So not invulnerable, just a layer of protection!" Sebastian said as he attempted to strike the elf in the same spot.

The attack was successful and more cracks in the ice spread from the impact point. Dormeir didn't feel like celebrating as he could feel part of his extremities going numb from the cold. He parried Arden's sword but was a little too slow to realize it was a feint and blocked the blow to his head with an ice-covered fist.

The lord went flying back into the wall and as he tried to get to his feet realized his balance was off and his sword was several feet from him.

Major Arden had dropped his sword and rushed Lord Dormeir as he tried to shake off the effects of having his bell rung. Sebastian blocked the first few strikes and got in a few of his own, but it was clear the tide of the fight had shifted with that blow to the head. The man still made the elf work for it and managed to last several more minutes before collapsing from cold-induced exhaustion.

"Unbelievable! Major Arden wins!"

The cheers went up. Some in the crowd were not happy with the use of magic in the melee fight but when the announcer reminded people that body strengthening is still enhancement magic, the murmurs stopped.

The announcer told the healers to bring Lord Dormeir to Deathwalker as he wanted to see to Sebastian's healing personally. Then he called down to Major Arden. "Do you need time or are you ready to face your final opponent?"

"Just a few moments and I will be ready to fight." Arden said as the blueish white sheen faded from his skin.

Cal and Mary Sue sat together in the stands. Having seen the impressive fight, Mary Sue spoke up. "See do not feel so bad about losing to him. Look at what he just did. You are still number one in my book Cal."

She leaned into Cal, and he put his arm around her. "Thank you for trying to comfort me, Mary Sue. Honestly, I cannot seem to care much about losing after you nursed me back to health. These last few days with you have been wonderful!"

The maid smiled at Cal, a smile that warmed his heart and made him want to promise anything and everything to keep her by his side. 'I still cannot believe she professed her love for me after I got hurt. I must be the luckiest man alive.'

———

"Now, for the fight we have finally all been waiting for... Sunderer and Major Arden! Let us cheer them on!"

The crowd was happy to oblige.

Sunderer! Sunderer!"

"Arden! Arden!"

"Yeaaaaaaaa!"

The chants and excitement continued and only got louder when the announcer's voice cut through it all. "BEGIN!"

Neither man held a weapon. Major Arden's was damaged in the last fight. Seeing his opponent without a weapon, Sunderer decided to discard his weapon as well. This fight would be an all-out brawl.

Major Arden immediately activated the ability or skill he had. The crowd knew this when the elf's skin took on that blueish-white sheen. The stands got excited as the elf moved with grace as ice seemed to form wherever he stepped.

Sunderer roared as he met the elf's charge with one of his own. "Rawwwww!"

When the two met in the middle of the arena there was an impact wave that everyone in the stands could feel.

Major Arden did his best to use his speed to his advantage to dish out blow after blow on his opponent. Most were blocked by Sunderer's massive arms. Ice started to form on the impact points, beginning to cover the giant of a man in a coating of cold.

Sunderer just slammed his wrists and elbows together in front of him and the icy coating shattered and fell. "You will have to do better than that little man!"

"Happy to oblige." Major Arden said as he increased the speed of his attacks.

Though the elf was now moving even faster that he did fighting Lord Dormeir, he could not seem to make much progress getting inside the guard of such a massive man. Sunderer moved far faster than expected from one so huge.

Any time too much ice would form on the Sunderer's arms, he would just slam them together and break the ice. If the big man got a blow in on Major Arden, it usually sent him sliding back a few feet, before he charged right back in.

Blow after blow the two danced around the arena. The crowd cheering the two men on the entire time.

After getting a lucky cut in on the giant of a man, Major Arden swung a punch with all his might thinking he finally caught the Sunderer off balance, when a massive fist met his and sent the elf flying landing on his back.

The Sunderer charged forward in a rage. "Puny man hurt me, let me show you pain!"

Major Arden was sure his hand and arm was broken but he didn't get much chance to think as the Sunderer grabbed his legs with one hand and started to hulk-slam the elf back and forth on the ground.

"Uhhhh..." was all Major Arden could croak out as his whole body ached all over.

It was clear to him and everyone the fight was over, Sunderer had won.

"Wow! Get some healers to that man right away! Everyone, congratulate our champion and winner of the Melee tournament!"

The crowd went even more nuts at that announcement.

Deathwalker stood and walked up to the announcer. He raised his hand and gave time for the crowd to die down. Looking to the stands and then to Sunderer, he spoke. "Such an impressive display of martial prowess fitting for a Melee champion. It is my understanding, Sunderer, that you long to find someone to serve who is worthy. They must defeat you in combat is that correct?"

"Yes! I cannot bend the knee to anyone who is not stronger than I am. Many have tried and all have failed." Sunderer answered.

"Then let all witness as I give you what you truly desire, a strong leader you can follow! I challenge you Sunderer to one-on-one combat!" Deathwalker immediately jumped from the announcer box balcony several stories up to land several feet in front of Sunderer.

"Do you accept?!"

Sunderer smiled and charged his new opponent.

# Chapter 27 – The Sundering

Sunderer was happily running full speed towards his opponent. Here in front of him was a man with guts if not brains. He would defeat him like all the rest.

Deathwalker did not stand there idle. He checked his current Strength stat.

***Strength: 323***

'For a magic user my Strength is absolutely ridiculous. I am like that meme with the wizard with ripped abs. This is gonna be fun.'

With that thought Deathwalker rushed forward. When the duke jumped down to challenge the champion of the Melee tournament, he had done so without a weapon. 'Why use a weapon when you have Omni-claws? Right?'

Both men swung their fist at each other. When the blows met each other, a massive shockwave could still be felt echoing in the arena shaking the entire coliseum. This time when dust settled Sunderer's hand was the one knocked back.

The massive man looked down at his hand then to his opponent. "Finally, a worthy challenge!"

Sunderer charged once again. Deathwalker met him blow for blow.

"Yea! You can do it boss! Rip his head off! Ha, ha, ha, ha!" Garry cheered.

Deathwalker had covered the skin under his clothes with his dragon scales to provide better protection. Glad he did as each strike from Sunderer hit like a freight train. Though the mage was dishing it out just as much as he was taking.

Shockwaves kept reverberating as the men moved back and forth across the arena. Both men could be heard laughing. It was clear they both were enjoying the challenge. The Sunderer finally had an opponent to go all out on and Deathwalker was just enjoying the physical challenge and preparing for a big finish.

The crowd kept cheering as the fight continued. The back and forth blows and the constant change of tactics kept everyone on the edge of their seats. They first started with punches and quickly switched to adding in elbows, kicks and other moves into the mix.

"I thought Deathwalker was a mage who specializes in healing." Lady Emma commented.

"Did you know he could fight like this?" Darrius asked his brother.

"I have not seen him fight unarmed. Though I have seen him with a blade. He is an excellent swordsman." Marius replied.

"I have never seen anything like this." Lord Dormeir stated.

Deathwalker picked up the various conversations here and there. He just smiled. His original plan was to keep his physical skills secret as they were not his specialty, but he could not pass up the chance to get such a powerful warrior to stand with him.

"You are a formidable opponent." Sunderer grunted.

The fight had passed the hour mark and yet everyone was still focused on the combat. King Alfheim, Elder Martha, Duchess Lightheart, General Mineheir, and the elf king's advisors finished the magical tournament for the day and joined the growing crowd.

"Please join us grandfather." Lady Emma gestured to the seat next to her.

"We had to end the magical tournament early today. The constant shockwaves were such a distraction we had to." Elder Martha explained.

"That and the spectators came here. And I can see why. Arden, did the Sunderer manhandle you and slams you around like a rag doll?" General Mineheir teased.

Major Arden, who stood behind his general sighed as if this was not the first time he had been asked this question. "Ugh, yes... sir."

"Ha, ha, ha, ha!" General Mineheir laughed.

"It is impressive to see the duke fight like this. I saw him fight in the capital, but it was so quick... this is on a whole other level. I approve." Duchess Lightheart commented.

BOOM!

Deathwalker had launched Sunderer into the arena wall. The Sunderer shook his head and charged his opponent once again. This time rather than meet the charge as he did every time before, Deathwalker sidestepped and swept the Sunderer's legs out from under him.

The Sunderer fell face first into the ground.

"Hmmm." Deathwalker grabbed one of the Sunderer's legs and started slamming the giant man back and forth.

"Ha! How do you like it!" Major Arden yelled out.

SLAM!

SLAM!

SLAM!

Deathwalker dropped the leg. The Sunderer was now lying face up in one of the craters his body had made from the intense impacts.

Deathwalker looked around at the damage. "I might have over done it just a bit. I'm going to have to fix the floor or get some earth mages to do it." Shaking his head he stuck his hand out to his opponent. "I thought it was only appropriate I defeated you the same way you gained your championship."

Sunderer grabbed Deathwalker's hand and let him lift him to his feet. Then the massive man took a knee and bowed his head. Doing so, he was still just as tall as Deathwalker in his human form. "You have given me what I wanted. You have proven yourself worthy to serve. If you will have me, I shall give you my oath of loyalty and fealty... my liege."

"I accept your oath with the same gravity that it is given! Arise no longer a wanderer, you have a home at my side Sunderer!" Deathwalker replied.

The crowd went nuts. The entire coliseum roared and cheered; it was deafening. No one had ever seen the Sunderer defeated. Greater even their duke was the man to do it, ensuring the Sunderer's strength was added to their Duchy.

DRAGONVIEN!

DRAGONVIEN!

YEAAAAA!!!

————-

## ——Deathwalker's Perspective——

"I really didn't think this through." I told Mrrsha.

"He is rather conspicuous." She replied.

"My liege please allow me to be one of your personal bodyguards!" Sunderer pleaded.

The giant of a man followed me everywhere and I do mean everywhere. I had to draw the line at the privy, I mean come on! In truth I wasn't to upset he wanted to be one of my bodyguards, but I had to keep up appearances to make sure he understood boundaries.

“I was planning on having you join our adventuring party and also working with General Marius and Commander Willis on matters of defense.” I explained.

Sunderer was in supplication. “Please my liege! I must see to your protection! It is my sworn duty!”

Garry laughed. “Yes! Bow before my master! Ha, ha, ha, ha!”

Draconis nodded. “I agree! It is only right he bow to you master!”

I groaned. “You guys are not helping.”

Lady Emma, who made General Marius escort her down to where we were snickering. “Psst. He, he, he!”

I gave her a stern look. “You are not helping Emma.”

She tried to compose herself but wasn’t trying very hard. “He, he, he, he! Hey, you were the one that wanted him to bend the knee. Ha, ha, ha, ha!”

I shook my head. Everyone thought it was so funny. Sure, the guy came up to my chest even in supplication with his massive size. That doesn’t make it funny.

“Sure, it does! What makes it funnier is we know how much this kind of stuff makes you feel so uncomfortable. Ha, ha, ha, ha!” Lilandra telepathically chimed in.

“Would you please get up. Or at least sit up.”

The Sunderer got up and then promptly sat on his rump, shaking the ground a little as he landed. “Is this better, my liege?”

I sighed. “Yes. At least this way we are eye level. If... and I do mean if I allow you to become one of my bodyguards, I expect multiple things.”

“Name it, my liege! It is my duty to serve!”

"First, I expect you to help wherever I need you. Sometimes that will send you away from me..." I raised my hand to forestall his protests. "That does not mean always, but I need strong, able-bodied people that I can trust and who can carry out important missions for me."

"I understand, my liege."

"Second, you follow the orders of Mrrsha, Prrsha, and Frrsha. You will have to fight my apprentice to see who follows who's order but you can do that later."

Sunderer looked at Draconis. "Not a problem."

"Hey!" Draconis protested.

"Settle it later apprentice."

"Fine!" Draconis harrumphed.

"Third, I there is one other I will introduce you to. Oh, and I will need you to coordinate with General Marius, his brother Darrius, and Commander Willis at times on important matters to ensure our people are protected too."

'He cares for his people. Yes, I have chosen well.' The Sunderer thought as he nodded in agreement.

"Fine. You can be my bodyguard."

I no sooner finished those words than Sunderer lifted me off the ground and wrapped me in a big bear hug. "Oh, thank you, my liege!"

"G-got it... big... guy. How about... you stop... crushing me." I croaked out.

"Oh sorry, my liege. I sometimes forget my strength." Sunderer said as he put me down.

"Hey boss, I noticed you didn't give him any instructions about me." Garry interjected.

"Oh yea, and this is my familiar Garry. He is a crazy ball of murderhobo, but I love him. So don't hurt him, but also take what he says with a grain of salt." I explained.

"Okay, little one. You can help me kill the liege's enemies." Sunderer patted Garry on the head. Though he meant them as light a pat, it made Garry bounce like a basketball.

Garry wobbled in the air. "Ugh. I feel a little dizzy. Did I hear him say I can help him kill stuff, or was that just my wishful thinking?"

"You heard correctly, Garry." Draconis answered his friend.

"Okay, good. I knew I would like this guy! But next time don't pat me, only the hot female variety can touch me." Garry stated.

"They must be of a certain temperature?" Sunderer asked confused.

"Yes! Smoking hot! Ha, ha, ha, ha!" Garry laughed.

"Now that that is settled, shall we all adjourn for the evening?" I asked.

—————

It took some serious convincing, but I got the girls to start to work with Sunderer. More importantly, they had to stay outside the bedroom, so I didn't have him hovering over me while I tried to sleep. Nice guy but a bit more zealous than Draconis, and that was saying something.

The girls hadn't been thrilled with the idea of not being able to sleep next to me, but I just needed some alone time. I still trip out on how this is my life now. My original plan was to go on a solo adventure. It had started out that way, but that was definitely not the case now. Eh, who am I kidding? I like people, some may drive me nuts, and some are completely infuriating, but I like helping heal those around me. Also, I am surrounded by some awesome people.

No real complaints other than I wish some of my friends from my old life could be here to share it all with. I do hope James is okay. My timetable pushed back even further in finding him just so I don't come apart at the seams.

A light whizzed in front of my face just before I opened the door to my private bedroom.

The little fairy whispered. “Oh, savior of fairy-kind, I came to warn you. There is someone in your bedroom. Advisor Mona.”

I really did like these little guys. They were the perfect messengers and spies. I nodded back. “Thank you for letting me know. No turning back now. Might as well figure out what she wants if I have any hope of getting some sleep tonight.”

The little fairy bowed in the air before darting off out of sight. I entered my room to find Advisor Mona sitting on my bed staring at me.

“Surprised to see me?” The fey woman smiled coyly at me.

I sat in a chair near a small desk I had in my room. After sitting down, I started taking my boots off. “Not really. I figured I would be seeing you at some point.”

“He, he, he, he. You are an interesting one.” Advisor Mona chuckled. She stood up and walked over to me.

“Most men, especially humans have a hard time resisting a fey’s allure.” Advisor Mona ran her slender index finger across my cheek giving me a sultry look.

I felt a surge of energy. It did not feel malicious, more a promise of what could come. “I am not one to be driven by my emotions. One thing I know about Winter Court fey, neither do they.”

Advisor Mona giggled as she sat in my lap. “One’s desires can stimulate the mind.” giving a little wiggle in my lap.

I shook my head. “Ha! Laying on a bit thick don’t ya think, my lady?”

She gave me a little pout. “You are very focused Duke Dragonvein. I have noticed when you set your mind on something your focus is unbreakable. Like an arrow focused on its target... or perhaps the hunter who shot the arrow.”

"Ah, she gets to the heart of the matter." I replied.

The fey woman put her hand to her chest with a look of mock confusion. "Why, what ever could you mean your grace?"

"You are an advisor to Queen Mab are you not?"

"I am." Advisor Mona's smugness and pride in her position roiled off her.

'Time to change things up.'

I picked her up in my arms, stood up, and turned around before promptly plopping Advisor Mona in the chair I was just sitting in. She had an initial look of surprise and confusion. That look turned into a sly smile. "I had no idea you like to manhandle a woman. Do not worry fey women can handle it rough."

I shook my head. "Laser focused remember."

Mona took on a puzzled look with my use of the word 'laser'. Deciding to get this little game wrapped up I figured blunt and direct is what I had time for. In truth, that is usually all I have time for. "It has been a long day, Advisor Mona. Let me answer some questions you have not asked. Yes, I love to hunt, and I only eat meat or things that come from an animal. It appears I have a way with animals, and I love magic. Critical thinking and logic drive my decisions and as you can tell my emotions are a bit... muted. Now, if you do not mind, can we call it a night?"

"I would not mind adjourning for the evening." The fey woman motioned to the bed behind me.

I sighed.

Advisor Mona waved her hand. "Fine, we can 'dance' some other time. For you to give me those answers means you have some idea of why I am here. I will say you are the most likely candidate to be the Huntsman in centuries."

The fey woman stood up and leaned into me for a hug. Her head came up to my chest which meant she looked up at me. Grabbing my head, she pulled me closer to her. “I will leave you for now. But know this, there are many benefits to being one of the Winter Court.”

Advisor Mona stepped back abruptly. “Until next time, your grace.” Then promptly turned around and left.

I just shook my head. “Yikes! That is one very dangerous woman.”

Prrsha burst in the room. “Alpha, are you alright?!”

“I am fine. The advisor just wanted to talk.”

Prrsha walked up to me and sniffed. “Are you sure? I can smell her on you. I could claw her eyes out for you.”

‘I think Prrsha might me a Yandere.’

“Yes, fey play mental games. This was nothing more than that. Oh, let’s not tell Garry about this. I’ll never hear the end of it.”

“Only if I can stay here tonight.” Prrsha countered.

“What about the Sunderer? I am not going to have him watching me all night.”

“Mrrsha is handling that. She is better at coordinating others, especially non-pumas. Frrsha only has eyes for you and our kind. And I would rather claw the eyes out of those that annoy us.”

“Ha! Ever my huntress.” I reached up and scratched behind her ears. “Fine, I’m going to sleep. Stay if you want.” I said sleepily.

# Interlude - Timberfall City - Northern District

"Why are we waiting in this abandoned, rundown building Chen?" Belinda was annoyed and not thrilled to be in such a place.

They had witnessed the upset at the Melee tournament. "Sister, calm yourself. I agree what we saw makes no sense." Carn put his hand on his sister's shoulder.

Chen chimed in. "It does not match any of our intel. He is a healer, nothing more. That is why he surrounds himself with powerful allies."

"Somehow that spoiled noble tricked everyone with some kind of illusion magic. There is no way his victory makes any sense otherwise." Belinda spat.

Carn nodded. "That makes sense. No way he could defeat the legendary Sunderer with brute strength. It must have been an illusion!"

"Now that things finally make sense again, why are we here again Chen?" Belinda turned her attention back to Chen.

"You will have your answer shortly." Chen answered as he leaned against the wall.

True to his statement a shimmering oval portal opened up in the middle of the room. Two people stepped through, entering the room.

All three original inhabitants of the room knelt down as they saw their commander, General Marks. Standing beside him was one of the Proletariat's greatest trump cards, the Archmage Lenn, he possessed the rare affinity of Space magic. His ability to open portals into enemy territory allowed their forces to circumvent even the most unassailable of strongholds.

“Rise.”

The three did as they were told.

“General Marks, Archmage Lenn, it is an honor to be in your presence.” Carn said as he kept his head down.

“We were not expecting you General.” Belinda stated.

“No. I told Chen here not to say anything. I wanted it to be a surprise. It is time to prepare for the invasion of Timberfall.”

“Everything is ready General.” Chen replied.

“Good. Any outliers or concerns?”

“The duke worked with the elves we think to create a magical shield over the entire city.” Sergeant Chen was the first to speak up.

“A magic shield you say?” Archmage Lenn asked.

“Yes, they tested it before the festival. The device has been set up at the town hall. It would prevent others from getting in when activated.” Chen explained what he had learned from Commander Willis.

“It should not affect my portals but will have to be destroyed if we want the army to scale the walls.” Archmage Lenn.

“Belinda and Carn, I expect you two to see to that when the time comes.” General Marks ordered.

“Understood General.” Belinda bowed her head.

“Yes, General!” Carn agreed.

“What else?” General Marks asked.

“The Sunderer has joined the duke. The noble used some magic tricks to win him over.” Belinda stated.

"That is a complication but not a concern. He is just one more person to wipe out. What else?" General Marks dismissed the news of the adventurer.

"We still do not know what happened to the duke's defender Grimhold." Carn offered."

Archmage Lenn spoke up. "Our spies saw him heading into the elven nation. It appears he and a woman made it into the Dwarven kingdom."

"That is not good. If the dwarves can be convinced to join the Kingdom of Nord it could make this upcoming war even harder." Sergeant Chen chimed in.

"Ha! I am not concerned about a bunch of dwarves." General Marks laughed.

"We have a delegation in their capital already. All reports show the negotiations are going well. We should have an agreement with them soon." Archmage Lenn explained.

"Ally with dwarves?!" Carn asked in shock.

General Marks further explained. "An alliance of convenience. They are not fans of the elves and their ability to strangle their trade. Our promise to fight the elves and wipe out Nord and their support of such restrictions has an appeal to those short thick-headed fools."

"But still dwarves?!" Belinda protested.

"Once we have wiped out Nord and enslaved the stuck-up elves we will take care of those dwarves. They will make good workers for the greater good. Even if they are less than a human. All things in time." General Marks sneered at the thought of tolerating the dwarves that long.

"You always think of everything General!" Belinda said in admiration.

"Of course, I do. Now, have you found what I asked you to?" General Marks eyes flashed with a dark hunger that he barely kept at bay.

# Interlude - Dwarven Mountain Kingdom

"We at the Proletariat are excited to help the dwarven people overthrow the oppression of the greedy elves." The ambassador commented.

"Your majesty, the ones you requested are here." The advisor to the king interrupted.

"Very well. Let them approach." The Dwarven King replied before turning his attention back to the Proletariat ambassador. "We will finalize these agreements after I deal with some internal Dwarven matters. I will summon you ambassador when I have finished."

The Proletariat ambassador bowed. "Of course, your majesty. I look forward to it."

After bowing the ambassador was escorted out of the royal hall. As he exited, he saw the dwarf male and female surrounded by royal guards. Seeing the annoyed look on the captain's face, the ambassador knew he was not happy.

'These two must be the two the Kingdom of Nord sent. To have that expression on the captain's face tells me all I need to know. Whatever Duke Dragonvein was attempting has failed. I must report this to the Archmage Lenn. Soon we will have these dwarves fighting the elves and making us their cold iron weapons. Such fools, but that is to be expected from non-humans.' The ambassador thought gleefully as he realized his mission would soon be over and he could leave the presence of these thickheaded dwarves.

——-

"Your majesty, I have brought Grimhold as ordered." Fenrir said as he bowed.

All the other royal guards bowed, Grimhold and Mezza joining them.

The king stared at Grimhold and Mezza. After a few moments of silence in the royal hall the king spoke up. “Who is this Dwarven woman? She does not look like a Mountain Dwarf. No, I would say she be a Hill Dwarf by the look of her.”

“I be Mezza, your majesty.” Mezza replied but kept her head down.

Grimhold squeezed her hand as encouragement before he raised his head high as if giving the king a challenge. “She be my betrothed!”

The king’s bushy eyebrows rose. “Betrothed?! What do you mean betrothed?! My nephew comes back after being away from home for years and now he tells me he has a betrothed!” The king slammed his fist on the throne. “I mean I get a man needs to make his own way, but coming home saying his is betrothed when his family has not even met the girl... what nonsense is this!”

“Nephew? Family?” Mezza squeaked out in confusion.

“Yes, the king is my uncle. Did I not mention that?” Grimhold replied.

Mezza immediately rose from her knees; all thought or worry about being in the presence of the king completely forgotten. “You most certainly did not Grimmy! I can guarantee you that important bit of information I would have remembered!”

“I wanted to tell you, but I wanted to be sure you wanted me and not my title. Ya do not know how many dwarves I have run off. I was waiting until we were officially betrothed, then Deathwalker asked me to come...”

“Grimmy do not give me that! By now you should know I do not care about such things. Cooking and family, that is what I love.”

“And I love that about ya...”

Mezza interrupted. “Do not try to sweet talk me ya pigheaded dwarf! I am about to give ya a wallop with my frying pan! I want a partner, do not keep things from me! Oooo, I am so mad...”

The king laughed. "HA, HA, HA, HA, HA! I like her! She has some fire in her belly! I can see why you like her nephew."

The king's words seemed to snap Mezza out of her rage and remind her there were more than just her and Grimhold around. Horror-stricken, she turned to the king. "I am sorry yer majesty. I should not threaten a member of the royal family."

The king waved her comment off. "No, ya should not, but it is understandable. Though do not blame my nephew too much. I asked him to not share his true lineage. He was only allowed to share such things with someone who saved his life. As you know, such an act is something the whole family must give thanks to and offer assistance to such a person."

Mezza bowed her head, then realization dawned on her. "That is why Deathwalker sent you, he knows."

Grimhold nodded. "Aye. I owe that man my life many times over."

"Who is this Deathwalker and why do you owe him your life my nephew?" the king asked.

"Deathwalker has saved my life multiple times and he even repaired and enhanced my armor!" Grimhold replied.

"I thought your mithril armor looked better than I remembered." The captain of the royal guards commented.

Grimhold nodded at his old friend before turning back to his uncle. "Deathwalker Dragonvein is one of the most honorable men I have met."

The advisor near the king spoke up when he heard Deathwalker's last name. "Dragonvein, as in Duke Dragonvein of the Timberfall Duchy within the Kingdom of Nord?!"

"Aye, that be him. If you doubt his honor, the system granted him a 'Hero' title for rescuing Timberfall and again for subduing an Adult Red Dragon!"

"A system acknowledged hero?!" The advisor gasped.

"Aye, and he be ma liege. I gave him my oath of loyalty and fealty!" Grimhold declared.

"Your what?!" The king shouted.

Grimhold did not back down. "What was I to do uncle? I have told you of what he has accomplished, my honor demanded it!"

Mezza came to stand beside Grimhold and took his hand in hers. She whispered, "I may be mad, but I respect you standing up to yer uncle for yer friend... and it makes me love you even more Grimmy."

Grimhold got so choked up by her words he just squeezed her hand back and smiled. He did not trust himself to do anything more or he might have lost control of his emotions.

The king looked at this quick exchange. "She has a spine too. Do you stand with my nephew for him or in defense of this Deathwalker?"

"Both! I love Grimmy and Deathwalker has always done right by me, Grimmy, and the people under him. To not stand for both would be to betray them, and I cannot do that... Though for Grimmy I would if he asked, I trust him enough."

"You are not mad at him any longer?" the king asked.

"Oh, I be furious, but that does not change my loyalty to him." Mezza stood; her posture even more resolute as she made her statement.

"Hmmm. Fenrir, you know my nephew more than anyone here, what are your thoughts?"

"He can be the most stubborn dwarf I know, and that is saying something as I know many stubborn dwarves..."

Grimhold winced as he expected Fenrir to dismiss his decision just as he had dismissed his decision to take on two young elves and continue being an adventurer.

"But he is a man of honor and sticks by his friends and his sense of duty no matter what. If Grimhold had given his oath he did not do so lightly. This Deathwalker Dragonvein must be at your level of honor my king." Fenrir declared.

Both the king and Grimhold's eyes widened at Fenrir's declaration. "You surprise me Fenrir... but you are right. My nephew is loyal to a fault and stubborn, but he does take after his uncle. I cannot deny that... Very well nephew I do not challenge your oath, but we must discuss this Deathwalker further. As for your betrothal..." the king looked at the two of them still holding hands. "She is willing to defy me which means she risks her own life, that shows how much she respects and loves you, nephew. I will support your choice for that alone, however, you have to tell your mother and get her blessing."

Grimhold cringed.

That simple act made the smile return to the king's face.

"Uncle, as I owe my fealty to Deathwalker, he asked me to deliver a message and an offer to ya. May I?" Grimhold asked.

The advisor leaned over and whispered into the king's ear.

The king nodded before turning his attention back to Grimhold. "Very well, but before you do that... I do have a matter we must discuss first, nephew."

"What is it uncle?"

"The human you saw as you entered the royal hall was an ambassador to the Proletariat. They have come seeking an alliance against the elves and the Kingdom of Nord." The king explained.

Mezza sucked in a breath. Grimhold had a frown on his face. "Ya very well know uncle that Timberfall Duchy is in the Kingdom of Nord. If we go to war, I am honor-bound to fight alongside Deathwalker."

"From what you have told me, that is expected. That is part of the problem." The king replied.

"But why war with Nord?" Grimhold asked.

"The elves." The king answered.

Mezza had a puzzled look on her face.

Fenrir looked to his king for permission before he explained further. "Nord is the elves strongest allies. King Alfheim's own daughters married the king and some of the dukes in the Kingdom of Nord. The two nations are bound by blood and family. If we attack one, we must plan to attack the other."

"I am a Hill Dwarf, so I do not understand what the reason is for the dislike of elves. Why attack them at all?" Mezza inquired.

This time the advisor spoke up. "Our mountain exits into the elven nation. This means if we want to trade with others, they or us must traverse through the elves' lands. For centuries the elves have used that against us and taxed or charged transportation fees, or a number of other excuses to bleed us dry."

"Plus, everyone knows the elves are just puppets to the fey. The Winter Court has complete sway and they do not like cold iron passing through any nation they control. This has made it difficult at best, impossible at worst to sell weapons to other countries. War means freedom from fey oppression." Fenrir chimed in.

"The king had already agreed in principle to the alliance." The advisor further shared.

"But uncle you have not signed yet? That means there still be a chance." Grimhold pleaded.

"A chance for what nephew?"

"Let me share Deathwalker's message and offer." Grimhold said.

"Very well." The king gestured to his nephew to continue.

Grimhold withdrew a letter and opened it. Then he read it out loud for all to hear.

*Honorable King of the Dwarves,*

*Through your nephew and my cook Mezza I have come to know what amazing and steadfast a people the dwarves can be. Like all races not everyone is the same, there are good and bad ones. Yet Grimhold is your kin and I have had the privilege to fight by his side and the honor to call him friend.*

*I also learned how much influence the fey have over the elves and I can only imagine their dislike of certain metals has led to adverse outcomes where trade is involved. A disadvantaged people can tolerate such things only for so long, so I have sent Grimhold to address this longstanding gap. I would like to offer an alternative solution.*

*I have created portal stations that allow for instantaneous travel between two stations. This dramatically cuts down on travel time and as you can expect costs. I propose an alliance with myself if you are concerned with the level of influence the elves have within Nord. I will have my people build a portal station in your kingdom. This would allow you to bypass the elves and the fey's restrictions. Timberfall gains the benefit of dwarven made goods. Plus, I am interested in promoting free trade, so I am willing to negotiate my portal fees to ensure a long-lasting agreement.*

*I welcome your decision good king.*

*Respectfully,*

*Deathwalker Dragonvein*

"Stable Portals?!" The advisor finally asked in exasperation when the king remained silent.

"Aye. He has built a few already. It be a most impressive invention. More importantly it means we no longer have to care what nonsense tariffs the elves try to impose on us." Grimhold answered.

Finally, the king started laughing. "Ha, ha, ha, ha, ha! I can see why you like this man! If this works, we have no need to bother with the elves or their blasted fey overlords ever again!"

"What is involved in making a portal station?" The advisor asked.

Grimhold held out another piece of parchment. "This is the list of materials and quantities needed to construct a portal station. Deathwalker sent a few construction crews shortly after we left. They should be here soon. If you allow them to enter and we can gather the necessary materials, I am told they can finish in about a week or less."

The king stroked his chin while the advisor took the parchment. After reviewing it the advisor handed it over to the king.

"It is not cheap but most of the materials will not be difficult to obtain. What is your decision your majesty?" The advisor asked.

"We will give this Deathwalker and his people a chance. If they are successful then I will agree to an alliance, but with him, not Nord or those pointy-eared bastards!" The king declared.

The advisor bowed.

"Fenrir."

"Yes, my king?"

"See to it these construction workers are escorted and treated properly. Let no harm come to them." The king ordered.

"As you command my king!" Fenrir bowed.

"What about the Proletariat uncle?" Grimhold asked.

"As you said nephew, I never signed the treaty. We will stall them for as long as possible. That will give Deathwalker a chance to prove this marvel solution works. Now, you better get to your mother, or I will never hear the end of it."

"Thank you, uncle." Grimhold took Mezza and pulled her along. "Now the real challenge begins.

"The real challenge? Grimmy what have you gotten us into?"

"Do not worry lass. My mother should love ya!"

Mezza heard the king say, “Yea right, ha, ha, ha!”

# Chapter 28 – Its Good To Be The Duke

"Good morning, your grace. Good morning, Ms. Prrsha."

"Good morning, Geeves." I greeted.

"Rarrrr." Prrsha stretched. "Morning."

Prrsha got up. "I am going to check on my sisters. Frrsha will be insufferable."

I looked at her in confusion until I realized what she was talking about. Frrsha was a bit single-minded when it comes to me. "Understood. I have a feeling my seneschal woke me up for a reason."

Geeves bowed. "Yes, your grace."

"Very well. Take a seat." I gestured to the chair by my small writing desk in the room.

Prrsha left the room and Geeves started talking once she closed the door.

"Sir, this is a bit awkward for me..."

"Whatever it is, just tell me." I stated.

Geeves sighed. "Very well. Mary Sue approached me. She has asked for my blessing and yours to pursue a relationship with Cal."

"Ah, that."

"Yes, that, your grace." Geeves nodded.

"Is this sort of thing common among the nobles? Staff members asking for permission that is."

"For high nobles it is common for their staff to share whom they are pursuing romantically to avoid any scandals or concerns. However, for those of us serving a duke or duchess, it is a bit more complicated."

Complicated? In what way?" I asked.

"To serve a ruler over a duchy is one of the highest honors. Much is on your shoulders. Those who are in your employ must comport themselves with that in mind. It has been a tradition in this kingdom for anyone in service of someone with such responsibility to ask for their guidance and input. Many take that as asking permission, but it is more than that. Mary Sue is checking to make sure you see no issues or problems in this match." Geeves explained.

I sighed. Such protocols seemed wrought with a chance for abuse, but I understood the intent. "Love should be tempered with rational thoughts. I understand that nothing is promised, and it is common for those in this kingdom to move rather quickly after meeting a potential partner. If the mind, heart, and spirit agree who am I to interfere. Tell her if all three of those agree that he is the one... then they have my blessing."

Geeves stood and bowed his head. "Most wise, your grace."

"Does Cal know she has asked for my decision?" I asked once I realized my friend might be a bit concerned.

Geeves smiled. "Yes. Mary Sue made a point to tell him. He is waiting to speak to you this morning. Apparently, he did not sleep very well last night once he heard the news."

"I am surprised he didn't try to barge in sometime last night." I commented.

"Oh, he did, your grace."

"What?"

"He did not get passed the Sunderer and a very agitated Ms. Frrsha. From what I hear, she threw him out the door saying if she had to wait until the morning he could." Geeves relayed.

"Ha! That sounds like her. Very well, send him in."

"Very good, your grace." Geeves bowed once again before letting himself out.

A few minutes later Frrsha opened the door. "Alpha, can I take up post as your guard? The Sunderer is here as well."

I had finished getting dressed while talking with Geeves. "I'll join you in my private suite's living room. Probably best to talk to Cal there."

I gestured to Sunderer to open the door once I was sitting at my table picking at the food on it. Cal came bursting in, sliding through Sunderer before he had finished opening the door.

"It is about damn time Deathwalker! I have been pacing all night! I have not slept a wink! You do not know what this is doing to me..." Cal word vomited as fast as he could.

"Sit down my friend. Have some food." I moved a plate in his direction.

"I cannot think of food at a time like this! I still cannot believe this is a rule in this kingdom. Had I known..."

I interrupted Cal's tirade. "Calm down Cal. I said if her mind, heart, and spirit agree then you two have my blessing."

"I mean I know that you are my friend, but this is..." Cal stopped mid-sentence as his brain finally registered what I said. Then he swooped in to give me a hug. My friend only took a few steps before Sunderer lifted him off the ground by the scruff of his neck.

"Let him down Sunderer. Cal is my friend. He just wanted to thank me."

"Oh, okay. Sorry, my liege." Sunderer said sheepishly as he set Cal down.

Cal looked back at the giant of a man. "How are you so fast for being so big?"

The Sunderer shrugged his shoulders. "I do not know. Just am I guess."

Cal turned his attention back to me and decided to stick out his hand instead of attempting another hug. I clasped wrists with my friend. “Congratulations Cal. I’m sure Geeves has already told Mary Sue. You might want to go talk to her.”

Cal didn’t even hesitate, he turned on his heels and bolted towards the door. My friend was almost out the door when I told him, “Let her know she has today off.”

Cal stopped and turned back to me. “You are the best friend a man could ask for!” After he said those words, he darted down the hall.

“He is very happy.” Sunderer commented.

“The man is in love. I can smell it on him.” Frrsha stated.

I knew the cat girls had a heightened sense of smell. “You can?”

“Of course, so can you alpha. It is that sweet smell that lingers.” Frrsha explained.

I took a stronger whiff. “Ah, yes. Now I can. It is strong. I’m still learning to pick out different scents and what they mean.”

“Alpha has learned much already from his time with the pride. We should visit them soon.” Frrsha purred.

“After the festival. Though you could go earlier if you want. Just be back before the hunt.” I offered.

Frrsha shook her head. “No. I will stay with alpha. What is your plan for today?”

“Later I will attend the Archery tournament finals. Before that, I was planning on seeing if Lady Emma wanted to practice some of her magic, then help me judge the cooking competition.” I answered.

———

“Your Fireball is getting stronger, Emma.” I commented.

“Thanks to your instruction. You are a good teacher DW.” Lady Emma smiled back at me.

Lady Emma was adamant that I drop the honorific and in turn I told her my closest friends called me DW as a shortened version for Deathwalker. She liked the nickname so much it was all she used when we were training.

A notification popped up in my vision.

***Royal Bloodline of Indomitable Will*** *perk activated! Your bloodline comes from teachers and knowledge seekers. You have chosen to guide and teach someone magic. They will gain knowledge faster. This bloodline perk triples the rate of growth of anyone you personally teach.*

*Your student's skill has gone from Apprentice rank to Journeyman rank!*

I imagine a similar one appeared to Lady Emma based on what she said next. "Have you ever thought of being a teacher? Perhaps opening up your own school to guide those with magic affinities."

I had to stifle a laugh. "You mean open, say a... school for witchcraft and wizardry?" 'Oh, the cosmic irony of a woman named Emma Watson from another reality telling me to open a school for Wizards.'

"Why is that funny? You look like you are trying to suppress a laugh." Emma pouted.

I waved my hands in front of me and rained in my random thoughts. "You just reminded me of something from where I come from." Then I changed the subject back to her suggestion. "Several on my mother's side of the family were teachers and guides. They did a great job in guiding the younger generations."

"You do not talk much about your past or where you are from." Emma leaned over and squeezed my hand to show her support.

"No, I guess I don't. One reason is my focus for the most part remains on what is needed right now. It is hard though, as they are all very far away. The other reason is my focus on getting stronger so I can find my friend."

"Is he lost? Why would you have to get stronger?" Emma asked.

It was just the two of us sitting on the meditation mat. Sunderer and Frrsha were outside the room ensuring no one disturbed us. The closeness of our proximity, her genuine interest and concern, it all felt very comforting. In a way it was far more intimate and open than I had been with anyone since coming here.

I ingrained this moment in my memory, squeezed her hand back before I replied. “In a way, he was taken. To where, I am not sure. But what I do know is I have to grow stronger. It is the only way to ensure nothing can stop me from rescuing him when the time comes.”

Emma smiled. “He sounds very important to you.”

“He is my best friend.”

“It does not surprise me how much you are willing to do for the ones you care about.” Emma praised.

I put my other hand on Emma’s. “I do what others cannot or at least so they don’t have to. I would do the same for you, Emma. I respect your passion to help our people. No matter what happens I am grateful we got these chances to get to know each other.”

Emma leaned in and kissed me. The kiss took my breath away and when we parted it appeared I was not the only one breathing heavily and a bit flushed.

“Wow, that was like Princess Bride level of a kiss!”

Emma looked at me funny. “Well, I am a princess and if my family has their way, I would be your bride, if that is what you are referring to. Where you come from, is such an amazing kiss an indication they are the one you should marry?”

Her question and comment made me laugh as I stood, and I pulled her up into a hug. “Ha, ha, ha, ha! That could be one interpretation. But it can just as much be how nice it feels to hold or be held by that person.”

"Not sure what I said that was funny. I will say I do feel safe in your arms DW." Emma replied as we just stood there enjoying the moment together.

Frrsha opened the door like she had some kind of radar or signal when I was opening up. "Oooo, are we hugging? Alpha gives the best hugs!" She practically pounced on us and forced her way into a group hug.

Her innocent antics just made both Emma and I laugh.

"Is this what I can expect should we wed?" Emma teased.

"Ha! Where is Garry when I need him to crack a joke?" My statement gave me the briefest pause. 'I do hope they are keeping the mayhem to a minimum.'

"We probably should be getting to the coliseum. We have to judge the finals. Mara versus Lord Longshot. Who do you think will win?" Emma asked.

"Not sure. Both are skilled archers. Either way one friend will win today and the other will need our encouragement. I plan to be there for both, regardless of outcome." I answered.

Emma smiled at me but said nothing. We left the training hall I had set up in the manor and made our way to the arena. The city was overflowing with people in various forms of merriment. I could also smell various dishes being prepared.

Bards were playing various songs celebrating the recent melee tournament. I heard a few talking about my fight with the Sunderer. It made me chuckle internally.

Later today would be the archery tournament, but first I must judge the cooking competition.

'It's good to be the duke!'

"You know I'm surprised Garry isn't here. Food is like his third favorite thing." I commented.

"What are his other two?" Emma asked.

"You don't want to know." I replied.

"I know." Frrsha said with a big smile on her face.

"Deathwalker! Deathwalker! Over here." I heard Alyce's voice calling my name.

I saw her over by a particular stand helping an older gentleman prepare some food. The smells of flavored, cooking meat made my mouth water.

I noticed a certain duo hovering near Alyce.

"Hey boss! We heard you are going to be taste testing and we thought we would partake, you know, to help! He, he, he!" Garry chuckled.

"Ha! Should be fun buddy. I see you are interested too, Draconis."

"I just wanted more kebabs." Draconis replied.

"That's fair. If they taste half as good as they smell." So, tell me about your stand Alyce."

"This my uncle's cart. He is known for using different spices and sauces to flavor his meats." Alyce explained.

"His kebabs are magically delicious!" Garry commented.

An older gentleman working at the grill gave a quick bow before he spoke. "It is an honor to have the Hero of Timberfall at my food cart. I am Tookin, a longtime friend to Betterman, which is why this one calls me her uncle." After pointing to Alyce, he turned his attention to Draconis and Garry. "It is also an honor to have our two protectors here again. I know Alyce and I feel safer having you two around."

"Yea we rock!" Garry gloated.

"Rock? Eh, no matter. Do you have kebabs for us?" Draconis chimed in.

"Of course! Here take a few as thanks." Tookin handed Draconis more than a few kebabs.

I gestured to the princess. “I am sure you both know of Lady Emma, who is helping judge the cooking competition this year.”

Both Alyce and Tookin bowed to Emma.

“It is an honor to make your acquaintance your majesty.” Tookin greeted.

“Nice to meet you, Lady Emma. You sure are pretty.” Alyce replied.

“That is very kind of you to say Alyce. It is nice to meet you both.” Lady Emma smiled.

“Yea, yea. What new stuff ya got for us?” Garry asked.

Tookin pulled out a large jar and a decent sized bottle. “Well, these two are my most popular. I glaze some of the kebabs in this and then dunk it in the sauce. I use large wooden barrels filled with a Moromi mix to create the salty flavor.”

“Wait did you say moromi?! Did you make soy sauce?!” I asked as I took some chicken and dipped it in the sauce. I immediately recognized the flavors. “You made miso and soy sauce! Oh my, this is amazing!”

“Ooo, ooo! Give me some!” Garry demanded.

Draconis not far behind him. “And I.”

“This is rather good!” Lady Emma declared.

Back in my old life I learned less than 1 percent of soy sauce was made the traditional way using large wooden barrels with a moromi mix to create the soy sauce. The flavor was night and day difference between the mass-produced stuff and the exceptional quality of traditionally made soy sauce. To be able to have that and miso again in this new world, my palette was doing flips for joy!

“You are familiar with the process Duke Dragonvein? Not many know of such traditions. It proves you are a connoisseur of fine cuisine.” Tookin commented.

“There is a region where I am from that takes it as their family’s honor to preserve this way of making soy sauce. I wish more would follow in their footsteps. It is good to know you are doing that process here Tookin.” I praised the man.

“You honor me, duke!”

“Tookin is showing me the process to make it. I want to help share this yummy food with the world.” Alyce declared.

Draconis hummed in appreciation of the flavors. “A noble goal little one.”

I ruffled her hair. “Glad to hear it, Alyce. You keep surprising me with all that you do.”

Alyce beamed and blushed.

I offered some to Frrsha and Sunderer. Both made noises of contentment. The food was gone in an instant.

“Thank you, Alyce, and you too Tookin. If you will excuse us. As much as I do not want to, we have several other food stalls to visit.”

“Yes, I agree with Deathwalker. Thank you for sharing your delicious food. I feel others will pale in comparison. It was a pleasure to meet you both.” Lady Emma waved by as she took my arm as I escorted her away.

————

# Chapter 29 – Cooking Competition

By the end of the cooking competition Deathwalker, Lady Emma, Frrsha, Draconis, and Garry were stuffed. Sunderer opted to stand guard, though Frrsha did get the giant of a man to sample a few of the items. They all had eaten various cooked and seasoned meats, pastries. The wide variety of dishes had been mindboggling.

"Boss, this idea... burp... was genius!" Garry groaned from overeating.

"I agree with Garry. This was one of the best days I have enjoyed since coming to this city." Draconis chimed in.

"How are you holding up Emma?" Deathwalker asked.

"I am quite stuffed."

"Not yet, but you could be." Garry smiled.

"Garry! What did we talk about when it comes to being around ladies?" Deathwalker chided his familiar.

"No innuendos with the classy ones. High society can be a bit stuffed up." Garry pouted.

"Stuffy was the word I used. But yes, we should be mindful of what we say around a lady." Deathwalker replied before turning to the princess. "My apologies Emma."

She waved the comment off. "I take no offense. Your familiar is an odd one, most of the time I do not understand his references and comments."

"See, she doesn't mind at all." Garry countered.

“That is not exactly what she said my friend. But enough about that, let’s get back to the competition. I think there is a clear winner. Tookin and Alyce.”

“I agree.” Lady Emma stated.

“I second that.” Draconis said.

Frrsha just nodded.

Garry burped, again. “Buurrpp! What you guys said.”

“Ha! That sounds like a glowing recommendation to me.” Lady Emma laughed.

“True enough. Let’s tell them. I am sure everyone would like to know.” Deathwalker replied.

———

Deathwalker and Lady Emma approached the speaker’s podium in the arena. “Good people! Lady Emma and I wanted to announce the winner of the cooking competition. First please give all the competitors a round of applause.”

The crowd clapped and cheered lightheartedly.

Deathwalker raised his hand to get everyone’s attention. “As you all know we will celebrate the end of the Timberfall Festival with a grand hunt. The winner of the cooking competition will lead the cooking of all that we hunt. Once prepared, the food will be shared with all of us. Now without further ado please show your appreciation for Tookin and Alyce!”

This time the crowd was deafening with the cheers and clapping. Several of them had made a point to visit Tookin’s food stand. Word of mouth had spread quickly during the festival. Alyce’s cheery disposition and quick wit combined with Tookin’s unique combination of flavors and dishes led the stand to sell out quickly every day. Their amazing kebabs were the talk of many a festival patron. A few of the bards had taken to writing songs about them. It was those songs that drew Garry and Draconis to seek them out in the first place.

‘Figured it would be good to remind them why this competition was important. Nothing like free food to lift people’s spirits.’ Deathwalker thought as he saw the shocked and embarrassed looks of Tookin and Alyce.

“Please join us for the finals of the Archery Tournament!” Deathwalker motioned for the two winners to come up to the judges’ box.

“You are most gracious Duke Dragonvein.” Tookin said in greeting when he entered the area set aside for judges and their guests.

“Nonsense. You earned it with your amazing cooking. Feel free to take a seat anywhere.” Deathwalker replied.

“Sit here next to us Alyce.” Lady Emma patted the chair next to her.

“Thank you, princess.” Alyce said as she took her seat.

“Deathwalker was telling me all that you do Alyce. Helping with your grandfather’s leatherworker business, assisting your mother at the Adventurers’ guild, and now helping your uncle with his food stand. Most impressive.” Lady Emma praised.

Alyce blushed. “Deathwalker talks about me?”

“Of course I do. You and your family were some of the first people I met in Timberfall. All of you were kind and helpful. Besides you three and Samuel are how I got my start.”

“I did not realize you knew no one, Deathwalker. You are so well liked and known now I forgot you were just a mysterious traveler at first.” Alyce commented.

“You know that when I talk to Samuel, he raves about you and Elsa all the time. He says you’re like a second daughter to him and that you will help Elsa with the tavern just so the two of you get time to hang out.” Deathwalker continued.

“Yet another thing you help with! When do you have time to be have fun or do things you like?” Lady Emma asked.

Alyce blushed again as she shrugged her shoulders. "Elsa and I find time to hang out as we can. Until recently Timberfall was much quieter, so we had more time on our hands. But I do not mind, I like to help others."

"That is most admirable." Lady Emma said.

Tookin interjected. "Duke Dragonvein, do you really plan to feed the entire city from the spoils of the great hunt?"

"Please call me Deathwalker."

"I could not, your grace. It would not be appropriate." The nervous cook replied.

"Nonsense. I prefer to be less formal. Also, to answer your question, yes, I plan to feed the entire city. I expect many of the nobles, their guards, and the adventurers to join the hunt. The forest is overpopulated with various beasts and monsters as of late. Something to do with the primary predators vanishing." Deathwalker answered.

"Yea, I wonder where they went." Garry deadpanned.

Frrsha giggled. "He, he, he, he!"

The others looked puzzled but let it go when Deathwalker changed the subject.

"My personal chef is out of town and will not be back any time soon. If you are interested, I would like to hire you as our personal chef. That is until Mezza returns."

The shocked cook nodded in his chair. "I would be most honored."

"Also, feel free to recruit any of the other cooks to help you in the feast preparations. I know it is far too much to put on two people."

"That is most appreciated Deathwalker." Alyce commented. She then turned to Lady Emma. "My lady, can I ask you what it is like to be a princess?"

"If you can call the duke Deathwalker, then you can call me Emma. As for what it is like, usually it is rather boring. I am required to attend various noble gatherings and balls..."

Garry laughed. "Ha!"

"Garry!" Deathwalker warned.

"But boss, she walked right into that one!"

"Later buddy." Deathwalker said before apologizing to Emma for the interruption. "My apologies."

Lady Emma waved it off. "I do not get it but no matter..."

"Oh, I just got it! Thank you for the mental image! Ha! That is hilarious Garry!" Draconis burst out laughing.

"Please ignore them." Deathwalker replied.

Emma shrugged. "Much of what I do Alyce is a matter of duty. I do get to help people as I can." She then put her hand into Deathwalker's, "Then there are the rare times like these where I can be myself and create amazing memories with those I care about. These are the moments that I cherish and help sustain me through the rest."

Deathwalker squeezed Emma's hand. "I wholeheartedly agree with that statement."

"Awe, see I knew I wanted to be a princess!" Alyce commented as she looked at the two holding hands.

General Mineheir entered the seating area and took one look at Deathwalker and Emma before smiling and speaking up. "My apologies for the interruption, but King Alfheim and the other judges should be here shortly."

"I appreciate you letting us know General. I hear two of the semi-finalists are from your retinue." Deathwalker greeted.

The general took a seat next to Draconis. "Yes Duke Dragonvein. They are two of my finest archers." He then turned to Draconis, "It is good to see you again Draconis."

The dragon in humanoid form grunted. "Eh."

General Mineheir tried to start up a conversation. “Perhaps we could spar again in the near future.”

“Who am I to deny you a beating.”

“I have been practicing, I think you will find...”

Draconis interrupted the elven general. “It will not matter.”

“You may be correct...”

“May be correct?” Draconis scoffed.

“Okay Sheldon.” Garry quipped.

Draconis looked back at the Shadow Gazer. “Are you feeling alright Garry? Why would you call me by another name? Surely, you know that makes no sense.”

“Don’t call me Shirley. Ha, ha, ha, ha!” Garry laughed.

Even Deathwalker chuckled. “Ha! That was a good one buddy.” He turned to his apprentice. “It is an inside joke Garry can explain later. I believe it would be good for you to spar with the general again.”

Mentally Deathwalker said, “It will teach you restraint. Last time you patted a soldier on the back for giving you directions you knocked him into the nearby wall.’

‘You heard about that?!’ Draconis telepathically replied.

‘Of course, Commander Willis keeps me well informed.’

General Mineheir smiled at Deathwalker’s recommendation. “Thank you, your grace. Fighting stronger opponents is how one grows stronger and pushes past their previous limits.”

“That I can agree with.” King Alfheim said as he entered the judges’ box. “Sounds like my friend is trying to fight your apprentice again Deathwalker.”

“That he is. Here, I saved you a seat next to me.” Deathwalker motioned to the open seat on the other side of him.

"I would have liked to sit next to my granddaughter, but who am I to pass up a chance to sit next to my new ally."

"Grandfather you are shameless! Deathwalker knows you want him to build one of his portal stations." Emma mock admonished King Alfheim.

King Alfheim shrugged at his granddaughter. "I never claimed I was not transparent in my objectives. Ha! I do hope you both know I have valued my time here in Timberfall. I have been able to repair my relationship with Emma and you have been most hospitable Deathwalker."

"Something tells me we would be stronger together than apart King Alfheim. You and your people have been excellent guests... for the most part." Deathwalker smiled at the end.

"Oh? Has one of my retinue been a bother?"

Prrsha who appeared out of nowhere next to her sister chimed in. "Yes. That frigid witch!"

"Where did you come from? Most impressive display of stealth." King Alfheim turned back to Deathwalker. "I am guessing she is referring to Advisor Mona?"

Deathwalker nodded.

King Alfheim sighed. "Ah, yes I have noticed her rather keen interest in you Deathwalker." He then motioned to Emma and Deathwalker holding hands. "Though I figured you would be used to interest from others. It is all I can do to keep my daughter from trying to spend what time she can with you."

Emma spoke up. "I thank you for that grandfather. Auntie can be a bit 'driven'."

"Ha! That is one way to put it." The elven king laughed.

"Oh, really father?" Duchess Lightheart interjected as she walked into the seating area with Elder Martha and Lords Dormeir and Simium.

"You know I only speak truth daughter."

"That does not mean I approve. I thought it was rather odd that you were monopolizing my time. Here I thought you wanted to catch up. I do not approve." Duchess Lightheart replied.

"Oh, come now daughter. I have greatly enjoyed my time with you. Do not make it out as anything other than giving my granddaughter time with our host. Come, sit next to me." King Alfheim patted the seat next to him.

"Very well. I did monopolize Deathwalker's time when he was in the capital." Duchess Lightheart said as she took her seat.

Lord Dormeir sat behind Deathwalker. "You do not pay Elder Martha enough." Sebastian said as he leaned in and motioned to the older elf and how she already had Duchess Lightheart distracted and smiling.

"I agree." King Alfheim whispered as he heard what Lord Dormeir said.

"Well, I second that and will have to see what I can do. Been having fun Sebastian?"

"Yes, surprisingly Lord Simium and I have much in common. He has been giving me some valid pointers for next year's tournament."

"Surprisingly?" Lord Simium teased.

"Oh, you know what I mean! I was paying you a compliment." Sebastian replied.

"Oh, is that what that was?" Lord Simium had a stern face before it broke into a smile. "Ha! You are fun to mess with my friend!" Lord Simium sat next to Sebastian and the two men clasped wrists.

"I am happy to see you two getting along. So, who are you rooting for?" Deathwalker asked.

"Mara of course!" Cal said as he and Mary Sue entered.

"Though I have been impressed with your sister's performance Cal, I will be rooting for Lord Longshot." Sebastian replied as the two newcomers sat on his other side.

"As will I, Calcius." Lord Simium answered.

“Hey, I am still rooting for my people.” General Mineheir chimed in.

“Either way this should be interesting.” Deathwalker stated.

# Chapter 30 – Archery Tournament

The arena was divided in half using a rather impressive wall that was created by Elder Martha and a few elven earth mages King Alfheim had offered to help. Rather than raise the wall himself Deathwalker had taken the elf king's offer. This prevented him from having to show any more of his magical capabilities to Advisor Mona.

The fey woman said nothing, but she watched him like a hawk. A predatory smile was always on her face any time he glanced at her. If Emma was not still sitting next to him holding his hand, Deathwalker was sure Advisor Mona would be on his lap again.

'Would this woman be classified as a cougar? Heck, I have three pumas by my side, and I have never felt so much hunger targeting me before. These fey are over the top.' Deathwalker thought.

"Be cautious my hunky master."

"What's up Lilandra? I take it you're seeing how Advisor Mona is acting?" Deathwalker telepathically replied.

"Yes. Elder fey do not think as humans do, especially those of the Winter Court. Once they set their designs on you it is difficult to deter them. That is one of the things they admired about the Huntsman, his ability to remain so focused on a target nothing would stop the hunt. She sees you as a prize. She only suspects you now, but what Mona knows so far has made you too interesting to let go."

"You sound like you know her."

"I do. Mona is one of the older fey. She is not one of Mab's advisors for nothing. To her, you are free game, at least while she only suspects you and has her doubts. The more she learns the harder it will be for her to delay notifying her queen. When that happens, you can no longer be claimed by her as you would belong to Mab."

"What do you mean I'm Mab's?"

"That is how the Winter Court thinks. They are cold and calculating. Never ceasing in their pursuit. Claim territory and survive the harshness of winter. It is that trait within the Huntsman that both attracts them and can allow you to lead. All of the Winter Court know the Huntsman is Mab's. If Mona ever loses her doubt of who you are she must abdicate any claim on you."

"Weird. Makes an odd kind of sense in a cold and calculating way, but still weird."

Emma squeezed Deathwalker's hand. "You seem distracted. Everything okay?"

He smiled back at her. "Of course. Just having a discussion in my head."

Garry chimed in. "Oh? I do that all the time, boss. Usually, it's just me convincing myself of something fun. And you know what? I have some great ideas! Not sure how much fun your conversations are but mine are awesome! I'd be happy to share them with you anytime, boss!"

"I appreciate that, Garry. Maybe later." Deathwalker replied.

Garry's odd behavior had briefly distracted Emma. When she was about to ask what Deathwalker meant the announcer spoke up.

"Welcome everyone to the last of the matchups for the Archery tournament! As you can see the arena has been divided by a raised wall into two sections. The arena is further divided by a line down the middle. The adventurer Mara will face off against Noral from the elven nation. While they are competing, another guest from the elves Alvamar will face off against Lord Longshot!"

The crowd clapped and cheered for their favored person. Mara's name was heard just as much as Lord Longshot. Some of the elves in the stands who were originally from the elven nation rooted for Noral and Alvamar as the two men were rather well-known archers in the army.

The town crier turned announcer gave the crowd a few moments before he continued. "Now these next rounds of matchups will be done differently. Neither competitor can physically cross the line marked in the ground. Targets will randomly appear on both sides of the line. The person who shoots the target first with an arrow, no matter what side it is on, gets the point. Opponents can attack their counterpart to distract them or take them out of the tournament as long as the attack is not fatal."

"You and the mages did an impressive job on the arena, Elder Martha." Deathwalker commented as he looked at the various changes in elevation and different obstructions on the field.

"Thank you, your grace. The earth mages and I felt they would need some options that could be used for cover against their opponent's attacks." Elder Martha commented.

"This should be interesting." Lord Dormeir stated.

"BEGIN!"

The announcer's voice snapped the competitors into action. All four of them took cover behind one of the various pillars placed across the arena.

Targets started to appear on the field. The first set of targets were easy to hit even while the four contestants remained behind cover. Each target would appear with a glow making it hard for them to go unnoticed.

The rate and difficulty of positioning fluctuated as more and more targets appeared. They only remained so long. Each target would vanish after a specific amount of time or sooner if one of the contestants hit the target with an arrow.

## ——Mara——

Mara knew she was going to need to take some risks if she hoped to win. Any time she stuck her head out, Noral would fire an arrow in her direction. Drawing two arrows from her quiver she adjusted the fletching on each one. Then Mara charged each arrow with a small bit of her mana.

Lining up her shots Mara fired the two arrows simultaneously. The arrows went wide. One ricocheted off a wall and hit the target. Mara heard a satisfying yelp as the second arrow ricocheted twice before cutting a gash across Noral's leg.

Cheers came up from the crowd after witnessing such an impressive move.

This made Noral grow cold, and he charged his own arrow. Pouring his mana into it he angled his bow out just enough and fired as he cried out, "Explosive Shot!"

Hearing those words Mara dropped to the floor just as the glowing arrow hit the pillar she was hiding behind and exploded. Bits of rock flew everywhere, several pieces hitting and cutting Mara up.

"AHHHH!"

Cal could be heard as the rest of the crowd grew silent. "You bastard! How dare you!"

Mara scrambled for another pillar, shooting an arrow at her opponent as she dove. She was bruised and cut in several places. It was only a matter of time before the Noral would fire again and elven woman knew it.

Alvamar was a fierce opponent. Multiple times they shot at each other only for the opposing arrows to hit each other mid-flight and veer off. It became common for them to rapidly fire at each other and then immediately shoot at a target. Longshot was loving every minute of it.

Both archers were clearly skilled and masters of their skill. Alvamar started to taunt the lord. "Give up while you can. No human can beat an elf!"

"It is funny how often I hear that from an elf right before I beat them!" Lord Longshot quipped back.

The human archer next few shots caused the arrows to bounce off the surface of a pillar and angle right at the elf. Alvamar was forced to duck down to avoid being turned into a pin cushion.

"Perhaps you do have some skill after all!" Alvamar replied.

The two got shots off but none of Alvamar's got close to hitting Longshot whereas Alvamar had to continue to dodge out of the way. The elf knew he was outmatched but refused to give up.

Then the two competitors heard the sound of loud cracks as rock shattered.

And that was when Lord Longshot got serious. He increased the mana being cycled through his body. Anthony knew it was time to use his trump card. Closing his eyes, he turned and fired multiple arrows in rapid succession high in the air.

The arrows flew over the middle wall of the arena as they found their target.

THUNK, THUNK, THUNK

In rapid succession each arrow sunk deep into an unsuspecting Noral. One in the shoulder, one in his left thigh, and the final one in his right arm. The man dropped to the ground as his body gave out.

"AHHH!"

"That is what you get you bastard!" Cal cried out.

If the crowd was silent before, you could hear a pin drop now. General Mineheir was the one who broke the silence. "How did he do that?!"

Deathwalker looked up into the sky and saw a hawk circling the coliseum. Other birds had flown by periodically, so most people never paid attention, but it was clear this one was following a pattern.

'That hawk must be Anthony's companion. My friend closed his eyes when he fired those shots. I bet he has the ability to see through the hawk's eyes. That is a powerful skill if that is the case.' Deathwalker thought.

Lord Dormeir confirmed Deathwalker's suspicions as he answered the general's question. "Little known fact. Lord Longshot has a hawk companion, and he can see through its eyes. I have seen him use that skill when we were putting down a monster surge in our younger days."

"Beast bonded or tamer skills are very rare. That is quite impressive." King Alfheim commented.

"Look Mara is getting up!" Emma noticed.

Mara saw her opponent was down for the count. It was not hard for her to figure out who stepped in to help her. She called out, "Thank you!"

Alvamar hearing Mara's words realized his peer must have lost control. He knew the man was one of the rare elves like General Mineheir who had Summer Court in their bloodline. Those with such origins tended to run a bit hot tempered.

Even if others were not convinced, it was clear to him what would have happened. His friend violated the tournament rules and most likely have killed Mara if Lord Longshot had not interfered. Alvamar's decision was clear. "Honorable judges, I forfeit this match!"

Mara did not miss a beat. She too turned to the judges' box. "I forfeit as well. Lord Longshot saved my life! He deserves to be tournament champion more than anyone!"

The silent crowd went nuts.

"LORD LONGSHOT"

"Lord Longshot!"

"Yes! Making him champion!"

"Champion! Champion!"

Deathwalker looked first to his fellow judges. All of them nodded in agreement. Then he looked to his friend Cal.

"Hey if this is what my sister wants who am I to argue with it. The man did save her life even if the judges may not see it that way."

Deathwalker considered his next steps. To him this was more of a grey area, but he knew this is what his people wanted. "Who am I to argue with acknowledging such an honorable act."

He let go of Emma's hand. Deathwalker still couldn't believe he had been holding it this entire time. The duke made his way to the podium. Giving a nod the Town Crier stepped as he bowed.

"Will someone please take Noral to the healers and treat Mara's injuries." Deathwalker pointed.

The fallen elf was still on the ground moaning and slowly bleeding out. Most had put him out of their minds with Lord Longshot's win.

Mara was covered in bruises and minor cuts. Luckily for her she looked worse than Mara felt. Several people in robes along with a few guards came out on the field. A few guards put Noral on a stretcher after the healers removed the arrows and closed the wounds. A couple healers saw to Mara's injuries.

"My duke if I may be impertinent." Lord Longshot spoke up.

"Go ahead." Deathwalker nodded.

"Can you do something about this wall?" Longshot asked.

Elder Martha rose to her feet and approached the podium. "If I may your grace."

"Of course." Deathwalker waved.

"The earth mages and I put a resonance in the wall that makes it easier for us to return it to the ground if one knows the spell." Elder Martha explained.

With a quick flick of her wrist the large wall dissolved back into the ground.

"Thank you, Elder." Lord Longshot rushed to Mara and the two healers treating her.

Longshot addressed the healers. "Will she be alright? If you need mana stones, I can provide them!"

"I will be fine Lord Longshot. It looks worse than it is." Mara smiled at his concern.

"Call me Anthony. Please." Lord Longshot replied.

"Very well, Anthony. I appreciate what you did. Noral caught me off guard." Mara took Anthony's hand.

"She will be fine. Most of the wounds have been closed already." One of the healers said.

Anthony raised his other arm and his hawk landed on it before moving to his shoulder. "This is my dearest friend, Talon."

"Nice to meet you, Talon. You are a gorgeous and majestic bird." Mara cooed.

Lord Dormeir leaned over to Cal. "Looks like my friend is rather smitten with your sister."

Deathwalker coughed loudly. "I do not wish to get in the way of a budding romance, so I will not ask you to stand Lord Longshot. However, it is probably best we get you two off the arena field. So, let me officially congratulate you as the winner of the Archery tournament!"

The stands had been murmuring here and there as they watched the display of concern from Lord Longshot. After Deathwalker's declaration the crowd went wild.

"So, gallant!"

"What an archer!"

"That hawk looks scary!"

"Heck yea! So fierce!"

"I love a good romance! What a lucky girl!"

"Have you seen Mara? Lucky guy is more like it!"

On and on the crowd joked and cheered even as Lord Longshot and Mara left the arena.

The Town Crier took the podium back to give out a few announcements. "Tomorrow morning will be the completion of the Magic tournament! After which, our beloved Duke will gather the hunters and share the details before he leads us in the Grand Hunt! It should be wild!!!"

Deathwalker took Lady Emma's hand. Before they left the stage, he turned to Tookin. "I encourage you to take this time to speak with and recruit the other cooks to work under you."

Garry spoke up. "Draconis and I can help if there is taste testing involved!"

Elder Martha chuckled. "Ha, ha, ha, ha! I can help you coordinate the other cooks if you require more than taste testers."

"That would be most helpful, Elder!" Tookin quickly agreed.

Alyce walked over to Garry and whispered. "Do not worry I will make sure you two get to try the food."

“Smart girl. Call on us anytime little one.” Draconis smiled.

“Yep! I knew I liked her!” Garry echoed.

# Chapter 31 – Timberfall Celebrations

Tookin and Alyce spent a good amount of time working with Elder Martha on hiring cooks. Many of the previous contestants from the cooking competition were selected. Several of those same contestants had tried Tookin's kebabs and knew they were delicious. To them it was an honor to serve in any capacity for a high noble. Working alongside a master chef was a large bonus.

"I believe that is the last of them we will need." Tookin let out a loud sigh.

"It is getting late. I am sorry for keeping you both so long." Elder Martha commented.

"No, we thank you, Elder. Without your help we still would be at it." Tookin replied.

"Still Alyce, will your family worry you are not home yet?" Elder Martha asked.

"It is way past my time to be home, but mom and grandfather know I am helping Uncle Tookin. I have been getting home late this week because we have been very busy with the festival. They will figure I am still working, which I am. Though you are right Elder Martha, I should be getting home." Alyce answered.

"I should probably stay and finish things up here. But I do not like the idea of you walking home alone this late." Tookin stated.

Mary Sue and Cal were walking by as they were talking. Her and Cal stopped. "We could take her home, Elder." Mary Sue offered.

"Are you sure it will not be a bother?" Alyce asked.

“Not at all. I remember what it was like when my sister and I lived on the street. Nighttime dangers should not be ignored.” Cal responded.

Mary Sue nodded in agreement. “Cal and I were just going to have a night on the town. Taking you home should be on the way.” She then gestured to the younger girl. “Come on, let us get you home.”

Alyce quickly joined them. “Thank you for this. I can walk fast. I do not want to be a bother.”

“Ha! Nonsense! Come on. While we walk you can tell me what you thought of the Archery tournament.” Cal assured her.

Alyce smiled. “Really?! With grandfather being a judge he has been sequestered here in the manor. Any time I see him and try to ask about the tournaments, he refuses to talk about any of the fights. Something about not being swayed and remaining impartial.” Alyce pouted a little at the end.

“Well, if your grandfather is not home, is your ma?” Cal asked.

“She might be. But lately she’s been busy with all the influx of adventurers, and she often just sleeps at the guildhall. It is okay though. I do not mind. I stay really busy.” Alyce explained.

“Alright. Come on let us get you home so I can enjoy the rest of the night with my Cal!” Mary Sue took Alyce by the hand, leading her out of Timberfall Manor.

———

It took them some time to get through the crowds and various festival goers in different states of inebriation. As they got closer to Alyce’s home the street was rather empty. At first the trio did not notice, but then the level of noise seemed to drop significantly.

“How odd.” Alyce commented.

“What is?” Cal asked.

“It is just that there are usually more people on our street.”

“It is rather late.” Mary Sue suggested.

"Even still." Alyce replied.

"There are a good number of guards. Perhaps something happened." Cal said.

"Look some are approaching now." Mary Sue observed.

"Halt! State your business!" One of the guards ordered.

"We are just escorting young Alyce here home as it is rather late." Cal answered.

"So, neither one of you live on this street?" A different guard asked.

"No. Like I said we were just escorting her home." Cal pointed at Alyce. "Now, how about you tell us what is going on?"

"We do not answer to the likes of you! This is city guard business!" A third guard barked.

A man in sergeant's uniform approached. "What seems to be the problem here?"

"Nothin! I was just telling these blokes we are only here to escort Alyce home."

"We can see she gets home. This is an active crime scene, so I am going to have to ask you to leave." The sergeant ordered.

Cal rested his hands on the hilts of his two sheathed swords. Seeing this several guards pointed their weapons at the trio.

Alyce spoke up. "It is okay Cal. These guards can take me the rest of the way home."

"Are you sure Alyce?" Mary Sue asked.

"Sure. I will be fine with the guards. This is probably the safest this street has been in a long time. Do not worry. Go enjoy your night."

Mary Sue put her hand on Cal. "She is right. The guards will see her home."

Cal visibly relaxed at Mary Sue's touch. "Alright. See you later, Alyce."

“You two love birds have fun!” Alyce teased.

Mary Sue took Cal’s arm and they slowly started to walk away.

Cal and Mary Sue were a couple blocks away when Mary Sue pulled Cal into a long passionate kiss. Cal temporarily forgot his concerns. After a few intense moments of kissing the two separated.

“Wow! What was that for?” Cal panted.

“Just felt it was time.” Mary Sue took Cal’s hand. “Come on, it will be light soon and you promised me more night out on the town.”

The two love birds spent the next several hours stopping by at different impromptu celebrations to join in the fun. It felt like they had traversed the whole of the city. Mary Sue and Cal enjoyed the overall atmosphere and upbeat attitudes of the patrons, but something kept nagging Cal.

“What is wrong? You are still tense.” Mary Sue asked as the sun started to crest on the horizon.

“It is those guards. I cannot put my finger on it but something about that whole situation bugs me.” Cal answered.

“Would you feel better if we go check on Alyce? I am sure she has to be up early to help Tookin anyway. We could escort her back to the manor or to the food cart if Tookin has already left.” Mary Sue suggested.

“Actually, yea I would.” Cal replied.

“Come on then, you big softy.” Mary Sue guided him away from the celebration that was still going strong.

As they were on the other side of town it took them awhile to get back to Alyce’s neighborhood. Once again, they noticed very few people on the streets but still a good number of guards.

“Look! There is that Sergeant from last night.” Cal said before picking up his pace, heading straight for the guard. “Hey Sergeant!”

Seeing the man from last night stalking towards him, Sergeant Chen frowned. “What do you want civilian?”

"You still doing whatever city guard business?" Cal asked but really didn't want an answer and quickly just kept talking. "Which I do not buy. I mean what takes you guys all night?" He then pointed at the sergeant. "We are about to head to Alyce's place. If I do not get a glowing recommendation from her, I will see to it you pay for it."

"Is that so?" Sergeant Chen raised an eyebrow.

"Yea that is..." A mithril dagger jutted out of Cal's throat cutting him off and spraying Sergeant Chen in blood.

The dagger quickly was removed. As Cal collapsed and just before he died, his eyes widened as he saw Mary Sue holding the blade.

"Finally!" Mary Sue bent down and wiped the blood off her blade on Cal's leather armor. "You really think I could care about some elf? I would never dirty myself with such filth. I am going to have to take a long bath after having your hands on me."

"You complain about needing a bath, look at me!" Sergeant Chen complained as he took a bit of cloth he had and wiped the blood off his face.

"Oh, quit complaining. You are not the one that had to kiss him." Mary Sue signaled a few guards. "Drag the body away. We do not want anyone seeing it until we are ready."

The two soldiers quickly did as they were told.

"Where is the general?" Mary Sue asked.

"Having his fun in the house." Archmage Lenn walked out from behind the side of the house and pointed back.

"That is perfect." Mary Sue snapped her fingers at the guards carrying Cal's body. "Put the corpse in the house. We want to make sure Deathwalker sees it before he witnesses our general's handiwork."

The two guards hesitated. This woman scared the crap out of them, but no one ever interrupted General Marks.

Seeing the looks on the two guards' faces Archmage Lenn spoke up as he cast a portal under the corpse. "Drop the body. The portal comes out in the house I was just in."

The two guards did as they were ordered, then quickly scurried off as fast as they could.

Mary Sue just smirked. "You are too easy on them."

Archmage Lenn shook his head. "You are just upset after having to be touched by an elf."

"What of it! Do you know how much I wanted to slit everyone's throats in that damned manor? Especially that pompous butler! He was always watching, and that damn contract prevented me from directly harming him or that noble." Mary Sue gestured towards the house. "But that lovesick idiot gave me the perfect opportunity to get out from under that old man's watchful eye."

"It will be over soon. Everything is in place." Sergeant Chen chimed in.

"After far too long... I finally get to see this place burn! Though we could kill a few more to help kick things off." Mary Sue smiled evilly.

"Save that bloodlust for what is to come. Now tell me what you have learned." Archmage Lenn ordered.

The pixie assigned to watch Cal took off. His charge had died so quickly, he didn't even sense any killing intent until after the elf was dead.

The little, tiny fairy beat his wings as fast as he could. 'I must reach Timov right away! Deathwalker must know what is coming!'

## ---Somewhere in Timberfall---

Draconis and Garry were walking along one of the city streets heading to yet another celebration where food and entertainment would be in surplus. Out of nowhere Garry stopped. This abrupt action made Draconis turn to his companion.

"What is it, Garry?"

"Not sure. I feel like someone just rolled a 1. And I mean major crit fail!"

"What do you mean a 1? Crit fail?" Draconis asked.

Garry shook himself. "Eh, whoever it is, who cares. Let's get some grub!"

# Chapter 32 – Unexpected News

People had gathered early for the final tournament of the festival. In truth many stayed up the previous evening and rather than miss anything they assembled in the coliseum. Vendors walked around offering teas and other items to help people wake up.

The festive mood and excitement over the last few days was infectious. It created an energy all its own. Many mini celebrations took place during the festival. Several who were not used to such excess went overboard. The amount of mead and wine sold this week set new records, making many alcohol merchants happy as can be.

Deathwalker and the other judges and guests were already present and excited to see the final rounds of the Magic tournament.

Mara was sitting next to Lord Longshot holding hands. After the Archery tournament they both stopped kidding themselves. The two had spent most of their free time together since meeting.

Mara had been concerned about dating a noble and how others might perceive their budding relationship. Anthony didn't care in the slightest. He found a woman who shared his passion for archery and helping others.

"It is good to see you two getting along so well." Sebastian commented.

"Mara was concerned people would not accept us. Especially as we have only met recently." Anthony replied.

"Nonsense! Sometimes love just works out that way. As long as you two put the other first and look out for one another you will be fine."

The two friends clasped wrists in acknowledgment of their friendship.

"What about you Deathwalker?" Mara asked.

"What about me? You are both my friends. I am happy you found each other."

Mara smiled. "I am glad my brother found someone too. I feel Mary Sue will be good for him. I do not like to see him alone."

Advisor Mona spoke up. "Perhaps, perhaps not."

Mara looked puzzled at the fey woman who still never took her eyes off Deathwalker.

Emma chimed in as she took Deathwalker's hand. "It is good to see love blossoming. Nothing in life is promised and the dangers are plentiful for our people. Love breathes hope into all who witness it."

"Well said my granddaughter. You speak like a wise ruler." King Alfheim said.

"Thank you, grandfather." Emma replied.

"When this festival is over, I want you to travel back with me. It is long overdue for me to name you, my heir."

Emma knew her grandfather's attitude had changed since he learned of her ability to wield magic. He had pulled her aside and told her how sorry he was to have kept her at arm's length all her life. His duty to his people outweighed his love of family. That and she reminded him so much of her mother it was easier at first to stay away. Now, however, he asked for her forgiveness and Emma gladly gave it to him.

Emma knew all too well the obligation of duty and how a noble had to consider their people. A royal had to go beyond just consideration. She knew her grandfather had to make an impossible choice. No Emma did not blame him as much as she blamed the fey with all their rules about magic and bloodlines. They were obsessed with such things.

"You warm my heart grandfather. I will gladly return with you. Perhaps Deathwalker can join us. I do believe you wanted to build a portal station, yes?"

"An excellent idea! But that is to be expected from my heir!" King Alfheim smiled.

———————

"You are shameless, grandfather!" Emma teased.

Deathwalker just looked at the two and laughed. "Let's figure it out after the festival is over."

"Very diplomatic Deathwalker." Duchess Lightheart commented

"I try." Deathwalker smiled back at the prim and proper duchess. Deciding to change the subject, he turned to her father. "Where is Advisor Nero?"

"Oh, yes. He said he felt ill after being out all-night celebrating."

"Ha! Tightwad cannot hold his liquor!" General Mineheir laughed.

"Quite right you are my friend. He asked to take the portal to Hargrave. We left a few of our healers there with the rest of my contingent." King Alfheim replied.

"Lilandra, did Nero really take the portal to Hargrave?" Deathwalker telepathically asked.

"He did. However, I sensed no illness when he traveled through the portal."

"You can sense that kind of stuff?"

"For the most part yes. If it could be a danger, I can detect it. Alcohol is a poison. If he had been sick from drinking, I could easily detect it when he went through. He lied." Lilandra explained.

"Yes, and this is not the first lie we have caught him in. Which makes me wonder why he was so interested in getting out of Timberfall."

Turning his attention back to the present, he overheard Elder Martha talking to Duchess Lightheart about a few of the semi-finalists.

Then he caught Mara talking more to herself than anyone. "I wonder where Cal is. He should be here by now. I hope he did not celebrate too much last night."

Tookin entered the judges' box and approached Betterman who had remained quiet this entire time. The leatherworker still could not believe he was among so many important people.

"I was wondering if you have seen Alyce?" Tookin asked.

Betterman looked confused. "What do you mean have I seen her? She has been helping you the last few days!"

Elder Martha heard the two men talking. "Cal and Mary Sue escorted her home last night before they joined all the celebrations."

"Where is Cal and Mary Sue?" Betterman asked.

"They are probably sleeping it off." General Mineheir suggested.

"Cal can hold his liquor. He went drinking plenty of times with Grimhold and the two of them knew how to drink." Mara said with a hint of concern in her voice.

Lord Longshot squeezed Mara's hand. "We can go looking for him. I imagine it would not be too difficult to find them."

A flash of light zipped by fast, stopping in front of Deathwalker. Timov made a little bow in the air. "Oh, great savior of fairy-kind, I have urgent news to report!"

"You have pixies working for you Deathwalker?" King Alfheim asked.

"Yes."

"Since when? I have never seen you with them." Elder Martha commented.

"Why did they call you the savior of fairy-kind?" Emma asked.

"How interesting." Advisor Mona said as she studied the little ball of light. Then it clicked. "That is my personal pixie!"

Deathwalker turned to the fey woman. "No, they were your personal pixie. That was voided when you sent them to spy on me. Now they work for me."

“For how long has...” Deathwalker cut Mona off. “Conversation for later!” Turning back to Timov who was anxiously waiting. “Go ahead. Give me your report.”

Timov saluted. “Yes, your majesty! The pixie I assigned to watch Cal has reported he was killed by the maid Mary Sue!”

“Nooooo!” Mara cried out in anguish.

Timov turned to the elf archer who was leaning into Lord Longshot for support. “I am sorry but it is true, my lady. Mary Sue was working with some city guards and an unknown mage.”

Commander Willis, who arrived just before Timov did, could not believe his ears. “What?! City guards? Which ones?”

“The sergeant was named Chen. There is little we know of the others involved.” Timov answered.

“I will rip that traitor in half!” Growled Commander Willis.

“We both will.” General Marius said.

“And I am helping!” Darius added.

“Hey if we are ripping people in half Draconis and I want in!” Garry declared.

BOOM

BOOM

BOOM

Explosions started to go off across parts of the city. Fire began to spread. People started to scream and panic.

Then they saw large boulders being launched over the city walls. The first boulder got through smashing into a few nearby buildings and killing those inside unlucky enough to be caught in its path.

After that first Boulder got through a shield sprang forth from Town hall in the center of Timberfall, quickly expanding to the outer walls. Just before more of the boulders could pass over the city walls the translucent citywide shield blocked the remaining catapulted stones. Each subsequent Boulder bouncing off the shield, crashing outside of Timberfall.

A soldier rushed up panting. He saluted to General Marius. “S-sir... the city... we are under siege! A massive army outside the walls! They are carrying the Proletariat nation’s banner!”

# Chapter 33 – Invasion

Mrrsha appeared shortly after the wheezing soldier gave his report. "Alpha, there are fires spreading throughout the city! Your suspicions proved true, many in the refugee camp are taking up arms against us and sowing chaos in the streets!"

"How many from the camp?" Deathwalker asked.

"Perhaps a third, maybe more. It is difficult to get an accurate account with the current level of chaos. Several in city guard uniforms are helping the infiltrators and attacking civilians!" Mrrsha answered.

"I am going to kill those traitors!" Commander Willis went to exact his revenge.

"Hold Commander!" Deathwalker ordered. "You will get your chance at vengeance."

Turning to General Marius. "Other than the special beastmen force, those in city guard uniforms cannot be trusted."

Commander Willis winced at his alpha's words.

Deathwalker continued. "Get soldiers on the battlements! We need to know what we are facing. Then get word to our secret base to send reinforcements. Their job is to begin sweeping the city. Stay in contact via communication crystal."

"As you command my liege!" General Marius replied before taking off.

"I am going to find that bitch and make her suffer!" Mara snapped as she was about to follow General Marius out.

"Mara, stop!" Deathwalker's words held such authority she froze mid stride.

"I need you to work with Lords Longshot, Dormeir, and Simium to get our guests to the portal hub!"

"What?! I am not leaving! We can fight!" Emma declared.

"Oh, you will have to fight. The way to get back to the portal and the manor is not clear. You will all have to fight your way to get there!"

Mara gritted her teeth. "I want that bitch to suffer!"

"I promise you Mara that day will come. For now, protect the king and our guests. If something happens to them, we could not only expect war with the elves, but Nord itself might turn against us if something happens to Emma and Duchess Lightheart."

"Where will you be?" Emma asked.

"I'll get to that. First things first." Deathwalker replied before he started to turn to people and give orders at a rapid-fire pace, his problem-solving brain in overdrive mode. "Commander Willis, your beastmen unit is the only one I trust, they need to start funneling our people to safety and start taking back our city. Mrrsha, Prrsha, and Frrsha go with them, they will need your ferocity. Do not hold back do you hear me?"

All four of them knew there was no room for discussion and gave a quick, "Yes, alpha" before they darted off.

"Elder Martha and Darius, this is your city. Round up as many adventurers and mages as you can, then start putting out these fires and help rescue the civilians. Help Commander Willis' beastmen, but do not trust anyone else in a city guard uniform.

"Draconis, when the rest of us leave the coliseum, I need you to make your way to Timberfall's Townhall. It is rather easy to figure out the citywide shield is coming from there. If these infiltrators manage to deactivate or destroy it, Timberfall will be vulnerable to those catapults and whatever forces are outside our walls."

Draconis nodded. "As you command, Master."

"Oh, see if you can subdue or capture anyone of these that might have information. But do not risk your own life or that of this city."

"It shall be done, Master."

Betterman and Tookin had immediately left to go find Alyce once the soldier had reported the city was under attack. "I am going to go with Timov to find Betterman and Alyce. We cannot lose one of our city leaders and someone I consider a friend." Then I will join Marius on the wall to help deal with our invaders. Plus, Cal deserves justice!" Deathwalker turned to Mara. "If I find Mary Sue I will make sure you get your vengeance!"

Mara nodded at him, rage boiling in her eyes.

"I will go with you, my liege. I am sworn to protect you!" Sunderer chimed in.

"No!" Deathwalker replied harshly, then softened as he continued. "I need you to protect Emma. I cannot stand the idea of something happening to her."

Sunderer put his fist to his heart. "I will protect Lady Emma with my life."

"Boss, what do you want me to do?"

Deathwalker turned to his friend and familiar and said one word. "Smash!" Then added, "Oh and have FUN!"

"Boss, I love you. Ha, ha, ha, ha, ha!"

————

The group made their way out of the coliseum. Luckily, they had a separate exit from the other spectators. They moved as one to get out of the arena. As they exited the giant building, adventurers could be seen already trying to help organize and funnel the civilians to safety.

BOOM!

This time the explosion was larger than the previous. Off in the distance it looked like the smoke from the explosion came from Timberfall Manor.

"How did they get inside the walls of the manor?!" Elder Martha cried out as she noticed where the new billow of smoke was coming from.

“We must be betrayed; it is the only answer!” Lord Simium replied. He hoped his son hadn’t been part of this mess. The sting of that betrayal still hurt.

“Alright people, time to do what we discussed! Sebastian and Anthony, protect King Alfheim, Duchess Lightheart, and Lady Emma! Mara, stay with Lord Longshot and help him defend our allies!” Deathwalker ordered.

Sebastian and Anthony moved their retinue into a protective formation. Mara moved to stand next to the man that had started to capture her heart, Anthony Longshot.

“Oh no! I am coming with you! I have magic now and can help!” Lady Emma demanded as she stepped out of the protective circle.

Deathwalker shook his head and put his hand on her shoulder, genuine concern in his eyes. “We discussed this. I do not doubt your capabilities, but this is war. You are now the heir to both this kingdom and that of the elves. If something were to happen to you, I would never forgive myself! Please stay with your grandfather and aunt. With enemy soldiers in the city, you’ll be safer together.”

Lady Emma hesitated. Her emotions warred within her. Everything she knew said she should stand by his side and have his back, yet deep down Emma knew Deathwalker was right. If something happened to her grandfather before he could officially announce his support for her and Deathwalker the elven nation would be thrown into chaos, perhaps even turn on the kingdom.

“Fine, but if you die out there, I will never forgive you!” Lady Emma declared before she pulled him into an embrace and kissed Deathwalker.

“Alright! Way to go boss!” Garry cheered.

“Niece! I do not approve!” Duchess Lightheart chastised.

The kiss was quick, yet Lady Emma felt short of breath and her magic felt like it was brimming to take on the world. She had not thought much about the act other than the fact if something happened to Deathwalker and she never got the chance to kiss him again, it would be her greatest regret. Pulling away, Lady Emma stepped back behind the protective formation and began channeling her magic.

Advisor Mona was conflicted. Her duty to Queen Mab required her to pursue this lead, but she knew if King Alfheim died that would irk her majesty even more. Deathwalker fascinated her and the fey woman was very attracted to the man, far more than she cared to admit. Until her suspicion could be confirmed she wanted him. Refocusing on her first charge, protecting Mab's puppet, the advisor fell into line near King Alfheim. 'If he does not survive then Deathwalker is not the one my Queen is looking for.'

"Draconis and Garry, with me. We will begin to route the enemy in the city, then each of you will do as I ordered earlier." Deathwalker ordered.

"What about the barrier?! How long can it hold the enemy at bay?" General Mineheir asked.

Deathwalker looked at the elf. "Hope it is long enough for us to end this madness so we can deal with the enemy at our gates."

Giving a quick glance to the older mage. "Elder Martha, do what you can as you go. We will take out as many as we can along the way."

Elder Martha looked resolute. "I will not fail you, my liege."

Turning to Draconis, "Just like I taught you." Deathwalker said as he grew wings out of his back to the gasps of everyone but Advisor Mona who had already learned he possessed this ability.

Draconis nodded as he grew his own wings. "I am with you master!"

"Timov, lead the way."

"As you command, your majesty!" Timov saluted.

Following the little ball of light, Deathwalker, Draconis, and Garry took off into the air, heading to the different smoke pyres that could be seen billowing up from the various fires the saboteurs started. Deathwalker was determined to help along the way.

The four fliers made their way in the air. Each one would strike out as they saw enemies. Deathwalker would cast Create Water over a flaming building to douse the flames as they flew by. After they quickly moved in a single direction, he knew it was time for them to split up.

“Draconis, head to the town hall and check on the barrier device. Kill any enemies you feel are appropriate, BUT make sure you take some survivors for interrogation later!” Deathwalker said as he pointed in the direction of the central building.

“As you command, master!” Draconis bowed his head before taking off in the direction Deathwalker pointed.

“Awe, what about me boss?” Garry asked.

“Stick with Timov and I. Use your ice spells to help put out the fires.” Seeing Garry’s face disappointed Deathwalker continued. “Oh, and anyone not with us...”

Garry perked up. “Yes?”

Deathwalker smiled wickedly. “Be your murderhobo self and kill them all!”

“Ha, ha, ha, ha, ha! You are the greatest boss EVER!” Garry said as he took off towards the nearest billow of smoke.”

## ———Not Too Far from The Coliseum———

SHUNK!

An arrow took out another Proletariat soldier.

"How are there this many Proletariat scum in Timberfall?!" Mara said in frustration.

Once the Proletariat saboteurs set their fires and did what they could to sow general chaos in the city they shifted to taking out high value targets. Several enemy squads swarmed the elven envoy once they were caught out in the open near Timberfall Manor. The envoy was not without teeth, protected by Lord Simium, Lord Dormeir, Lord Longshot, Mara, Duchess Lightheart, and Lady Emma.

"Kill the elves!" A proletariat saboteur cried out as his squad charged the group.

Lord Longshot put an arrow in the infiltrator's eye in response. "I do not know Mara. We must get the elves to the portal."

"We are going as fast as we can, but there seems to be no end to these ruffians." Lord Simium said as he held his flaming sword cane in his hand.

About ten enemies were approaching from one side while fifteen were charging at them from the opposite side. Duchess Lightheart looked at her niece. "Care to show me what Deathwalker has been teaching you?"

"With pleasure." Emma smiled.

"I will take the ten on the left, try to hold off the ones on the right until I can join you." Duchess Lightheart did not bother checking if Emma agreed.

The elven duchess raised her hands and veritable blizzard hit the oncoming soldiers. The men were first slowed as they had to lean into the intense cold wind buffeting them. Then the cold started to set in right before shards of ice zipped by, impaling several. All ten were taken out of the fight. Three were incapacitated and seven were fatally wounded.

The higher-level spell took the wind out of Duchess Lightheart. She knew stopping to rest was not an option. Turning to help her niece, she found that was unnecessary. All fifteen were dead or severely wounded. Some were impaled from Ice Lance and others severely burned from fire.

"I approve." Duchess Lightheart said to her niece.

"Thanks auntie!"

"I agree, most impressive granddaughter." King Alfheim commented.

Some other enemies had tried to approach from behind but the Lord Dormeir, Lord Simium, and General Mineheir made short work of them. An enemy arrow zipped by General Mineheir's face, as the elf shifted to look at his new opponent. The enemy archer had already nocked another arrow when two arrows, one to the head and one to the heart took the man out.

Looking back the general saw both Lord Longshot and Mara. "Thank you, both."

Mara just nodded. Lord Longshot shut his eye. A moment later he opened them and pointed. "Talon sees more coming from that direction. I suggest we pick up the pace."

## ———Timberfall Townhall———

Draconis flew as fast as he could to his destination. In route an archer tried to take a shot at him. He dodged the attack, but the aerial maneuver made him lose the momentum he had built up.

"Why you little shit!"

The dragon in humanoid form covered his body in scales. Then Draconis altered his course to deal with the pest. He picked up speed and barreled right at the archer on the roof of a nearby building. It was a simple matter for him to literally tear right through them.

Draconis was covered in gore. "Uck! Guess I will clean myself up later." He looked down at the archer's remains. "That is what he gets for bothering me. Stupid human."

That resolved the man continued his flight to Timberfall Townhall. As he flew closer, Draconis saw several soldiers outside the building. "Well, this should be interesting."

Draconis dropped to the ground, making a superhero landing, emulating what he had seen from the various movies and shows Garry had shown him so far. The move startled the Proletariat soldiers, and they all drew their weapons.

"Now, why would all of you be here? You know..." Draconis was interrupted when a nearby soldier carrying a spear jabbed him. The point of the spear harmlessly bounced off his scale covered stomach.

"How dare he!"

Like lightning, Draconis moved. He grabbed the offending soldier by the head and slammed him into the ground. The man's skull was crushed in an instant. Slowly rising to his feet. "Now, as I was saying before I was so rudely interrupted, you know you insects are in my way."

The enemy soldiers started to tremble as Draconis smiled wickedly at the same time he unleashed his killing intent.

"My master asked I take a few for questioning. I will throttle back my strength." Draconis said as he moved.

The dragon turned man pulled his punch as he hit the first guard. Even though Draconis reduced his strength, he still punched a whole right through the man's chest, his fist coming out the other side. "Damn it! You humans are complete weaklings." He tried to pull his arm out only for it to get stuck in the damaged armor. "Son of a..." Draconis cursed as he swung his arm around trying to dislodge his fist from the corpse.

Relaxing his hand as he flung his arm hard sent the corpse flying into a group of soldiers bowling them over. "Ah, that's better! Now, where was I? Oh yea!"

Draconis resumed his attacks. Trying to subdue when he could, but often not hitting his targets too hard and crushing or fatally wounding them. One soldier took a swing at him with a sword. Sadly, for the soldier, Draconis grabbed his arm and ripped it off. Then he subsequently used the severed arm still holding a sword to impale another soldier with the blade.

"Man, you guys are weak. Though I think I am getting closer to regulating my strength." Draconis said more to himself than his foes.

It only took Draconis a few more minutes to take care of the remaining soldiers, both outside and on the bottom floors of Timberfall Townhall.

"Well, well, what do we have here?" Draconis commented as he entered the upper floor.

Belinda, Carn, and the five battle-hardened soldiers with the twins all turned to look at who just spoke.

"Who are you?!" Carn exclaimed in shock at some random redhaired man covered in gore appearing at the stairs.

"It is one of the duke's retainers. Some pompous noble, he will be child's play. I will deal with him, take out that barrier, brother." Belinda declared as she drew her blades.

Carn trusted his sister and knew no noble could match her skill with the blade. He burst into the final room where the city shield was housed.

Smirking, Belinda licked one of her blades. "It has been a while since one of my blades bathed in a nobleman's blood. This should be fun."

She took one step when Belinda felt an aura of murderous intent hit her like a wave that caused her to stagger mid-stride. The twin blinked. One second, she was staggering and the next second the squad of five men between her and this new arrival were dead. To her it happened in an instant. She blinked again and the redhaired man right in front of her.

'How?! When did he kill them?!' Belinda thought before Draconis slammed her into the nearby wall, knocking her unconscious.

Carn turned back when he heard his sister be slammed into the wall. "You bastard! I will kill you!" Carn cried out as he charged.

"My master said to keep a few alive for interrogation. I guess you two will do. I think I have finally perfected how to control my strength." Draconis said before punching Carn into the other wall.

Carn went flying. He hit the wall with a loud thud before sliding to the floor just as unconscious as his sister.

"Tsk-tsk. You humans are so fragile." Draconis said as he picked up his two new prisoners and dragged them into the room with the barrier device.

## ———Commander Willis———

"We must hurry!" Mrrsha ordered.

"You are sure your sister found Chen?" Commander Willis asked as he ran alongside her.

"Prrsha is the one of the best trackers in our pride. If she says he is there then she is there." Mrrsha replied.

'How are they even communicating?' Commander Willis thought before he asked. "Do you have a communication crystal hidden somewhere?"

"What? No. Thanks to our alpha, we can communicate telepathically." Mrrsha answered as if it was the most obvious thing ever.

"Really? Do you think our alpha would bless me with such a gift?"

"Do not know. We are his disciples, pledged to him for all eternity." Mrrsha stated with pride.

"I would gladly do so! He is the most honorable man I know! Our pack has grown stronger than ever thanks to Deathwalker!"

"Then ask him in private when this is all over. Come, we are almost there." Mrrsha scaled a two-story building rather than navigate around it.

"Damn cats." Commander Willis cursed.

Mrrsha just smirked at the wolfman.

After a few more turns they arrived at an alleyway where a squad of men dressed in city guard uniforms were passing through.

"CHEN! YOU TRAITOR!" Commander Willis roared when he saw the man.

This traitor had undermined his command and turned the guard into the exact opposite of what it stood for. It would take the citizens years to trust the guard again thanks to a few bad apples. But earning back that trust started right here when Willis brought this man to justice.

"Commander, how good of you to join us. You are outnumbered and outmatched. I have been holding back my strength just waiting for when I could take you out!" Chen taunted.

Mrrsha and Commander Willis were surrounded by thirty men plus Chen.

Commander Willis charged Chen only to get backhanded through a wall. Chen chased after him.

Prrsha and Frrsha dropped down from nearby rooftops.

"That leaves ten of you for every one of us." Mrrsha commented.

The sergeant goes flying between the cat girls and the guards right through another wall. Commander Willis stalked out of the humanoid sized hole in the wall and charged after Chen.

"They should have brought more men. He, he, he, he!" Prrsha chuckled as all three sisters extended their claws.

# Chapter 34 – Cold Logic

## ———Betterman's Leatherworks———

Deathwalker noticed one of the buildings currently burning was one of the first places he had ever visited in Timberfall, Betterman Leatherworks. Changing direction, he cast **Create Water** to douse the flames. Seeing their house in the back was partially collapsed, Deathwalker dropped to the ground and entered the building to check for anyone that might be caught in the rubble or hurt.

"Go take care of some of these other fires. I will deal with this." Deathwalker ordered Garry as he entered the building.

"You got it, boss!"

Reaching out with his all his senses including **Tremorsense**, Deathwalker searched for any sign of life as he moved through the remains of the home. As he went further into the building, he did not sense any life, but he did sense something else. A faint magic coming from deeper inside the house.

Deathwalker moved toward the energy he felt. It was like blood magic, but wrong in some way. As he moved towards the area where the feeling of wrongness was coming from, a corpse blocked his way. He immediately recognized Cal's body. "No!"

Quickly moving to the body, Deathwalker had heard his friend was killed by Mary Sue, but to see it with his own eyes was different.

Lilandra spoke in his mind in the hope of offering comfort. "I am sorry master. I know you considered him your friend."

Hearing the djinn's voice in his head was like a lifeline. "Lilandra, does resurrection magic exist?"

"It does, but you are not high enough of a level and your mana pool is not near enough." Lilandra replied.

"But it is possible, I could bring Cal back?" Deathwalker hopefully asked.

"Not in your current state master. Such a thing would require you to be not only much stronger, but not be dying yourself. Your mind, soul, and body are shattered in different ways. I am sorry master." Lilandra lamented.

Shaking himself, Deathwalker opened his bag of holding wide and put Cal inside. He may not be able to store living things, but he would not give up so quickly on his friend. With that done, he rose to his feet and continued further into the building.

He entered what Deathwalker thought were the remnants of a bedroom. There on the bed, he found a mutilated corpse. It was the source of the corrupted magic he sensed. Even mutilated he could tell who it was. Even as badly damaged as it was there was no mistaking little, sweet Alyce.

Deathwalker dropped to his knees next to Betterman's granddaughter. Her dress was torn, glowing words were carved into her flesh.

"Careful master, that is foul magic!" Lilandra warned, but Deathwalker stopped working.

"That Blood magic I feel, but it does not resonate with my core. It is like it's been twisted or corrupted somehow." Deathwalker replied before his brain registered something he had read in the Infinite Library that triggered his Insight.

***Ritual of Twisted Empowerment***
*Description: the combination of Eldritch and Blood magics are used to grant the caster a part of the life of the sacrifice in the form of permanent stats. This blood sacrifice ritual requires both the defiling and killing of an unwilling victim while channeling Outsider power.*

“What the heck is Outsider power?” Deathwalker had asked himself back then. He remembered vividly reading about the abhorrent act, in some ways the downside of eidetic memory. The victim was tortured, raped, and then when their suffering was greatest, they were murdered. For all their effort, the caster got a few stat points at most from the victim. The younger the victim the higher the stat gain, something about younger victims held more lifeforce. Such a thing was horrendous, it was a difference of gaining maybe a handful of stats compared instead of one of two from an older victim. It made no sense to Deathwalker, but he knew some did not care what they had to sacrifice on their quest for power.

Now Deathwalker was seeing the results of such an evil act, and it made him sick. His **Power of 13** was nothing like this, sure it took, but in combat or as part of a hunt, there was honor in that. “This...is just wrong. Wait is this magic preserving the writing even from the soot and other damage. What madness is this?” Deathwalker said to himself as he had tuned Lilandra or any of the others who tried to reach him telepathically. There was a firm mental wall that went up.

Distraught and lost for a moment, Deathwalker finally focused and read the message left.

“Let this be a lesson to our enemies. My friends and I relish this power. No one interferes with my fun, and what fun she was! Oh, I do so hope the duke sees this note before his city falls! Signed, General Marks”

Deathwalker was stunned. “This evil scum killed such a sweet and innocent girl and is bragging about it, hoping I would see this! I am going to see this man and everyone like him suffer! I will find a way to make them all pay! No quarter will be given to any of them!”

Turning as he stood up, Deathwalker felt a cold fury take hold of him, something dark and primal. That was when a memory came rushing forward.

Words Mother Winter had said to him echoed in Deathwalker's mind. ***"You have lost your heart and compassion, your emotions are stunted and fractured. Not all of them are gone exactly. Your drive and passion to fight cannot be separated from you. However, I and my daughter know better than most the dark path pure cold logic can lead you to. Be careful, with a cold heart you will need a code, or the result will be horrible atrocities. You are of Spring, but that means a part of you is of Winter, remember that. Winter is cold and calculating. We do not care about your feelings and nowhere is safe, you either become the Hunter or end up the hunted."***

It was like a switch flipped in Deathwalker's brain. Logic dictated such cruelty must be met with the fiercest and most brutal response. "Death is too good for them. I will find a way to make them suffer. No mercy!"

What Deathwalker did not notice during his musings was the ambush falling into place. Fifteen Proletariat infiltrators covered the exit to the building. Several equipped with bows, nocked arrows and prepared to fire the moment their target stepped outside. When the surrounding soldiers started to get a feeling of unease, a mix of someone watching them nearby and a growing danger coming from the leatherwork shoppe, the original plan went out the window. They switched to the backup plan and tripped the trap they set up earlier to collapse the building.

His familiar and disciples all felt it along their bond. Their master had just taken the gloves off. Garry was having the time of his life when he felt a one-word command in his very core, "MINE!"

Bursting out of the rubble, Deathwalker let out a bellowing roar as he flew into the air.

"RROOAARR!!!"

The sound echoed throughout the whole city causing everyone to pause. They could feel the cold killing intent that began to radiate outward. Worse, they felt the gathering of massive amounts of mana.

The roar caught the Proletariat off guard. The momentary pause cost the fifteen infiltrators. As Deathwalker flew out of the building he cast several Overcharged Chain Lightning spells hitting all his would-be-ambushers. However, this was not just a simple overcharged spell. He attempted something he hadn't done since he fought the krythid, channeling his unique ability through one of his spells.

With his mind crystal clear, all doubt removed, Deathwalker used the **Dual Casting** skill with **Power of 13** and **Chain Lightning**. The empowered chain lightning hit all the ambushers, lighting them all up like a Christmas tree. All fifteen dropped to the floor dead, nothing but burnt husks. Deathwalker paid them no mind, their deaths were not enough to quench his vengeance. Ignoring the slew of notifications, he rose further into the air while continuing to draw on his power.

## ———Near Timberfall Portal Hub———

The escort finally had the manor and portal hub station in their sights. There was smoke coming from the manor.

"Oh no! We must go help them!" Emma declared.

"We cannot, my lady." Lord Simium stated.

"Simium is right. We must get you and the others to the portal!" Lord Dormeir insisted.

"Is that Elder Martha?" King Alfheim asked.

"It is. And those look like adventurers." Mara commented.

Elder Martha and several others made their way to the group. "It is good to see you all alive. My apologies for having to go coordinate the rescue operation."

“Nonsense Elder. This city is under your protection. That is to be expected.” General Mineheir complimented.

“How bad is it?” Emma asked.

“Bad, your highness. We are still counting the dead and doing what we can for the wounded. Darrius and several others have been helping establish a protective circle where the civilians are being escorted to.”

“What happened at the manor, are they alright?” Emma had a look of concern.

“The structure is intact but there is significant damage. From eyewitnesses that survived Mary Sue was the one that set off the attack.”

Upon hearing the name of the woman who killed her brother, Mara immediately shifted all her attention. “Where is that bitch?”

“Gone, but not before killing Geeves and several others. This whole thing is mess.” Elder Martha replied.

“Do they know which way she went?” Mara pressed.

“No, they were too busy fleeing for their lives.” Elder Martha answered.

“Damnit!”

“Do not worry, my love. We will hunt her and the others that did this!” Lord Longshot said with determination.

“Yes, we will make them pay! This I approve!” Duchess Lightheart stated.

“They made a mistake attacking Timberfall when we were here. When I return, I will rally every elf to march against the Proletariat!” King Alfheim declared.

“I will gladly lead our forces into battle against these scoundrels!” General Mineheir commented.

Lord Longshot took out another target. “Maybe we can save that for after we have full control of the city.”

The group saw more Timberfall soldiers pouring out of the portal hub building. There were well over a thousand. Lieutenant Daniels was leading the force as it immediately established a perimeter and started to methodically move one block at a time with large pike shields up to protect them against enemy archers hidden in the buildings.

Lieutenant Daniels approached and then saluted. “Elder Martha.”

“Lieutenant. Where did all these men come from?” the city noble asked.

“Duke Dragonvien and General Marrius established a secret base linked to the portal network. We have been consolidating our forces there so we could spring into action should we be attacked.”

“Deathwalker planned for an event like this?” Advisor Mona asked.

The soldier did not know the woman but figured she was with the other nobles. “Not exactly. He kept feeling like something was off since he woke up from that crow incident.”

“What crow incident?” Advisor Mona narrowed her eyes.

Elder Martha got the conversation back on track. “What was his feeling?”

“Duke Dragonvien wanted somewhere his people could train yet be ready at a moment’s notice. After we interrogated that treacherous noble, some additional measures were considered.”

“What treacherous noble?” Lord Dormeir asked.

“My disowned son.” Lord Simium answered.

“What?” Lord Dormeir said in shock.

“Deathwalker kept it a secret to protect my honor, but the truth is my son was poisoning me and working with some clandestine organization to replace me.” Lord Simium explained.

Lieutenant Daniels interjected. “After we learned of his involvement we pulled more of our forces from other locations and centralized them. Mrrsha, Prrsha, and Frrsha should be working with Commander Willis and his men to be the first strike, then we flood the city with overwhelming force. Once the city is secured, we will prepare to take the fight to the enemy outside.”

“How bad is it outside? We have not been to the walls.” General Mineheir asked.

Elder Martha answered the general’s question. “I have a communication crystal tied with Commander Willis and one tied with General Marrius. Inside the city we estimate several hundred infiltrators, at least a third of the refugees were saboteurs. Beyond the city wall, there is over three thousand Proletariat troops.”

“That does not bod well Elder. We have just over a thousand soldiers pouring into the city now. We should have no problem taking back the city...” Lieutenant Daniels was interrupted by Lord Dormeir.

“The problem will be us keeping it.”

“Agreed. Perhaps you all should take the portal to Hargrave or the capital. You would be much safer there and you could begin to plan a counter offensive.” Elder Martha suggested.

“I am not leaving!” Emma declared.

“Granddaughter, I do not like that idea.”

Emma shook her head. She then turned to Sunderer. “If I stay, you will make sure no harm comes to me, right big guy?”

Sunderer nodded his big head. “I will protect you with my life, your majesty.”

“There it is settled.” Emma stated.

“No this is most certainly not settled, niece. I do not approve.” Duchess Lightheart interjected.

Lord Longshot jerked and looked up into the sky. “Something has Talon scared!” Then he shifted his gaze to where his Duke was floating in the air. “It cannot be.”

Everyone looked up to see what Lord Longshot was focused on. Then they were hit with the aura of killing intent and the fluctuations coming in waves from massive amounts of mana being channeled.

“Is that Deathwalker?” King Alfheim asked as he looked in the direction of a man with wings hovering over Timberfall.

“It is!” Emma stated.

“I knew he was a mage and healer, but this… I have never felt anything like this!” General Mineheir looked on in awe.

“How much mana does he have?” Duchess Lightheart said as she could feel the tidal wave of mana gush out of him.

“That feels like Grand Scale Magic or even possibly Pinnacle grade! Unbelievable!” Elder Martha gawked.

Mona knew of only very few beings capable of doing what she was witnessing. The fey woman could no longer pretend or hold off any longer. “I must inform my Queen!” Advisor Mona stared at the sight before taking out a special thin rod, casting a spell into it, then snapping it in two.

## ———Garry ‘Smash’———

Garry was busy flinging one target after the other, having the time of his life. He would periodically cast Ice or Water to put out a fire. Usually that would make one or more Proletariat saboteurs come out of the woodwork and attempt to stop him. To Garry’s benefit, this just meant more targets to unleash mayhem on.

"You get an Ice Lance to the face, and you get an Ice Lance to the face! Ha, ha, ha, ha, ha!"

"I love it when boss lets me go all out like this." Garry said before his attention made the **Shadow Gazer** look upward. "Is that killing intent I'm feeling from the boss? Oh goodie! This feels like a warm blanket of awesomeness!"

Just then a Proletariat soldier shot an arrow in Garry's direction. It was easy for the little murderhobo to dodge the projectile.

"How rude! Don't interrupt me basking in my boss' killing intent!" Garry said as he used **Telekinesis** to first rip the bow out of the man's hands. Then lifted the soldier off the ground.

"Ahhh! What is happening?!" The Proletariat soldier cried out as he was lifted into the air.

Garry brought the man to just out of reach of the **Shadow Gazer**. "Now, now. Stop being so rude. Come let us get a better look at the awesomeness that is my boss!"

Just as he was about to rise another soldier jumped down blade extended hoping to impale the Shadow Gazer. The soldier froze in the air. "Really. Dumbass? Can't you see I have your buddy floating in the air? Bunch of morons! Now stop interrupting the show!"

The three rose higher and higher in the air, drawing closer to Deathwalker, who was now hovering over the city just on the other side of the barrier facing the invading army.

AHHH!" the two trapped men cried out in fear.

"Don't you feel all that awesome mana gathering? This is so exciting!" Garry said, ignoring the men's pleas.

"Please let me go! I promise I will run far away!"

Pleeeese!"

“Some people just can’t seem to appreciate the finer things in life. Ugh, stop yapping, I am trying to watch my master at work. Something tells me this is going to be totally awesome!” Garry said without even looking at the man hovering next to him.

“I beg you… please let me go!” the man was openly sobbing now.

The other man had stopped pleading and instead was doing everything he could not to look down.

Please, please, let me go! Do what you want to him but let me go!”

“You bastard!” The other soldier said.

“Fine! I was trying to broaden your horizons but oh well. Sure, I can let you go! Boss did say ‘smash’ after all. Ha, ha, ha, ha!” Garry gave a wicked grin.

The sobbing man realized too late the error in his request as Garry released his **Telekinesis**.

Garry moved an eyestalk like he was both watching and listening to the man fall.

“AHHHhhhhh…”

SPLAT!

“Yea! That’s the stuff!” Garry sighed in satisfaction.

Looking at the other enemy soldier he was holding. “Now don’t interrupt the show!”

The man clamped his mouth shut even harder.

“Better.” Garry said before all his eyes turned to Deathwalker. “I don’t think he was even this pissed off when we fought the krythid. Wonder what he does this time?”

## ———Somewhere in Timberfall———

General Marks felt the massive amount of magic flood the area. “He is capable of casting Grand Scale magic on his own?! Damnit! Had I known that I would have prioritized his death.”

Looking at Mary Sue. “Why did you not mention this in your report?”

Mary Sue shrugged. “The man kept his secrets close to his vest. I tortured that old man, and he still told me nothing! Stubborn old fool!”

Turning to Archmage Lenn, “Can you get to him?”

The space mage shook his head. “No, he is too far to get to. Plus, that much mana wreaks havoc on my portals. Space magic requires precise calculations.”

“Damnit! Time to go! All our planning, for nothing!” The general knew when to retreat.

“We dealt a blow to the elite. It is only a matter of time before this kingdom falls like all the rest.” Mary Sue commented.

“At least we will soon have weapons crafted by the dwarves. Let us leave this place.” General Marks consoled himself.

When the space mage had not yet opened a portal, General Marks turned to the man. “Well, what are you waiting for?!”

“What about Chen?” Archmage Lenn asked.

“Who cares about him? He is on his own!” Mary Sue answered.

General Marks smiled at his most trusted operative. “I could not have said it better myself.” His smile turned into a frown as Archmage Lenn still hadn’t used his magic. “Open a portal you idiot and get us out of here!” General Marks pointed up at the hovering mage as massive formations began to form. “Or do you want to stick around for whatever THAT is?!”

Archmage Lenn could feel the killing intent and massive amount of mana being gathered, it scared the crap out of him. "N-no, G-General. A-at once!" The space mage said as he began casting his spell.

'Worthless space mage. The only thing they are good for is a quick retreat. They have no talent for using their magic for combat. Such a waste of space.' General Marks thought as he impatiently waited. The man knew Archmage Lenn was indeed very capable in combat and had been their greatest asset, the man's cold demeanor just irked him at times. "My apologies old friend. I am just pissed off that our months of planning has been wasted."

The portal opened up in front of the trio. "I have learned to ignore your tirades. We will get our revenge for this slight." Archmage Lenn said before walking through the shimmering portal.

Mary Sue followed quickly behind. General Marks took one last look at the man who had ruined everything. "This is not over Deathwalker. You will fall like all the rest." Were the last words he spoke before stepping through the portal as it began to close behind him.

As the portal was closing Chen appeared, running for his life. He was beaten, had a broken arm, and claw marks everywhere. "WAIT! Do not leave me!"

The fleeing man dove for the portal in desperation. The sergeant could see Mary Sue looking back smiling at him waving as the portal closed just before he reached it.

He hit the ground and rolled to his feet. "That psychotic bitch!"

"Nowhere to run now traitor." Commander Willis growled.

"I still have a few tricks up my sleeve wolfboy." Chen taunted.

He withdrew a poisoned blade and chucked it at his pursuer.

Commander Willis easily parried the blade back with his sharp claws.

Chen once again found himself diving out of the way. Before he could get up...SPLAT! His leg was crushed by a falling body.

Garry had moved to get closer and saw the fight out of the corner of one of his eyes. He decided it was the perfect time to drop his other prisoner. He could be heard yelling down at Commander Willis. “You’re welcome! Now stop playing around and look what the boss is doing!”

## ———Above Timberfall, Near the Outer Wall———

Deathwalker looked down on the thousands of enemy soldiers. There were archers, spearmen, calvary, foot soldiers, and some mages. They even had catapults. How the army showed up without anyone knowing was a serious concern. He thought it probably had something to do with that space mage Timov told him about.

Once Deathwalker learned Betterman’s shoppe was where the little fairy had witnessed Cal’s demise, he sent Timov to work with General Marius to help coordinate their defenses. They only had so many communication crystals and the pixies had claimed him their king. That was still a bit odd.

Though none of that mattered to Deathwalker right now. His people were good at what they do, and he trusted them to get the job done. They would see to routing the enemy within the walls. But the thousands of enemy troops outside the walls were not something they were ready for. It took time to recruit and train an army. Time seemed to be up now. This many enemy forces would mean hundreds of casualties, and that was if they won, and that was a big if.

Putting the rescue of his friend aside, Deathwalker currently wanted two things. First, deal with the enemy at the gates. Then, hunt down those sick bastards who murdered Alyce. His vivid memory brought back the horror he had just witnessed earlier. His friend was dead, and an innocent girl was... 'No, nope. Time to close off that line of thinking off.

Pouring cold logic on his brain, it washed away the turmoil of emotions and cleared his mind so he could think. He needed something to deal with these bastards. Last time Deathwalker had to deal with a large force he had used Gravity magic to crush his enemies. The problem was the area he would have to control was massive. Far more than anything he has done before.

"Man, what I need is one of those orbital bombardment satellites that can nuke someone from space!" Deathwalker said to himself. "Wait a minute, that gives me an idea!"

'More than Gravity Magic was going to be needed. Perhaps Gravity Magic could be the foundation of the spell. I know I shouldn't but add in some Time Magic and a bit of elemental damage... yes! The idea is taking shape! I'll have to use my font for the Time Magic part. The girls are going to be so pissed, but it has to be done!'

Deathwalker poured all the mana he had been gathering into both his core and Infinite Well of Time Magic, visualizing exactly what he wanted. He was rewarded with a new notification.

***Congratulations! You have created a new spell! Please name your spell!***

Deathwalker thought of the name he wanted, and the spell description appeared in front of him.

**Spell: Grand Scale Magic: Orbital Bombardment**
*Mana Cost: Channeled (Adjustable)*

*<u>Description</u>: This spell combines Gravity, Time, and Space magic to blanket an area of the caster's choosing with a strong gravitational field preventing movement of selected targets, making it impossible for them to avoid the devastation from the stars above. This area must be visually seen or can be scried for additional mana cost. Targets within that area are first suppressed by Gravity Magic. This gravitational field is combined with Time magic to lock down the area. Caster can instead use additional mana to only freeze specific targets. Once in place a hole is opened in the sky using Space Magic. Then one or more giant meteors covered in flames and lightning descends from the sky.*

*<u>Please Note</u>: As you are the creator of this spell casting time and mana cost are greatly reduced.*

***<u>Warning</u>**: Use of this Time Magic spell will reduce the time it takes until you unravel.*

'Now that is what I am talking about! The extra cost of shortening my life sucks, but my mamma didn't raise no quitter.'

Deathwalker cast his newly created spell.

A massive gravitational field blanketed the battlefield in front of Timberfall. As it spread the field encompassed almost all the area the Proletariat soldiers were in.

At first the enemy didn't notice anything. Sure, they could feel the killing intent and massive gathering of mana, but they had no idea what was happening until it was too late.

As there were no allies on the field Deathwalker did not need to hold back. All at once the gravity increased exponentially. Most soldiers were brought to their knees. The calvary collapsed. Only those with body strengthening Magic remained standing.

Panicked shouts could be heard even from where Deathwalker hovered.

"What is happening?!"

"I cannot move!"

"What are you complaining about? I am stuck in the latrine pit!"

"My horse's legs are broken!"

"Let's get the hell out of here!! Ahhh!"

"This cannot last forever! Hold strong men!"

"If you have body strengthening magic use it! We just have to move outside the area of effect of this spell!" One of the lieutenants said as he very slowly and painfully made his way towards the outskirts of the battle formations.

A few of the other higher ranked soldiers and mages that could do the same started to make their way towards the edge. Each one had to shuffle their feet along the ground rather than take full steps. They had quickly surmised the best way to overcome this was to get out of range. However, the progress was slow going.

Unlike Deathwalker's other gravity based grand scale magic spell, **Grand Scale Magic: Gravity's Master**, he could not keep increasing the G-force intensity on his targets. But he didn't have to, that is where the Time Magic aspect comes in. The spell drew on his Infinite Well of Time Magic causing immense pain to course through not only his body but his mind and soul too. He almost passed out from the pain, but Deathwalker held on, and the Time magic clicked into place.

The lieutenants and mages using body strengthening magic all froze mid-shuffle. Then a massive hole in the sky opened up, revealing the stars and other celestial bodies. The light partially darkened almost as if that part of the ground had a cloud overhead.

All eyes were fixed on the hole in the sky. Even those that were fighting had all stopped in a mix of rapt fascination and morbid curiosity. They rarely even blinked.

Then what was darkened started to light up as massive meteors covered in flames and lightning began to pass through the event horizon. As they descended those trapped in the spell could only look on in utter horror. They were all witnessing their own demise.

Those in the city said silent prayers for themselves and their loved ones. No one wanted such destruction brought upon them.

Deathwalker probably would not have unleashed this new spell so close to the city if not for the Pinnacle grade shield in place over Timberfall.

BOOM!

BOOM!

BOOM!

As the meteors landed, they did not just instantly kill what was hit, those anywhere near the impact site were vaporized or thrown far away. The ground shook so violently that many people in Timberfall could not remain standing as they fell, despite the shield taking most of the impact.

All the fighting spirit vanished in the enemies within the city. Hard to want to fight when you can barely stand. Also hard to be motivated to attack the home of person who is literally flinging meteors at people.

People cried out and many prayed the shield would hold. Some even prayed for the ground to stop moving. All waited with bated breath as the calamity given form pounded the ground outside.

BOOM!

BOOM!

BOOM!

BOOM!

BOOM!

On and on it went. The bombardment was as relentless as its creator, Deathwalker. After what felt like hours to those who bore witness, when in truth was only several minutes, the meteors stopped falling. The hole closed and the light in the sky brightened with the rays of the sun.

Deathwalker looked upon the battlefield. There were massive craters everywhere, the ground looking like the pockmarked surface of the moon. Some parts of the earth were still smoldering. Very few bodies could be seen, though some disfigured body parts could be picked out of the wreckage.

“This is going to take the earth mages weeks to fix.”

He refused to look away. Deathwalker had made this choice. He did not regret it, but a part of him had a greater understanding of those who created the atomic bomb. Three thousand lives snuffed out in an instant, and something told Deathwalker he was just scratching the surface of what magic could do.

Doing one last detailed scan of the remnants of battlefield to see if he saw any movement. Seeing none, Deathwalker finally decided he had engrained the aftermath fully in his brain and turned his attention to Timberfall. The source of that foul magic was gone. ‘My guess is he fled after my little display. Time to find Betterman.’ His heart felt heavy as he thought about what came next.

Garry floated up to him. The Shadow Gazer had a mixed look of awe and satisfaction. “Boss! Did you see the ground, you flipped the bitch!”

“Great Clone High reference buddy.”

“That was TOTALLY AWESOME! Why did you not tell me you could do stuff like that?! Can you do it again!” Garry continued enthusiastically.

Deathwalker couldn’t help himself. He laughed “Ha, ha, ha, ha, ha!” and with his laughter the stress of what would come next, did not seem as overwhelming. “Thank you, buddy. I needed that.”

“I had so much fun today, Boss! Thank you so much! BEST DAY EVER!”

# Epilogue

## ———Dwarven Mountain Kingdom———

“What is your decision, your majesty?” The Proletariat ambassador asked.

“I am afraid I have to disappoint you ambassador.” The king replied.

“What?”

“Yes. We are pursuing other avenues.”

“Other avenues? One of those avenues would not be Timberfall is it?” The Proletariat ambassador inquired.

“What if it is? What does that matter?” the king asked.

The Proletariat ambassador had a smug look on his face. “Simple. Timberfall should have already fallen to the Proletariat. It now belongs to us! So, as I was saying...”

The pompous human was interrupted by the dwarven king. “Sounds like you need some updated information.” The king waved the communication crystal his nephew gave him.

Then he looked to his guards. “Get this man out of my sight. I want him and his escort out of this mountain.”

The dwarven guards saluted. “Yes, my king!” They then surrounded the Proletariat ambassador.

“This way ambassador.” One of the guards said.

The Proletariat ambassador turned back to the king as he was getting escorted out. "You will regret this dwarf! Mark my words!"

Grimhold walked out from behind the throne. "I am gonna miss him! Not! Ha, ha, ha, ha!"

"The Proletariat are a bunch of racists. This Deathwalker seems to be an honorable man who appreciates dwarven culture. Our conversations with him so far have been quite enjoyable." The dwarven king replied.

## ———Winter Court Palace———

"Princess, what is it?" The servant asked.

"Mother has received news of the Huntsman returned. In a rural place called Timberfall." Maeve shared.

"How is this any different than the other false claims?"

"Advisor Mona was the one that notified my mother. She used a rare one-time use artifact. For her to use such a thing and not just send a messenger fairy..."

"Means it is most urgent." Her servant finished for her.

"Precisely. It also means Mona has some significant evidence to back it up." Maeve continued.

"Then the Winter Queen herself will go?"

"Yes. Mother is leaving the north after so long and there is no way I am letting her go without me." Maeve said with excitement.

"We should get you packed right away." The servant suggested.

"Yes. Get whomever you need to help. I want to be the first to bring the Huntsman to my side."

## ———Timberfall Council Chambers———

The aftermath of the battle was evident all over the city. Builders and Laborers were working on repairing the various collapsed and damaged buildings. The earth mages on hand were working on smoothing out the terrain and road outside of the city. Several earth mages were brought in from other cities to help.

All festival activities were put on hold while all the repairs were made and until the duchy could figure out the next course of action. Duke Dragonvein hired Tookin and the other cooks to help feed everyone. One meal was provided once a day to those that asked for it, while three meals were given to anyone helping with the rebuilding effort.

All the city guards were relieved of their duties until a formal investigation could be completed. Commander Willis was leading the investigation personally. They were not allowed to leave the city, but many were helping with the various repairs. There was no shortage of guards as the large number of soldiers were filling in. Crime was practically zero and there was little unrest due to all the soldiers patrolling.

All the enemy soldiers captured were put in makeshift prisons made by the earth mages. Any of the infiltrators not captured were being routed out with the help of Garry, Mrrsha, Prrsha, and Frrsha, even Draconis was providing his muscle as needed. Commander Willis' beastman hunters were under the direct command of Mrrsha while he was busy with determining which city guards could be trusted.

Deathwalker's heart nearly broke when he told Alyce's mother and grandfather what happened. Betterman was inconsolable and was currently living with his best friend Tookin. He refused to leave the house. Clara was living at the Adventurers guildhall. She had thrown herself into her work and according to Darrius, the bereaving mother would cry herself to sleep. She asked him to watch over her while sleeping and the guildmaster was glad to be there for her.

Adventurers had been hired to fill in wherever there were gaps in resources. Some gathered herbs for healing. Others went hunting for food or adding to the restoration efforts.

What was left of the Timberfall city and duchy councils were assembled. Lady Emma, Duchess Lightheart, and King Alfheim also attended. Sunderer was standing behind Emma as he had never left her side since Deathwalker charged him with her protection. The three guests had decided to remain to determine next steps for the duchy along with how the kingdom and the elven nation could help.

King Alfheim spoke up. "Deathwalker, I know I am only a guest here and this may sound self-serving but hear me out."

Deathwalker gestured for the man to continue. "From Timberfall we can launch a counter offensive. Either way the duchy will be on the front lines of this war. If we could build a portal station in the elven nation, we could more easily bring our forces in to assist. The Proletariat tried to kill me and some of my kin while we were here. I am committed to joining this war effort."

"I do not take it as self-serving. I will have to travel to your capital to finish the portal station after my team builds it. All this will take time, it would be wise to begin construction right away." Deathwalker replied before turning to his head trader. "Can you arrange for the construction team to head there when they can?"

"It shall be done, my liege."

"My duchy will help share the burden of the costs to build. We are the closest territory to the elves and this would allow me to see my father more often than every decade or so." Duchess Lightheart offered.

"And we will cover the rest of the costs." King Alfheim agreed.

Emma giggled. "He, he, he, he! Once my family sets their mind to something it is hard to deter them."

"So, I have noticed." Deathwalker replied.

"I have already sent Captain Saunders to begin rallying my men." Lord Dormeir spoke up.

"I will begin my recruitment efforts. We may have to consider drafting soldiers." Lord Simium stated.

"Start with volunteers before we have to move to drafting people. I am hoping there are plenty of people out there upset and wanting a chance to defend their homes." Deathwalker replied.

"Speaking about the attack, Mara is adamant about taking the fight to the Proletariat." Lord Longshot shared.

Deathwalker sighed. "Make sure she knows we will not let this go."

"I have her working on training the new archer recruits." Lord Longshot explained.

"Good idea. Best to not have her with idle hands. It will take time to gather and train a large enough force to March on the Proletariat." Deathwalker complimented.

"Could we recruit from the refugees?" Clarisse asked.

"You must be joking!" Ron scoffed.

"No, I think Clarisse is on to something. Many lost their homes to the Proletariat. Such a thing can be a powerful motivator." Elder Martha interjected.

"But they attacked us!" Samuel slammed his fist on the table.

"Then we do some extra screening. We are already interviewing everyone to help rout any hidden infiltrators. Put them through whatever we need and limit what information we share." General Marius offered.

"I am surprised you would suggest such a thing." Samuel countered.

"Give them hope. It can be a powerful motivator." Paul suggested.

Timov darted into the council room and was whispering something in Deathwalker's ear the zipped out of the room.

"What are your thoughts on the refugees, Deathwalker?" Elder Martha asked.

"There is merit in Clarisse's idea, but I agree there is a danger too. General Marius has a good compromise."

"Thank you, my liege." General Marius bowed his head.

"However, I would like some additional insurance." Deathwalker stated.

"Insurance?" Emma asked.

"Yes." Deathwalker said before turning to King Alfheim. "Is it possible to hire Advisor Mona?"

"Excuse me?" King Alfheim asked in confusion.

"From my understanding, she has some strong mental magic capabilities."

"She is fey. You never make deals with their kind." Elder Martha cautioned.

"Of that I am more than aware. Leave that to me." Deathwalker said.

"She is technically not my subject. If she agrees, leverage her as you see fit. I mean what I said that the elven nation will join Timberfall in this fight." King Alfheim replied.

Duke Watson, Emma's father, had made his way to the council chambers after arriving via the portal hub. He burst into the room, catching the tail end of King Alfheim's words. "I would hold off on that, your majesty."

"Father! What are you doing here?" Emma asked.

Duke Watson ignored his daughter's question. "My apologies for the interruption. May I speak Duke Dragonvein?"

“Of course.”

Duke Watson turned towards King Alfheim. “We received word that Queen Mab is on the move. I have orders from my brother to clear a path and not interfere. She is laying claim to Deathwalker and is coming here to confirm her advisor’s suspicion. You know as well as I do King Alfheim the Winter Queen will destroy anyone who gets in her way.”

King Alfheim’s face was pale. “The Winter Queen has not come down from the north for centuries.” He then stood, facing Deathwalker. “I must return to my people. They will be terrified. Queen Mab will pass through our nation. I apologize Deathwalker but our nation will not be able to help until this is settled.”

“I understand. Go in peace.” Deathwalker replied.

As elven king started to leave, he paused. “What of my granddaughter?”

“That is the other reason I have come.” Duke Watson stated.

“Father?” Emma asked with concern. She did not like where this was going. Growing up she had heard stories of Queen Mab and how cold and cruel the Winter Court could be.

“Deathwalker, my brother rescinds his royal decree asking you to marry into the family.” Duke Watson shared.

“Father! No! Do not do this!” Emma rose to her feet and was on the verge of tears.

Duke Watson finally looked at his daughter. “I am sorry Emma, but I do this for you. If Queen Mab considers you as a threat to her claim in any way... I cannot stand to lose you as I did your mother.”

Emma looked at Deathwalker. “Let me sort this out. I do not want any harm to come to you either.”

Hearing his words broke her heart. Emma knew Deathwalker was right, but she could not bear it right now. She stormed out of the room before her tears could start to flow.

Deathwalker looked at Sunderer. "Please go after her. I need you to keep protecting her even more now."

Sunderer bowed. "As you command, my liege." The giant of a man left the room, following in Emma's wake.

"I doubt that is all you came to say Duke Watson." Deathwalker said.

"You know?"

"I do."

"Your information network is quite impressive." Duke Watson commented.

"Would someone tell us?" Elder Martha asked.

Duke Watson nodded. "With this latest development serious actions are required. The fact that a path is to be cleared for Queen Mab and her retinue all the way to Timberfall means no kingdom support can be risked on this current conflict."

"Meaning what Duke Watson?" Duchess Lightheart pressed.

"Meaning Timberfall stands alone. They will receive no support from the Kingdom of Nord and I am to also retrieve you Duchess Lightheart. This will remain the case until the matter with the Winter Queen is resolved." Duke Watson explained.

"My sister cannot be serious! After everything he has done for this kingdom, and your daughter... what is my sister thinking? I do not approve!" Duchess Lightheart could not believe what she was hearing.

"What does that mean for our duchy?" Lord Longshot asked.

Deathwalker was the one that spoke up. "It means we are no longer part of the Kingdom of Nord."

"Those are treasonous words. Be careful Deathwalker." Lord Simium cautioned.

"No, Deathwalker is correct. The Kingdom of Nord has succeeded their authority over the Timberfall Duchy. We can take no chances against the Winter Court." Duke Watson confirmed.

"What about trade?" Paul asked.

"The portals Deathwalker has built technically belong to him. We cannot do anything about those." Duke Watson answered.

"Huh?" Clarisse had a clear look of confusion.

"In other words, it is a loophole they can exploit and will." Elder Martha explained.

Duchess Lightheart rose to her feet. "I will not let this stand. I will speak with my sister at once."

The proud woman stormed out not to dissimilar to her niece.

Deathwalker turned his attention to Duke Watson. "Is that all Duke Watson?"

The man deflated some. "It is. I am sorry this has come to pass, but I must think of the Kingdom as a whole."

"Tell yourself whatever you wish. We no longer are allies. Please get out of my territory." Deathwalker replied.

Duke Watson nodded and left the room.

"Never was a fan of that guy. He reminded me of some pompous doctor who plays second fiddle to his smarter brother." Darius commented.

"Now what?" Ron asked.

"Timberfall has operated by itself before, we can do it again." Elder Martha said encouragingly.

"Elder Martha is right. The Proletariat is not going to leave us alone and they are not our only neighbor. We must prepare."

"Will we have time?" Clarisse asked.

"I would say so. That display by Deathwalker set them back quite a bit. They will need to rebuild their forces." Lord Dormeir explained.

Deathwalker thought to himself. "This actually works out perfectly, minus what happened with Emma. Now I no longer am beholden to anyone but the people in my care. Any territory we take from the Proletariat is ours. I will carve out our own kingdom. Grimhold has done an excellent job with his kin. With cold iron weapons and other dwarven crafted armaments we will have our war supplies. Plus, a little insurance for when the fey arrive. Lots to do. Time to wrap this up.'

Deathwalker rose to his feet. "Let us do the same."

——End of Book 2——

# Afterword

I wanted to thank you for reading the sequel to my first book. This creation is a labor of love. I started writing out of love for fantasy and science fiction but that has grown into a joy of finding ways to remind all of us that we matter and are better together than apart. Hopefully you will continue this journey with me.

The Third Path of Creation series is part of a larger universe I am creating that will span several stories and take us all on a journey of adventure and discovery.

I also wanted to take this time to thank my family and friends who have been supportive through the good and rough times. My family came here with nothing, they talked funny and prayed differently than others, but they came together and helped each other rise. Their stories have inspired me to create and pursue my own calling.

"We are not meant to live this life alone. We are more alike than different; we just have to look past the surface." That fundamental truth has always stuck with me and is a part of my writing. My hope is you will enjoy these stories and find something in them that speaks to you.

If you like these words or enjoy these stories, please leave a positive five-star review, it does make all the difference.

# About the Author

ItalianDragon has a love for all things creative from art to fantasy and science fiction. Writing with a belief we are all more similar than different and just have to look for the similarities. Coming from an immigrant family who taught him the importance of self-accountability, critical thinking, and looking out for one another. You are bound to find such relatable reminders in his writing. ItalianDragon's writings include cultural, popular, and nerd references to add to the humor and fun easter eggs we can all relate to.

Please click the link to follow the author on Amazon.
https://www.amazon.com/author/italiandragon

www.ingramcontent.com/pod-product-compliance
Lightning Source LLC
LaVergne TN
LVHW010626110826
845149LV00014B/2790

* 9 7 9 8 9 9 0 7 4 1 3 6 2 *